Praise for Behind the Veil

Behind the Veil is a two-time winner of the 2024 Aurora Awards, earning first place in both the Young Adult and Science Fiction categories.

"In *Behind the Veil* an ominous landscape pairs with an overbearing council and a blindly loyal main character to create the perfect setup for a dystopian novel that portrays loyalty, friendship, and what it means to face the consequences of our actions. Creative, unique, and addictive, this book will fit perfectly on your shelf next to The Hunger Games and The Maze Runner." —*E. A. Hendryx, award-winning author of Suspended in the Stars*

"Award-winning author Samantha Rae Ortiz comes onto the Christian fiction scene like a blockbuster with her new novel *Behind the Veil*. A fantastically original and a deeply immersive story, thrilling to read—with relatable characters, clock-ticking suspense, terrible secrets, and a fateful choice. What a fun new read from a very talented new artist!" —*J. A. Webb, Winner of the ACFW Genesis Award and author of the Seeker Series*

BEHIND THE VEIL

WHISPERS OF EDEN
BOOK ONE

SAMANTHA RAE ORTIZ

ISBN (Hardback): 979-8-9985076-0-1

ISBN (Paperback): 979-8-9985076-1-8

ISBN (Digital): 979-8-9985076-2-5

Cover design by Hannah Linder, www.hannahlinderdesigns.com

Developmental Manuscript Assessment by Laura Burge, www.literarylaura.com

Copy-edit by Joanna K. Harris, www.gracepossible.com

Commissioned art: Character Cards: Kassi Roos (@kassiroosartist), Nyine City Concept Art: Catherine High (@catherinehigh), World Map: Antonio G. (@kitsunekei1)

To the many who walked beside me on this journey.
To the few who shared the narrow paths.
To the One, without whom there'd be no road to walk.

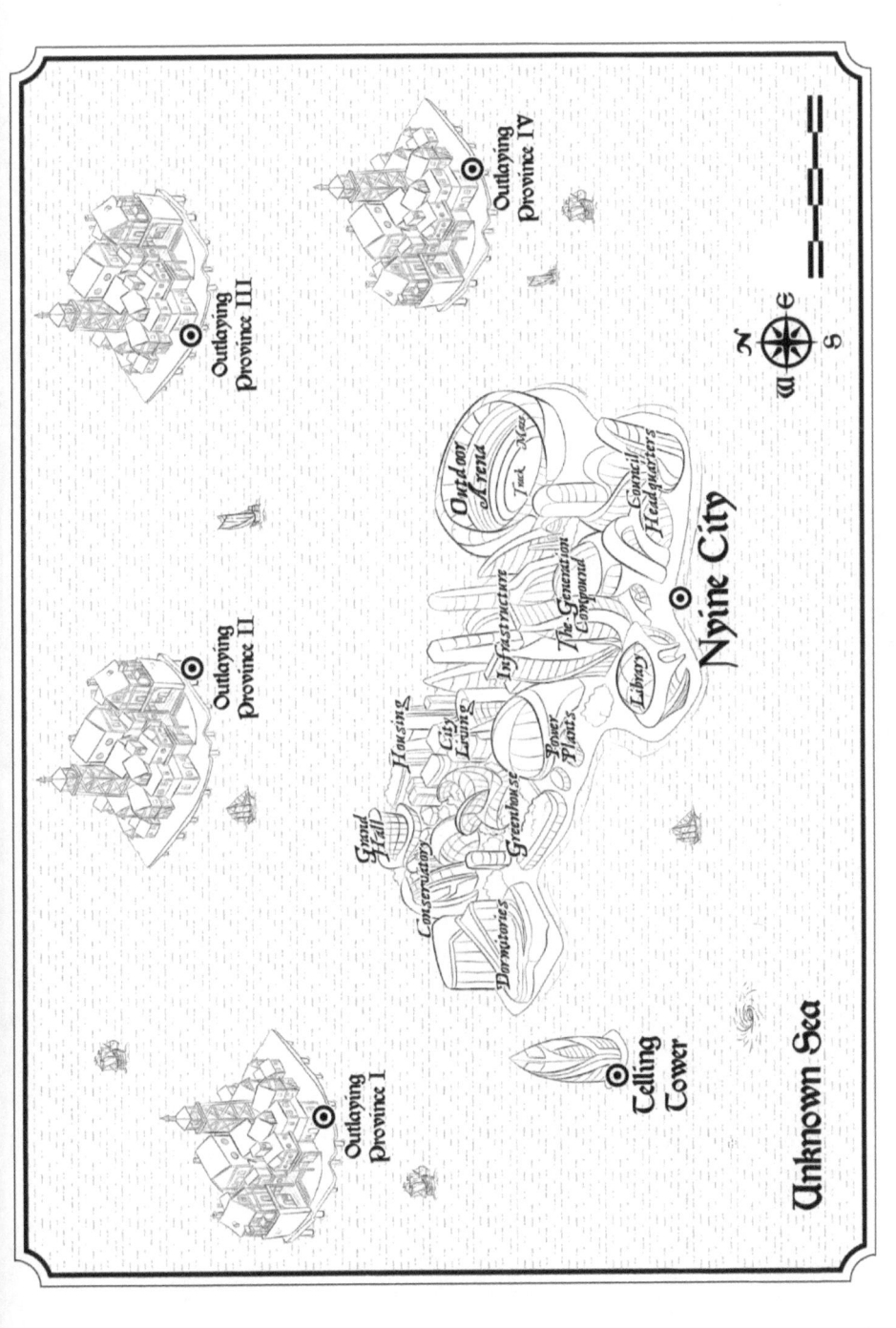

Outlaying Province III

Outlaying Province IV

Outlaying Province II

Outlaying Province I

N
W ✦ E
S

Housing

Grand Hall

Conservatory

Dormitories

Greenhouse

City Living

Power Plants

Infrastructure

The Generation Compound

Library

Outdoor Arena

Track Maze

Council Headquarters

Npine City

Telling Tower

Unknown Sea

CHAPTER ONE

L AYDEN PRIER WAS CRAWLING out of her skin, and she hadn't even left her body yet.

For the past thirty minutes, she'd watched her peers rise from the wooden pews when called, anxiously counting the minutes between their disappearance behind the large oak door and the Guardian's reappearance, the next candidate's name ready on his lips.

The entire process seemed to take mere minutes.

However, when it had come to her turn, those minutes passed and then some. For some reason—some unknowable reason—the door remained closed, her name uncalled.

The Grand Hall stood in a hush all around, with its golden dome soaring upward and light shining in through honey-colored windowpanes set in dark-stained walls. Row upon row of watchful eyes reminded Layden every second why she was there and that she could no longer turn back. Whatever awaited her behind that door was now as inevitable as the rains that flooded their world.

And yet, apparently, inevitability could be delayed.

In the back of Layden's mind, she knew she should be grateful for her stolen time—a few more minutes to draw her own breath, to feel her own heartbeat—but she couldn't keep her thoughts from running to the room beyond. What could have happened to make them stop like this? Surely it wasn't planned...

The crowd watched her with wary eyes, as though the delay were somehow her fault. And maybe it was. Maybe she'd given the Council a reason to doubt her candidacy. Maybe they'd seen her on the ledge outside her window that morning, which now that she thought about it, could have looked suspicious. Uncommitted. Or worse.

Only...it wasn't what it looked like. She'd only wanted to get one more glimpse of the sea as the sun rose, the vast expanse of water stretching beyond the horizon, never-ending and unbroken all around, punctuated only by the glistening buildings of Nyine City. To her, they looked like monsters rising from the sea; no hard angle to catch the eye, only curves and smoothness and movement. Beautiful. Her childish heart sometimes pretended to see land, eyes squinting so tight that the hard line of the horizon fooled her for the briefest of moments. Exhilarating.

However, that morning, Layden hadn't wanted land. She hadn't wanted myths and legends, just the world she'd always known. Unchanged and familiar. She needed to feel her toes go stiff against the metal in the chilly morning air, and relish that they were still hers. She needed to study them carefully, every pockmark, scar, and line that made them unique. The stories behind each.

They'd served her well as far as lesser appendages go.

Layden turned around briefly to survey the crowd, the bright light illuminating every face. It was fairly common for the residents of Nyine City to attend the annual Transfer Ceremony, their presence a show of support for the work of the Conservatory and the purpose of the Trials. But being that Layden's world rarely stretched beyond her den, not one face was familiar.

Part of her wondered if her parents were there, watching. Parents sometimes were. But she doubted hers would've made the four-day sea journey from the Outlayers—not for her, at least. And even if they had, they probably wouldn't recognize her anyway. She'd been only five seasons old when collected. Now she was nearly fifteen.

If she was honest, she wouldn't have recognized her mother's face either. In her mind's eye she recalled dark hair and tanned skin, but nothing else. This might have distressed her if she'd been particularly attached. But the truth was that being the youngest of five, brought into the world mainly to increase her family's workforce, Layden hadn't been close to either parent. Or her siblings.

Layden turned her attention back to the door and pressed her shaking hands against her fine, white dress, the silk folds becoming stiff and damp in her sweaty palms.

"Come on," she whispered to herself fervently, as though she could will the Guardian's unfeeling face to come back through the door. Funny, she'd feared him at first—he seemed the harshest of all the Guardians she'd seen roaming the halls of the Conservatory on their wordless observations and nameless missions. Now all she feared was his absence.

Her Guardian, however, did not obey her silent pleas, and in the accusatory silence of the Grand Hall, all thoughts whittled down to one. Either something had gone wrong with the Transfer...or something was wrong with her.

If it was the Transfer, all she needed to do was wait patiently for her summons.

If it were her...

Almost without thinking, Layden found herself standing. Murmurs and gasps rang out from the crowd and those around her on the benches. Someone whispered her name, a cautious warning, but she didn't turn to see who it was. She couldn't. Nothing else mattered now but getting through that door. Her entire life had led to this moment. She was ready—ready for the Transfer, ready for the Trials. No one would stop her. She wouldn't let them.

Layden exited her row and crossed to the door as confidently as her trembling limbs would allow. Manni's face swam before her mind's eye. He'd walked these steps not a half hour ago, rigid with nerves. If only he were here now to cock his head and give her his one-sided smile. He'd know if she were doing the right thing.

But he was already through the door and onto his next Assignment, and anyway, not even he'd boasted the steeliness of resolve their years of preparation had promised them.

Layden's shaking fingers connected with the cold brass handle, the rich oak of the door smelling overpoweringly like treated wood. The door was heavier than expected, almost too heavy for her. But Layden was determined and threw the whole weight of her small body back to wrench it open. This was it. She was ready.

Or...that's what she thought.

Unfortunately, no amount of calculation, courage, or resolve could have prepared her for the scene awaiting her on the other side.

Her new Guardian stood in the middle of the room, his arms around the shoulders of another woman. She was elderly, in her seventies at least, rail thin but embracing him strongly in return. She was crying. A lot. His hand cradled her head to his chest, his face lowered to her hair, filled with compassion, maybe even anguish.

Layden moved into the room and closed the door behind her, instinctively feeling like she should hide what was happening from the people beyond.

But what exactly *was* happening?

The whole thing was largely out of character for the day. This wasn't some detached scene of resolved fate and duty. It was charged with all the emotions for which they'd been told, "there was no room." And while she hadn't even met her new Guardian yet, she couldn't understand what he'd be doing in a situation like this.

As Layden stood there, searching for understanding, one thing became clear: this moment had been private, and she'd grossly intruded on it. The heat drained from her cheeks as she realized what a mistake she'd made. The pit in her stomach turned cold and froze over.

Both the woman and the Guardian broke apart as soon as they noticed Layden, the Guardian's expression immediately returning to stone. Though perhaps it had always been. Perhaps she'd imagined such compassion, for no trace of it was left. She couldn't even envision it back. The woman, however, gave a small smile through her tears.

"Hello, young one," she said into the silence.

The Guardian briskly put his hands behind his back and stared off beyond them both. Layden was wrong; his face may not have reflected compassion, but it wasn't stone either. He looked angry. Harsh. Terrifying.

"I'm so sorry," Layden managed to choke out. "I thought this was a test."

Even to her ears, her words sounded foolish. Weak.

The woman smiled kindly, but the Guardian cast her a look that resembled disgust.

"Well then," he spoke curtly, "it seems it is time."

The woman nodded soberly and walked to the back of the room. Layden's eyes followed her, noticing the space for the first time. It wasn't what she had expected. The air was thick with an acidic, chemical smell, and while the room had the same dark walls and lush carpets of the Grand Hall, the furnishings were odd, metallic, and cold. The tables were covered with equipment she didn't recognize, and there were consoles with bright lights at every turn. It all looked terribly out of place, and had she not been so sick to her stomach already, it would have unsettled her greatly. The oddest part of the room was the set of glass doors on the back wall. They sat in the wall and domed outward slightly, opening at hinges on the side.

The old woman had taken her place in front of the one on the left, and the Guardian stood by the other on the right. Then they faced her expectantly and waited. Layden looked between the two of them, momentarily confused.

Until she realized. This woman was her Assignment.

Revulsion overcame her and threatened to bring her to her knees. She should have known immediately...their first Host was supposed to be older, in their seventies at least.

Hearing the theory was one thing. Facing the reality was much, much different.

Layden swallowed against the lump in her throat, her heart panging in turmoil. This whole time she had only been thinking of herself, what would change for her, what she would lose. What she stood to gain, even. But what of this woman? What happened to her? No one had prepared Layden for a situation wherein she'd *meet* her Host, face to face, living, moving, speaking. Crying.

Layden fought the violent urge to be sick.

The old woman crossed to her swiftly and took her hand. She gazed into Layden's eyes with compassion and smiled again. How was she able to smile?

"I'm the one who should apologize. I tarried too long. You should not have had to meet me," she said softly.

Layden took a steady breath but could not bring herself to speak.

The Guardian opened the doors with a gentle glide of his palm and helped the woman inside. He spent a few moments securing her, and while Layden couldn't quite see what he did, when he stepped back and closed the door, the woman was unconscious. Then he turned to Layden and met her eye for the first time.

"Take your place. We have wasted enough time," he said quietly.

Layden didn't move because she couldn't. He waited for a moment but then took her by the elbow and guided her into her chamber. His direction was unexpectedly gentle.

She watched him in a haze as he secured her arms and legs in small metal harnesses. He placed several patches of wires on either side of her temples, measuring their spacing with meticulous care. She could hardly control the trembling of her limbs and was covered in a cold sweat, but the Guardian made no indication he even noticed.

"We will take good care of you," he said, his words only an echo of ones already spoken. "You will not feel a thing. All will be properly explained at the orientation following the Ceremony. If you are ready, we will begin."

He did not wait for her answer, however.

The Guardian backed out and closed the door, moving out of sight. Layden's breathing became loud and labored, but she could still hear the chamber hum as something powered on. For a while, there was nothing, and she thought she might die from waiting.

Then without warning, her muscles seized against her will and a violent force coursed through her veins. It felt physical at first, but then it moved beyond physical, as though her consciousness had been hurled straight out of her skull and thrown far away. Far from the room, from her body, from anything tangible. In this far-off place she felt everything—light, color, even heat—fly through her mind's eye as though it were hurtling thousands of miles per hour through space.

Then it stopped. She stopped.

For a few moments she perceived nothing, halted between spaces. She no longer felt sick, nor could she sense the cold metal around her; she existed momentarily with no perception of form. It was not dark for she could not see; it was not cold for she could not feel; she simply was. The feeling—if one could call it that—was unnerving to say the least.

Then, almost without transition, she began to perceive again. She was again aware of the prickling of hairs on her arms and back of her neck, the blood coursing through her veins, her heart pumping within her.

But no. Not hers. She could tell. The hairs, the skin, the blood, they were foreign.

Layden opened her eyes to see another's reflection before her in the glass. No longer her own, but the woman's. Her skin crawled and the nausea returned.

The door opened, and her Guardian stepped before her, freeing her from her harnesses. She felt his fingers against her skin, different than before.

"Welcome, Layden Prier, to the Generational Trials."

Layden awoke reluctantly, coming to consciousness in a haze. She didn't remember falling asleep after the Ceremony...had she passed out? That wouldn't exactly be hard to believe. The bed she lay on was narrow and hard, but she didn't want to move. She knew as soon as she did, she'd have to face what had just happened.

Her mind had been transferred to the body of another.

Even wording it so definitively in her head sent a chill down her spine. But it was true. The mass of her body was different, and the texture of her skin felt papery to her fingertips. Even her heart was beating differently, its rhythm not her own.

How had she not been prepared for this? The education at the Conservatory had been thorough, steeped in a culture of excellence and competition, all preparing her and her den mates for this moment: their Trial.

Layden shuddered, realizing with bitter shock how little she truly knew. Her body was in stasis. Was it the same for the Host mind? And if she didn't pass her Trial, if she couldn't do this...what exactly happened?

Naturally, there'd been rumors circulating around her peer group for years, everything from being sent back to the shanty docks of the Outlayers to banishment in the sewer treatment plants. The worst of the rumors involved horrifying stories of disqualified minds being separated from their bodies and put into a dreamless sleep for eternity. But Layden and her den mates were too old for ghost stories now, and the prevailing theory had shifted.

It was likely that, should they be denied a spot on the Council, there would be other opportunities to contribute within Nyine City. True, the Council didn't allow just anyone to live and work on their man-made island, but it made sense that they'd need to maintain the numbers. The greenhouses, powerplants, and warehouses all required a steady, trusted workforce. And then there was the Defense League, entrusted with the security of the city and Outlayers.

However, while Layden had spent years waiting for these theories to be confirmed, no one had ever concretely done so. This vagueness was compounded by the fact that Layden didn't remember anyone in the Outlayers who'd returned from a failed Trial, nor had she ever met a city worker. She'd been largely isolated within her den for the majority of her time at the Conservatory. There were other dens, of course, and new students coming into the Conservatory every winter, but her den didn't interact with them either.

Layden cracked her eyes open and looked around. The room was small, with nothing more than a few empty cots around her. From the room next door, a voice echoed, and a blue light leaked through, spilling onto the wall opposite Layden. She listened for a while, but when she couldn't make out the words clearly, she finally eased herself up to investigate.

As she swung her legs off the bed, she got a glimpse of blue veins showing through pale skin and a shudder ran through her body. This was her new reality. And it threatened to overtake her. Layden took a breath and pushed the sensations from her mind.

Don't look at anything too closely. That's how you make it right now.

Her knees and ankles throbbed dully as she stretched them, and the muscles in her back ached. However, when she tested her legs, she found them stronger than expected.

Layden entered the adjacent room and discovered that the voice speaking was actually a recording. The room was dark except for that blue light from the projection. Some chairs faced the wall where a few shell-shocked viewers sat, staring blankly ahead. Layden chose a seat in the corner and drew thin arms around a bony frame.

"This spurred the first members of the Council to thought, and then to action. Realizing it was useless to convince citizens to care for a dying world, they knew they'd first need to create a world worth saving."

The voiceover was female, her tone grand and weighty, and although the video was at the end of the track, Layden already knew what it would say. She'd been learning about the Council since the day she was born. This remarkable group of nine individuals, led by Grand Councilor Nyine herself, had saved the world from its own, sure destruction. While the planet faced global Monsoons and a devastating virus that nearly rendered humanity extinct, they pioneered the scientific discoveries that ultimately saved mankind. Then, when order had returned once more, the Council founded the Conservatory and initiated the Trials in order to identify candidates worthy of joining them. Candidates like Layden, who had been granted the chance to become a part of something more. On paper, Layden knew it all.

And yet, for some reason, as Layden sat and listened with ears not her own, all the things she thought she knew were suddenly colored in a different light. She found herself listening carefully, hoping for some explanation of her present state. Something beyond the childhood histories she knew like fairy tales.

After a moment, the projection gave way to a passive screen, and Layden's heart sank in the oppressive silence.

That is, until a voice rang into the stillness of the room.

She hadn't noticed him before, but now she saw their Guardian standing in the corner of the room. He was still in his ceremonial garb of white silk tunic and pants, his black, chin-length hair slicked back. The rest of his features were lost to the shadow of the projector as he moved to stand in front of it.

"Welcome," he said, his voice quiet but clear. "You have just undergone your first Transfer. Your Hosts have given themselves willingly to further the Council's cause of educating you by way of the Generational Trials. You would do well to care for their bodies as your own. It is an honor to host and a responsibility to inhabit. Any abuse or neglect of your Host will result in your immediate dismissal from the Trials."

Even in the darkness, his eyes searched them shrewdly, and she could see the line of his jaw flexing between each thought. He took a pace to the right as he continued.

"If your performance is exemplary, you will have the opportunity to transfer five more times, progressing down through the Generations. Within each season there is something to gain, a lesson to be learned, and it would behoove you to remember the Council cares about more than your contributions and achievements. It seems there was something crucial, something hidden deep within the Grand Councilor's journey—a revelation as it were—that changed the way she viewed the world. It is because of this revelation that we have the world we know now. To rule alongside her, as you have the chance to do, one must see the world as she does." He looked around the room, and his voice softened almost imperceptibly. "It is not a simple task. And I do not have to remind you that the Council has not added a member to its ranks in over fifty years. I am your Guardian. You will be with me for the duration, and I aim to deliver the first worthy candidate the Council has seen in years. Live in your moments, learn beyond what is taught, and, before you know it, you will see your body once more."

The reminder of her lost body was too much to think about and much too soon. All resolve she'd felt at the Ceremony hours ago disappeared like raindrops in the ocean. *How am I supposed to do this?* Tears rose to her eyes unbidden, and her throat closed with fear and doubt and panic.

Then, out of nowhere, a quiet whisper answered her silent cries, echoing in her chest with a clarity that defied reason.

You can. And you must.

Layden let the thought wash over her as she looked up at the Guardian once more. His eyes met hers and she felt something pass between them—an unspoken challenge that felt solely for her.

She wiped her eyes and took a deep, slow breath. She could do this. She must.

"Orientation is tomorrow at 6:00 a.m. This hall leads to your rooms. Get some sleep."

CHAPTER TWO

L AYDEN WOKE RELUCTANTLY THAT next morning, peeling herself out of bed only for the fear of missing her orientation. There were no windows in her room—hardly anything at all for that matter—nor was there any way to tell time. This was strange, as the Guardian had been clear that she report at 6:00 a.m. exactly, but she had been too tired to notice, let alone ask about it, the night before. Thankfully, the rigor of the Conservatory had stood for something in the end, and her body woke quite naturally in what she supposed were early morning hours.

Any other day Layden would've brushed her teeth and washed her face, maybe even put her hair into a braid or a bun. It was always a bit untamable which had always annoyed her, but as she saw the Host's dry, white wisps out of the corner of her eyes, she knew she would've given anything for that to be her biggest problem.

Mercifully, neither was there a mirror in her small, stark room, so Layden was free to sweep the hair back and pretend her residual self-image was as it had always been. Chestnut hair: wild, as stated. Brown eyes: a fleck of gold in the right one. Neither was particularly unique, as the Council often chose analogous phenotypes to bring simplicity to the gene programming. Still, they'd been hers.

Unfortunately, the charade was doomed to failure. It took her longer than usual to complete the simple task of getting limbs into cloth-ing—her mind knew they weren't hers after all—and the moment she growled in frustration, Layden's ears had to face the sound of another's voice. A rich, deep voice. It might have been beautiful had it not brought back afresh their traumatic meeting the day before.

All of this was enough to make Layden want to crawl back under the covers and stay there until someone came looking for her. She longed to be at the Conservatory again, or anywhere else for that matter, so long as it was in her own body. Her mind and heart were tempted toward mortification, and she might have given in, had she had less faith in the Council.

Ever since they'd rescued her at a young age from a harsh life where the only goal was survival, Layden had eagerly placed her hope in the future they offered. For many years, joining the Council had been the goal and the prize. They were the shining beacon for all humanity, and joining their ranks was her chance to do something truly good, truly worthwhile. So, it was hard for her now, to have to reconcile what they just put her through. An act both violent and violating, obtuse and obscene.

Layden took a breath and shook her thoughts clear. It would be okay. Orientation would help...reorient her. After all, there had to be a reason to all this. If the members of the ruling Council had endured this very thing, and with far less guidance, then it stood to reason she could too.

And, if she made it through to the end, she may just have a chance to save a dirty-faced, bright-minded, shanty-Outlayer girl like she'd been. That would make everything worth it.

Layden exited her room, following the quiet murmur of voices coming from the end of a long, cold hallway. As she walked toward them, she passed many other doors like her own, heavy concrete and unmarked, until she came upon a double archway that stood open revealing a large meeting hall. While her room and its surrounding aesthetics were stark and devoid of color, this hall was more like the Conservatory had been.

Both hers and the boys' hall—strictly guarded by their den mother but which every student had made the adventure to sneak between and see—had been warm, vibrant, and luxurious. It had been such an honor, and a bit of a shock that first night she'd been collected as a child, to fall asleep in that large bed. Before that, Layden had only ever known the floor of her hut and the heat of her brothers' bodies crammed in nearby.

Then again, she would've preferred either option to the night she'd just endured.

The Guardian was nowhere to be seen, but a few others, about as old as she, were already there. That was a good sign. The Meeting Hall itself was spacious and airy with a platform to the left and rows of chairs facing it. The carpet beneath her feet was lush and red, and the walls were stained a dark, rich brown. Light streamed in from one small window, high in the pitched ceiling, creating a dim haze that illuminated particles of dust floating silently in a world of their own. The whole space had a vaguely musty scent, and Layden suspected the thick carpet.

There seemed to be enough chairs for about fifty people, which made sense, but admittedly surprised her. Two dens started at the Conservatory every winter comprised of children collected from all four provinces of the Outlayers. Each den had twenty-six members—though Layden's den had one less than that—who lived and learned under the tutelage of the evaluators and den mother. Apparently, they'd be sharing their Trials with this second den, though none of them had met before now.

Layden searched the faces around her for Manni's before remembering with a pang that she didn't know what he looked like anymore. The thought made her throat close up. As she filed into a row of chairs and took a seat, her heart pounded in her chest. She was surrounded by people she might rightly know, but there was no way to tell... It took everything within her not to sob aloud.

"You all right, Dennie?" a voice rasped in her ear.

Layden startled and turned to see a man beside her, his dark gray eyes shining compassionately. And while she didn't know his face one iota from the rest, she recognized the glint within almost immediately.

"Manni?" she exclaimed, standing up and embracing him tightly.

Manni laughed softly and hugged her for a moment before pulling away. His eyes appeared moist in the hazy light. "How'd you know it was me?" he asked.

"You're the only one who calls me that."

"Ah, right," he said, smiling again.

Dennie had started as Manni's nickname for all their den mates, until he'd realized it was also one of Layden's short-names—not her most intimate short-name, but certainly one that denoted familiarity—and had made it hers exclusively. Layden hadn't been wild about it at the time but had been eager for his friendship. To this day she was not the best at making friends. Now, she was nothing but grateful for anything that tethered her to something normal.

"And how'd you know it was me?" she asked in return.

"Oh. Besides chewing your lip, you're a creature of habit," he responded.

"What?"

"You're sitting in your den-ordered place."

Layden looked around and blanched. Salt it. "Yeah, so you could find me," she responded, annoyed despite herself.

Manni laughed loudly, a low, mature laugh that sounded nothing like the Manni she knew. "This place is much nicer than my room," he mused, taking a seat beside her.

Layden followed his eyes and nodded. "It's like they mean to shock us or something. Lux to discomfort."

"Ha. Like after yesterday we'd be thinking about missing our beds."

Layden caught his meaningful look but decided she wasn't ready to talk about the Transfer, though she was grateful to hear him being honest about it. He always was one to look things straight in the face. She was a push-down and avoid kind of person. That's why they worked.

"Though, both are better than the docks, I suppose," he continued.

Layden gave a false shudder and scoffed. "I didn't even have a bed at the docks."

"No? I did. It was a big tub over in the corner. True, I shared it with fish. Actually, now that I think about it...yeah...no. It was the fish's bed. The fish were sharing their bed with me."

Layden laughed deeply, grateful for the shaky release of emotions, even if they were laced with more than merriment.

"I was hoping you'd find me." She wiped her eyes. "Actually, I was counting on it."

But instead of Manni's steady, reassuring reciprocation, she felt him withdraw slightly.

"Oh? I didn't think I was much on your mind after yesterday."

Layden paused for a moment, surprised by his tone. She'd almost forgotten about that. He'd asked her to meet him before they'd been collected for the Transfer, and she'd planned to. Then she'd glimpsed her face in the mirror and realized for the first time what she was about to do. What she was about to lose.

"Oh. I—I'm sorry," she stammered. "I just needed time."

"No worries, Dennie. I get it," he replied, his smile tight.

Discomfort grew in Layden's chest. She could understand why he might be upset she stood him up, but she wasn't used to him being so sensitive, let alone offendable. True, they'd both been through a lot, but she was the changeable one. He was the rock. She counted on that. Layden tried to think of something to say, something that would let him know she *had* been thinking about him. That she always did and always would.

Her mind trailed back to the peculiar nature of her Transfer—what she'd witnessed between their Guardian and her Host. Even though she was still processing it herself, she'd already framed how she was going to explain it to Manni. He was good at helping her understand things like that, and it might be exactly the peace offering she needed. But just as her mouth parted, ready to divulge all the details, she noticed someone observing the room from the platform.

Their Guardian. She hadn't even noticed him enter; he'd come in as stealthily as he was watching them now. Apparently, that was his thing. He stood imposingly on stage, dressed in the traditional long sleeve shirt, tunic, and pants they were all given, except his were all a dark shade of charcoal. He wore a cloak as well that looked black but could have been dark green. From where she sat, she could see few other features besides his black hair and shrewd eyes that watched them like a hawk.

No. Not them. Her. And very directly for that matter. Her heart stopped for a moment, and she closed her lips tight. His cold eyes warned her that it would be unwise to retell the tale of the night before as she'd been about to do.

From the beginning, she'd known she shouldn't have seen what she did. It wasn't until this moment, however, that she realized that doing so might have put her at odds with their Guardian. That was the last position she wanted to be in. He was meant to be the one looking out for her intake and also rating their progress for advancement.

How could she have been so stupid? Taking matters into her own hands when years of tradition told her it would have been fine if she'd only waited! It was just like her to misread the situation and act rashly. If Manni had been there, he would've talked some sense into her. He always did.

Layden leaned forward slightly and swallowed hard against the lump in her throat. She was an idiot. If she were the Guardian, she would have disqualified her before she'd even had a chance to transfer.

Still, he hadn't, had he? In fact, hadn't there been something akin to a challenge in his eyes last night? *Prove me wrong*, they seemed to say.

Layden breathed deeply and made herself an internal vow. Until she knew differently, she would say nothing to Manni, or anyone, about what she saw. She would prove she could be trusted. She would right this wrong, no matter what it took.

Manni followed Layden's eyes to the platform. "I can't believe he wound up being our Guardian," he said, distrust in his eyes, "out of everyone we could have gotten. He only worked with us, what, once when we first arrived? Even then, he made me uneasy. And why is he *staring* at me?"

Layden couldn't respond. For one, she didn't remember working with their new Guardian ever. For two, she didn't know how to tell Manni that the Guardian was actually staring at her. Not without explaining why. Thankfully, the Guardian broke her gaze and took center stage. Those who were still ambling around took their seats, and all were silent in a matter of minutes.

"We greet the morning and are thankful," their Guardian began. "With eager minds, we embrace all knowledge. With open hands, we embrace all tasks. With willing hearts, we embrace the Council. With repentant souls, we embrace the past."

His voice had an effortless resonance; rich and deep and commanding silence and his eyes held them expectantly as though they should respond in some way. But respond with what?

Eventually, some began to realize they were meant to repeat his words, and a smattering of people tried to echo back. After a few pathetic attempts, the room fell silent again.

"I hope, for your sakes, you will do better tomorrow," the Guardian responded coldly.

Layden glanced around to see confused faces; how could they be expected to know something they'd never heard before? Such childish expressions on elderly countenances would have been amusing had circumstances been different. Layden wiped her palms on her tunic and fought to swallow.

"You," the Guardian commanded loudly, "join me on the platform."

Layden snapped her attention toward the front and locked eyes with the Guardian. She knew he was speaking to her even though the hall was large and he was distant. Those around her swiveled in her direction, confirming what she'd feared, but she remained rooted in her seat, unable to obey. He did not command her again but held her gaze with such intensity she became like a wilting plant under a bright sun.

The seconds dragged on as Layden willed her Host's body to stand, but it seemed at odds with her. She couldn't tell if it was an effect of the Transfer or else paralyzing fear, but she was so frozen that she almost didn't notice when Manni stood to his feet beside her.

"What are you doing?" Layden whispered, her arm thawing enough to grab his sleeve in protest. But Manni gently shook himself loose, his own gaze trained unflinchingly forward.

All eyes shifted to Manni, and Layden realized—perhaps too late—that he'd mistaken the summons for himself. He walked to the end of the row and then crossed to the platform, and all the while Layden wanted to stand and stop him. To explain. However, with every step he took, she felt further rooted to her seat.

As Manni approached, the Guardian remained silent, though Layden could tell that he had most certainly meant to call her. Oddly enough, however, he did not correct the mistake. Rather, he turned and gave Manni his full attention.

"What is your name?" the Guardian asked once Manni stood before him.

"Emmanuel, of den Prier, sir."

"Guardian."

"Sorry. Guardian."

"Emmanuel Prier, pray, enlighten us on the meaning of the words just spoken."

Several moments of strained silence passed before Manni opened his mouth to speak. "I'd need to hear them again, Guardian," he said uneasily, "but I believe they were a pledge to the Council."

"A pledge," the Guardian repeated. "And why would the Council wish for you to recite a pledge?"

"I suppose...to secure our allegiance?" Manni proffered.

"Does the Council not already have your allegiance secured?"

Even from where she sat, Layden thought Manni's expression was...complicated. She willed him to answer as the Guardian's eyes bore into him.

"Of course, Guardian."

"Why do you answer with such reticence, Emmanuel Prier?"

"I—I don't know."

"You do not know. If the Council were here before you now, is that the attitude you'd present? Are those the words you'd choose?"

"Of course not, Guardian," Manni said quickly, his voice wavering dangerously.

Layden knew Manni well and could tell he was hanging on by a thread. Still, he was doing far better than she would have. The Guardian, however, did not seem to share her admiration. When he spoke again, his tone was firm, chastising, but also heavy with warning.

"Let this be a lesson to you all. Conduct yourself, at every moment, like you are in the presence of the Council. You very well may be."

Manni could not answer at first, but eventually he nodded some form of his understanding. Apparently satisfied, the Guardian straightened up.

"Good. Now, get out."

Manni's head snapped up in surprise. The silence that existed before compared nothing to that moment. No one breathed as they waited for either the Guardian to explain or for Manni to obey. As for Layden, her insides turned to ice as she thought about how she was supposed to be up there; how the Guardian had meant to make this spectacle of her.

"Out!" The Guardian's roar caused Manni to startle and back away. "Return to your room and stay there. You will not speak to a soul; you will not eat. You will learn these words like your life depends on knowing them, and if you fail to impress me, tomorrow will look much the same."

Manni wasted no more time descending the platform and rushing from the room. His eyes were cast downward, but his expression unnerved her. She'd expected fear, maybe humiliation, but instead, she saw anger. Anger and maybe even resentment. Whatever it was, it made her blood run cold, and she desperately hoped the Guardian could not see what she did.

Once Manni was out of sight, she turned her attention back to their Guardian while trying to shrink into her seat and become invisible.

"Mark these words," he continued. "Your soft days in the Conservatory are over. Your world has changed. Ignorance is no longer an excuse for negligence. Doubt, no longer an excuse for lukewarm devotion. And friendship is not an excuse for dependency. In these Trials, you will not succeed by relying on me or even one another. You and you alone are accountable for your progress...and your conviction.

"There is much against you and *nothing* for you. That is the path the Council had to follow. That is the environment in which they thrived. They did not blaze it for lesser souls, but for those who could propel themselves through adversity and come out the other side. They blazed it for the conqueror in us all. It is your turn to do the same."

He looked around at them one last time and then descended the platform and exited the room swiftly.

The hall remained in perfect silence long after he had gone.

CHAPTER THREE

L AYDEN WASN'T A STRANGER to feeling out of place. In fact, one could say she was quite used to it.

It didn't seem to matter where that place was—the Outlayers with her birth family, the Conservatory with her peers, or, well...whatever this place was, with whomever they were to each other now. No matter where she went, it felt as though everyone else played by rules she'd never been taught, operating on subtle clues and hidden cues she never picked up.

That is, except when she was with Manni.

Ever since they'd been moved to the Conservatory at five seasons, he'd been her lifeline. Manni was always game to explain, to cover for her gaps in understanding, and Layden had relied on him heavily to keep her off the fringes of their little society, a dangerous place for anyone.

So, it was difficult now to know if what had just happened was her fault, or if she was in big trouble. Not without his perspective.

Layden walked the hallways stealthily, her heart racing a mile per minute. Sneaking away like this was surely grounds for disqualification, and it wasn't lost on her that his help would be moot if she were caught. But as she walked the cold hallways alone, she suspected she might be in shock. She needed Manni to help her understand what had just happened, and she needed him now.

It shouldn't be that hard to find his room. Everyone else would be at second meal for a while longer, and the lights by each room indicated whether a door was locked. Plus, she had a suspicion her den was on the same side of the hall and still in alphabetical order.

Soon enough Layden passed her room and counted backward to E—for while everyone called him Manni, his full name was Emmanuel—and, sure enough, the light by the door shone orange.

Shifting her weight slightly, Layden knocked almost inaudibly on the cold slab of concrete. There were a few moments of silence, but then she heard a click and hiss, and the door slid open.

Manni stood on the other side—well, Manni's Host, an elderly gentleman with a slightly rounded back and inquisitive eyebrows. He looked pale.

"Layden?" he asked, fear entering his eyes. "What are you doing here?"

"You didn't think I'd let you starve, did you?" Her voice was steadier than she felt.

"You shouldn't be here," he said, looking behind her. "You could get us both kicked out."

"Then scoot aside and let me in so no one sees."

Manni did as she said, and Layden closed the door behind her, hiding shaking hands as she unraveled a small bundle from the folds of her tunic.

"Sorry it's not much. There wasn't much to begin with," she said.

Manni eagerly grabbed the half-eaten barley loaf and meager piece of fruit she'd saved.

"Oh, and something else," she continued, producing a small piece of paper on which she'd written the pledge that morning.

"You unexpected genius, you," he responded, his mouth full. His eyes roved the pledge. "Best memory around, I've said it once and I'll say it again."

"Yeah, well, employ your own and learn that, okay?" she said, unable to keep a small smile down. "Don't be caught out tomorrow. I need you back."

Manni stopped reading and eating and looked up at her with those inquiring eyes.

"What happened?" he asked immediately.

"Why do you think something happened?"

"You may be in someone else's body, but you've got your own language, Dennie. Out with it and get back before they discover you've come here."

Layden wrapped her arms around herself and took a breath. "It's been...so strange," she said, fighting tears that came fast and unexpectedly. "For first meal we had to wait in long lines in the cantina—like back in the Conservatory—except the servers just ignored us. Some people tried asking for food, or what we were supposed to do, but they said *nothing*. No one knew what was going on. Eventually, we were shepherded out of the cantina and sent to a warehouse-like room, where we received clothes, materials, and codes for our lockers. By the second meal I was so hungry, and my feet and back hurt so bad, that I just had to..."

"Had to what?"

"I took a seat at a table instead of waiting in line. I was toward the back of the room, by the doors. I didn't even think anyone would notice and it was supposed to just be for a second."

"You got in trouble?"

"The opposite! As soon as I sat down, someone came and brought me food, saying that my 'independence served me well,' whatever that means, and basically reprimanded everyone else for being sheep! Both dens had to wait to eat until I was done eating. It was awful. I've never seen so many people loathe me all at once. And that's saying something."

"That's saying something."

"I scarfed what I could, waited till the others were eating, and snuck out for the restrooms. Be honest, I'm sunk, aren't I?"

She flicked tears away from her eyes as Manni watched her with a thoughtful expression. At length, he shook his head and leaned against the side of his bed.

"It's just a game. They're all in on it; the servers and workers. Must be part of the Trials for them to pit us against one another."

Layden thought about that for a second, and about the Guardian's warning just a few hours ago. He had just said they couldn't rely on each other during these Trials, hadn't he? Maybe he was trying to make them distrust one another so they'd keep their distance. There was a small ache deep within that hated that thought. It felt wrong in her bones, but also, maybe, inevitable. Perhaps they were supposed to do this alone. But she just couldn't imagine a world in which she didn't rely on Manni.

Layden looked back to Manni, her eyes roving his unfamiliar features. His face had turned cold and pinched, like he was holding back more than a few choice words.

"It's all very sink or swim, isn't it?" he said at last.

"I suppose." She paused for a moment, a memory surfacing unbidden. At length she said. "Remember that last time we went to the Telling Tower? Before it was banned?"

Manni smiled and crossed his arms. "I remember you trying to convince me you couldn't swim so that I wouldn't push you off. Monsoons, that was funny."

Layden laughed and shook her head. It had been a preposterous lie, as swimming was as crucial as walking in their waterlogged world. "Don't know why I thought that would work."

"What are you trying to say, Layden?" he asked, his countenance turning somber.

"I dunno. I guess, if they're expecting us to sink, then maybe they don't remember who he's dealing with."

Manni's eyes held her own for a long time, a new kind of resolve glinting within. "You mean kids that have been trained to live in the water?"

Layden nodded and they regarded each other a moment longer.

"Second meal has concluded. Proceed to E45, off the southeast quadrant."

The announcement came from overhead, ringing loudly in the bare room.

"What was that?" Layden asked, startled.

Manni cocked his head, his brow knitting together. "The announcements?"

Layden paused. She had not gotten an announcement in her room. Had she? No, she must have done; she probably just slept through it.

"Go," he said, opening his door. "And thanks for the food."

"See you tomorrow," she said.

Layden left and walked down the hall toward the cantina where the rest of the students were filing out in a herd. Some vied for the front of the line, perhaps to stand out like Layden had inadvertently done. But there was not a lot of room in the hallway, so the jostling ended quickly. Layden tried to slip into the crowd but was still noticed by many distrustful eyes.

Eventually, however, the group arrived at the room marked E45, and the line began to enter. As they did, it became clear there wasn't enough room for them all. Short, backless benches, with little space in between them, populated a small, square classroom. Layden pushed her way to a bench in the back corner.

Most of their Hosts did not give off an odor, per se, but with all of them cramped together, the room was overpowered with exhaled breath and the scent of some kind of skin cream—or maybe a hair cleanser—clearly used by all of their Hosts. Layden sat back to try and gain space from it. Those without a seat were left to stand awkwardly between them, waiting.

Thankfully, they didn't have to wait long. After a few moments, their Guardian entered the room and stood at the front. Layden was blocked by several tall men who left only a gap through which she could see him, but she didn't mind being hidden so much.

The Guardian had shed his cloak and looked much more informal now, and when he spoke, his voice was quiet and lacking the ceremony from earlier. In fact, he seemed almost bored.

"As you have by now figured out, I will be your Guardian throughout your Trials. So, unless otherwise stated, all your instruction will come from me. Let us begin."

He paused for only a second and then began to pace the room, reciting what, from Layden's understanding, was a rote recounting of the formation of the Council. He listed the conditions of Earth-that-was, the melting of the ice caps, the Monsoons that flooded the planet, and the rampant Sterility that threatened to wipe out humanity with its aggressive spread.

"But of course, that was not to be humanity's end, thanks to the unparalleled leadership and direction of our very own Grand Councilor Nyine. Every one of you is here because of the way she pioneered the world we know today. She herself led the team that uncovered the science of gene manipulation and growth acceleration, which directly contributed to seeing the first new life born in half a decade."

The Guardian paused here, seemingly letting this sink in, but Layden shifted impatiently. They'd been listening to this for years. After all, they were all a direct result of this technology. It was because of the gene manipulation that Layden possessed advanced intelligence, retention, motor skills, and other capabilities far beyond that of someone her age. And the accelerated growth genome? It was how she was alive at all.

The theory, tested true, had been to program the mother's womb in a way that grew and delivered a baby before the effects of the Sterility kicked in at five months. The Sterility was a savage virus, one they'd yet to eliminate from their world, affecting every woman in some way or another. For most, it made it impossible to carry a child full-term. For others, it had additional effects, spreading beyond fertility complications into cancers and organ failure.

Thankfully, the Council's lead scientist, Reginald Hargrave, not only found a way to manage the virus but also circumvent it. In combination with altering the fetus to keep up, the accelerated gestation period succeeded in delivering the first viable birth in half a century. With this new breakthrough came a whole new class of humans, developing twice as fast as those unaltered. Layden and her peers, as well as others before them, lived their lives in seasons—a six-month period encompassing the development of an average Earth year. In other words, five years meant ten in growth for her.

Most considered this a small price to pay for seeing the first new life in decades. Layden had simply never known any different.

"Now, for the next four hours and every morning within the coming week, we will be going over these accomplishments in detail. It is more important than ever for you to understand the evolution of the Earth-that-was into our world today."

The Guardian stopped for a moment, but Layden could tell by the abruptness that it was not his intention to. Through the gap in front of her, she saw him looking to his right.

"What is it?" the Guardian asked curtly, his tone full of annoyance.

A quiet voice mumbled something in return that she couldn't make out.

"I see," the Guardian responded icily. After a second, he said, "There is not enough room for all of you because there does not need to be. Within a short amount of time, there will be plenty of space for those who have earned it."

Layden felt the tension in the room rise instantly as all considered these words. It was hard to know exactly what he meant, but it was ominous all the same. What qualified as a short amount of time and what would cause a dismissal were questions at the front of her mind. And if the system was so poised to disqualify, surely she was closest to striking out...she and Manni, right? But the Guardian didn't elaborate; he merely continued, his tone more emboldened than before.

"During your time in my care, you will learn the art of stewardship over both your bodies and your minds, through vigorous care and study. This is the path we've chose for the Year Seventies Generation. Our challenge for you is that you would not only become contributing individuals to Nyine City, but grateful ones. The ruling Council sacrificed much to be where they are today, and if you wish to join them, you must understand sacrifice in all its forms. I've been appointed to teach you by any means necessary." He paused for a moment, the silence hanging heavy, before continuing on. "When your name is called, please stand. Abisen Prier."

Roll call. Great. Layden's hands went clammy at the thought of all eyes on her again so soon. Being noticed like that did the opposite of making her feel seen. It made her feel like a sore thumb standing out in a crowd that did not, and would not ever, approve of her. A peculiar pang of loneliness resounded within, aching deep in her bones.

Layden watched Abisen's Host stand—a small woman, wiry and taught—and tilt her neck to the side, pushing her shoulders back in a stretch; that looked like Abisen.

You are not alone.

The thought rose to her mind unexpectedly, but Layden let it wash over her like a calming wave. She wasn't alone. It felt like it, but she wasn't. She'd spent most of her childhood with these people. She'd known Abisen since she was five seasons and knew she was athletic and agile, with a keen mind for the fastest sport and unparalleled coordination. Layden even knew her mannerisms enough to recognize them outside her body. That wasn't nothing.

Maybe they could get through all this together. If they were willing to try.

"Thank you. Able Quain," the Guardian continued.

The man named Able stood to his feet shakily and Layden angled to see a shorter man, stocky, with untamed ear hair. The second den was Quain then. Layden had yet to hear their name. Two dens, fifty-two candidates per Trial. Well, fifty-one in theirs. Again, there were only twenty-five students in den Prier. There had been twenty-six, but they'd lost one, a young girl, that first winter.

Layden's turn came as it should have, right after Kaden Prier and Katherine Quain were named. But when it was time, the Guardian paused. A chill ran down Layden's spine as she remembered the uncomfortable scene she'd intruded on, and how he'd meant to make a spectacle of her not seven hours ago.

"Layden Prier," he said, his tone gravelly. Apparently, he remembered too.

His brief hesitation before calling her name had piqued everyone's interest and once again, they swiveled to find her. She wanted to hide but knew it would be pointless. If the Guardian wanted to punish her, he would probably do so now, and she had no way to prepare herself for defense. She was helpless.

Slowly, she stood to her feet and stepped clear of the people blocking her from view.

"Present," she said, for lack of something else to say.

She waited for him to respond, to move on, to dismiss her from attention, but he did not. He simply stared with narrowed eyes, as though mulling over a difficult decision.

Maybe because she was in survival mode, dumb with fear, or in some manner of the aforementioned shock, her eyes began to take in every detail of their Guardian as if her life depended on it. His dark hair was cut at chin length but slicked back, perhaps in an attempt to hide a slight wave. It might even have a curl to it were it left out. He looked much younger than she'd previously thought—Layden hazarded not even past thirty—and while few looked their actual age those days, he lacked the chemical sheen that Long-Life products left behind. From far away, his eyes had seemed the usual brown or gray, but now she could see they were green. How had he come to have green eyes? No one had green eyes anymore.

"Is there something you wish to say, Layden Prier?" he asked her curtly, breaking her from her thoughts. His tone was cold, disdainful even, but she could also tell he was put off guard by her lingering stare.

And there it was again, as she stood utterly exposed and alone, that small voice inside of her, whispering the dream of unity. Of togetherness. She couldn't help but listen.

"Yes," she began, "there is."

Her heart beat wildly as she turned her attention to the room. Inwardly she was alarmed and imploring herself to remain quiet and sit down. But the words came tumbling from her mouth before she even knew what she was saying, as if they weren't even her own.

"I'm sure you're all scared. I know I am. No training could have ever prepared us for this, and that's just something we must accept. But I think we can. I think we can do more than accept it. But not alone. Den of Prier, I am the same Layden I ever was. We may not have been friends, but you *know* me, and I know you. And I think we will handle the challenges ahead better, well...if we remember that."

Heavy silence filled the room. Some of the faces around her were still suspicious. Others, confused, as her peers processed what exactly she'd said. Others still looked terrified she was speaking at all (which she recognized because, frankly, it was how she felt).

But she ignored them all and turned back to her Guardian, unable to avoid his cool, green eyes, made sterner by the narrowing of his eyelids. His lips thinned and it looked like he was biting back words. At length he spoke once more, his tone now low and menacing.

"You speak of unity as if it is grand, but you, Layden Prier, are weak and immature. These are the words of a child. If you are not prepared, if you are not willing, to pay the price this life demands, then you are no more welcome here than those whiling away their days on the docks, living only to live, understanding nothing of the weight of death or the responsibility of life. So. Let me be clear. The next time you speak out of turn in my class you will be out of this establishment before you blink those wide, naive, eyes of yours."

All faces that might have seemed sympathetic to her words quickly looked away as if they too had been reprimanded. Mind blank with panic, Layden fell into her seat. The Guardian continued on with roll call, but Layden couldn't pay attention to the names of the people she was supposed to know. She sat frozen, both unable to process what had just happened, and also unable to move on.

But then, the touch of cool skin on her hand silenced her thoughts. The woman beside her, while staring intently ahead, grasped Layden's hand tightly in her own. And for the rest of the class, she did not let go.

CHAPTER FOUR

*I*T IS A QUIET *and moonless night, the twilight hours of the deep winter months. From her window, she can see the waters surrounding the city frozen over and solid twenty feet down in some places. The glimmering surface of ice stretches as far as the eye can see, smelling almost metallic in its frostiness, but fresh and pure too. It's a time she waits for all year.*

Tonight, however, she will not be able to enjoy it.

Somewhere in the distance, there is noise—a loud thud, no, a pounding. It has awakened her, and she is sitting up in her bed of soft, down blankets, her ears searching intently. Then, the unmistakable sound of broken glass, hushed whispers, urgent and emotional, and the soft treading of heavy boots on carpet.

Layden climbs out of bed to investigate, her curiosity outweighing her fear, and opens her door. Dim lights of the electric torches illuminate the hallway with a strange glow, and she can just make out the broken window at the end of the hall. No alarm has sounded.

But there is crying.

She walks toward the noise and notices Constance's door is also open. There is another voice, soothing whispers, trying to console. But the crying grows hysterical as footsteps thud nearby. A bright light blinds Layden, and her courage runs out.

She turns and runs. Runs hard, runs fast, back to the safety of her room.

Layden lay in her bed, in her cold compound room, thinking again on the dream of a memory. It came to her often, always ending the same, with her running back to her room. For some reason, this bothered her. She wanted it to end differently; she wanted to know why Constance cried, and who consoled her.

Unfortunately, Layden *had* run back to her room that night, and no matter how hard she tried to change the events in her mind, there was no way forward in this dream.

Her peer, Constance, had been a tiny girl, blonde and fair-skinned. Idyllic featured. All quite uncharacteristic for gene-modified children. She'd stood out right away. And perhaps that's why her family mounted a mission to bring her back—for that's apparently what Layden had witnessed, though she hadn't known it at the time.

She learned later, after a standard eval session, that after being denied their daughter's return, Constance's parents had taken an ice rig across the sea to a window at the end of the girl's dormitory hall. This window had been overlooked for protection, being normally inaccessible by several stories and patrolled by the Defense League perimeter guard.

However, when the water turned to ice, the intruders were given a stable surface on which to mount an entry into the grounds. All they'd had to do was wait for the right moment.

Layden's heart had twinged with admiration—and a bit of envy—when she'd learned that. Her evaluators had been clear that her parents had not asked for her back. Not once. This, apparently, was normal. Most parents became accustomed to the change and realized it was best for them all. Her den mother was convinced this bit of information would reassure Layden; but reassure was the wrong word.

Layden sat upright in bed. She'd been awake, but only half so; now a sudden panic rose within her that she might be late. She slid out of bed quickly to check. The light on her door shone blue—an indication that it was day, as a locked door shone amber—so she opened it a crack. She wagered it was early morning, as nothing but silence filled the hall, but it could've been midday for all she knew.

Layden closed the door and got ready to leave, pulling on her white undershirt, slate-gray tunic, and pants from the day before. She'd only been given the one set of clothes the day before, and she wasn't sure where to get clean ones which made her feel like she'd missed some crucial instruction. Then again, the material didn't look worn and was breathable, anti-wrinkle, and scentless, so maybe they didn't need fresh ones every day.

As she finished dressing and slipped on her shoes—an uncomfortable, flat, cloth-build that made her toes feel cramped—Layden recalled the pledge the Guardian had posited to them, hoping the knots in her stomach would lessen if she practiced a bit. She couldn't afford to get in any more trouble. She had to be prepared.

"We greet the morning and are thankful..." she began, her voice trailing off quietly.

Was she thankful? All she felt was dread. All she'd felt since she transferred was dread and fear and loneliness. She shook her head.

"I greet the morning and am thankful," she repeated, more forcefully this time.

She wanted to be thankful. There had to be a point to all this. She could still remember the look in the Grand Councilor's eyes as she promised Layden a better future. And Layden had believed her. This may be hard, but it would lead to somewhere good and pure. It had to. The only thing standing in her way, as the Guardian had said, was her lack of resolve.

"We greet the morning and are thankful," she continued with force. "With eager minds, we embrace all knowledge. With open hands, we embrace all tasks. With willing hearts, we embrace the Council. With repentant souls, we embrace the past."

She spoke it through again for good measure, and once she was certain she had it down, she left her room and made her way to the meeting hall. The sun was just rising, its pink, hazy light streaming in through the one window in the high-pitched ceiling. Unfortunately, the hall, like the corridors, was also empty. Again, that feeling that she'd missed something big made her heart race and her limbs go weak.

The chairs from before had been replaced with large, flat cushions, laid out in evenly spaced rows. For lack of other direction, Layden picked one and sat down, crossing her legs and settling in.

"I'm just early," she tried to reassure herself. "Early is good. Early is prepared."

Layden watched the door for a few moments, but when no one came in, she rose to her feet again.

"Where *is* everyone?" she uttered to herself.

Just then, a door to the right of the platform opened, and, to her mild alarm, the Guardian entered. He walked across the front of the hall, the heavy fabric of his cloak rustling behind him as he ascended the platform. He did not notice her at all.

Layden quietly slid back down to her cushion, trying to remain discrete while feeling wholly conspicuous and intrusive. The feeling only intensified when he went on for several minutes not noticing her, completely absorbed in some papers, mumbling to himself, and staring off into space. His countenance was not nearly as harsh without an audience, but she still dreaded the second he looked up and spotted her there.

Maybe she should center herself, and if he did notice her, she would say she'd come early to do just that. That would be a reasonable excuse, right? And she could claim she hadn't noticed him...preparing...or whatever it was he was doing.

Layden took a breath in through her nose and calmed her heart, trying to picture something peaceful. The Shallows came to mind immediately, as they often did, and she focused on them, trying to place herself there.

While she'd only been there once, Layden held an obsession with the Shallows. Though its name suggested the water was less deep there, in truth, the land was simply higher. The topography around Nyine City to the east was perhaps once a mountain range, and a mound of earth rose from the water. It was strange looking, like the Telling Tower, clearly from a different era. Nothing grew on it for it was only rock, and it flooded each Monsoon season. But if one wanted to stand on real land for a time, this was the place to do it.

It was places like these that the children would talk and dream, exchanging rumors of parts of the world where land still existed, dry and open, where trees still grew. Though, a tree outside of a greenhouse was as unlikely to be seen as a sea monster (there were plenty of rumors about those too). Mostly, Layden thought these were fairy tales, stories the uneducated and children alike told for entertainment. Still, it was fun to imagine.

She focused back in, recalling the scents to her mind: the stone ground down to dirt, the water lapping over the slick rock's surface, depositing brine and sea. Salty and earthy. She could smell it all now, as though it were right under her nose. For a moment she was mildly impressed with herself, never having recalled something so well she could actually perceive it again. In fact, it was so real, she started thinking she was there.

Layden cracked open her eyes and took a peek at the stage. The Guardian was no longer there. Layden relaxed and let out a breath.

"What were you thinking of just now?"

Deep tones startled her, nearly causing her to tip off her cushion. Layden looked up to see the Guardian standing directly beside her. She scrambled for a moment against her old limbs and stood as fast as she could.

"I'm sorry," her voice rasped in its unfamiliar way.

"I did not ask for an apology."

Layden took a breath and tried to decide if she should lie or be honest. What did he want to know, exactly?

"The Shallows, Guardian," she answered before she could decide. The earthy, stone scent still lingered strongly and prompted her to share.

"The Shallows? Why?" he asked, his eyes narrowing slightly again.

Layden couldn't help but wonder if he ever smiled; the evidence in the lines on his face would say no.

"I—I like the idea of ground above water," she said, heat rising to her cheeks.

That was not a thought she shared with many. She had been taught early on not to dwell on the past, or things that could no longer be. Look forward, her evaluators would say. So, she kept her fascination with the craggy mountain to herself. Unless startled into confession, apparently.

"I see," he said.

His tone and expression were both hard to read, but she didn't seem to be in danger.

There was silence for a moment as she stood before him. She felt so young, like a child being reprimanded, and yet she could feel exhaustion in her bones, and she had hurt her hip from her small stumble off the cushion. It was an uncomfortable paradox to feel so old and yet so young.

Thankfully, before the Guardian could ask anything else, they were both interrupted by someone entering the room.

"Manni!" Layden exclaimed, as her friend came closer. But then she cast a nervous look to the Guardian. Was such enthusiastic friendship even allowed after all his speeches about independence?

The Guardian glanced from Manni to Layden but said nothing. Then he abruptly walked away. Manni finished making his way to Layden, keeping his head down as the Guardian passed.

"What was that about?" he asked quietly, his eyes following the Guardian.

"Nothing," she said, then, "I don't know."

"I tried to find you at the baths, but you clearly finished early. Don't know how you avoided the lines though." He took a cushion and sat down.

She followed suit, though very slowly, her neck and ears growing hot with alarm. The baths? That's where everyone was? She didn't remember being told anything about baths.

"How did you know where to go if you weren't in any classes yesterday?" she asked delicately.

"The announcements?" he half asked, half stated.

Layden said nothing but a cold chill ran down her spine.

"Are we supposed to, you know, center or something?"

Layden shrugged distractedly. The confirmation that she most certainly was not getting these announcements in the morning shook her. She heard the rest throughout the day, but there was obviously something wrong with her room. She contemplated if she should say something to the Guardian, if he didn't already know.

"So, what did I miss yesterday?" Manni asked.

Layden brought herself back to her friend and looked over at him. She couldn't imagine how anxious he must feel to be starting the day so behind the others, and truly he was behind. In comparison, a missed alarm was nothing to complain about.

"There's lectures every morning and then a practicum. I'll help you out as we go," she said, "but I can say now that we learned a bit more about the Trial. There are six Generations to progress through, and if we are selected to move on, we receive the next Host in descending age until we reach the Twenties. Each Trial is designed to take a full six-month season, give or take, and we'll be evaluated at the end of each. If done in the proper timeline, our bodies will age appropriately, and the one we receive in the last Generation will be our own."

"So, the next time we see our bodies, we'll be twenty?" he paused as though disturbed, but then he covered it with an old-man smirk. "I guess that's fine. At least we get to skip the rest of the adolescent hormones anyway. Why different ages though? What's the point?"

Layden couldn't answer. It occurred to her briefly how much time had been wasted at the Conservatory, learning everything but these things. Surely, her evaluators could have spared a day or two to go over all this.

At least the Guardian had confirmed, mercifully, that the minds of each Host had been carefully placed in stasis for the duration of Layden and her peers' inhabitation. He'd even gone so far as to reassure them that all Hosts had willingly volunteered, and that after they'd served their term, they would be allowed to return to their normal lives. Layden couldn't help but notice that his eyes had unflinchingly avoided her own as he'd explained that though, bringing fresh questions about his relationship with Layden's Host to the surface once more.

"I'm sure they have their reasons," she said finally. "This is the Council we're talking about. They organized the Outlayers in the face of extinction, established the Conservatory. They run all of Nyine City with precision. They don't do anything half planned."

"Did the Guardian go into much information? Did he teach, I mean?"

Layden sighed heavily. "Yes, a lot, but it was mostly on the Council. Stuff you already know. I'm sure you'll catch up, and anyway, it's just context. We're supposed to create something worthwhile to present to the Council."

"Worthwhile?"

"Yeah, an invention, a product. An idea."

"Anything else?"

"Well, the most crucial thing—and mind you, I'm reading between the lines, not my strong suit—is that the Guardian could disqualify us at any turn, for any reason. In fact, he seems to expect for more than half of us to be gone. And soon."

"Did he say where we go if we get disqualified?"

"No. That topic seems to be avoided at every turn, and I'm not gonna be the one to ask," Layden said quickly, trying to keep her hands from shaking. "But I'll tell you one thing, it didn't sound like there needed to be much of a reason. He just kept saying things like *if our resolve proved unworthy*, or *if the candidate isn't good material for shaping*, and whatnot. Also, the Guardian is evaluating us, but so are the nine members of the Council. They're keeping track of everything we do."

"Well, that doesn't bode well for me," Manni said darkly.

Layden wanted to say, *you and me both*, but she couldn't without elaborating on everything since the Transfer, and she had vowed that she'd remain silent. She had already gotten so much wrong. She needed to get this right, even though she wanted Manni's insight—and honestly, his comfort—more than anything in the world at that moment.

Either way, even if she did feel permitted to talk about it, there wasn't time. The hall was almost filled with people coming fresh from the baths. So instead, she mustered a kind of half smile and said, "Nonsense. A charismatic genius like you is sure to be fast-tracked through at least one of the Generations."

"That can happen?"

"Apparently, though it's rare. The Guardian was clear it wasn't something any of us should be expecting. I don't think he likes us very much."

"I don't think he likes anyone very much."

Despite the tension and the weight of what they carried, Layden couldn't help but laugh. "I'm so glad you're here," she said, subtly taking and squeezing his hand. "I missed you."

Manni looked at her briefly and smiled. "Yeah, me too. Missed food more, but yeah."

Layden laughed again. "You had some yesterday. It's not worth missing."

Her attention turned back to the Guardian on the platform, noting his gaze was fixed on her yet again, almost as though he were looking through her. She hoped she could do enough to convince him she was worth keeping around, but she had a sickening feeling her fate was already decided. Her throat was tight as she swallowed, but she did not break his gaze.

CHAPTER FIVE

THE DAY PROGRESSED MUCH as it had before, except now she had Manni by her side. It was surprising how comforting a familiar presence could be, even if he resembled her old friend by mannerisms and speech only.

Layden had met Manni the very day they'd been collected. He was chosen right after she was, his hut being down the boardwalk from hers. They were only five seasons old at the time, but he'd been conscientious enough to tell her not to worry. She remembered that.

Manni soon proved to be charismatic and intelligent, a reluctant and unvoiced favorite among his teachers and den mates. When he was younger, he had a vibrant energy that made others gravitate to him, but over the years he refined slightly and developed a more calculated focus. Layden suspected he reserved his most somber thoughts for her.

In those moments, she felt his charisma was a mask and she was seeing the real him, particularly as they drew near the Trial, and he began to retreat into darker and gloomier moods. While these were abrupt and slightly confusing, she wanted him to know he could trust her, like she trusted him. She'd always felt she could tell him anything.

Which was why it was difficult to have so much she *couldn't* tell him now.

She could almost feel the wall grow thicker between them as the days wore on and she continued to be withholding. Especially as the special treatment continued at mealtimes, and the Guardian's disdain became less concealed in the classroom. And she'd be daft to think Manni didn't notice how icy the students were to her; no one dared associate with her after her little speech.

And yet, every time his eyes turned to hers in question, or he tried to inquire, she'd find a way to dismiss him. She could tell it hurt.

Layden glanced at Manni now, as he sat beside her in the classroom. His back curved slightly at the shoulders. It looked like it was hard for him to sit up straight. But he didn't complain, just stared forward, listening intently to the lesson. It did help that they had nearly a whole bench to themselves, something Layden would have been happier about if it hadn't meant so many people weren't there.

The Guardian let them know at the start of that day's lesson that five of their fellow students—two from den Prier, three from Quain—had already been released from the Trials the previous night. This shocked them all, and it took a while for the pallor to leave the faces around Layden. Someone had dared ask the reason for their dismissal, but the Guardian's answer had been completely evasive, with more verbiage about worthiness, and lacking the right potential. So much so that Layden had to wonder if he knew the reasons himself.

Layden shook her head slightly, trying to recover her focus. She was finding the instruction hard to follow. The Guardian had finished with the history of the Council—a more detailed version than she'd been taught in the Conservatory—and had segued into the prolific medical and scientific contributions of its nine members. Gene accelerations and alteration, cell revitalizations and preservation, extinction theory and counter attacks against nature's genocide of humanity, and on and on.

Layden understood that there was a lot to appreciate, but she was overwhelmed by the sheer quantity of innovations pioneered by the original Council members. It made her feel quite insignificant and wholly unqualified. She knew she was intelligent and had a keen memory, which often filled the gaps in her lack of understanding, but she didn't have a scientific mind. She had never excelled at mathematics, nor had she found any passion in studying technology. Yet these subjects seemed crucial. What could she possibly have to offer that would be different or unique?

"What does all of this have to do with your journey?" the Guardian asked suddenly. His question brought her out of her reverie. "It might seem a waste of time to unravel the details of our daily lives, the ones woven in so effortlessly that we barely give them pause. But this practice is the reason you are here today."

He paused for a moment and looked around. When he resumed, his tone was nearly conspiratorial in nature, as though letting them in on a well-kept secret.

"You do not live in the world-that-was, so you cannot understand the spirit of it. You will never have to feel the blood that once pumped through the veins of a people dry out and blow away, powder in the wind. No longer a pulse, no longer a light. There were only dark days and darker days ahead. If you find yourself here, without interest, without desire, without a craving to understand why you were created..." his voice trailed off, his thoughts unfinished.

His tone had changed, warming slightly from the calculated lecture into an earnestness they hadn't yet heard. They waited for him to continue, but for a long moment, he simply let his words hang in the air.

Layden and Manni exchanged glances. She wouldn't say it, but while both moods were unnerving, she preferred this impassioned nature to the cold one. It seemed far more genuine.

It did not last long, however, and in seconds his eyes were once again narrowed in that piercing way.

"Well," he finished at last, "let us just say, I have no time for the disinterested."

Manni and Layden trailed behind their peers so they could talk. After another painful meal in the cantina, he had finally taken her aside and insisted she explain. The look in his eyes was too imploring and concerned to ignore and she'd relented to disclose her theory—or some of it anyway.

It was her belief now that the stunt at the cantina and the lack of announcements in her room were a result of her mistake during the Transfer. It felt, at this point, like the Guardian was going out of his way to put her at a disadvantage. While she couldn't tell Manni all of this, she hoped he'd recognize the pattern and back her up.

"So...you think he's got it out for you?" Manni asked.

"Don't you think?"

"But why?"

Again, she hesitated. "It doesn't matter why. You asked what was going on and that's what I think."

"Still, could be a coincidence."

Layden chaffed but stopped herself from speaking out. She supposed if she wasn't going to tell him the full story, she couldn't expect him to arrive at her conclusions. "Maybe," she said finally.

"Look, we're all on edge. You weren't the one sent away on day one. You also haven't been dismissed yet, have you? If he wanted you gone, it doesn't seem like he needs much of a reason."

Layden steadied her breath. "Yeah. You're right," she said.

"I honestly think things will calm down in a few days. Those running the show had to set the tone, the status quo—it's a classic militaristic tactic. Once we get into our practicum, our work will speak for itself, and we'll be able to breathe a little."

Layden glanced at him sidelong. He'd always been interested in strategic history. And while students weren't normally encouraged to obsess over things-that-were, Manni was often given free rein because he was so good at everything else.

As they walked in silence, following their dwindled group of peers, the corridors became brighter and wider, and they entered a different part of the compound. The light and space brought new breath to her lungs, and the tension in her began to ease. She remembered that she'd been chosen for a reason, scientific mind or not and Manni was right; their practicum was an opportunity to prove that.

Eventually, Layden's group stopped at a set of doors and waited for the Guardian to display his access and unlock them. As the doors slid open, they were met by a brilliant, natural light—*sunlight*—pouring out full force. As Layden crossed the threshold, she was met with the scent of fresh air, as large floor-to-ceiling windows stood open to a courtyard to their right.

None of them had seen the outdoors since the Transfer. It had only been a handful of days ago, but it felt like months to Layden. Through the windows, she could see a thick but manicured carpet of grass, the likes of which Layden had only ever seen in the greenhouses. Planted in the center of this courtyard was a broad, towering tree. Its stunning trunk was white and smooth, its branches spread out and bearing bright pink blossoms.

Layden had never seen a tree with her own eyes. Much like the Telling-Tower and the Shallows, its presence in her world was jarring. But that only intrigued Layden more.

"Layden, let's go," Manni called, tugging her gently by the arm.

The Guardian led them to another set of doors and stood aside so they could walk through. As Layden crossed the threshold, the first thing she noticed was the sound of her feet on the floor. They thudded and echoed the way they had at home on the docks. The way they did on wooden planks. She looked down to see glossy beams of timber, edge to edge, leaving no gap, marvelously polished and preserved.

"What in the sea and stars...?" Manni exhaled beside her.

Layden followed his eyes upward as they pushed into the room.

The beauty of the courtyard had stunned her, but as she entered this new space, she nearly lost her breath. Walls of golden wood beams stretched heavenward all around, and a ceiling that boasted ornate arches, massive and imposing, loomed overhead. Where had they found this much timber that wasn't waterlogged? And in such good condition? Windows as tall as she gave an all-encompassing vista of the glassy ocean outside.

But none of that impressed her as much as the actual contents of the room. Every inch of wall not claimed by a window was lined with physical books, hundreds of volumes climbing all the way to the towering ceiling. The air was thick with the scent of them, a heady mix of dust and the oxidation of their ancient pages. It made Layden light-headed.

"I'd heard...but I had no idea." Manni exhaled, his eyes roving the bookshelves to the top of their height.

Layden had no words to respond.

Every one of them knew what a book was, but few had held one in their lives. Most physical copies saved from the flood had been digitalized due to the shortage of paper, but the Council had tried to preserve those still in existence, housing them in a hall called the Library.

Layden knew this but had never imagined it to be so extraordinary. Nor had she expected to see it, short of joining the Council. Layden's heartbeat quickened. The silence, the beauty, the vast revelation that lay before her, layers and layers deep, buried in words on all sides, took her breath away. How many eyes would see this rare place? How many feet would walk across its floor and bathe in the light and scent of it? Her bet was, not many.

The Council was generous to all but unashamedly kept precious things like this secure and reserved for members of the Council and a select few. That few apparently included herself now.

With fresh eyes, Layden began to truly realize the privilege of the life she led. Not only was she overwhelmed by the honor, but that desire to prove herself worthy of it glowed stronger than ever.

The Guardian moved to the center of the hall and watched as they spread out, necks craning upward. Layden discretely made her way to the nearest window and looked out onto the waters. She realized at that moment that she still didn't quite know where their current compound was oriented in relation to the Conservatory.

From her current position, she could see almost the whole city rising from the water. There weren't many sharp angles to it, not like the Outlaying provinces where all houses were square and squat. Rather, the buildings spiraled as they rose and curved in large arches, their foundations connecting underwater. Each surface was covered in white panels—designed to convert energy from the sun into power—giving them an almost blinding, reflective surface. And when the sun set behind them, they looked like sleek, white eels, towering into the sky. The view never grew old.

But she wasn't there for the view. Layden was looking for something specific, and, after a moment, she found it. The Telling Tower. It was distant and stood at a different angle than she was used to, but having found it, she was able to orient herself within the city.

This tower was one of the only pre-flood structures that remained in view from the Nyine City, its foundation plunging far into the water below until only a few windows remained above the surface. It looked from a different era, its edges sharp, the façade black and slippery with moss that had grown on its stone walls. It sat eerily out of place beside the white curves of the pristine city.

Layden could also see power plants, greenhouses, and even some of the entrances to the underwater sewer systems running the length of the city. Workers were out, traveling to and fro, but their tasks were unknown to her. They were distant specks only; ants working diligently for the hive. From here she could just make out her old dormitory jutting out from the back of the Conservatory. It was a faraway—further than she remembered traveling the night of the Transfer. She absolutely must have passed out.

Layden moved from the window to the nearest bookshelf, lifting a tentative finger to one of their bindings. It was supple and rough at the same time. The covers were many colors, but one in particular—a deep green—caught her eye. She liked this color; it reminded her of earth and growth and the courtyard. Engraved on the binding was a small silver tree, its roots and leaves forming a concentric circle. Her heart quickened. Was she allowed to take it, she wondered? Her instinct said no, but a whisper in her heart said differently.

It belongs to you, that whisper said.

Layden knew that wasn't true—and rather entitled to think—but she wanted to believe it all the same.

Deftly, her fingers moved to the top of the binding and slipped it gently out of its place. It wasn't large, maybe a bit bigger than her hand, so she tucked it into the hem of her pants, pulling her tunic down to cover it. She could feel it there pressed against her stomach, but there was barely a bump to be seen.

The whisper that had moved her forward soothed her with unspoken confirmation, and her pulse pounded in her neck in an unexplainable way.

For some reason, it felt as though she'd recovered a long-lost posses-sion, something treasured she'd been searching for her whole life. And now she'd found it.

CHAPTER SIX

A S CASUALLY AS SHE could, Layden rejoined the group, following her peers as they gathered around the Guardian. When he had their attention again, he addressed them quietly, his tone rich and hushed with reverence.

"As you have most likely realized by now, this room houses what we know to be the last physical copies of writing in existence, recovered during and after the flood and brought here for preservation and protection. Even after our most valiant effort, it is merely a fraction of what the world held before. You are some of the few privileged to make use of them and I trust you understand what an honor this is. The Council wants only the best for its potential members.

"Through the corridor behind me, you'll find rooms for your work." The Guardian gestured to a large set of doors opposite where they entered. "Should you need assistance finding any resource at all, refer to the individual consoles located on each desk. Otherwise, you are free to browse and retrieve books, as long as they stay within the grounds of the Library. The digital archives are comprehensive; however, the Grand Councilor believes there to be something about the use of physical references that are conducive to retention. Take advantage of her predispositions."

Layden felt the book press against her stomach like hot lead. The Guardian had just given them permission to take and study, but she still felt disobedient—mostly because she had no intention of returning it.

"Your goal, once again, is to contribute an idea, product, or system that will benefit the Council and our society," the Guardian continued. "Remember that innovation often comes from questioning. Pursue a thread and with any luck, you will see it unravel. Get to work."

He cast one final glance around before turning to leave. Layden instinctively stepped back, hoping to remain unnoticed. But as he wove through the group, the students parted in such a way that he passed right beside her. Their eyes met unintentionally, and his stride faltered, his lips forming words she would never hear.

For without warning, Layden could hear nothing at all.

Nor could she see. One minute the room was there, the Guardian's narrowed eyes before her and the next there was nothing but black. Layden blinked rapidly and shook her head, but it was no use; she couldn't clear the ink that had spilled before her eyes. She reached out her hands instinctively and tried to move, but, in her disorientation, she tripped and fell forward onto her knees and hands with a heavy thud. She could still smell the lacquered wood of the Library floor, could even feel it under her hands. But her other senses were mute.

As she knelt there trying to quell her panic, a bright image flashed into view. Pink blossoms floated before her mind's eye in sharp relief against the black—vivid and dancing in circles as if they were really there.

Pink blossoms, like the ones she'd seen on the tree in the courtyard.

Then, as suddenly as they appeared, they were gone. Her hearing returned slowly, all sounds muffled and distant. A few people were murmuring in confusion, and the ground vibrated below her as feet shuffled her way. A pair of calloused hands grabbed her arms and helped her up off the floor and as soon as they did, her vision snapped back into place. When she looked up to see who held her, she saw a man she didn't know yet.

"What just happened?" The Guardian asked, demanding her attention. He did not seem in any way concerned with her fall.

"I'm sorry, Guardian," Layden replied, unable to say more.

The strange moment had come and gone so quickly it left her with a jarred sensation, and she felt like she was going to be sick. But she couldn't bear the thought of doing so in front of him, so she took a shaky breath and tried to regain some composure. After a moment, when no explanation seemed forthcoming, the Guardian turned away, apparently willing to dismiss the moment. That is, until something on the floor beside Layden caught his attention.

Layden followed his eyes. The book! It must have tumbled out of her belt when she fell.

The Guardian stooped down and recovered it slowly, brushing it off. At first, he seemed puzzled, maybe annoyed, to find it there, but then his face went white, and he rose angrily, coming down on Layden in an instant.

"Why do you have this?" he barked. Behind his anger, Layden thought she saw surprise, almost fear. She opened her mouth to answer, but no words came out.

"I asked why you have this—where did you find it?" he demanded, his voice booming through the cavernous room. He looked momentarily like he might hurl the book down on her if she didn't speak soon, but a voice stopped him.

"I dropped it, Guardian. It's mine."

The Guardian's fury turned on the man beside Layden as he, for reasons Layden didn't understand, took the blame for her.

"I grabbed it a second ago," the man said innocently enough. "I thought that was allowed..."

There was a charged silence as the Guardian considered his words. Layden didn't know why this man was covering for her. Clearly, he felt it was nothing too egregious, as the Guardian had just given them permission to take these books. Maybe he pitied her and wanted to give her a moment's reprieve from the Guardian's caustic attention. But as they stood there, Layden knew this was different. There was something about this book specifically that she wasn't meant to have. And judging by the man's trembling hands, still gripping her shoulders, he was realizing it too.

"Mathis Prier am I right?" the Guardian said between clenched teeth.

The man pressed his lips together and let go of Layden, all color draining from his face. Layden willed the man to answer, but he remained as frozen as the waters in midwinter.

"Guardian—" Layden tried to interject.

"What is it, now?" he asked her harshly, his expression making her heart stop. "What does Layden Prier have to say *this* hour?"

Danger riddled every line of his harsh countenance, and she recoiled, biting her lip so hard the taste of copper flooded her mouth. The Guardian seemed ready to release more words upon her but as his gaze locked onto hers, once again, he faltered.

For a fleeting moment, something unreadable flickered in his eyes. At length, he regained his composure. However, the expression replacing his fury was even icier than before.

"Mathis Prier," he said, returning his attention to the man at her side, "I would not waste your time defending this young woman; she would not do the same for you. Her judgement is flawed, her actions rash, and her constitution weak. Anyone found in her company risks the danger of being classified much the same...that is, for whatever little time they are left in my care."

This thinly veiled threat rang loud with her impending fate and brought fresh tears to her eyes. He was right. Twice now she'd let others take the fall for her, and for what? Her error in judgement at the ceremony had sealed her fate that first day, and there was no repairing that. She could see clear as day.

It was just a matter of time before the Council acted on it.

Finally, the Guardian turned and made the exit he'd attempted to make twice before, leaving them without a further word. After a few minutes of dense silence, the group began to disperse, whispering to one another on their way to the study corridor. The man, Mathis, lingered for a moment in shock, but then scurried away without so much as another word.

Manni found Layden where she stood and took her by her thin, wiry arms, leading her slowly to the corridor. The hallway was long and narrow with doors that opened on a series of elongated study rooms on either side. Layden followed Manni to the first available room and directed her to a chair. She fell into it heavily, her whole body shaking, and her mind obtusely preoccupied with the fact that the Guardian still had her book.

"Take a few breaths," Manni said, leaving her briefly to lock the door.

Layden did as he said and focused back on her surroundings. The room was long with a low ceiling and lined with waist-high shelves laden with books, artwork, and dioramas of various kinds. In the middle was a long, polished oak table with one of the consoles the Guardian had mentioned. Manni placed his fingertips on the surface and the system opened for him with a pulse of light. Manni engaged the device for a few moments before a soft, calming whistle of birds sounded within the room.

"What's that?" Layden asked.

"I thought it might calm you down. Or maybe I thought it would calm me down." He laughed tensely.

"How did you know how to do that? What is it?"

"It's just a soundscape in the archives. They're not hard to find. They've been helping me sleep."

"What do you mean helping you *sleep*?"

Layden's confusion was soon mirrored in Manni's face. She most certainly didn't have a console in her room, but it was apparent he did.

"At night, I turn this on," he continued slowly. "They have other sounds too. Waves, wind blowing. Anything's better than the silence of this place pounding in my eardrums."

Layden didn't respond. She couldn't. Her cheeks burned with shame as everything crystallized in that moment. It was clear now that the Guardian and the Council behind him had decided to send her home since day one. She didn't know what they were waiting for, but how else could she explain all the uneven treatment? She was being made a spectacle, and the grand finale would be her dismissal. It was a miracle she had lasted this long.

If only she had just stayed in her seat that day.

"Are you okay?" Manni asked, taking a seat across from her.

"I don't know what to say to that," she answered spreading her fingers and lowering her forehead to the desk.

"I know. But you can talk to me." He slid his hands forward and took one of hers. His palms were large and clammy, smelling strongly of the acrid hand balm they were given.

"Maybe it's best," she said after a moment, "if I don't."

"What do you mean?" he asked, his brow knitting slightly.

Fresh tears came to Layden's eyes. "You heard the Guardian; I'm barely treading water here! I honestly don't know what he's waiting for, but my time is coming and when it does, you shouldn't be anywhere near me."

Manni was quiet for a long time. He didn't try to refute her, but neither did he reassure her. "But...*why*?"

His eyes fixed her with a piercing stare that demanded the pieces of the puzzle she'd denied him up until now. The ones he knew she'd been withholding but had been too respectful to push for.

Layden sighed heavily. If she was going to be dismissed soon, maybe it didn't matter anymore if she kept this secret.

"You were already through by then," she began, "but when they called my name for the Transfer...well that's the thing, they didn't actually call my name. We were all waiting for what felt like forever. In the end, I decided I had to do something, because I didn't know if it was a test of my resolve or something, you know?"

"Okay," he accepted. "So, what did you do?"

"I went in," she said, lifting her shoulders helplessly, "without being called, and I saw..."

"What?"

She closed her eyes and tried to keep the tears from breaking through. She gestured to her person with one hand and in a raspy voice managed, "My Host. I met her. Before she was sedated. The Guardian was with her, and they were...hugging each other."

"Hugging? The Guardian?"

Layden nodded.

"So, he knew her."

Again, Layden shrugged. Manni was silent for a moment, clearly thinking on what she'd shared.

"Did he say anything?"

"He didn't have to. The look on his face made it evident I'd messed up big. In the moment, I didn't care. I was too disturbed by meeting my Host. But the next morning I began to realize the mistake might have cost me everything."

"Did you hear him say anything though? To your Host, I mean? Were they talking about anything when you came in?"

That was an odd question, and Manni seemed more than curious; there was a reason he was asking. Layden shook her head.

"No. Nothing."

"Ah, well," he said after a moment. His tone was a little too light, like he was trying to keep it that way. "It is odd. But it does explain something I'd been curious about."

"What's that?"

"Well, this grudge, vendetta, whatever you wanna call it, seems specific to you. *Layden Prier.* He even said 'young woman' earlier, referring to you. He isn't seeing some random old person in the Trials. He knows you are in there, and it's you he doesn't like."

"Is that supposed to make me feel better?"

Manni paused for a second. "No, but it might explain why you're still here. It's not what the *Council* thinks of you. It's what he thinks of you. It's personal. And for the most part, he's not letting it get in the way of his job."

Layden felt her chest expand just a little in hope. "Do you think he resents me for inhabiting someone he...cared about?"

Manni's face drew in contemplation, but he didn't seem convinced. "Something tells me he wouldn't make a very good Guardian if that were the case."

"Yeah. Probably right."

"At any rate, I think if you keep your head down, you'll be okay, Dennie. For real. No speaking out, no falling over in the middle of libraries..."

He said this last bit as a joke, even chuckling, but she could only manage a thin smile. So that's what it had looked like? That she'd just fallen over? She let out a shuddering sigh.

"Is that all?" he asked, as if he could read her mind.

She chewed her lip and met his eyes again. It was never a bad thing to tell Manni, that was apparent now. But what had happened in the Library...she didn't know what it was, or how to speak of it yet. It had been so abrupt and strange, as though she had been dreaming with her eyes wide-open. It was one thing to share her fears of dismissal, but if she told him she was...no. There was nothing to tell! It was clearly just a stress moment. Lack of sleep most likely.

Either that or she was going crazy.

Layden shook her head and looked away.

"Why did he get so angry about that book though?" Manni asked the air more than her.

Layden said nothing, having no more energy for speculation. "We'd better get to work," she said, even if just to end the talking.

"It'll be okay. We're in this boat together."

Layden nodded but was unable to offer a smile. She heard his words, but they did little to convince that lonely ache in her bones.

chapter seven

"I T'S BEEN FAR TOO long. When will we see if the recruits hold any promise?"

The Grand Councilor watched as Henry shifted in his seat anxiously. While his words were bold, his tone was only a little more confident than a mouse. He was sitting very close to her desk, which she could tell made him uncomfortable, but he didn't dare move back; the chair was where she wanted it, and he sat where she wanted.

"What I mean is," he modified after her prolonged silence, "I am not sure how to keep the...occurrences...from interfering with my work. None of us are anymore."

Occurrences. She had insisted her Council members call them that. What the Council faced at the moment was a problem unique to any past leaders in history, that was for sure. But she couldn't risk the decline of morale with terms like conflict or struggle... Now that she heard him say it though, she decided she hated it. She also hated that he felt the need to tell her, of all people, how difficult an *occurrence* could be, and that he came to her to speak on behalf of *her* Council.

But she didn't remark on any of this. It was important to her that he felt heard.

"There may not be a way for you to avoid him anymore," she said simply, a small, pitying smile rising to her face. She could tell by the look on Henry's that this wasn't what he wanted to hear. "Perhaps you can attempt to work together."

"Work *together*? He doesn't want to work with me!"

The Councilor's eyes narrowed, and she lifted her chin slightly. "You have always known the risks, Henry. But let me ease your worries. New recruits are coming through as we speak. Several are extremely promising. As always, I am sensitive to our timeline. I understand you are fifth in line for a change in...partnership. However, if you don't think you can cope any longer, perhaps we can work out another solution. Perhaps you need a break?"

Henry's face drained of color, and he shook his head slowly. "No, Grand Councilor. I understand it's important to take our time. I believe in the Trials, and I trust your judgement with the recruits. I apologize if it seemed I was doubting you."

"Oh, Henry," the Councilor said, all lightness, "I know you meant nothing by it."

"Thank you," the man said again, looking like he wanted to stand and leave.

"You may go now," the Councilor permitted.

Pity. He had once been so strong. Such an agile mind. Now he seemed all fear and trembling. Ah well. At least there were others she could count on. Speaking of which.

"You may send Guardian Cherut in now," she said as Henry made his way to the door. He turned back only fleetingly to acknowledge her request and left without a second look.

Those first weeks proved harder than Layden expected, and she hadn't been expecting an easy run. She'd never been so tired, nor felt so alone, even now that Manni was with her. She was happy for his companionship, but there was that nagging ache that insisted she keep him at a distance. While Manni had had reassuring thoughts about the Guardian's vendetta, it still felt like the storm was about to hit at any moment. And when it did, he couldn't be anywhere around her.

The dream surrounding Constance's kidnapping had taken to making a nightly appearance, which didn't surprise her, for it had been known to resurface when she was anxious or stressed. She wasn't a stranger to its repetition and wouldn't have given it a second thought, except her subconscious seemed to be struggling against the dream more fiercely than ever before. It constantly urged her toward the light in the next room, toward the conversation she couldn't hear, as though they were the missing pieces to a puzzle she'd yet to solve.

After waking from the dream for the fifth time that week, Layden sat up in bed and rested her head against the wall. Her eyes were heavy and her brain in a fog, but she knew all too well that sleep would elude her from that point on. It was for the best. After all, she still wasn't receiving any sort of waking call. But she was managing. Most mornings her body woke close to the appropriate time, and the rest of the time she gauged the noises outside her room.

At that moment, Layden couldn't hear anyone in the hall, but the light by her door told her she was free to leave. She rubbed her eyes and climbed out of bed, eventually managing to pull on her clothes and shake off the grogginess. As she slipped on her bath slippers, her mind began filling with the tasks of her day. She had a lot of work to do. Even after a solid two weeks of cramming, she didn't have a clue what she'd present to the Council at the end of the season. Not an inkling, an idea, or even a path to walk down.

The Guardian had advised her and her peers to verse themselves on the accomplishments of the Council, with the end goal of discovering something new to contribute to the world. But it soon became obvious that it would be nearly impossible to learn everything they'd done—at least not by the end of her Trial. Each member of the original Council had been prolific, stockpiling achievements that were the result of several lifetimes of study. The current members weren't dullards either, though it would be fair to say their achievements had waned somewhat in the recent years.

Yet, none of these accomplishments were relics of the past. Their benevolent acts and scientific discoveries weren't just written in books or taught in lessons; they were felt in Layden's day-to-day life. The most notable example being the Trials, which had begun as a means to elevate promising citizens and allow them a chance to contribute to the larger organism of their world.

Layden didn't remember much about being collected, but she remembered being excited and honored, especially when the Grand Councilor herself had told Layden that she had a light too bright for the life lived by the rest of her family. From that moment, the Council had become her ideal, and Layden wanted nothing else but to be worthy of that compliment.

It was for this reason that Layden found herself more interested in the personal lives of the original Council members than their accomplishments, even though she knew the Guardian would disapprove of her priorities. Who were the people behind the tasks? The personalities and passions of the ones who'd saved the world? Sadly, there was not as much material on this as she wished.

Two of the members had been married to one another. A few were teachers and the rest were the head of their fields: socio-economy, anthropology, even biology. The Grand Councilor herself had been the head of a scientific foundation of bright, like-minded individuals called the Nyine Foundation. Incredible individuals, all.

Layden put her forehead in her palm and took a steady breath. She was still here. That was clear. But the ground didn't feel any less precarious than it had at the beginning. She still felt like that girl of five seasons, hoping she could prove herself worthy.

Out in the hall, Layden felt the stillness of the compound, its sleeping inhabitants tucked away in their chambers. Perhaps she had time to hit her study room before the baths were open. If she could choose a direction by the end of the week, she might be able to catch up to the timeline she'd drawn out.

However, no sooner had she begun walking than she was arrested in her footsteps by a strange feeling. It prickled her skin and churned her stomach, and her vision began to cloud again. She reached back to the door to stabilize herself, shaking her head in an attempt to clear it, but the waves of black spread before her eyes until she could no longer see.

She fumbled for a moment, plunging into the hall and hitting the wall across the way, thinking only of finding help. As she stumbled along, following the wall with her hands with barely controlled panic, a brilliant flash of white took over the black.

And she could see.

The bright light around her told her she was outside, no longer in the compound but somewhere else entirely. Rather than seeing walls and floors or her outstretched hands, she stared downward at a pair of feet pressed together, bare and tan. Were they her feet? They were youthful, not an adolescent's but not an old woman's either. She could feel them like they were her own. She could also feel the surface beneath them, gravelly, loose, and sandy. It was earth. Ground. Dirt.

Layden stared at it, astounded at the sight. Her limited experience in the Shallows told her ground was much different—smooth, black, slick. Yet she'd read about earth like this, seen photos. As she stared, a pink blossom tumbled into view; a wind was moving. It blew in more petals and shifted a white skirt across the tanned legs. She could smell the air—fresh, fragrant, and sweet. She couldn't look up, or anywhere else for that matter, so she simply stood and watched the blossoms as they rolled across the toes in great numbers.

And then it was gone.

While its arrival had been gradual, its departure was instant, leaving behind nothing of this bright visage within the dark hallway of the compound. Her arms still stretched before her beseechingly, and her breath was frozen in her chest. When she was able to recover it again, she wiped her eyes and drew a shaky breath, casting a look around.

Her immediate thought was she was grateful no one had witnessed this bewildering experience, but that soon passed as she realized she wasn't, in fact, alone. Several feet away from her, a man stood watching her.

The Guardian. She cursed under her breath. She didn't know why she was surprised. It was always him.

"Layden Prier," he said quietly, "what are you doing out here at this hour?"

"I—don't know." It was all she could manage. How could she tell him what she'd just seen? For a moment she'd felt swept away somewhere else, to some other time, standing as some other person, and she had no explanation for him.

"I'm sorry," she tried again. "I'm confused. My door was open—isn't it morning?"

The Guardian didn't respond but took a few soft steps toward her. She could see, even in the dim light, that he seemed as confused as she. Though for once, he was not angry. His mouth opened slightly, like words were poised on his tongue.

"It is early yet," he said slowly. "Perhaps you had better head back to bed. Wait a further three hours."

Layden nodded slowly, slightly surprised she'd be let off so easily, and turned back to her room before he could ask any more questions. Sick to her stomach, she closed her door and gingerly climbed back into her bed.

As she replayed the moment over and over, she began to feel even worse. At first, she'd been relieved he hadn't been angry, but the more she thought about it, the more she was sure she'd come across as quite mad.

Why had her door opened when it was clearly the middle of the night? It had been her only real method of telling time, and now she wouldn't be able to trust it! Why was this happening to her? Was this the Guardian's doing too? A test, a trick, a way to catch her out? Then again, if it was, why was he confused to see her out?

A thought came to her without her knowing, a whisper to her heart answering her very question.

He understands what's happening to you, it said.

But she shook the thought away. That was nonsense. At the most, he probably suspected she was sleep-walking. At any rate, she had to prepare herself; as if he didn't have enough justification, being mentally unstable had to be enough grounds for dismissal.

Thoughts of how she could explain things away took over her thoughts, but when she found she had no believable explanation, she buried her face in her pillow, smothering her angry tears.

She remained that way for what seemed an eternity, until eventually, finally, she began to hear commotion in the hall. Layden slid out of bed without any further invitation. Her room felt like a prison, and the quiet voices in the hall rose like the sun after a frightful night.

It was finally time for the baths.

The baths were an uncharacteristically relaxing experience at the start of an otherwise demanding day. While it had taken her a bit to figure out the routine—the rest of the students having already been instructed—Layden quickly found solace and peace in this time of day. It gave her a chance to think and process and to lay out her day. Not to mention, it was oddly reassuring. Things may have been hard and jarring, but how could they doubt the Council's heart for them when the baths existed?

She filed in behind the others through the glass doors already fogged over with steam. The baths were housed in a large, square room, its center an open courtyard smelling like burning charcoal and filled with rows of benches built of light wood. This portion of the room acted as a sauna, designed to conduct heat within the large, open space. The perimeter was lined with private bathing chambers, around thirty in total. Each chamber was big enough for one person to perform their bathing routine, after which they would dry off on a bench for the remaining time.

Layden made her way along the left side, grabbing the shower at the farthest corner, adjacent to those along the back wall. Ever since she learned these particular baths were reserved for another Generation, she always tried to get close, hoping to catch a glimpse of an advanced recruit as they exited. But no one ever did. In fact, Layden and her peers hadn't run into anyone else from a different Generation yet. But it made sense they would all be at the same compound together. Nyine City was only so large, and it was probably beneficial to keep all recruits in the same area. Still, she wondered where exactly the other Generations were housed, and what it would be like to advance.

Layden tried to read the names on the doors before she went into her own bath. The exclusivity of these reserved chambers had a kind of paradoxical effect on her; she felt both insignificant and hopeful. There was a twinge of excitement at the thought of anything, ever, being reserved for her, even if felt far away and impossible.

Once in the bathing chamber, Layden took a breath and looked around. She liked this space. The air was fragrant with herbal scents and soap; the counters and walls were white marble and gray slate. A small counter lined the wall to her left with just enough space for their care regime and a towel. There was a mirror above the counter and a metal chute and clothes dispenser opposite, where Layden had learned she could deposit old clothes and receive her new ones—another mystery solved. At the back of the chamber was the shower. She palmed the console that turned on the water then stretched out her hand, feeling it as it warmed

As she stepped into the water, she dipped her head and let the stream drench her. She stared at her feet, lined with age and purple veins, and thought of pink blossoms.

CHAPTER EIGHT

A S EFFICIENT AS ONE tried to be, it was impossible to finish showering in less than twenty minutes. The regime was extensive and directed by a small holographic projection, the products listed with their corresponding body parts as one progressed. When she was finished, a quick and powerful spout of air dried her in seconds, and she stepped out and wrapped herself in a towel.

After the shower, it was ear drops and foaming mouth rinse, nasal spray and face cream, lip balm and hand ointment...so the process went. The last thing was a full-body cream whose properties were activated by heat. That was what the sauna was for.

Layden exited her chamber and crossed the courtyard to one of the benches, sitting down alone. She'd have to remain for a few minutes, or until the product started tightening on her skin. This was what made the lines so long. No one would be able to use her shower till she was done there.

The thick, warm air pressed in around her, tempting her to nod off. She was tired. After all, she'd hardly slept. The peculiar vision and the Guardian's reaction weighed heavily on her heart, but she tried to shake them away; she'd already spent the whole night obsessing about it all.

The bathing hall was quite beautiful, but she found herself, once again, wondering how the Council had found so much unpolluted and dry timber. Her thoughts ran to the tree in the courtyard, how rare it was with its pink blossoms. But that only led back to her waking dream and the pink petals tumbling across her feet. Layden shook her head again. It was a good thing she had a full day of work ahead of her.

At least she'd have some relief from her tangled thoughts.

Layden stood, ready to make her way back to her chamber to neutralize the toner and get dressed, but before she could, she heard a voice calling her name. She turned to see Manni's Host ambling her direction.

"Hey," she greeted. "Did you just get here?"

"Sort of. I was waiting for you to come out so I could talk to you."

"Won't you be late?" Layden looked around at the line of people waiting for a shower.

What she really wanted to ask was, why the urgency? She saw him regularly enough, though admittedly they'd been so consumed with their studies, they hadn't had a real conversation since that day in the Library.

"Is something wrong?"

"Did you notice...anything strange this morning?" he asked rather enigmatically.

"What do you mean?" Immediately her mind ran the incident that had left her stumbling through the hallway in the middle of the night. But that couldn't be what he meant.

"Anything out of the ordinary?" he asked again.

"I suppose there are fewer people here this morning," she said on a whim; he seemed intent that she guess.

"No, before the baths."

"Just tell me what it is I was supposed to have noticed, Manni," she said, sitting back down and fighting annoyance. She needed to go back to bed.

Manni followed and sat beside her, looking around conspiratorially. "Our doors unlocked in the middle of the night last night." His eyebrows raised slightly, and his eyes widened just enough to convey a restrained kind of excitement.

Layden, however, felt her chest constrict slightly. Yes. She had noticed that. "Do you know what happened?"

A corner of Manni's mouth curled up almost imperceptibly. Layden recognized it only because it was a trademark characteristic of his. He was proud of himself but trying not to show it.

"I was on my console last night and I stumbled onto the compound's security system."

"How do you *stumble onto* a security system?"

"It wasn't deep security, just like, locks to doors and stuff. I tested it on our floor, and it worked on my door. Then I overheard some other recruits talking about it this morning in line for the baths. What about you? Do you remember hearing a click in the middle of the night or anything?"

Layden bypassed the dozens of questions swirling in her head and went straight to what really concerned her. "Why would you do that Manni? Don't you think that's a bit reckless?"

"Yes, probably," he said, but the half smile remained.

"Don't do it again," she said more forcefully, alarmed by his lack of remorse. Then she lowered her voice and looked around to make sure no one could hear them. "It's one thing if it was an accident. But if the Defense League found out—or the Guardian, or even the Council—that you're doing it on purpose...we don't have carte blanche here, is all. They could think you're trying to undermine them or something."

Her tone was perhaps a bit harsher than she intended. She knew she should be concerned for him like she said she was, but, honestly, she was angry. Angry and annoyed. She needed things, some things, to remain the same so she could have an ounce of control.

Not to mention she never would've run into the Guardian if her door had been locked.

"Yeah. Okay," he said quietly.

Layden could see she'd deflated him, maybe even made him mad. She took a deep breath and tried to be kinder. "We've already seen so many people leave. It's barely been a month. I don't want you disqualified over something stupid like that."

After a small amount of time, he responded. "How many does that make?"

Layden sat back and sighed. "If I've kept track properly—"

"I'm sure you have."

"Twenty-three."

"'Soons, that's crazy." Manni exhaled darkly. "If the Council could tell they weren't good enough so quickly, why make them go through the Transfer to begin with?"

"Obviously those recruits weren't what the Council needed," Layden responded, looking away.

"Recruits, huh?" Manni laughed wryly. There was something tense in his features. "Not just recruits, Layden. Your peers. Your friends. And if the Council had used the Conservatory more wisely, then those twenty-three *recruits* could have been spared...well, all this."

Layden felt herself prickle under his insinuations. First, to behave so recklessly, and then to criticize the Council... Not to mention she wouldn't dare to call any of them friends. But she kept her mouth closed, not wanting to hop out of one fight and into another.

"So. D'you think they went back to their families?" he asked.

Again, Layden didn't respond. It seemed like they'd talked this to death, but the fact that she still didn't know bothered her more than a little. And if that was what happened, the idea of being cut out of the

Trials just to be sent back to life at the docks...it made her sweat turn cold.

"I don't think that would be so bad," Manni said at last.

"What? You wanna go back?" she asked him, slightly surprised.

Manni arrested her with a strange look and held her gaze for a moment. "You're saying there isn't at least a *part* of you that wants to go home?"

Layden paused to think, watching as the lines to the baths thinned and more peers left the benches to get dressed for the day. For all their childhood speculation, it surprised her that she and Manni had never had this particular conversation. It's true the Conservatory had encouraged them to look forward, but she supposed it would have been natural for other children to have spoken about home. Still, she'd never wanted to—after all there wasn't much to talk about.

She barely remembered her father. Her mother had been morose and distant, and her brothers hadn't given her the time of day. Manni was the closest she had to family now, and he was here with her. But even as she thought these things, a strange feeling welled up from within, choking her words.

"I doubt it's that simple," she finally replied.

"Maybe not," Manni persisted, "but if you could, would you?"

"What's there to go back to, Manni?" She crossed her arms. "An arranged union and partnership with some person I barely know, and the ordeal of having children just so we have more hands to fish and dive and haul?"

"Not all unions are arranged, and you wouldn't need to have children. Not if you didn't want," he said quietly.

"Okay, so, the other option would be to go it alone? Keep the mouths few so there's less to feed. And do *what*, Manni? Dive for soil like my mother? Fish for days on end like my father, who I barely knew because he was never home? We have a chance to do something great here. To *be* something great. Why are you entertaining anything different?"

Manni was silent again. She cast a sideways glance at him. She didn't mean to be sharp, but what was with his carelessness earlier and now all this talk of leaving? He was making her think of things she didn't want to and making her nervous on top of it.

"Yeah. You're right. It was a dumb thing to say."

"I didn't say you were dumb."

"I'd better go shower or I'll be late." He stood and offered a tight smile that didn't quite reach his eyes. "I'll see you in the Meeting Hall."

Layden sat for a moment longer, her ears and neck burning with some hidden discomfort. And deep in her bones, the loneliness echoed.

To Layden's surprise, Manni had met her like he'd said. He didn't mention their conversation from before, but his manner was reserved. However, there was no time to talk about it, even if he'd wanted to. As she took her seat beside him, they were greeted by a couple of other students filing in the row in front of them.

"Good morning, Manni. Layden."

It was Abisen's lithe seventy-year-old body that approached them, a haughty spring in her step. She was easily in the best shape of any of them. Following her was Mathis. While he'd stood up for Layden so readily that first week, he'd since taken the Guardian's advice and kept his distance. Even now she thought she saw a bit of reluctance when he greeted them.

"Morning—want us to move in?" Manni asked.

"Nah, it's okay. We could each have our own row if we wanted. We're dropping off like flies," Abisen said, shifting her feet and crossing her arms.

"We were just talking about that," Manni responded.

Layden felt herself withdraw a little. She didn't want her and Manni's topics of conversation open to others, though she didn't quite know why.

"Watching us go one by one?" Mathis asked, his narrow eyes trained down on Layden.

Oh, that's why.

"Excuse me?" Layden said, her jaw jutting forward in offense.

"Hey now," Manni said mildly to them both. "We're all in the same boat here."

Mathis practically snorted. "Please. She's a tidal wave. Not to meant she's been *singled out* more times than the number of weeks, and she's still somehow here. I'd say she knows something we don't. Tell us, Layden, what exactly did you do to get on the Council's good side, when even the Guardian hates you?"

The blood rushed to Layden's neck and cheeks, and she stood up to meet Mathis's eye. He was clearly trying to provoke her, but she didn't have the words to respond yet.

"Come on, that's not fair." Manni said, standing beside Layden and putting a staying hand on her arm.

"He's not wrong," Abisen said. "Your girlfriend obviously has favor with the Council, or else she'd be way gone."

When Abisen said it, it didn't sound like an insult—almost the opposite—but Layden was offended anyway. "What could I possibly have done to win favor with the Council? And *when*?"

"Layden, don't," Manni interjected.

Layden shot him a look. For some reason, his placation made her angrier, like she was some child to be reined in.

"What do any of you know about any of it? There's been more against me from the beginning than any of you have had to deal with. If I'm still here, it's because I'm earning it. Just like you."

"Whatever that means," Abisen said rolling her eyes up and away. "Look, we didn't mean to insult you. I just meant you'd be an idiot if you didn't see that you were on the track for advancement."

"No more than any of you!" Layden insisted.

She hated how defensive and unpersuasive her words sounded coming from her lips. Especially as she could tell she wouldn't change their minds. Somehow it felt worse to know that people hated her because they thought she was getting special treatment—when the opposite was so clearly true. She preferred them distrusting her or avoiding her because the Guardian hated her. The latter made sense; the former made her limbs shake with anger.

"Yeah, okay," Abisen said, throwing her hands up. "We'll just sit over there."

Layden's blood curdled as she watched them walk away, her brain spinning with words she longed to call out after them.

"Was all that necessary?" Manni intercepted, before she could say anything else.

Layden blanched. "How can you take their side? You know what I've been going through!"

What she was living with was the opposite of favor. In fact, after her run-in with the Guardian last night, outside her quarters past curfew, when she'd appeared *way* off the deep end, it was possible she'd be disqualified this very hour. He was probably preparing the paperwork now.

She was about to say that to Manni, her words poised on her tongue like arrows, when the Guardian entered through the side door. As he made his way to the front of the room, the students rose to their feet. Layden felt the color drain from her face, and she stood on wobbly limbs.

Without prompting, they all recited the pledge they'd come to know by heart, then waited for the Guardian to acknowledge their words.

"You may be seated," he said finally. "But before we begin our day, there is something that must be addressed."

Layden sat back down, her every nerve on edge.

"Last night there was a malfunction within our security system. Everything has since been corrected and further safeguarded, and it will not happen again. However, some of you managed to find your way out at unsanctioned hours. As you know, our curfew is strict, and it is strict for a reason." His eyes found Layden in the crowd with ease.

Her pulse beat in her neck, and a cold sweat broke out on her forehead and temples, clammy and instant. This was it. Out past curfew. Out of luck. Out of chances. She sensed Manni's head turn and look at her, but she buried her own gaze downward, staring at the veins in her Host's rigid feet. The Guardian finally had real grounds to dismiss her, and the coldness in his eyes had said it was time.

At least Abisen and Mathis would be proven wrong, Layden thought darkly.

"Be reminded that you are to remain in your rooms for the duration of the night, rising only when the announcements toll for the morning."

There was a pause and Layden dared a glance up. Was that it? Was that all he was going to say? She felt Manni release a breath beside her.

"You may begin to center," the Guardian allowed, looking around the room dispassionately.

Layden knew she should be relieved, but instead, she felt weak and in shock. Why hadn't she been reprimanded? Did he think she was just sleepwalking? Or maybe he was still figuring out what to do. Or...were Abisen and Mathis, right? Had she done something to gain favor with the Council? Wracking her brain, she couldn't think of a single thing. She'd only ever met the Grand Councilor once and so had everyone else who'd been collected. It was customary.

She turned and received an odd look from Manni. What was he thinking right now? Was he starting to believe Abisen and Mathis too? He didn't even know about the waking-dream yet, or breaking curfew, but he had read the moment between the Guardian and her, clear as day. Manni knew something had happened, and he could no doubt tell by her face that she'd expected trouble, but that the trouble had not come.

At any other point in her life, she would have poured the details on him like a torrential rain. But the more details she gave, the less it made sense—and the less it made sense, the more likely he was to think exactly what she couldn't bear for him to think. Even from where she sat there were two likely options: she'd rigged the game, or she was going mad.

That aching, loneliness throbbed within, and she bit her lip to the point of bleeding, reopening the cut that had never quite healed, just to feel something different.

The Guardian descended his platform and began walking among the students. Layden took a deep, shuddering breath and closed her eyes quickly. There was less chance of him interrupting her if he believed she was engaged.

Breathe, Layden. Deep breaths. Calm breaths, she instructed herself.

As she clenched her eyes tight, trying to think of other things, the visage from the night before flooded her mind. Her stomach dropped. She didn't want to think of this anymore! She didn't care what it was. She was tired. She wanted to sleep.

But it did not leave her. In fact, the picture crystallized before her. Nothing else in the room but the feet below her, the pink blossoms tumbling over her toes. She could feel the wind. It played across her face and tickled the hair on her arms. Layden barely noticed it happening, but in an instant, she knew the dream had returned. It consumed her view and paralyzed her movement.

But the view was changing now.

Her eyes lifted from her feet, away from the white skirt dancing around her legs, and beheld a dirt path in front of her. Someone else was there, but they were standing far away. A man with dark hair, dressed in white. Layden couldn't see his face, it was blurry and distant, but his arm extended in her direction.

And then the scene was gone. Suddenly, she came back to herself, her sight returning with hardly a warning.

"Layden Prier," the Guardian's tones rang out into the hall.

Layden looked up to see herself standing in the middle of the hall, her hand outstretched toward the front of the room as the man's had been. All eyes stared at her. Some seemed frightened, others hostile. But as she turned to look down at Manni, his expression chilled her most of all. He looked concerned. Very concerned. And a bit terrified. It was the exact look she'd imagined he'd have when he learned about the waking-dreams. It was the exact reason she hadn't told him.

"Come with me," the Guardian said.

Layden stumbled forward, having no better option herself.

CHAPTER NINE

THE COUNCILOR SAT BEHIND her desk calmly and tapped at her console with practiced fingers.

"Please send in Guardian Cherut," she said to the intercom that sat before her. It was time for their weekly meeting, but she had reason to believe this one would be more interesting than the last.

A second or two passed before the door opened and revealed the man she'd summoned. Jeremiah Cherut was one of her most trusted Guardians, though it was underselling him a bit to say this was his only role. She watched Jeremiah with appraising eyes as he entered the room and stood before her. When she smiled, she tried to make it warm and inviting.

"Hello, Miah," she cooed softly.

The man shifted uncomfortably, but it just made her smile more. She didn't use his short-name exactly, but it was close enough to presume an intimacy. He didn't like it when she did—oh yes, she could tell—but she didn't care. She'd never use it in public, of course, but in her own office, she could say whatever she wanted.

"You wanted to see me?" he asked shortly.

She looked him over for a moment. The dark hair cropped mid-length, almost hiding the wave, and slicked back with careless fingers. The green eyes. So uncommon. Some day he would explain to her how he came to have those eyes. But today was business, not pleasure.

"I actually believe you have something to tell me," she stated.

"You speak of the girl," he said, surmising her meaning.

"You clearly think she's doing well enough to stay, though I haven't seen anything out of the ordinary. Until recently. I beg you, explain to me what has been happening within the last twenty-four hours."

He nodded. She could tell she took him by surprise, but, to his credit, he hid it well. After all, he should know by now that nothing went on in that compound without her knowing.

"I am not sure, Grand Councilor. I was on my way to figure that out when you summoned me. The girl is in my office now, awaiting my return."

"But she *is* having visions."

Jeremiah didn't respond at first, but after a moment he nodded. "It is likely."

"Good. I wish to speak with her."

"I do not think that is the best idea, Grand Councilor."

She raised her eyebrows.

"That is," he continued carefully, "I am in the process of quashing a bit of a rebellious spirit."

"So? There have been many before like this."

"She is very taken with the Council. Any encouragement from yourself and she might prove to be unmanageable."

"In what way?"

"She speaks out of turn. Tries to rally others. If you endorse her, she may feel she has the right to do so."

"I see," she said, considering this. "Well, I trust your judgement as her Guardian. Has the separation helped at all?"

He paused again. Of course, she'd noticed he'd been trying to isolate her. She'd given him the benefit of the doubt that he had valid reasons. Isolation was a common technique to cull an excess of entitlement, though the girl's particular case seemed a bit dramatic.

"I believe so. She has one close friend. But she seems to be making more enemies these days."

"It's sobering," the Councilor said thoughtfully. "But she will need to know how that feels."

Jeremiah nodded.

"Well. Keep a close eye. When you deem it prudent, bring her to talk to me. It might be premature anyway if the visions don't persist."

"Yes, Grand Councilor."

"Miah, I have asked on more than one occasion that you call me Miranda."

The Guardian's mouth twisted imperceptibly, but, in the end, he gave her a small, tight smile. "I respect you too greatly to break such convention," he said.

The Councilor's smile only widened. In another life she would have called this charming repartee, but in their tightly run world, they could not be slave to the baser instincts of attraction and chemistry. Especially not between those working together. Still, it was tempting, even despite the large age gap. Age could be worked around, after all.

"You may leave," she granted him quietly. "Miah? Keep a close watch on the girl." She didn't bother with details, she knew he'd infer her meaning.

He hesitated slightly then nodded one final time before leaving the room. He did so quicker than she'd hoped.

Layden was shaking all over. She had never been more terrified in her life, and that included the moments before the Transfer. She sat in the Guardian's antechamber, awaiting his return. To be dismissed, surely.

All she could hear was the sound of her heavy breathing and the pounding of her heart in her eardrums.

The room was large but dark. Its main source of light was a wide window, draped and covered, the sun sneaking through a corner where the cloth had slipped away. She sat in front of the Guardian's desk at one end of the room, the door behind her to the right. Much of the space was clear, but stacks of large cushions and pillows were piled in various corners. She wondered what he needed so much space for, and why he didn't use the lights. Looking up, she could see them in the paneled ceiling, but they were covered over with more thick swathes of cloth. Layden stood tentatively and walked to the window. Standing on her tiptoes, she lifted a corner of the drape back and peered outside.

The view was the same as any view, endless waters spanning as far as one could see, but it was a welcome sight.

"Layden Prier," a voice rose from behind her.

Layden turned to see the Guardian entering the room then closing the door behind him. He walked briskly toward her causing her to lean back defensively, but she quickly realized his eyes were only on the window. As he pulled the drapes back and let in the full light of the day, it revealed a beautifully ornate carpet in the center of the room, as well as—more astonishingly—many, many books. Where there was a space along the wall, there was a shelf fully stocked. She'd never heard of people keeping so many books to themselves. There were also candles on any flat surface she spotted, no doubt how he kept the place lit at night with the covered lights. All of it was...not what she expected.

"Please, have a seat," he said, gesturing toward the chair.

Layden sat gingerly as he moved around the other side of the desk. In the natural light, she could see his face and hands more clearly. The products she was using these days gave her Host's skin a waxy look, but he didn't have that. He looked, for lack of a better word, unrefined. It wasn't a common look among those in Nyine City, and it brought back vague and distant memories from childhood.

"Guardian, I was unwell earlier, but I'm feeling better. I can return to class," she ventured, her voice trembling.

"I am glad to hear that," he said judiciously as he tidied some things on his desk.

It, too, was covered with papers, books, and candle wax. Hadn't they made a wax that didn't drip like that? Her eye caught a book on the corner of the desk; it was small and green. Her heart leapt. Was it the same one he took from her in the Library? The Guardian swept it up with some others and deposited them in a drawer before she could check for sure.

"I know I haven't been the most ideal candidate," she began again, seizing his silence. "And I know I've made a lot of mistakes. I've never apologized for walking in on you and...my Host."

He stopped what he was doing and stared at her, his expression growing dangerous. But she had to say what she needed to say. She might not get another chance.

"I just wanted to say, if it makes any difference, I do *not* want to go back to the Outlayers." Tears welled in her eyes, and she scrunched her nose to keep them from spilling over.

"What?" he asked her stiffly.

"I want to be here. With everything in me. I don't want to go back."

"Who said you'd be going back to the Outlayers?" he asked. His tone was low and quiet.

She paused to take in his question. At first, she thought this meant she was wrong for assuming she'd be dismissed. But then a thought crossed her mind that maybe she was wrong to assume she'd be *sent to the Outlayers* when dismissed. She was too afraid to inquire which it was.

"No, Layden Prier, it seems you are in my office on entirely different grounds."

Layden forced herself to swallow.

"I am here to ascertain what is happening with you. Three times now I have witnessed you falter, faint, and show up in corridors you have no business traversing in the middle of the night. Now, I have a suspicion as to what's going on. But it will be best for everyone if you will explain it to me, in full, without me having to make assumptions."

Layden's mouth fell open awkwardly. She hadn't expected a chance to explain herself. Now that she had it, she wasn't sure what to say.

"Well," she began haltingly, "I have been losing sleep—a reoccurring dream from childhood; it might be in my files. Also, I don't have a console in my room?" She posed this as a question so as not to sound accusatory. "So, I've been waking throughout the night, anxious I'll oversleep."

The Guardian merely gazed at her, his expression unimpressed.

"I have been feeling strangely," she continued under his stare. "Nauseated, disoriented. My vision...goes..."

"Is that what happened today?" he said after a time.

Layden didn't know if she should explain about the vision, or if it was better left unsaid. The possibility of coming across as crazy was still a danger. "Not exactly."

"Layden Prier. This may very well be your only chance to explain. Do so."

"I had...a dream."

"Yes, you just said. A reoccurring dream from childhood."

"No. This is a different one. More like a daydream? The same thing happened to me last night, when you, well, when you ran into me."

"What was this dream about?"

She thought she saw a flicker of curiosity glinting in his eyes, though his face remained disinterested. "I'm not sure it's a dream exactly," she back peddled. "I see it so clearly, but I tend to lose track of where I am. I don't recall falling asleep either."

"What do you *see*, then?"

"I see my feet, Guardian."

"Your feet," he repeated blankly.

"Well, they're not my feet, or rather, *her* feet." She gestured downward. "They're someone else's. But I can feel them beneath me, on dry ground."

His right eyebrow rose. "Dry ground?"

"Yes, it's brown and flat, and I can almost feel the pebbles beneath my toes."

"Almost feel?"

"I *can* feel them," she said more decisively. "And as I'm staring, flowers—like the tree in the courtyard—pink petals tumble across my toes. And then I look up, and there's a man, standing down a path from me, facing me."

"And what else?"

"That's all. I think maybe more will come, though. The man wasn't part of the dream till this morning. I might dream it again."

"What makes you think so?"

Layden shrugged slowly. "It feels...unfinished."

"I see."

The Guardian was silent for a few moments, likely collecting his thoughts, while Layden sat feeling exposed. She had been sure he'd find her disturbed, but he wasn't acting that way.

"Dreams aside, it is my job to inform you that you will be continuing under my private tutelage for the remainder of the term. You will carry out your day as normal, except that you will do your practicum in the morning, and your tutoring will take place in the afternoon."

"Why?" The word came out choked. She didn't know whether to feel excited or terrified. Why the individual attention? Was this good or bad?

"I have been told to keep a close eye on you. The Council has yet to determine whether you'll be of use to them, or whether you'll be a detriment. But as of right now, you are a distraction."

Layden's cheeks went hot. A distraction to the other candidates. So, she would be completely alone all day.

"Yes, sir," she answered absentmindedly.

"Guardian," he corrected her. "I am your Guardian."

"Yes, Guardian," she said. Though she did not feel remotely like his relationship with her reflected that title. If only she could have requested a different tutor, someone who didn't hate her as much. But things didn't work that way. She could tell he liked the arrangement about as much as she did.

He stood and gave her a small nod, and she inferred she was dismissed. She rose and walked to the door.

"I will see you this afternoon. For now, I suggest you make use of the Library. End of term is fast coming."

Layden left his presence in a stupor, not regaining any kind of mental presence until she made it to the double doors of the library. As she was entering, a group of people blocked her way. They were younger than she was, possibly in the Year Fifties. They wore green jumpsuit-like attire and heavy boots, and their bodies were lean and muscular. Some looked at her with confusion, others annoyance, like they didn't understand what she was doing there.

Layden hurried aside and let them march through as a unit, not quite in step but not out of it either. She scrambled through the door and made her way to the study rooms.

With every step she took her bones felt heavier, and that deep sense of isolation constricted within her like a coiled rope. She wished she could turn to someone, anyone, and divulge all her fears and doubts. But she wasn't likely to be able to, not with the Guardian keeping her wholly separate from everyone.

And without her around, there wasn't anything to stop her peers—or her friends—from believing whatever they wanted about her.

CHAPTER TEN

L AYDEN'S CHEEK WAS STUCK to her book, the moistness of her skin fusing to the gloss of the page. Her fingers reached up and peeled it away gingerly, and she realized, yet again, that neither were hers. She still wasn't used to waking up in someone else's body, but after three months, the adjustments were taking less time.

She sighed. It appeared she'd fallen asleep in the study rooms again. It wasn't the first time and probably wouldn't be the last, but it was unfortunate all the same.

Her private tutelage with the Guardian had come with a few perks—such as getting to be out past curfew and all hours' access to the cantina—but it also came with a price. The Guardian was relentless in his instruction, and her brain was fried from staring at books and screens full of information she was quizzed on almost incessantly. Not to mention his daily questioning about her now *persistent* visions.

Visions. That's what the Guardian had begun calling them. He took more of an interest than she'd expected, inquiring often if she'd seen anything new. Unfortunately, while they were happening regularly, nothing within them was changing.

But at least she wasn't *distracting* anyone anymore, because she was never around anyone to begin with. Her only social interaction for the last two months came during the hours she spent with the Guardian—though even calling that "social" felt like a stretch. She didn't even keep the same meal hours as everyone else, preferring to use the morning hours to study before her sessions with the Guardian, and often eating late at night after they were done.

She did occasionally see her peers on their way to the baths and study rooms and was even running into more recruits from other Generations now that she was on an adjusted schedule. It was hard to tell what the different Generations were up to, but occasionally she'd see the Year Sixties in the Meeting Hall doing extensive centering, or a group of Fifties marching somewhere together. The Forties she encountered were often lost in thought, sometimes staring out windows or contemplating the tree in the courtyard for what seemed like hours. But no one spoke with her.

Not that she blamed any of them. The latter didn't know her, and the former had good reason to avoid her. Her last big interaction with them had been that day in the Meeting Hall where she'd tranced out and been carted away by the Guardian. Now, whoever was left from her intake—and those numbers appeared to be dwindling weekly—seemed to view Layden as some mysterious, mythological creature; they were in awe when they saw her and fearful because they didn't understand her.

But mostly she was too busy and too tired to think or care about any of that.

Except when it came to Manni. He was one person Layden never seemed to run into, and the one person she wished she would. A few times she'd thought about stopping by his room again, but she couldn't afford to mess up anymore, and honestly, her push-down-and-avoid tendencies were working overtime. She hadn't gotten to explain things when she had the chance—in some ways she'd chosen not to—and now she had to live with that. Not to mention their last real conversation had been a fight about the Council, where she'd staunchly defended their way of life and criticized him for being honest about how he felt.

Salt it, he *should* be mad at her.

Still, it was hard to think he might be doubting her like the others—or worse, be jealous of her private tutoring. She could only hope he was giving her the benefit of the doubt when he thought of her.

Layden sighed and rubbed her forehead. Tapping the screen of the console, she looked at the time. It was only an hour till the morning announcements. Her body ached and she thought about going back to bed, but it made more sense to head to the baths. Layden stood and gathered her things, lingering on a sheet of paper with an idea she'd scribbled late last night. On second thought, she sat back down and began to make notes on it.

Layden and the Guardian worked together in his office for close to six hours a day, and often they worked through dinner, which was fine with her. Because unfortunately, she still was no closer to choosing a path for her presentations than she had been three weeks ago.

She'd thought about creating a new Long-Life product, but the Council's advancements had been so prolific that anytime she had an idea, no matter how small or large, she'd find out the Council had already pursued it. And while she'd been studying biology and chemistry with the Guardian extensively, she was still just barely grasping it. She could spout answers fine—her ability to recollect complex detail fooling even the Guardian—but she didn't have an organic understanding of any of it.

On top of it all, she often wondered if all the studying was even worth it. One time she'd dared to ask the Guardian if it was her mind or the Host's brain storing the information, and if she would remember any of it when she advanced to the next Host. The Guardian had explained—after chaffing at her assumption she'd advance—that the consciousness was just as involved in learning as the brain was. What she desired to transfer would transfer. As the science of Host technology was held close to the Council's vest, she would have to take his word for it.

But it wasn't all a struggle. In addition to her keen memory, she seemed to be able to hold an inordinate amount of information about the Earth-that-was. History, socio-economic relationships, politics, even the start of the Council—she drank it all in like a sponge. She remembered these facts and dates like they were a part of her own life, especially when attached to a story that intrigued her. And even though he was clear her time would be better spent on the hard sciences the Guardian seemed almost to approve of her fascination.

"I am surprised you have taken such an interest in this," he had said to her as they sat in review one day. "There are not many who care where we have come from. But there is much to learn from putting ourselves in the minds of the Council at that time in their journey. Your attention shows a layer of awareness not often displayed in one your age."

Layden didn't know what to say to such overt praise. It was the first compliment he'd ever given her and one of the few times his manner had warmed from its stern and disinterested gaze. So, she simply stayed quiet and did her best to hide her reddening cheeks.

"But it is not all worth your time," he continued after a moment.

"What do you mean?"

"Mythology, deities, the spiritual bent of humanity as it were. I noticed you have a book on the leaders of one of the organized religions of the eighteenth century. A notable, if not fruitless, aspect of humanity."

Layden thought about this for a moment. "It's interesting though that so many people would believe in a deity of some kind; something that could create and destroy them. It's not a concept we covered at all in the Conservatory, and yet it seems a lot of people believed in something beyond themselves in one form or another."

The Guardian moved to his desk and began to tidy some papers, looking up only briefly to give her a noncommittal nod. "It was, indeed, a large part of our communal history. A way to soothe the fear of mortality."

"The only thing is, I can't seem to find any of the original texts," Layden continued while there was space to muse. The longer she could keep him from neuroscience the better. "I see references and quotes to multiple religious works of the Eastern and Western world-that-was, but the archives don't hold any copies. Isn't that odd? If it was such a huge part of history, as you say."

"Not really," the Guardian said, his tone edging on bored. "The Council, along with many in their time, believed that religion was the cause of most of the suffering in the world. False hope, the abdicating of one's responsibility, the ethnocentric and egocentric mindsets, and prejudices. In their minds, it was better to eradicate religion from our daily lives and remove the temptation to return to it."

"But we center," she dared to persist. "That has its basis in Eastern mythologies and spirituality, right?"

He seemed surprised by this observation but responded quickly. "We center to order the mind, nothing more. We do not pray or seek some greater enlightenment. Any terms that have been borrowed from ages past have little to do with what they used to mean. The Council has adopted and pioneered their own meaning for these words."

Layden nodded her understanding.

"Believe me," he concluded, "you would be unwise to bring anything that concerned this topic before the Council."

Her expression must have seemed less than convinced because he stopped and looked directly at her. "Do you understand? Barring your personal time—which I can hardly believe you have much of—continuing down this path would be unwise."

Layden had nodded and assured him she would heed his advice, though she'd replayed his words in her head afterward, sure that he had been implying she could, in fact, study on her own. So, she continued her fascination with the Earth-that-was in all its forms, finding deeper and more extensive rabbit trails, until she was up till three in the morning and falling asleep on the books, her cheek sticking to the page.

Layden put her papers down once more and took a breath. She knew she could do nothing with all the things she was learning, but nor did she feel able to stop.

Because that quiet whisper in the depth of her chest told her this knowledge wasn't wasted. Who knows, perhaps she could find some parallel, something that had been that could be again, only greater. Perhaps she was fascinated with the pulse of the world-that-was, as the Guardian had said, for a reason.

The sun had just begun to set, and the Guardian's office was filling with darkness. Layden rose slowly, aware of the tight muscles within her aged body, and accepted a long matchstick from the Guardian to help him light the candles. There were so many that this normally took a few minutes, but Layden was anxious to continue their session, so she moved faster than normal. She had questions to ask. She moved the flame from wick to wick, watching the pearl of fire start small, catch, and grow.

When she finished on her side of the room, she turned to see the Guardian staring at her. What was he thinking when he did that? And was he aware he did so, openly and often? She'd always been told staring was rude.

"What is it?" Layden dared to ask.

"You seem almost eager to continue today."

Layden shrugged. "I was hoping to ask some questions."

"Have I ever been able to stop you?"

Layden ignored the jab. "I have some specific questions," she clarified.

The Guardian gathered the excess matchsticks, placed them in the
timber box beside the back wall, and moved over to their study area. He
had rearranged his office to accommodate their study, setting up a board
to write on and a workbench to do some of the more hands-on work. She
usually sat on a stool at the bench while he stood by the board or walked
around the room when he talked. Depending on what he had planned,
books and materials would be set out when she arrived. Today she had
come in to a makeshift chemistry set, and they had worked on reverse
engineering some of the Long-Life products most of the afternoon.

"Well, go on then." He made his way over to his desk and took a seat.

She mirrored him and sat on the high stool at the workbench. "It has
to do with the subject that I've chosen for the presentations," she began.

"I am happy to hear you have chosen one," he said, though he
sounded, at most, indifferent.

"I think I have. I'm interested in the conception of the Trials. The
beginning of all of this. But there isn't much information. Mainly historical accounts, but nothing in detail."

"And your question is?"

"Do you have any books you can recommend?"

He paused for a moment, then replied, "Have you checked with the
archivist?"

"Yes, of course. She said to speak with you."

"Hmm. I will see what I might have around. Until then, as always,
you can ask me any question you have."

Layden nodded, relieved. "Thank you, Guardian."

She paused, knowing she'd have to be careful with how she worded
her next question. The truth was that since she and Manni had last
spoken in the baths, she'd thought a great deal about what he'd said. She

realized his criticism of the Council had made her angry because at her core she feared he was right. Some aspects of the Trials so far—mainly the hasty dismissals of her peers after they'd already endured the Transfer—*did* feel careless and, dare she say it, even cruel. But she didn't believe the Council was cruel. So, if she could prove they had simply overlooked that dynamic of the Trials, then maybe she could help improve it.

"I'm wondering about the Collection process," she began cautiously, "and the qualifications for being chosen to join the Council."

"Ah," the Guardian said, his brow furrowed, lips slightly parted in hesitation.

"Not that I want to know for myself," she said quickly. "And I understand if you can't tell me. I just want to know why there haven't been any Council replacements or additions since that first Generation fifty years ago. I thought maybe I could help with both processes. Make them more...efficient."

"I see," he replied.

She waited for him to say more, but he didn't.

"I'm not insinuating that the Council doesn't know what they need in a Council member," she tried again, motivated by the niggling doubt Manni had planted that day in the baths. "But maybe there's a way we can make the years in the Conservatory work better for us all. Or even find new ways to look for potential in recruits before they're taken from the Outlayers. It seems to me that a lot of us didn't even make it past the first month here. If the Council knew so soon, why couldn't they have been able to tell back at the Conservatory? And maybe if I'm going this direction with my presentation, I can examine the Collection itself. Make the transitions easier on the family, and the children." She paused and bit her lip, waiting for his feedback.

The Guardian's face, however, was inscrutable. "You are assuming the Council wants the transition easy," he said delicately.

Why wouldn't they?

"I suppose it is an assumption," she said slowly. "But is it an incorrect one? I can't see what could be gained from making it difficult for everyone. I think I could make a good case for a transitionary program. Familial visitation even."

"The Council wants the children to adopt the Conservatory as their home. The severing of family ties is for the child's good. And the Council's."

"But it's *not* always the best, and the Conservatory isn't a home. That's precisely my point."

"Do you speak from everyone's perspective, Layden Prier? Or solely your own?"

Her neck went hot as his words sunk in, and she suddenly doubted her every intention. Was this truly Manni's doubt? Or was the Guardian, right? Did she miss her family after all? Was it she who was looking for a home? That persistent ache of loneliness quivered in her bones, and she drew her arms around herself, constricting tight as if she could squeeze the feeling away.

There were a few moments of silence where he seemed to consider her and her nonanswer.

"Well. While I cannot tell you which direction to pursue, I will fill you in on the beginning of the Generational Trials. Perhaps that will help you make your decision."

Layden nodded, trying not to appear too relieved or eager.

The Guardian leaned back in his seat. "Let's see. We have spent much time speaking about how the Earth was before the floods. The wars, the civil unrest. We have also spoken on the formation of the Council itself. But the Trials arose out of something quite different. The Council arose out of desperation, the Trials out of hope.

"You see, for you to fully grasp this, I must tell you something that few people know. It is not kept confidential, so much as simply not spoken of. The people who live today do not understand the times as they were. They see a mended society and a bright future. The truth is hard to comprehend when not seen through the eyes of that time. Only because you understand it better than most do I even dare mention this."

Layden tried to keep her face neutral, but he had never spoken so frankly with her, like she was no longer a tedious student but someone worthy of conversation.

"You have learned about all the members of the Council, both the present members and the original—now recorded as deceased—correct?"

"Yes. The Grand Councilor is the only one who is still living, all others having been replaced by the first round of the Generational Trials."

"The Councilor is still living, yes. But so are the others."

Layden had to replay his words several times before she could speak. "I'm sorry?"

"It was simpler to record the original Council members as deceased, but they are all, in fact, still alive."

"I don't understand," Layden said, shaking her head.

"After their experimentation with Host Transfer, the Council members knew they could not simply abdicate the Council. The science they had discovered within the Host technologies was equivalent to the power of immortality. Naturally, it would be irresponsible to let that fall into just any hands. Additionally, to the world, the Grand Councilor spoke of secrets—mysteries and revelations she and her Council had gleaned from their time with their Hosts—and a new way of looking at humanity. They needed time to teach and guide the future generations properly. But during their journey, their original bodies had...expired."

He paused for a moment. When he resumed, his tone was quiet and cautious. "You are aware that the Host's mind goes into stasis, and I am sure you have surmised your body does as well."

"I suppose so, yes," Layden said breathlessly. They'd been told precious little about all this, but Layden assumed it was more complicated than her body lying in a med-bay somewhere.

"The human body, when separated from the mind, must be kept in specific conditions if it is to be inhabited again. Yours is in a growth-enabled cryo-chamber, so that while you are inhabiting this body, yours is not only safe but growing, ready for you to inhabit it the next chance you get. This advanced form of cryo-tech is necessary, as the body does not live long without a mind. Unfortunately, the same cannot be said for the other way around..." He trailed off, as if lost in thought.

"What do you mean?"

"You are familiar with the term Sectioning?"

Layden felt her blood run cold. She nodded. For the worst crimes against the Council and its people—murder, sabotage, destruction, sexual deviance—there existed a procedure that separated the mind from the body, storing them apart from one another. It was rumored that in this state, the mind did not sleep but was awake every moment, devoid of any form of physical sense. Forever.

She shuddered.

"A mind, it seems, does not need a body to live on. Needless to say, this consequence is reserved for only the most dangerous and destructive individuals." The Guardian shook his head and returned to his original line of thought. "At any rate, the body does need periodic and specific communication from, well, anything, and the cryo-tech fulfills the role of your brain in this instance. However, this technology, even in its simplest form, was not discovered until much later in the Council's collective journey. Hence the Collection. Hence the Trials."

The Guardian paused and looked at her pointedly, as though she should be inferring something important. But she had no idea where he was going.

"I don't understand," Layden finally said.

"The first Generational Trials were not used to find replacements for the Council members. They were begun to find suitable, long-term Hosts for the Council members."

There was a moment of silence as Layden tried to process this.

"What?" she asked again. She knew she sounded like a broken record, but she didn't want to risk misunderstanding something this big.

"They had planned to live in one last Host, while they scouted potential from the next Generation of recruits—recruits who would truly be able to replace them and rule in their stead. So, while they planned to utilize the Trials as they do now—allowing candidates to prove themselves worthy of serving on the Council—it could not happen right away."

"So, for the past fifty years, it's been the same Council members...living in other people's bodies?" Layden was mortified. She couldn't imagine what it would be like to stay in her Host's body for the rest of her life. "But what about the mind? I thought the transfer wasn't meant to be permanent. Where did the mind of the Host go?"

She knew she was pushing her luck as soon as the words left her mouth. These were clearly things they'd not been told for a reason. He had shared a lot with her, but would he share this?

The Guardian lifted his chin slightly and regarded her for a moment. "I don't presume to know all the details," he said carefully, "but I do know that those who have given their bodies so that the Council could live on, did so willingly and sacrificially."

"Willingly," Layden repeated slowly.

The Guardian nodded.

"But the Councilor...I've seen pictures. She looks just as she did. Older, for sure, but it's her face."

"Older, yes, but not old enough. Do the math."

Layden paused. "It's been fifty years since the Council added a member...but she'd already transferred once before that?"

The Guardian nodded. "The dates are not precise; record keeping failed us at that time. She was in her forties when she formed the Council, but seventy-five when they first pioneered the Host technology. Another ten years passed before the first Trials yielded the Council members' long-term Hosts. And, you are correct, it has been fifty years since then."

"One hundred and thirty-five?"

"Yes, one-thirty-five, give or take a few years."

"So...how?" Layden asked, beginning to feel queasy.

"The Councilor inhabits the body of her daughter," he said simply.

Layden was speechless at the thought. Her *daughter*?

"You see what a sacrifice it was, for them both. To have a daughter at all, after the Season of Sterility, but then to give her up? To let her give herself up so that the world could continue healing? That is not something everyone could do, and it is why the Grand Councilor had to do it."

Layden fought another shudder. She studied her Guardian's face; his features poised in magnanimous awe. But she did not feel awe. She wouldn't say it aloud, but she couldn't fathom how anyone could act *that* sacrificially. Choosing the greater good over the life of your own flesh and blood? Over your own life? She knew she should think differently if she wanted to govern with these people, but, faced with this hard truth, her own humanity emerged like a whale breaching the surface of the sea.

"How did she have the daughter?" Layden asked quietly.

"She was genetically assisted, like every other woman in our world. A fertilized embryo was implanted and assisted at the correct times so the gestation process could continue unaffected by the Sterility."

"But her daughter *looks* like her," Layden said, unable to move on.

The Guardian shrugged. "It was early on. Perhaps the process was not as streamlined. Instead of a uniform genotype and phenotype combination—the reason you and your peers have the same eye and hair color and exceptional ability to learn—they may have used her actual genetics. The process is much more efficient now."

Is that what happened to you? Layden wondered, glancing up at his green eyes. But she didn't dare ask that one aloud.

"All of this information is to offer perspective on the Generational Trials and why there has not been anyone to replace a Council member since its inception. The Council are not looking for more Hosts. Those who replace them will replace them for good. That is not a burden they can hand to just anyone. A worthy candidate must, above all, be trusted with the temptation of immortality."

Layden nodded, trying to be thankful for the insight. However, all she could think of was that there hadn't been one person worthy of replacing a member since the Council's formation. How did she stand a chance?

The Guardian seemed to see the doubt on her face for he interrupted her thoughts. "If you use this information, do so indirectly."

Layden nodded.

"Come. I think we have had enough for the night. I suggest you get something to eat and retire early. We have a long day tomorrow if you are going to begin your research."

Layden was surprised. "You're helping me?"

"Of course not. But, as the materials you seek are hard to find, I will assist you there. Spend the night thinking of an angle that will convince me this is worth pursuing. I will give you one day. Otherwise, you will have to come up with something else."

Layden nodded eagerly, ignoring the contradiction that his approval of her topic was, in many respects, more help than most of the students were getting. Regardless, his sudden shift in attitude gave her confidence. She left his office with much to think about and feeling both lighter and heavier than she had before.

CHAPTER ELEVEN

L AYDEN WALKED TO THE cantina to get some supper as the
Guardian had said, though she wasn't planning on the extra
rest, even though her body ached from head to toe. Her Guardian
had given her some books to start her off, and she wanted to review
them. She also didn't think she'd be able to sleep after the conversation they'd just had. It was already consuming her thoughts so much
that she didn't even notice someone else was in the cantina until
she'd gotten her food and turned to sit.

"Manni!"

Her friend looked up, his face mirroring her surprise. "Layden?
What are you doing here?" He gestured to the seat across from him.

She took it, setting her tray down.

"Working late..." she said, her words trailing off. She still felt
self-conscious about the private tutoring, and all the things that led
to it. She stilled her shaking hands and wondered again what Manni
might be thinking.

His eyes met her own and then looked away quickly; his expression became cloudy. "Yeah, me too," he said. His voice sounded
weary.

An odd tenseness took the place of the excitement they'd first
felt to see one another.

After a moment, he broke the ice and spoke again. "It's this
presentation," he said. "I'm really...stuck."

Layden's interest was piqued. She felt a little guilty about it, but she was relieved to hear he was having problems too. "Yeah? Well, if it makes you feel any better, I just found my topic today."

"Really?" He looked alarmed, which made her cheeks grow hot, but she was hoping this little concession would make him feel better about things. About them.

"Yeah, well, I hope. The Guardian is going to tell me if I'm allowed to continue with it."

"Well, at least you have something," he said.

They both returned to their food.

"What's it like?" he asked after a moment.

"What do you mean?"

"To work with him, one on one?" He seemed self-conscious about asking but also strongly curious.

Layden thought for a moment and then proceeded carefully. "It's a bit like when you're deep under water, and you're all turned around and can't find the surface. I don't think anything I say is ever what he wants to hear. And..." She thought back to her many hours with the Guardian, trying to find the right words. "He has this way of presenting something directly—a thought or idea—but then expecting me to interpret it and arrive at a completely different conclusion. As you know, that's not my strong suit. But if I miss his meaning, he gets angry with me. When he goes dead silent, that's when I feel like I've *really* missed something. I don't know."

She looked to Manni to see if he understood. But his expression was oddly disheartened.

"Don't pity me." She half-laughed, looking away. "It's my fault I'm there."

"I'm not pitying you," he said. "And you didn't ask for the visions."

Layden paused, wondering what exactly he'd heard about them. She supposed word had to have gotten around at this point. "The *visions* have nothing to do with it. He told me on my first day of tutoring that I had become a distraction to the rest of you."

"Okay, Layden." His laugh mocked her. "Say what you will. But there's no way you're going to convince me that you're in private tutelage, in the Generational Trials, because you're being punished."

"Then you don't understand what it's like," she countered tersely.

It was Manni's turn to bite his tongue and return to his food. They sat in tense silence for a few moments before he spoke again. "What, uh, what is it?" he asked tentatively.

He meant her thesis. They weren't supposed to share, but at that moment she wanted things between them to go back to normal so desperately...she decided to tell him. Maybe it would even serve as an apology for their last disagreement.

"I'm looking into the Collection and the years at the Conservatory. Maybe even the transitions."

Manni perked up in interest, and his eyes held hers for a long moment. Layden tried to read his face, but it was one of those moments where his Host's features were too unfamiliar to interpret.

"It's like you said. Some of this seems...inefficient. I don't think the Council is doing it on purpose, mind you, but maybe I can help."

Manni sat back in his seat, a smile rising to his face. "I'm sure you can, Dennie."

Layden felt hope rise. "Really?"

"Absolutely."

She paused again, smiling back.

"What would you do?" His open posture and bright eyes encouraged her to keep going.

She tore off a chunk of bread and sat back. "I think I can come up with a transitionary plan where the children are better assessed for potential, and maybe even given a choice. Where they can clearly see what's being offered. Maybe even a compassionate-release term for those not coping?"

Manni nodded. "Your best bet would be to present it in a way that works for the Council's benefit. Who knows how many families they've had petitioning to have their children back," he added.

Layden stopped short and watched as Manni stirred his food around. His words triggered more heavy emotions within her. All of this was bringing up powerful memories of her own transition period, and while it had been a long time since she'd allowed herself to think of those things, apparently that ache for family lived deep in her bones.

"Do you know if yours asked for you back?" she asked quietly.

He laughed bitterly. "Yes. Apparently, a lot. And the Council almost granted them their request. But I guess they saw too much in me," he said this last bit with not a small measure of bitterness.

"You think the Council said no because they didn't want to let you go?"

"I know as much. The evaluators said everyone has a chance to get their child back if the parents make a good case. But I know that mine wanted me and couldn't have me."

"*How* do you know that?" Layden had a hard time believing the evaluators would tell him that. Even at this stage, she could see how that information would confuse a child and send the wrong message about the Council. Manni looked unwilling to say more.

"Please. If I'm going to make a difference, I should know as much as possible. There's clearly something I don't."

"Oh, there's nothing else really to tell," he said. Even with his Host's features, she could tell he was lying. "I hope you can figure something out," he said with finality, beginning to gather his utensils and trash.

She knew he wasn't going to say more, but she was thankful he had opened up in some measure. Layden returned to her food.

"Do...do you want to meet me here tomorrow?" he asked tentatively.

"You mean, at night?" she asked.

"Yeah. I assume that's when you eat now?"

She nodded.

"All right. I'll see you then."

"Are you allowed out?" she asked.

"Of course," he said. "The Guardian spoke with the kitchens since I'm working late on my concepts. I need the extra time if I'm going to make it worthwhile. See you tomorrow." He picked up his tray and left, giving her a small smile as he did.

Layden was left alone once more, processing the plethora of emotions running through her. The loneliness eased a little with the prospect of nightly dinners with Manni, but that didn't fully quench the feeling that seemed to follow her around. And, as petty and unfounded as it was, a new feeling was surfacing that she didn't know what to do with. There was no reason why Manni shouldn't be receiving special conditions, and she of all people could not begrudge him a little ease. Still, while the Guardian was Guardian to them all, Layden couldn't help but feel a stab of envy. For the first time, she got a taste of what everyone else might be feeling.

Layden stood outside the Guardian's office, hesitant to enter. She knew he was waiting for her, but she was anxious. If what Manni said last night was true, and the Council never intended to give the children back, it weakened the odds that the Guardian—or the Council for that matter—would respond to her ideas. Then again, if there was no changing the process once a child was collected, that made the evaluation and transition process even more important.

The books the Guardian had given her hadn't helped much either and she'd spent most of her morning trying to understand why he'd chosen them at all. The first was a historical overview of the concept of allegiance, be it to countries, religions, or cultures. She'd read about how people's faithful allegiance to causes or movements could affect momentous change, or in some instances bring about war. She also read about how, in some cases, allegiance was required or even demanded by a ruling power.

It was through reading this section that Layden fully understood what Manni had said their first day, that the Council was seeking to ensure their allegiance through a pledge. But she had a hard time deciding if her allegiance to the Council had been her choice, or if it was something required of her. She didn't like that she didn't know the answer. On one hand she could say she definitely chose the Council. On the other, it seemed the Council chose her.

The other book the Guardian had given her was a stark, data-oriented report on the Generational Trials. Den names, Generation year, dates of entry, and dates of dismissal. At first, she hadn't been sure what to even do with the sheer amount of information, but she did note right away that there was a section for "categories of release." The papers did not give much away, but she might be able to decode the terms with his help.

Finally, she entered the Guardian's office and took her seat. He was already at his desk, but he didn't look up when she entered. He seemed to be studying something and taking a note or two every few seconds.

"Guardian," she prompted tentatively, but he did not reply. She tucked in her lips and sat back to wait. That's when she noticed what he was reading. The small, green book he'd taken from her that day at the Library lay beside him.

Finally, he lifted his gaze to her. "Forgive me. I had an urgent letter to finish." He stood and pulled the papers with him, folding and tucking them into his tunic. Then he tidied his desk and swept the book unceremoniously into his desk drawer again.

"What is that book?" she dared to ask. She didn't expect an answer, but his attitude had changed the last time they met, and she thought she'd hazard a try.

He paused for a moment, and it looked like he was considering telling her. But, alas, his mouth curled in the sort of grimace that masqueraded as a smile, and he diverted the topic. "What have you come up with for today?" He walked around to the front of his desk and leaned back against it so that he was only feet from her.

Layden took a steady breath and sat up straighter. "Well," she began, "I *think* the dismissal data on the Trials can help me figure out what the Council is looking for in a candidate."

"How?"

"If I know what they don't want, perhaps I can extrapolate what they do. But I might need help understanding what the terms mean."

A small light came into his eyes, and he nodded slowly. "Go ahead."

Layden pulled out her lists and thumbed through the pages. "There are subcategories for each of these, but these are a few of the main ones. S.S.?" she asked, looking up.

"Subpar, substandard. They were not performing up to the expected standard."

"Okay. What about O.C.?"

"Obstinate, contrary. Mostly displaying an inability to work cohesively with other members."

"Obstinate...okay." She looked at the next one. "M.T.?"

"Myopic, tactical. Unable to see the bigger picture. Narrow-minded."

"There are a lot of those," Layden said. "Especially toward the end."

"Hmm," the Guardian murmured. "Any others?"

"U.D?"

"Untrustworthy, disloyal."

Layden looked up into the Guardian's cool green eyes and tried to catch the meaning of his tone. But there wasn't anything there but a frank invitation for her to continue. "There are a lot of those too."

"What other leads have you come up with?"

Layden didn't want to transition away from the categories just yet, but she put her papers in her lap and met his eyes again. "You asked me if it was just me who thought the transition into the Conservatory could be improved. I can answer that I'm not the only one. I believe if we extended the process, allowed the parents to see their children in increments during their seasons in the Conservatory, it might make the whole process smoother and less painful."

The enthusiasm seemed to fade from the Guardian's face, and he shifted forward and moved behind his desk again. Historically, she wasn't great at reading people, but she didn't have to be a genius at body language to see she was losing him.

"At this point, it's not just painful for the candidates but for the Council as well. I know they deal with resistance every winter," she continued before he could dismiss her, "from families and probably students too. My ideas could aim to alleviate this."

The Guardian looked up. "What do you mean by resistance?"

"I know that at times parents petition the Council for their child's return from the Conservatory, sometimes repeatedly. Surely the Council has better things to do than sit for these cases."

The Guardian watched her for a moment, his eyes narrowed, and lips pursed in thought. He didn't look convinced, but he didn't refute her either.

"The petitions only occur for two weeks out of the year. I hardly call that an inconvenience," he finally replied.

"What about those parents who go to more extreme lengths to get their children back? You don't think those are a threat? A waste of resources?"

His gaze arrested her immediately. He seemed surprised. "And how much could you know about that?"

His reaction gave away that she was on the right track, so she decided to gamble. "Enough."

His eyes narrowed, calling her bluff. "I think you do not know the half of it."

"If all I know is half, then the Council is dealing with far more than they need to," Layden quipped quickly. "Not only would my program be helpful to those in the Conservatory, but I think it would curtail a lot of those repeated petitions and...unrest."

"Or perhaps it would increase it all," he countered.

Layden shook her head. "I don't think so. My evaluators were clear that my parents never asked for me back and that likely they became used to my absence, as happens with most families. The visits could taper off gradually and adjust both the family and child to the change."

Layden was speaking with passion now, and the Guardian seemed to be responding to it. But when he opened his mouth to speak again, his question was not what she expected.

"And did you, Layden Prier? Get used to it?"

She choked back a surprising pang in her chest. She wanted to say yes, to brush off the question and prove her point. But she couldn't. Lately, her every limb felt weighed down with loss. It felt like she was missing much more than the life she knew before, but a whole multitude of family—brothers and sisters and friends. She swallowed against a lump in her throat.

"Don't dismiss me, please," she entreated. "I know I'm on to something. I have this memory from seasons ago...I was only a child, but it's so strong I don't think it'll ever leave me. A young girl from my den, and her parents, fighting for reunion."

"To what memory do you refer?" he asked quietly.

"Constance's kidnapping. I was there, apparently, and it's the reoccurring dream I mentioned; it comes nearly every night now." It felt amazing being able to speak of it, because the dream had been nearly as persistent as her visions lately.

"What exactly do you remember?"

"Constance crying, and her parents trying to comfort her. I'm walking toward the noise when I'm confronted with a blinding light, and I run back to my bed."

"Are you sure they were her parents? Was anyone else there?"

Layden shrugged, finding these questions odd. Then she realized she'd been assuming that for a long time. "Well, I guess I'm not sure. It's what my evaluators told me. But I never did see the parents myself."

The Guardian was quiet. When he spoke again, his tone was genial. "All right, you may continue to build a case for this. I will have a few more materials pulled for you. However, I would not neglect the first half of your proposal. I doubt this 'transitionary period' will stand on its own."

Layden nodded. She could work with that.

"You are dismissed for the day. I suggest you put in a few hours in the study rooms."

Layden rose, ready to leave. But as she did, a thought came to her mind, and something clicked. "Guardian, do you think they're memories?"

"What are?" he asked. He seemed like he had already moved on from their conversation.

"The visions. I wonder, is it possible they're memories from my Host?" Hearing it out loud, it made even more sense. After all, hadn't it seemed like the Guardian and her Host knew each other?

The Guardian became attentive again. "Why do you think that would be possible?"

"I don't know," Layden replied. "Maybe I wanted part of her to remain, and so it did. Didn't you say our will influences the Transfer?"

He shook his head dismissively. "It does not work that way. You only take things with you that you have already acquired."

"There's something else, though, about the vision. Something I haven't told you." She felt certain now, and if he would just hear her out, maybe he would know for sure too.

"What is it?"

"The man in my vision, well, I think he's you."

"What do you mean, he is me?"

His words cut through the air with icy precision, and Layden felt once again like she'd made a mistake.

"I—I'm sorry Guardian, I don't know what I'm saying," she retracted.

"You would not say such a thing lightly, Layden. Explain yourself now."

She had been so sure a second before, but his reaction made her doubt herself. She cursed her loose lips. Maybe he would explain it away, and then she'd accept that and never mention it again.

"I don't know. Your—his face is not visible. But I think..." She couldn't believe she was saying this. "I think, it always feels like you. And, after all, you seemed to have known her..." She paused again, her cheeks burning. "My Host. I thought that maybe it was her memory of you."

He stared at her for a while, his eyes intensely locked on her face. She feared she had done even worse by mentioning her Host and his connection, but she couldn't think of anything else to explain it.

"The woman in your dream, the feet you stare at, are they young or old?"

Layden knew he knew this, but she quickly obliged with an answer. "Youngish," she replied.

"And the man?"

"Older, I suppose. Not much older than you, though," she said.

"Then I would like to point out that if the woman in your vision was your Host, the memory would have been, what, fifty, sixty years ago? In which case, I would not be the same age I am now. Either that, or the feet beneath you in the vision would be aged like hers are today."

"Yes." Layden breathed out. "You're right." She felt utterly senseless not to have caught that.

"The most likely explanation is that you have imposed my likeness over his because of the hours we are spending together." He looked away from her, clearly done talking.

Layden cleared her throat and tried to stop shaking.

"That is all. Go to work," he said. Layden left immediately, cursing herself the entire way to the study rooms.

chapter twelve

*A*LL SHE SEES IS *black. Dark, thick, unrelenting black. It invades her senses completely and keeps her from all measure of time and space. She knows neither where she is, nor why she is there.*

Until, gradually, very gradually, she begins to perceive again. Not everything, but...something. A smell? Dank and musty, familiar but lacking a name.

Then, a light.

At first, imperceptible, but eventually bright enough to allow her to finally see.

She is surrounded by rocks on all sides, floor to ceiling. They curve inward around her, making her feel choked in the enclosed space. A cave. She somehow knows the name, even though she's never been in one before. She struggles to move and find her way out, but the light, now larger than her palm, hovers before her and demands her attention.

And as she gazes at it, she begins to relax.

And as she relaxes, the light, like a burning flame, begins to grow.

Soon it is so large she must recoil, pressing her back against the slick surface of the rock wall, feeling the wet and the cold soak through her clothing, and the heat from the flame on her face.

Then, at last, the moment she's been waiting for without even realizing it happens; a voice, deep and beautiful—layered in pitch and volume but somehow still in unison—begins to speak to her.

She can't understand the words. They aren't muddled, but rather ones she doesn't know. Regardless she can feel the message deep in her chest, and it overwhelms her.

The light goes out.

This was the vision Layden had only moments after waking, and for the first time, Layden began to believe the visions were about her after all. While obscure and confusing, the experience felt so personal.

But it certainly wasn't a memory. She'd been in a cave in the vision. Layden barely had a reference for caves, let alone experience in one.

The Guardian had disagreed with her last theory, and now she was convinced she'd been wrong as well. Which meant...what? They were visions of the future? But there were no more caves, no more land, so that couldn't be it. Either way, she had to find time to relay this new development to the Guardian. Surely, after all his persistence, he'd want to know immediately, right?

Layden rushed through the baths, determined to tell the Guardian first thing.

Excitement dared to grow inside her, and she was beside herself with the mystery of it all. She couldn't believe it. She'd had a *second* vision. It was both terrifying and exhilarating.

Layden ordered her words in her head as she walked, trying to think of the best way to explain what she'd seen, but when she reached the Meeting Hall, she didn't see the Guardian anywhere. A handful of students were settling in, and a quiet hum of voices echoed within. She tried to be discreet, but many noticed her. In no time, all attention shifted her way, and the room went silent.

For some reason—perhaps because her nerves were shot from not enough sleep—their prying eyes enraged her. Or maybe it was because, once again, their very attention reminded her how separate from them she really was.

"What are you *looking* at?" she called out, unable to keep the spite from her voice.

Several people startled, and the murmur resumed. More words of anger built within, but a familiar voice stopped her from bursting.

"Layden, what's going on?"

It was Manni. She took a deep breath and turned in exasperation. "I'm just waiting for the Guardian. I have to tell him something important," she said quickly.

"About your presentation?"

"No. Something else." She turned to leave. Maybe she'd go to his office or catch him on his way over to the hall.

"Didn't you hear? He's not going to be with us today. The Council is sending someone else."

"What about my lessons?" Layden chaffed.

Manni didn't respond at first, but he put a calming hand on her elbow. "Hey, maybe you can join us today," he said his eyes shining hopefully.

Layden cast about for direction but couldn't think straight. Finally, she turned and followed Manni. It would be fine. She just had to make it through the morning and then she could tell the Guardian everything. Layden sat down and tried to close her eyes, but she couldn't bring herself to relax. Her mind was too abuzz. Instead, she surveyed the room before her. There were under twenty candidates left.

Glancing over at Manni, Layden wondered if he was doing well. If the Guardian had given him special privileges too, then clearly his idea had potential. Then again, maybe they were all receiving accommodation at this stage. Shame bubbled up. Somewhere along the line, she'd begun to believe she was special. Important. Different. How pathetic she was to think she'd ever be.

"What's wrong?" Manni asked her again, no doubt sensing her tenseness. He grasped her arm gently.

Layden pulled away tersely.

"Layden, come *on*," he said, his frustration clearly growing. "Tell me! Let me help you!"

That wretched feeling in her bones ached silently and made her feel hollow with helplessness. Manni couldn't help her; another Guardian wouldn't be able to either. The only one who could, wasn't there. Layden stood again, fighting a fresh wave of tears.

"I have to go," she mumbled.

"Layden!"

"I'm sorry," she only barely managed as she turned and quickly left the room.

A full week passed and there was still no news from their Guardian.

Layden had been getting less and less sleep, her new vision occurring more and more often. Which was terrorizing. The visions were tolerable if they meant something. If they had a purpose. But without the Guardian to, at the very least, express interest, they sat in her heart like an unmarked checkbox. She realized that she had become accustomed to his validation of the visions, and that without it, she felt more lost and alone than ever.

And she was stuck. She needed his approval and direction for her idea. The thought crossed her mind that she shouldn't need him, that perhaps the Council were pulling him out at this crucial time so she and the other candidates would work on their own. But something within told her that wasn't the case. A tiny part of her was even a little worried.

Why would she be worried about him? His cold and distant annoyance tainted most of their interactions. She should be glad he was gone, and a part of her *was* grateful for a break. But a larger part of her knew she couldn't move on till he returned.

With all these thoughts swirling in her mind, Layden found herself outside the Guardian's office door one afternoon late in the week. She had to know for sure if he was gone or just avoiding them all. She knocked once, then again, and when no one answered, she tried the panel beside the door. Much to her surprise, the door slid open.

Layden peered into the dark room. The drapes covered the window completely, but otherwise everything was as it normally was. The Guardian's desk was clear of everything but candle wax; the cushions and the books were all in their proper places. The air was thick with a strange scent, almost like dust but mustier. She walked forward to his desk and slid her fingers gently over its surface. Something felt thrilling about being there when he wasn't, like she was on the edge of a forbidden secret. For this reason alone, she knew she should probably leave, but a small whisper told her to stay.

It's yours. Find it, it said.

Layden swiftly circled the desk to one of the drawers—the one she'd seen him keep it in—and opened it. There it sat, the small, green book, tucked away beneath some papers. She grabbed it quickly and closed the drawer quietly, ready to leave and go back to her room.

"Layden Prier," a voice rang into the room. "I must admit, you lasted longer than I expected. I am impressed at your...independence."

Layden leapt away from the desk, hiding the book behind her. Her first thought was that the Guardian had been hiding in the shadows of his office, waiting for her. But the voice wasn't his. In fact, it wasn't even a man's.

A woman stood in the doorway, an elegant frame in silhouette against the bright light of the hall, her face in shadow.

"I just left some of my things here," Layden lied, bringing the book out from behind her back. It would be useless to hide it, as the woman had clearly seen her at the desk drawer.

The woman stretched out her hand, and Layden put the book in it, maintaining a safe distance. She didn't want to give the book over, but if she hesitated or was possessive over it, she was sure the woman wouldn't believe her.

Thankfully, the silhouette merely leafed through it briefly and handed it back. "Odd book to need for your studies. I hope you won't be proposing we bring back a dead language," she said, a smile in her voice.

Layden took the book back, at a loss for words. She still had no idea what the book was, but the woman's tone and expression told Layden she was more in jest than accusation.

"Of course, not...ma'am," Layden managed.

Finally, the woman stepped inside and turned on the lights. They were dimmed by the cloth covering them, but they were enough to fully show the woman's features. In realizing who this was, Layden's heart nearly stopped in her chest, and her neck grew as hot as a fire.

"Grand Councilor!" she managed breathlessly, bowing her head quickly.

"Please, call me Miranda."

The Grand Councilor herself! Layden hadn't seen her since being collected ten seasons ago, but she still had the same piercing eyes and pearl-white smile. Her hair hung down her back, long and lackluster gray. Layden remembered it all like it were yesterday.

And yet, she felt oddly twisted up inside. After the conversation with the Guardian three weeks ago, Layden had briefly wondered what it would feel like when she saw any of the current Council members again, knowing that they actually resided in Hosts of their own. Now that she had, the answer was...complicated.

"It has been a while since we met," the Grand Councilor said, moving further into the room. "Do you remember?"

Layden nodded, still in shock. "Yes, of course."

"Collection days are often memorable, it's true. Tell me, dear," she cooed, "have you had any visions lately?"

Layden's heart quickened as she tried to process both the shock and the Councilor's question. So, the Council did know; Layden hadn't known how much the Guardian was reporting, but it made sense that he would mention the visions. A part of her was thrilled, wanting to tell the Grand Councilor everything. But there was a strange warning in her heart to stay silent.

"No, Grand Councilor," she said finally, not even fully understanding why she lied.

The Councilor watched her for a moment. "Come, dear, no need to be so afraid of me. I'm just a person, much like you."

Yes, you're exactly like me, a mind in another's body.

Again, Layden was surprised at the thought, and even more so at how it made her feel. She was both in awe of the Grand Councilor and slightly repulsed.

"You know, I think he's relatively fond of you," the Grand Councilor said, walking slowly to the window and delicately pushing the drape aside. "As fond as he can be of another, that is. I've always found Jeremiah to be a bit...withholding. Haven't you?"

Layden couldn't respond, her tongue thick and throat tight.

"And I don't think it's just because you're in this Host," she continued, waving a hand casually in Layden's direction.

Layden watched the Grand Councilor as she moved around the room, lazily touching various things in the Guardians office. She viewed a book or two, patted the dust out of one of the Guardian's pillows, even played with the candle wax, throwing Layden a unsettling smile as she did. She was graceful, that was for sure but there was an irreverence in her seemingly-casual movements that spoke louder. She was the one in control. While she was here, this space was not the Guardian's, it was the Councilor's.

"You know about my Host?" Layden asked, swallowing against the lump in her throat.

"Oh, yes," the Councilor said. "He had a fondness for this woman whose body you now inhabit. He doesn't think I know, but there's very little that goes on around here that I don't know about." She smiled wide at Layden as if it were all game. "Though I prefer to allow others the illusion of their privacy. There's a difference between knowing everything you can use and using everything you know. You'll learn that."

Layden nodded stiffly. She wasn't sure how she was supposed to respond to that, so she listened attentively, as a good student would.

"Well then," the Councilor stopped and clasped her hands in front of her. "Please don't let me interfere with your day. Your Guardian will be back this evening. Though, I'm not sure I'd call on him till tomorrow. I expect he'll be tired from his travels."

"Yes, ma'am," Layden said, taking a few timid steps toward the door.

It was not lost on Layden that for someone who desired more than anything to be in league with the Council, she'd never wanted to leave a presence so desperately.

"And Layden, do be sure to share your visions with your Guardian. If you do have more. I think you'll find I'm quite interested."

The halls to the Guardian's office were dark and quiet except for the low hum of the electric torches. Layden walked softly once again, not wanting to alert anyone to her presence. She knew she should wait till morning, as the Grand Councilor had said, but the vision had come again. While she wanted to sleep more than anything, she didn't think she'd be able to until she told him.

Not to mention, she felt plagued by the fact she'd lied to the Grand Councilor. Lied to her face! What had possessed Layden to do that? But it was okay...she could make it right. If she could tell the Guardian now, then he could tell the Councilor first thing in the morning, and she needn't ever know Layden had been hiding anything.

Surely, the Guardian would understand her hesitation to share, and she had a feeling he'd back her up. This was a strange feeling to have confidence in, seeing as at the start of the Trials the Guardian had nearly been her mortal enemy. Strong words for someone past the throes of childhood drama, and yet, they applied. Almost without her noticing, he'd become her ally and the Council something she was understanding less and less.

Layden reached his office and stopped outside the door, reevaluating her decision. On the one hand, she knew it was presumptuous, inappropriate, and just plain crazy to be there at this hour. But, in the end, the thought of another restless night spurred her forward.

As Layden approached the door, she saw it was already slightly ajar. Upon closer attention, she could even hear someone inside talking.

It was the Guardian's voice, though in tones she'd never heard before. He seemed angry, but quite a different kind of anger, almost anguish. She thought for a second that he was talking with someone else, until she didn't hear any other voices talking back. In fact, the longer she listened, the more the sounds resembled the rantings of a madman. Talking with himself, pleading with himself.

Layden knew immediately that she should leave. She took a couple steps back but in the next moment the door slid open and revealed the Guardian on the other side.

"Mairi!" he whispered to her. He looked only half lucid.

"I'm sorry," Layden said, utterly terrified. "I didn't mean to—" She turned away, about to make a dash for it but he called out and stopped her before she could.

"Layden Prier?" It seemed like he was just noticing her. "Come back here."

Layden took a breath and faced him again.

"What are you doing here?" he asked. As he stepped into the hallway, his face cleared.

"I'm sorry, Guardian. I shouldn't have come at this hour."

"No. You should not have," he said. But he didn't look angry. "Come."

Layden hesitated, but when he stepped aside and gestured her in, she followed.

The room was lit, but only half so, which drew the eye to the large space in the center. There were blankets on the floor and several pillows strewn about. Did he sleep there? Maybe it was all those seasons of being under the strict eye of the den mother in the Conservatory, but it didn't feel right being in his office when it became his bedchamber.

The Guardian followed her gaze. "You are right, you should not be in here at this hour."

Layden nodded and made for the door without any hesitation. To her surprise, the Guardian followed, closing the door behind them.

"Let us take a walk." He didn't wait for her to answer but began striding away from the room.

This was a mercy because Layden could scarcely hide how uncomfortable she was. She tried to gain on him, but her muscles were tired and sore. Sometimes she forgot she wasn't a spry young woman and pushed herself beyond what she should be doing.

The Guardian paused a moment and let her catch up.

"Where are we going, Guardian?"

"It is a nice night," he replied cryptically.

They walked along in silence for a while until the destination revealed itself. Layden found herself on the other side of the courtyard where she'd first glimpsed the miraculous, pink-blossomed tree. On this side there was a door, which the Guardian keyed open then stepped aside to let her through.

Shaking with excitement, Layden stepped outside in the courtyard and took a deep breath. She had not tasted fresh air in months. The wind was cool on her skin, and it blew her gray hair in front of her eyes. As she looked down, she saw pink blossoms tumbling across the ground, and her heart stopped. The reminder was potent.

"Guardian, I had another vision," she said suddenly, turning to him.

He regarded her for a moment but didn't respond. Then he moved over to a bench facing the tree and took a seat. Layden followed but remained standing.

"Please, you must be tired. It is late, after all." He gestured for her to sit beside him.

She hesitantly obeyed.

For a moment he sat quietly, looking upward and paying Layden no mind. She could see why he was fascinated with the sky—an Aegean blanket bejeweled in stars. But she had just told him she'd had another vision. After his persistent inquiry before, his silence wasn't what she expected. Not to mention, she'd been burdened with this for a full week. It would at least be courteous to act like he cared.

Layden looked around, drawing her arms around herself. She worried they'd be seen, and she wasn't even sure she was allowed in the courtyard. But as the silence wore on, she finally began to surrender to it and relax.

At that moment, he spoke.

"I heard the Grand Councilor conversed with you while I was away," he said into the night air.

Layden dared to turn his way. She watched the wind move through the hair that dangled just below his ears, bringing with it a waft of something earthy, barely perceived beneath the scent of a strong soap. And for a moment, the man beside her was just a man, and not her Guardian. He looked tired.

"Just this afternoon actually, yes," she finally responded.

"What did she say?" He continued to stare upward.

"She told me you were coming back tonight. She asked me if I had any more of my visions."

"Did you tell her of this new one?"

Layden shifted uncomfortably. "I—I told her I hadn't had any new ones."

The Guardian turned his head quickly. "Why is that?"

What look was he giving her now? It was hard to tell in the moonlight. He seemed surprised, but not angry. Was he pleased or the opposite?

"I've been asking myself that all day. I think I just wanted to talk with you before telling anyone else," she said. "Maybe I doubted myself."

The Guardian returned his eyes to the tree. "That was probably a wise decision."

Layden felt the burden lift and she let out a breath.

"Did she say anything else to you? About where I had gone?" he asked her hesitantly.

Layden paused, taking in his almost anxious countenance, and wondered what exactly he was concerned she knew. Her thoughts ran back to the way the Grand Councilor spoke of him, how she knew about Layden's Host and the Guardian's relationship, how she seemed to know a lot. Layden had always assumed her allegiance to the Guardian and her allegiance to the Council were one in the same. Why did that feel different now?

"No," she answered quietly. "Nothing about where you'd been."

She hadn't noticed how tense he was until she sensed his body relax beside her.

He let out a small, weary sigh. "Well, I think it is time we hear your vision then," he said.

Relieved, Layden explained quickly, but with detail, about the surroundings and the fire-like light, the voice, and how she couldn't understand it but that it emotionally affected her. He listened attentively.

"This voice. Is it speaking a different tongue?" he asked when she had finished.

Layden paused. "A different language?"

He nodded.

That thought hadn't occurred to her, mainly because there was only one language in the world. She knew there had once been others, but not for a long time. However, after considering that possibility, she knew it wasn't the case.

"No, I don't think so. That would be the logical conclusion since I don't know what the voice said. But I suppose it was more like someone speaking with a very advanced vocabulary. I recognized it as my language, but I didn't know any of the words."

The Guardian's face grew contemplative. "Thank you for sharing with me," he said after a few moments.

Layden nodded, wishing she felt better. She had to admit she'd expected more of a response.

"Perhaps it was time you returned to your room. Unless you have anything further to tell me?"

Layden shook her head. Then she spoke before she realized she was going to. "Where *have* you been all week?"

He seemed surprised at her question but not unwilling to share. In fact, she thought she saw an eagerness to converse, a relaxed kind of openness about him. Though, it could have been a trick of the moonlight, for she didn't think the Guardian possessed such a mood, let alone that he would share it with her.

"Do you remember our conversation about the families' petitions for their children, post-Collection?"

"Of course." She thought about it daily as she tried to rework her presentation.

"I was not sure if I could support your pursuit of this subject, but I have just returned from an investigation into one of these families. The Council discovered a plot to retrieve a child who was collected this past winter."

Layden sat up straight. Was he allowed to tell her this?

"I was sent to try and thwart it before it happened. A young family wanted their boy back. They were desperate for him. But their request was denied due to ineligibility; that ineligibility being purposefully vague of course, as always. I met with the parents and persuaded them to see the reason, for the time being. It was not easy, but I believe I bought them time."

"Bought who time...the Council? Time for what?" Layden asked. The way he was speaking it almost sounded like he was sympathetic to this family.

The Guardian looked at her like he had forgotten she was there. After a moment, he sat up straighter, his voice returning to its more officious tones.

"Yes. Time for the Council to deal with the family through official channels," he said, "before things get out of hand, and they must use drastic measures. They are never truly in danger from such plots, but it is not good for morale and of course the unrest is not their true heart."

Layden thought about this and nodded.

"What I am saying is I believe the Council might have more of a need for your concepts than I originally thought," he finally said.

"Guardian. There is something I need to ask. I am afraid to ask it, but if I am to keep going, I need to know. Even if I don't like the answer."

"That is very wise of you."

"Do families ever have their petitions answered in their favor?" She found she had a hard time keeping her voice from shaking. "That is, has anyone ever received their child back after the Collection?"

"No," he said softly. "Of all those I know who have petitioned, no one has ever had their child returned to their family."

It was as Layden feared and Manni had spoken. She sat in the dark and thought about what this could mean.

Before she could ask more, the Guardian spoke again. "Come now. It is time for you to get some sleep."

As she undressed in the dark, the lights having been turned off long ago, the small, green book fell to the ground with a dull clap. She had almost forgotten she'd tucked it in the waist of her pants earlier in the day. She stooped down and fumbled for it, finding it with her fingers, barely making it out in the glow of the orange light. The tree etched on the binding stood out to her fingers, and again she thought of the tree in the courtyard—the very one she'd just sat under, talking so openly with her Guardian.

Cracking open the binding, she tried to make out the words, but they were handwritten in faint ink and too difficult to read in the dark. The ones she could make out didn't make sense to her. Was this what the Councilor had meant when she mentioned studying a dead language? She wouldn't have thought about it had the Guardian not mentioned the idea not twenty minutes ago.

Her mind went back to the voice in the cave. Two instances where the words had seemed familiar enough, but, ultimately, wholly unintelligible. It was strange, that was for sure.

Regardless, it didn't matter to Layden whether she could read the book. It still felt nice to have something to hold in her arms, and that whisper in her heart told her that the book belonged there. She moved to her bed and climbed in, tucking the book in the crook of her arm. Though she never had held a book to sleep, deep down in her bones, she felt nostalgic about the dusty pages resting close to her face, the cover rough under her fingers.

Though there was much on her mind, she fell asleep quickly.

Chapter Thirteen

S INCE THEY'D DECIDED TO keep each other company nearly two months ago, neither Layden nor Manni had missed a single late-night supper, not even after she'd rejected his help in the Meeting Hall the day the Guardian had disappeared. That didn't mean things hadn't changed between them, however, and she knew that was mostly her fault. Manni had wanted to share the burden she carried—she could see it in every glance he gave her—and part of her wanted to lean on him as she always had. But she was starting to understand that she had to hold back, not just to preserve the way he once viewed her—as a strong, trusted friend of sound mind and loyal comradery—but also for his own good.

The information from the Guardian had been troubling at first, but, in the end, she'd decided to give the Council the benefit of the doubt. She had realized that the Guardian was able to talk to her that openly not because he wanted her to distrust the Council, but because he trusted *her* to see things through the perspective of the Earth-that-was, putting aside the judgement of her modern lens.

For that reason, she could not confide such sensitive information to Manni. She cared about him deeply, and in the past that would have looked like sharing everything. Now it looked like protecting him from things he wasn't able to hear. Within him a cynicism was emerging that scared her, and, for his own good, she wouldn't do anything to encourage it.

"There you are," Layden said as Manni entered the cantina. "Cutting it close, aren't we?" Her words stopped short on her lips as she caught a look at his face.

His energy was urgent and concerned her slightly, but not as much as when he sat opposite her and took her hands in both of his. His palms were large and enveloping; they made her own fingers feel small and as fragile as icicles.

"We don't have much time," he said, his tone hushed.

"Time for what?" Layden looked around.

"We're friends. Right, Layden?"

"Of course," she said carefully.

"We've always been friends. I've always considered you to be much like a sister to me."

Layden hesitated but smiled and nodded for him to continue.

"I don't know what has changed lately. I get that you don't have to tell me everything, and I don't need to know. I only need to know if you feel the same way I do."

"What are you talking about?" Layden asked, the uneasy feeling within growing.

"I've found them, Layden. The disengaging mechanisms for the outer compound. We can get out of here tonight."

Layden blinked at his words. What had he said? All she could think was that he was holding her hands too tightly and that he smelled overpoweringly like that acrid hand lotion.

"What? Get out of here and go where?" she asked.

"Just trust me, Layden. You trust me, don't you?" A small, anxious smile wavered on the face of his Host.

"Manni, this isn't the time for a childish adventure. We're not in the den anymore. Not to mention, you're about as fast as a tortoise. Even if we wanted to, we'd never get away with it, and we'd be released from the Trials immediately."

His countenance took a turn for the serious, his features almost contorting to disgust. "Do you think that little of me? Layden, I'm talking about leaving this place. For good. But we have to go now. I stumbled on it accidentally, and if I use it more than once, I'm sure they'll find a way to block it."

"Leave? In this body? And we have presentations in a week!" She pulled her hands from his grip.

"Listen to yourself! Presentations? We have a chance to *get out of here*. We can figure out our bodies later. Just trust me!" His tone had become frustrated, almost angry.

But that was nothing compared to the alarm Layden felt at hearing such words. "What are you *talking* about? How could you ask me to leave?" she whispered with force.

"Layden—"

"If the Council found out, if the *Guardian* found out what you've asked me to do, it could ruin everything!"

"The Council! The Guardian! They aren't your friends, and you know that!"

"Keep your voice down," Layden whispered, her teeth bared. She stood and distanced herself from him.

Manni paused for a second and looked at her as though he couldn't comprehend her reaction. He stood and held her gaze for a moment. "But...you spoke with the Guardian the night he got back..." he continued, his tone turning cautious. "Surely you must have found out where he goes, and why."

"Of course, I did," she said, unable to keep a haughty lilt out of her tone. "He told me the Council sent him to help deal with a troublesome family. He's trusted me with information like that on more than one occasion, because I don't run scared the second I find out something's different than it seems, Manni!"

Manni stared at her for a moment. She thought he'd have a rebuttal for that, or at least a quip, but he said nothing.

At length he whispered, "Do you really not remember anything?"

"Remember *what*?" she spat.

His manner was disconcerting, and she almost asked him again what he was talking about, but as he stared at her with his Host's large, watery gray eyes, she realized that a bigger part of her didn't want to know. Not one bit.

Again, Manni said nothing for a long time. At length, he took a breath and looked down. "You trust him then? You trust your Guardian?"

Layden felt halted in her tracks by his words. She searched her mind and the space in her chest that felt full of confusing emotions. "I respect him."

"Do you *trust* him?"

"Yes. I do," she admitted. "I didn't always feel that way, but I've come to realize he only wants to make us better."

"And do you trust me?"

Layden felt a lump form in her throat, and she found herself without words for a second time. At length, she finally said, "Did you know my mother tried to keep me from the Collection?"

Manni paused. "I remember you were late."

"She didn't even tell me it was happening. I knew nothing about it. She clearly didn't think I was bright or exceptional enough to even be considered." Saying the words brought hot tears to her eyes, though it had been many seasons since she'd thought of these things. "I told myself that I would never let another person keep me from my destiny again. I was *made* for this, Manni. I can feel it in my gut. I was made to...help make things better. You and I have been through so much together. You've known me at my weakest and been my lifeline. But if you jeopardize my future...if you try and make those decisions for me like she did..." She trailed off delicately, unable to get the words out.

Manni's eyes were wide, and brokenhearted, and she knew he understood. She took a breath, not wanting to leave angry, but not having anything else to say. Then she turned and left.

The tension in the air was palpable. As the week ended, one thing and one thing only hung on all their minds. The presentations. Layden had been used to having the study rooms to herself late at night. Now she had to share them with the remaining fourteen candidates in her intake. While there was plenty of space, their frantic last-minute preparations clouded her concentration. Not that she could blame them. Everything rode on what they brought before the Council, and in the single sixth-month season they'd been given, every second counted.

Layden kept much the same schedule. Except the fact that she hadn't returned to her dinners with Manni. She wasn't mad at him, so much as afraid he'd bring up the same conversation again. And anyway, she had too much work to do.

Every day she doubted her ideas more. They sounded weak and childish—visiting hours, transition periods...she was barely taking herself seriously. She tried to remain confident because of what the Guardian had told her. Not that she could use any of his information in her presentations, of course, which complicated things further.

Layden walked into the baths in almost catatonic fashion, feeling as drained and tired as the rest of her peers. She slipped into her preferred chamber and began her usual routine without thinking—washing, rinsing, lathering, foaming, drying, and sealing—all the while hoping it would take her mind off everything. It did not. She should have tried to sleep more the night before instead of staying up so late. She'd barely gotten anything done anyway.

Before she knew it, she was done with her shower and out into the sauna, sitting on a bench and breathing deeply in the warm air.

"Layden. Please, don't leave." A voice spoke from above her.

It was Manni, and it took everything in her not to do exactly that.

"I just wanted to talk to you. I won't take long."

Layden looked around to see if anyone was watching them. "Sit down," Layden said in a hushed tone.

Manni obeyed immediately, but his body language was still a little too imploring for her comfort. Anyone watching would notice something was off.

"I was wrong to have suggested what I did."

"Yes, you were," she said immediately.

"I just...it just seemed easier to leave," he said finally.

His expression showed shame, but even more so, helplessness. It was not one she was used to seeing, either on his or his Host's face. He had changed, but, then again, so had she.

"The future is just so uncertain."

"I know it is, Manni. It has been for a long time."

There was silence for a moment.

"Just know this, Layden. Whatever you decide, I'll follow that. I am there with you the whole way. No matter what I have to do to make it happen."

Layden regarded him carefully. She knew his words shouldn't comfort her, after all, he had no say in whether they progressed together. But she was comforted, and she did believe he'd be there. He always had been.

"Anyway, do well today." He stood.

"Manni," Layden replied, catching him. He turned back slowly and met her eyes. "You too."

He nodded, and she watched as he walked away.

CHaPTer FourTeen

NO ONE HAD TO present till that evening, but they'd been excused from their daily routine all the same. Layden was grateful for that. She didn't have much left she could do, but she wouldn't have been able to concentrate if the Guardian had insisted they study.

The dread within her was nearly paralyzing that morning, but she'd made herself shower, dress, and walk to her study room. Hopefully, she could alleviate the pressure in her chest with some more preparation. She cracked her portfolio and took in the variety of scribbles, diagrams, and prose she planned to read. Shuffling them around, she reorganized them for what had to be the hundredth time.

There was no specified time limit for the presentation, which Layden admitted had unnerved her to learn. The Guardian had made it clear she was to take whatever time it took to explain herself thoroughly. There'd be a time for the Council members to ask questions to clarify at the end, but she'd do better not to leave room for questions in case they weren't asked.

Layden's main concern at this point was that her brain wouldn't function properly by the time she got to present. If there was no time limit, who knew how long it could take for her turn to come, and she hadn't been sleeping well for months. She thought for a moment that she should get some rest right then, but she didn't want to risk oversleeping. The way she felt now, she was likely to pass out and not wake up till tomorrow.

Layden passed her hands over a couple of sheets and shifted their order within the pile. Standing, she cleared her voice and tried her opening lines. They sounded awkward and uninviting without an audience. Or maybe they were just awkward and uninviting. She tried again, giving them more gusto. They sounded worse. She sat down, abandoning the practice; it was only making her more anxious. Her body was heavy with exhaustion, and her head ached slightly.

Out of the corner of her eye, she noticed the small, green book lying on the table. She didn't remember bringing that out. She swept it up and placed it back in her locker, worried about what a memory lapse would do to her presentation. She really should sleep.

Then it dawned on her. While her room didn't have a console, surely the one in the study room could be used as an alarm. She searched its menu and found what she was looking for then gave it a practice try for thirty seconds. The alarm rang loud enough.

That was all the reassurance she needed to lay her head down on her books and slip deep into sleep.

"Layden! What are you doing here?" a voice called out sternly.

Layden startled awake with a racing heart. She looked up and saw the Guardian at the door, the hall dark behind him. Her heart leapt. What time was it? The screen showed that it was nearly an hour past when she'd set her alarm! It hadn't gone off—how had it not gone off?! The presentations were due to start any minute. She jumped to her feet and gathered all the materials at hand, her heart racing so fast she could barely keep up with it.

"Go on!" the Guardian said, stepping out of her way as she bolted from the room.

Running as fast as her old bones would carry her, she made her way to the Meeting Hall, fears abounding in her mind. What if the doors were already closed, or the location had changed? Skidding to a halt, she stopped in front of the main double doors. Relief washed over her. They were still open, and moreover, students were walking around inside, speaking with one another. She took a deep breath and walked in, her limbs trembling with adrenaline, her heart still pounding.

The room she'd known before had been transformed. Layden and the fourteen remaining candidates had their own table and chair. These were ordered in rows facing the platform, which now held a long, high table draped in a thick, dark blue cloth. A single podium stood facing this long table, and Layden assumed that's where they'd be presenting.

Layden moved to one of the empty tables and sat down heavily, smoothing back her wispy hair and attempting to catch her breath. Looking around, she saw that other students had set out their presentations on the table before them. Some had working apparatuses, which moved and made quiet noises. Others had books and prototypes of some kind. Some had consoles at their desks—had they requested them?—but others, like her, looked meek with a small stack of papers .

Her eyes found Manni nearby, who was already staring at her. He seemed angry for some reason and looked away quickly. Clearly nerves weren't treating him any better. On her right sat Mathis, who simply gave her a grim nod and began to spread his papers out before him. Clearly, even he lacked the energy to nurse his animosity toward her.

Layden opened her portfolio and slid out the pages she'd ordered so meticulously before, but which were now in a pile of undetermined order. What would she have done if the Guardian hadn't woken her? She would have missed her presentation, that's what. Been denied advancement, and then...what? Well, that was the problem, wasn't it? That's why all of them sat there, pale and still, their expressions void and hyper focused. No one knew what would happen if they failed to please the Council.

As if they had received their cue from her thoughts, the current nine Council members, including the Grand Councilor herself, entered the room and walked up onto the platform. Layden watched as they took their seats along the table, the Grand Councilor in the middle and the rest filling in spaces on either side. Layden had never seen them assembled like this before, and her heartbeat quickened at the sight.

She recognized the faces of each one and knew their names, along with all the areas of the city they were in charge of. Sephora Holmes: Ethnobotanic Greenhouses; Zachary Onieda: Defense League; Henry James: Arts and Culture, and so on. Of course, because of the information the Guardian had shared, she knew the minds behind those eyes were none other than the original members of the Council. She repressed a small shudder and tried to ignore the feeling of her skin crawling. After all, shouldn't she be more honored that she stood before the original Council? And ultimately how was she any different, occupying a Host herself? If she was going to live this life, she was going to have to toughen up.

The Guardian walked in a few steps after the Council and closed the doors behind him. He mounted the platform as well, but kept to the corner, facing the students. "Please stand," he instructed them.

How his tone had changed from the beginning of the Trials. He seemed to have lost interest in his sharp, intimidating tones and adopted a—slightly—more familiar manner. Though it occurred to Layden that maybe his intimidating figure was simply rendered less so in the light of the Council. After all, she knew the Guardian better now, for all his unpredictability and severity. The Council, however, was still larger than life and nearly mythological to her.

She and her fellow students followed the Guardian's instructions, reciting their pledge immediately upon standing, as they had become accustomed. She could see the Grand Councilor smiling down at them with apparent satisfaction.

"Please take your seats," she said magnanimously. "And please forgive our tardiness. We do not take these proceedings lightly, but we were waiting on one of our ranks." She cast the smallest of glances to her right.

Was she talking about the Guardian? Had he kept them waiting so Layden would have a chance at being on time? She shook the thought away; that was deluded and vain, even for her.

"I am very eager to see what you all have to show us today. I know you have spent the last six months learning, absorbing, and producing something of merit. While we rarely advance everyone who makes it this far, we appreciate the work you have put into the past season. Every contribution is a gift to us."

Her tone was kind and gracious, but her words sat uneasily with Layden. They'd made it this far, but that was not good enough. Not yet.

"We will begin in alphabetical order, as I am sure you've all been expecting. Abisen Prier. Please rise and make your way to the podium."

Layden watched with a lump in her throat as Abisen stood and walked forward. She could tell Abisen's legs were weak beneath her, even though she often had more command of her body than anyone. There were several moments of uncomfortable silence as Abisen set up her materials. Her movements were clumsy and nervous. But when she opened her mouth to speak, her tone was confident and authoritative, her words well-chosen and clear.

Abisen was presenting a bio-monitoring ingestible pill that would deteriorate at a slow rate and send out micromodules as it did. These modules traveled through the blood and into the vital organs, transmitting signals full of information back to a receiver. They could also be programmed to relay any kind of information in their vicinity, from disease and abnormalities to things as day-to-day as heart rate, metabolism, and anti-oxidization. It was smart science. Smarter than anything Layden could have thought up.

"Thank you, Abisen," the Grand Councilor said when it seemed Abisen had finished. "I will now open up the floor to the Council for any questions and comments."

There was silence for a moment, and Abisen looked pale and gray, but at length one of the members spoke. His name was Jonathon Gilchrest, a sleek-looking man with beady eyes; Layden knew him to be in charge of the infrastructure of the whole of Nyine City. His question was mild-mannered and unobtrusive enough, simply asking how long the modules lasted in the system, or rather, how often one would have to ingest this pill. Abisen seemed relieved and answered with alacrity. Only someone observing her closely would notice how white her knuckles were as they clutched the podium.

When no one appeared to have any further questions, the Councilor spoke. "And do you have a working prototype?"

Abisen shook her head tightly. "It's only a thesis at this stage. I have worked out all the formulas and I'm sure it can be done. I just ran out of time."

Layden waited expectantly to see if this was acceptable; she hoped it would be, not for Abisen's sake, but for hers. If the Council were only impressed with fully developed scientific projects, Layden's concepts would not pass by far. Thankfully, the Councilor nodded and smiled, releasing Abisen. It seemed she'd done well.

But not all were as lucky as Abisen. It turned out that, when the Council was unimpressed, they were relatively transparent about it. And there were no prizes for half answers. One member from den Quain bumbled through his concept—something to do with fortifying food with mood regulators—but he hadn't worked out any of the math. Nor had he given much thought to how it would benefit the Council—at least it seemed like he hadn't.

That being said, there didn't seem to be much discrimination as to what kind of contribution the Council approved of, which made Layden breathe a bit easier as the night wore on. As long as an idea was well thought out and advantageous to society, the Council apparently considered the idea seriously. Though, none of the candidates knew what kind of marks were being tallied up for or against them.

Few did exceptionally well, but it was clear Manni was one of them. If he wasn't her oldest friend, she probably would've been wishing the same thing the rest of those narrowed eyes did—that he'd have a sudden aneurysm, die, and give up his space to one of the lesser of them. But he *was* her friend, no matter what they'd been through lately. So, when he stood with confidence before the Council, she was relieved. This was the charismatic, bright mind she had known since childhood, and it was good to see him.

He had an opener of sorts, an anecdote about a simple man, with simple needs, and the lengths he'd go to in order to protect the smallest seed, because he knew the seed wasn't just a seed, but his hope for a better future. He knew one day others would come to him to buy seeds from the harvest he reaped.

"Every person has treasure," Manni continued, "something that represents their hopes and holds the promise of their dreams, and every person deserves the chance to protect that treasure. Because no matter how evolved we become, there will always be those who choose to rob, who try to destroy what we value."

Manni paused at this moment and looked at the Council in front of him. Layden wondered for a moment if she'd missed something because the energy in the room became electric in an instant. All the members' faces stared down at him, waiting for him to continue, and his eyes, while distant from her, looked steely. But when he did continue, Layden thought she'd imagined the moment, for his voice was light and compelling.

He moved out from behind the podium and delivered the rest of his thesis.

"A state-of-the-art security system designed as a small relay within the brain, keeping the owner notified at all times of the status of their treasured possession. This data won't be displayed on a console but will operate in league with one's own brain waves, sending gentle pings at regular intervals to inform the owner of his treasure's location, status, and security. All as a simple piece of knowledge. It will be like the owner simply 'knows.' This technology is complete with a nonintrusive installation and can be available to anyone who wants it."

But he didn't end with a mere concept. Manni had already developed it technologically and made a first pass at a prototype that worked on a basic level. The Council exchanged looks of approval and murmured among themselves for several seconds.

The Grand Councilor was the first to ask a question. "This is all very intriguing. But may I ask, what kind of item can this device pair with?"

"Do you mean, what objects can we track? It can be as large as a house or as small as a seed. The device simply needs something unique to the object, so it can be aware of its place in relation to itself."

"Unique? So, should I wish to track a person, a lock of their hair perhaps?"

Layden watched Manni recoil slightly, and she understood why. The thought of someone tracking her—knowing instantly where she was at all times, and via a lock of her hair no less—felt incredibly intrusive.

"I must admit, I hadn't considered tracking people. There could be complications," he said.

"I cannot see why there would be. It seems the principle would be the same."

"Yes, I suppose. It wasn't developed with that in mind though," he said.

"Yes, it was," the Councilor replied coolly.

When Manni spoke again, his voice was no longer as confident as it had been before. "I'm sorry, but I don't know what you mean."

The Grand Councilor was silent for a moment, but at last she curled her lips into a reassuring smile. "It's as you said, every person has treasure. You designed this to secure all manner of treasure. And I must say, you did a splendid job."

Manni seemed unable to speak, but he managed to mumble a word of gratitude.

"That is all, Emmanuel. You may take your seat."

And he did. Layden watched him as he walked back to his table, his face having waned a little whiter than usual. Still. He'd done great, and that wasn't just her opinion. She could tell by the way everyone looked at him now that they all thought as much. They were envious. And while she didn't like the idea of tracking a person—or being tracked for that matter—so what if the Council had other uses for his idea? That was a good thing, wasn't it? It meant that he was on to something.

Layden was relieved Manni had done well, but even more relieved that she didn't have to follow him. As it was, every third thesis seemed to be more advanced and developed than hers. While no one had yet to surpass Manni with a brilliant idea and a working prototype, with each fellow student that rose, Layden felt increasingly disheartened.

Then, much faster than she wished, Layden was up next. She watched in a haze as Kaden Quain answered questions from the Council. Were they pleased or not? She couldn't tell, nor did she care. With each passing moment, Layden oscillated between rehearsing answers and formulating various escape plans. At this point, she was convinced of her own ineptitude. If she was about to be rejected, maybe she'd save herself the trouble and leave before she humiliated herself.

"Layden Prier," a voice finally called.

Layden watched as Kaden made his way back to his desk. He looked like he wanted to be sick, and she felt how he looked. Rising to her feet, she shakily gathered her papers in her hands. A few flew off the surface and fell to the ground, and she had to stumble awkwardly to pick them up.

"Greetings, Councilmen and women," she began once she made it to the podium. She spread out her papers before her but seemed unable to read anything on them.

Focus. Just read what's in front of you till you get your sea legs.

Sea legs, that was a funny expression. Probably more apt when there was land and the time spent on the sea was the minority of life. True, the rocking of the docks in the Outlayers could get so bad sometimes it felt like you were on a boat, but Nyine City was firmly set. She wondered briefly if she'd struggle to adjust should she get sent back. She shook the thoughts away. *Focus!*

"Forgive me," she said, forcing her mind to think. "I appreciate the opportunity to speak to you all." She paused and looked over at the Guardian. He gave her the smallest of nods, and, for some reason, her mind began to clear.

"We have heard some remarkable ideas today," she began. "I am honored to be among such minds and their innovations. I do care deeply about the improvement of our society. Unlike Abisen, Manni, Kaden, I lack the scientific inclination that would allow me to develop something of such high caliber. But I do believe that my thoughts will fill a unique need, not only for us but for the Council as well. I hope to convince you of that as I continue," Layden concluded.

She hadn't written those things down, but she felt the need to say them. At this point, Layden felt her best bet was to take her presentation out of the same league as the others. To show it was of a different, not competing, nature.

"Thank you, Layden. Please continue," the Grand Councilor prompted graciously.

So, Layden began.

"Each year, fifty-two children are collected and brought to the Conservatory, with the Trials in mind. And yet, a mere fifth of each den make it through to the last Generation. And as we all know, no new member has been added to your ranks in over fifty years. My thesis, in short, surrounds this whole process, from Collection to Conservatory to Trials. And if I may be so bold, suggests ways to improve and refine it."

A few Council members shifted in their seats and exchanged a look or two, but she'd decided at the start that she'd have to ignore such body language if she was going to keep her nerve. Continuing, Layden detailed her plan to scout potential pupils before the Collection. She maintained, firstly, that students should be collected at a later age when strengths, weaknesses, and personality had developed further. She outlined a series of targeted evaluations to be conducted within small pre-Collection groups in each Outlayer. A new role—Pre-Evaluator—would be established, tasked with spending time in the Outlayers to uncover the more elusive characteristics necessary for progression through the Trials.

"Pray tell, Layden, what are some of these elusive characteristics you speak of?" the Grand Councilor asked.

No one had yet been interrupted mid-presentation, and Layden couldn't tell if this was bad or good. Nonetheless, she chose to answer speedily.

"From what I have inferred from some relatively stark Trial data, the Council seems to favor individuals who are competitive but also cooperative, loyal but able to see the big picture and make choices based on that. While those may seem like contradictions, I wager they're all necessary traits to becoming members of the Council. In addition to the intelligence testing, you might also check for problem-solving capabilities and other critical thinking skills. There are also certain temperaments that seem favored over others. Whatever you do look for, these earlier evaluations could help weed out the unqualified from the potential, saving you all time and resource." Layden paused to see if she had a response.

"How very astute of you, Layden. However, you discount the Conservatory's purpose in engendering such qualities in all the children we collect."

Layden faltered, but only for a second. "I'm sure the Conservatory does indeed cultivate desirable characteristics, but I also know certain things can't be taught."

The Grand Councilor seemed to consider this before speaking again. "Please continue," she said.

"Thank you. I would also add that it would drastically reduce the number of children who are raised apart from their families only to be dropped from the Trials early on."

The Councilor's wide and unsettling grin rose in response, but it was the voice of another who interjected. Layden knew his Host's name was Richard Hopper, and he was in charge of the Science and Technology division. His wrinkles were deep, and he had big, bushy eyebrows that seemed to move on their own.

"What if potential recruits are missed among those rejected early on?" he asked.

"I think my adjusted Collection age helps avoid missing potential. Additionally," Layden continued before she could be interrupted again, "I believe the children should be eased in when they are chosen—for example, periodic visits from family, even transitional programs to help them adjust."

"What would you say in response to the Conservatory being a place to foster culture?" Sephora Holmes asked, her bright eyes peering intensely from behind heavy lids. "If children are collected later in life and allowed to retain parts of their previous life, aren't you robbing them of the chance to immerse themselves in their better one?"

Layden's mouth twisted slightly. Despite the questions, Layden was no longer feeling deterred. Besides the fact that it felt like a collaborative conversation now, she was beginning to realize that she was the expert here. She knew the experience of the Collection and Conservatory better than anyone seated before her. Their questions showed as much.

"A child enrolling later in life wouldn't miss as much culture as you think, because they would be at the appropriate age to choose to leave their family, thus adopting any habits and patterns willingly. Culture once bought into does not take as long to adopt. Force it upon someone, however, and you often get the opposite of your desired effect."

This seemed to quiet the Council members, so she looked to her pages trying to remember her next thought. But her eyes could not decipher any of it.

"I would love to hear any further questions you have for me," she finished haltingly.

The Council members began to murmur among themselves, but eventually Sephora spoke again.

"Layden Prier, I can see that a great deal of thought has gone into this, and you speak with the passion of someone who desires to see improvement. However, as you must know, change of this nature is not easily rendered. For what benefit would we undertake such a reformation?"

That was what Layden had forgotten. But she was ready to answer. "In addition to actually finding worthy candidates that fit your unique needs for the first time in fifty years? I believe the current process creates...dissatisfaction among the people, and, therefore, far more work for you all."

"What do you mean, dissatisfaction?" Richard asked, his brow undulating ominously.

Layden wondered if she should remain vague during this part, but a small nudge inside her told her to relate the full event. So, for the next few minutes, she detailed her reoccurring nightmare of the night Constance's parents attempted to recover their daughter.

"I don't pretend to know how many times this has happened in the history of the Collection. But I doubt the incident with Constance was the first. I *know* the Council has its reasons for keeping the children who are petitioned for—" Layden paused for a moment and gave the Councilor a very pointed look. "And I trust the Council with those reasons. Still, it cannot be easy to deal with such occurrences or to be on constant watch against attempts like these. I firmly believe these are symptoms of the issue I have outlined, and my solution stands. Parents must have time to adjust, and children, time to choose."

She paused and looked at the members of the Council, no longer avoiding their eyes. "And they will choose you, Council. I know they will. Especially when shown just what a privilege it is to live here in Nyine City. The loyalty of all will be unwavering."

The Council was silent before her. There were no more questions, but neither did they dismiss her.

Finally, Layden decided to act in a way that would denote confidence, and she spoke strongly. "Thank you for your time. I hope, whatever the outcome of today is, I have helped secure your future in some small measure."

CHaPTer FIFTeen

O NE BY ONE, THEY reentered the Meeting Hall and lined up as instructed. Layden surveyed the row of solemn, elderly faces, realizing that it was the last time she'd see any of them again, regardless of their outcome. If they continued, they would receive new Hosts, and if they didn't...well, she doubted they'd be attending any post-Trials reunions.

"Thank you for your patience." The Grand Councilor said as she flashed an eerily calm smile.

When they had started this evening, that smile had seemed comforting. In their current circumstances, it felt...inappropriate.

"Please step forward when your name is called. Beau Prier. Heddah Prier. Inez Quain. Kaden Quain. Rebekah Prier."

Layden watched as the Host bodies, containing the minds of her fellow candidates, stepped forward. It was an odd group to be summoned, and she wasn't sure what the line represented. A few of them had done well, particularly Inez who had one of the stronger presentations. But Beau had lost his train of thought at least three times and hadn't been able to answer many of the Council's questions.

"I am pleased to inform you that we are impressed by the potential we have seen tonight, and we offer you advancement to the next level of Generation. Each of you will proceed to the Generation of Sixties after a short Reacquaintance Period in your own body. Congratulations."

Layden felt a shiver of fear run up her spine. The people before her had had promising ideas, and if they had lacked scientific backing, they had made up for it with creativity. But she was having a hard time processing their advancement. Especially in light of the fact that it meant her dismissal. It's true that the Council's reaction toward her had not been clear, but when she thought of Manni and Abisen, she became even further confused. Those two had been incredible.

Nevertheless, Layden had not misheard the Grand Councilor.

As Layden watched the students accept their success, clearly relaxing and smiling with relief, the revelation began to sink in, like a heavy weight on her chest; she had not been chosen. She had *not* been chosen. The room reeled around her.

"Please exit the main doors and form a queue in the hallway. Your Guardian will meet you and explain your next steps in a moment."

Layden watched as the five left the hall, their faces elated. She would have envied them had she not been consumed with the already icy stabs of dread.

"Please step forward when called," the Councilor spoke again. "Candice Quain, Isaac Prier, Paul Quain, Seth Prier, Wendem Quain."

Another odd group. The next five candidates timidly stepped forward with hope in their eyes and fear on their faces. None of them knew exactly how this part went—was it possible they would get their outcomes five at a time? Was there hope for her yet? Layden could see Candice shaking.

"To you five, we are also incredibly grateful. However, we do not have a place for you within the next Generation. If you would please exit the side door and follow the Guardian to the room behind this hall, there will be someone waiting to assist you with your next steps."

While the Grand Councilor delivered this verdict with the same unaffected tone one might use when announcing she'd run out of the candidate's favorite cookies, her words had the effect of a flash grenade. The five candidates stood seemingly in shock, their faces pale and frozen in surprise. Layden had to remind herself to breath. It was one thing to worry about being dismissed, another thing entirely to hear the verdict for real, and without explanation.

Why hadn't they been given an explanation? It seemed only kind that more be said.

But more was not said. In fact, the Guardian had to walk forward and usher the five out of the room. Even then, their steps were stiff and slow, their complexions white as ash. She wished she knew what was in store for them. She wished she could comfort them. And at the same time, she knew she didn't feel half as bad as she should, because beneath all of it was a glimmer of hope.

Layden gazed down the row of those that remained—Manni, Abisen, Mathis, and Yuna. These four had been standouts in Layden's eyes.

"Please step forward, Abisen Prier, Emmanuel Prier, Layden Prier, Mathis Prier, and Yuna Quain," the Councilor spoke in that unchanging peaceful manner, as though she had not just given them world-changing news.

"While I have you before me, I would like to commend you all for the fantastic work you have done. Abisen and Yuna, your scientific prowess is unmatched by any of your age. Our laboratories are already receiving your proposals and will begin implementing your ideas first thing in the morning. We are extremely impressed."

Both girls looked like they were fighting to keep their shock and pride from their faces, Yuna's manifesting in sheepishness, a slightly more becoming expression than Abisen's emerging haughtiness.

"Emmanuel," the Councilor continued, "outside your work today, we recognize your keen ability to spot vulnerabilities within our systems, and that is valued. Over the past six months, you have challenged the Defense League extensively, as you found your way inside our infrastructure and...explored."

Layden's blood went cold at these words, but the Councilor didn't seem upset. In fact, she smiled.

"Do not be alarmed, we know your curiosity was innocent. You may have felt like you were breaking a rule, but there was no malice in your actions. As there didn't seem to be any real threat in your prodding, we were content to let you move about and see what you could truly do. It was of value to us to see where we were weak, and we believe your thesis highlights similar needs in our world."

"Yes, ma'am," Manni said, bowing his head slightly. Layden could see him shaking ever so slightly.

"Mathis, perhaps you have been underestimated at times in your life. You have a quiet nature and unassuming manner, but the Council knows when it sees potential. Your ideas are creative and innovative. We know there is more to come from you. Your reservoir has just barely been tapped."

Mathis seemed to be blushing, but, to his credit, he only nodded his head humbly. Layden wondered if he would ease up on her now that he was receiving his own attention.

"And, of course, Layden Prier," the Councilor continued, demanding Layden's gaze. When the Councilor had it, she smiled kindly. "It is true I had planned on advancing you because of your visions. I am not ashamed to say it."

Layden's peers turned to look at her. Out of context, the term "visions" seemed supernatural and strange, and she cringed inwardly at what they must be thinking.

"Neither should you be. Not everyone could have handled such things as you have done, while also continuing your work and presenting what I would call a solid thesis. You have good intuition and are not afraid to be bold and perhaps the two things are related. Either way, such a keen observer can be a valuable part of a team; someone who sees holes and wants to mend them. You have identified several weaknesses in the Collection process, and we will be addressing those once we review our best options. In addition, your heart seems to be, almost unwaveringly, for the betterment of our governing. That loyalty is not easy to find. Nor will it go unappreciated."

Layden felt the tightness in her chest loosen a little and give way to relief. To excitement even.

"I am sure you are all wondering what will become of you. Indeed, we do not have much precedent that would prepare you for this, so I will spare you any more suspense. We would like you all to progress within our Trials. But as Layden so succinctly put it, we have yet to find candidates suitable for our ranks in over fifty years."

Layden noticed the Councilor's language. She did not lie, but she wasn't specific in her details either.

"Therefore, in a bold step of trust, we will be advancing all five of you, not just a single Generation, but two. You will be rolled in with an existing group of other candidates in the Year Fifties. While the Year Fifties do not have a set finish date, you five will need to Showcase at the end of your first season, so we can decide whether these advancements continue."

"What will happen if we aren't ready in six months?" Abisen asked.

Layden thought she was bold to interrupt the Councilor, but the Councilor didn't seem to mind.

"If we need more time to assess you, there are a few options available to us. I am fairly certain we will know what we need to know at the end of the six months. You all have given us cause to believe in you, but you still have much to learn. So, I suggest you focus on doing just that."

Layden shot Manni a look. She knew this was an honor, and yet, her excitement had been replaced with apprehension. There most likely was a reason the Year Fifties didn't have a definite finish date; to be given one seemed unfair.

"Now, I would stay and elaborate further, but that is what we have your Guardian for. Thank you for your efforts this season. I look forward to seeing you again very soon."

The Council members dismounted the platform and exited through the main doors, the Guardian reentering from the back hall as soon as they were gone. His face was pale and grim, and the question about what happened to dismissed candidates burned in Layden's chest. At the same time, she had never wanted to know less.

The Guardian did not speak at first but rather gestured for them to follow him out into the main hallway where the first five candidates waited. Their expressions were transparently suspicious to see Layden and the others. Some even seemed resentful, like the presence of Layden's group dampened the privilege of being advanced themselves.

"You have all had a long night," the Guardian finally said in a soft, but official tone. "And it is not yet over. Before we place you within your new Assignment, you must transfer back to your own bodies and spend a day reacquainting yourself with them. It will be easier to adjust to than a Host's body, but it is still necessary. Keep in mind, your body has aged in season with you. It may not be as you remember."

Layden tried to prepare herself for whatever that might be like, but all she felt was relief at the thought of spending even one day in her own skin.

"At the end of the day, you will transfer to your new Host. For half of you, that will be one within the Generation of Sixties." He gestured to Layden and the four on her right. "You five will receive your Year Fifties Hosts."

Understanding came upon the other five candidates, and a barrage of expressions were aimed toward Layden's group. Amazement, confusion, resentment, envy, anger.

"Come this way," said the Guardian. "There are more of you than usual, and I would like you all to have some sleep before tomorrow."

Layden stepped out of the chamber with her own toes, watching with her own eyes as her own hair fell around her shoulders. It had grown long in the last six months, but it felt and smelled like her own. Her elation was unmatchable. While she'd become accustomed to her Host in some measure toward the end, returning to her natural body made her realize just how foreign the other had been, and how that feeling had never really left.

The Guardian stood observing her as she tested out her feet and stretched her legs. He'd told her that there would be a bit of atrophy in her muscles—part of the reason she'd spend the day readjusting—but Layden didn't care about any of that. She could scarcely keep the tears from her eyes.

The chamber beside her displayed the body of her Host in stasis, and Layden couldn't help but linger. Touching its surface gently, she exhaled hot breath that fogged up the cool glass. She couldn't explain it, but she felt grateful to this woman and sad to leave her. Though Layden hadn't truly known her, it felt like leaving a friend behind.

"What will happen to her?" Layden asked the Guardian.

He hesitated. "It is policy to not use a Host more than once. Likely she will have her mind reinstated, and she will be released to live her life in peace. She did her duty."

At any other time Layden might have inquired about his lack of certainty. Why, even now, could he not give her a straight answer? Did even he not know? But today, her heart was too worn to ask.

"It's strange. I feel like a piece of her is still in here." Layden touched her forehead. "But I know that's not possible. I mean, there wasn't anything of her in there in the first place." Layden stated this rhetorically, but it was an odd enough sensation to bear speaking about.

"The things you experienced were unique to the state of inhabiting. There is your consciousness, and then your consciousness within her body. It is an experience even the Council has been unable to put words to."

"I feel like I've lived another lifetime."

"Yes. Well, that is the point, is it not?" the Guardian said quietly.

Layden considered this for a moment. "You know, at the beginning of all this, I spent so much time trying to understand why we needed to undergo these transfers at all. Now I'm not sure I would have even understood if somebody had tried to explain it. Maybe that's why no one ever did."

"Layden Prier, come. Others are waiting." He moved forward and took her by the elbow, much like he had six months ago.

"Thank you," she whispered to the glass one more time. Her heart hurt. She would miss the woman, even though the woman had only been her.

"Come, Layden," he said again, this time more gently than she had heard him speak yet.

"Maybe now you can tell me who she was," she said suddenly, looking up at him.

He paused for a moment and looked back at the woman in the chamber. His jaw clenched ever so slightly, but he only turned and led Layden away.

Manni and Layden rested against the metal fence surrounding the track. From where they stood, they could see the whole outer facility—still sheltered within the high, white walls of the compound but spanning further than one might expect. It was the largest amount of man-made ground that Layden had ever seen. An oval athletic track stretched perpendicular to the fence, beyond which a hill sloped downward, carpeted with imitation grass. To the right, down in a shallow valley, a set of sandstone walls stood without roofing, vaguely reminiscent of what people before used to call a maze. Layden had read about those once and the structure excited her. She could hear voices in the distance, somewhere within the maze, and she noticed workers in gray jumpsuits maintaining the grounds, though they were all too far away for any more detail than that.

For their reacquaintance day, Layden and the other four in her group were confined to the track and a small, sparring square sheltered by a canopy. Layden noticed the soft mat flooring and drew the conclusion the space was for physical training. She had to admit, it had been a while since she'd been up for anything more than a walk, but her own body felt nimble and full of energy in comparison to the one she'd recently inhabited. After a full morning sprinting around the track in bouts, she and Manni were now rehydrating under the canopy and watching the others.

After they'd transferred back the night before, the Guardian had explained that the reacquaintance was necessary so that their bodies didn't forget their minds and vice versa. The ideal period between these "reacquaintances" was six months—which is why most periods in the Trials aimed to end in a season—but it was relatively safe to remain outside their bodies for as many as four seasons. Any more than this and the owner risked their mind disassociating with their own body and treating it the same as a Host's. While one could get good at living within a Host's body, life would never be as synced or coordinated as with the original.

"For some reason," Manni said, interrupting her thoughts, "it feels different being back. Like I've changed."

"You mean, your body has changed?"

"No. I mean, like I'm more than I was before. Like something came away with me."

"Yeah. I get it." Layden straightened up and chewed her lip. "The Guardian was trying to explain it last night, but I have to admit, it didn't make much sense."

She moved her fingers absentmindedly, touching each of them to her thumb in turn—they'd been given various coordination exercises like this to help them readjust—back and forth, touch, touch, switch, switch.

"That's not the only strange thing," she continued. "I've been trying to put my finger on it, but I haven't been able to yet."

"Try," Manni encouraged.

"I've felt a very specific way over the last six months. A feeling deep in the bones. And now that I'm back in my own body, it's like that feeling has just gone away."

"What feeling?"

Layden thought for a moment. "The best way I can describe it is a deep, aching loneliness. I tried to fight it at first, but, in the end...well, I thought I'd be stuck with that feeling forever. Now it's just gone."

Layden glanced over to Manni who gazed back at her. His hair and eye color looked like hers, his skin too. But there was so much about his face that was just him. Manni. Though there was no question his body had changed as well; he'd grown. A lot of growth happens in a season. His dark hair, once short, was now below his ears; his jaw, once an adolescent's, now resembled that of a man's. His limbs had grown too but were thin and gangly.

"I think I know what you mean," Manni replied at last.

"Yeah?"

"For me, it was more like...helplessness. Maybe inadequacy."

"Helplessness?"

"Yeah, like I couldn't help anyone. I couldn't help myself; I couldn't help the Council. I couldn't help...you."

Layden turned and met his gaze. It was apologetic, and entreating. She looked away.

"Yeah, I remember a couple of conversations where that feeling might have surfaced," Layden said with a light laugh. For some reason, this conversation was making her uncomfortable. She knew it was hard on her to lose her sounding board when she was separated from Manni. But she hadn't expected that separation would affect him as much as it seemed to.

Manni laughed and shook his head. "I know. But it's gone now. I don't feel it even a bit, and I can't *make* myself feel it either."

Layden nodded as she returned her attention to her peers on the track. She wasn't sure what any of it meant, but it felt good not to be alone.

"Promise me. Whatever we're feeling in the next six months, we stick together. Okay?"

Layden paused and thought about this before nodding. They'd managed to keep their friendship intact, but in retrospect, only barely.

"Hey, you two," a voice called out.

Manni and Layden turned their attention to Abisen and Mathis who were walking toward them from the track. It was still strange to see their actual faces, though their mannerisms remained much the same.

Abisen, naturally, retained her strut. "Where's Yuna?" she asked, while weaving her hair into its customary tight braid.

Layden thought she could see the faintest hue of dark red in Abisen's hair. Layden had never noticed it before. Maybe it was the sun.

"She's over there." Manni gestured to an open space beside the track.

Yuna was sitting on the artificial grass, pulling it up with her fingers and studying it.

Layden felt bad she hadn't noticed Yuna over there by herself. It had to be hard, being the only one from den Quain with them.

"Well, go get her," Abisen said to Layden, pointing at her watch. "They should have our Hosts ready by now."

Layden recoiled a bit at the demanding tone, but Manni put his hand on her arm immediately.

"I've got her," he said.

He slid under the railing and walked over to Yuna. Layden watched as he spoke a few words to her. Made her smile. He extended a hand to her, and she tucked her dirty blonde hair behind her ears. Layden didn't know exactly how such color variance occurred, especially after the Guardian had explained the process of phenotype simplification to her, but she was beginning to notice more differences among her peers. None as dramatic as Constance's blonde hair had been, but different enough to make Layden wonder. Could you really take variety completely out of the equation?

"What d'you the Fifties will be like?" a voice sounded behind her.

It was Mathis. She turned toward him, noting how his complexion was waxy and pale. He was now a little shorter than Abisen, who had shot up in animated stasis. His face was a little rounder than hers too, still not having outgrown his childlike cheeks.

"Well, we'll find out when it's all over, won't we?" Abisen said practically.

Layden felt she was beginning to understand. But that didn't make the walk back to the Transfer chambers any easier.

CHaPTer SIXTeen

THEY'D BEEN INSTRUCTED TO meet the following morning at the sparring plaza after they'd gotten a full night's rest. Even with permission to sleep, Layden's body woke with the dawn. She couldn't be sure if that was from the rigor of her mind's schedule or the pattern of her new Host's body, which seemed used to physical regimes. Either way, she wasn't alone. By the time she got to the plaza, the others were already there waiting for their new Guardian.

She'd been surprised—and not a little bothered—when she'd found a different Guardian waiting for her at the Transfer the night before. He'd introduced himself as Commander but assured her his role was much the same as her previous Guardian. Since the qualified candidates had split into two groups, and their Guardian could not be in two places at once, the Council decided that Layden's group be rolled into the existing Year Fifties and under the Commander's direction.

Year Fifties were customarily divided into groups of five, training, eating, bunking, and breathing together. Naturally, Layden and the others would remain one of those groups. The main disadvantage of their early progression was time—the current Fifties had already endured two Generations together. And with Year Fifty lacking a defined end date, multiple dens had merged, forming a close-knit community of twenty individuals who already knew each other well, regardless of the isolating culture of the past Generations.

Their Commander finally arrived and stood before them, his hands clasped behind his back, showcasing his brawny, rounded shoulders through the sleeveless tunic. He was middle-aged with facial scruff and bright eyes. So far his demeanor was coarse and gruff, but not in an intimidating way. He seemed simple, focused, and disciplined.

"The Council is comprised of intrinsically unique individuals, cut from a different cloth than the rest of the world. But none of them would have achieved what they had, had they not all learned to work as a single, cohesive unit. While you may never see military battle, your ability to learn how to be a part of a corps is a skill the Council greatly desires to see in their successors.

"Out here at dawn, you'll train with me," he said. "After which, you'll hit the showers and get your morning meal. Following that, it's off to your lectures, where you'll study the dynamics of teamwork and leadership. It's vitally important to understand the role each individual plays within a team—when one member is incapacitated, the whole team suffers. You must learn this deep in your gut, and you don't have the luxury of time, so learn it quickly and learn it well.

"Your afternoon training is back here, with an added emphasis on strategic theory and practice, which will take place with the rest of the company of Fifties. Then it's dinner, and the lights go out at 20:00 hours. You may stay up later if you'd like, but you'll regret it soon enough."

Layden watched her new "unit" nod their understanding. They seemed to be listening readily enough with unclouded expressions, but she couldn't keep her frustration with the fact that their Guardian had been replaced from her mind. She wondered if any of the others were even thinking about the change. Probably not. After all, she was a little surprised *she* was thinking of it.

"All right, that's enough talk," the Commander said, cupping his hands together. "Let's begin with a series of exercises to wake those bodies up. I know the Transfer is new, so it will take time to acquaint yourself with your Hosts. But work fast. We don't have time to dawdle."

The Commander elaborated on each exercise, informing them that their goal was to discover exactly what their bodies were capable of. He gave them suggestions as they started and pushed them when they were hesitant to go further. The work was hard, but there was plenty of rest, and Layden decided to take the time between sets to get to know her friend's new faces as well. They'd had only seconds to reintroduce themselves before the Commander began.

Manni's Host was a middle-aged man of average height. He wasn't extraordinary in appearance but still had a powerful look about him—strong, with a well-developed physique, hair buzzed close to the scalp, and a nose slightly flattened at the bridge that looked like he'd broken it a few times. Throughout the morning, he proved to be stronger than he looked, out-lifting, jumping, and sprinting the lot of them. His eyes were brown and had a steeliness about them, a hardness that shone intensely during concentration.

Abisen's Host was close behind him in agility and speed, no doubt because she possessed these things in abundance in her natural body. Layden heard the Guardian's voice echo in her head. *The consciousness brings along what it wants to bring.*

Unlike Abisen's last body, she was almost as tall as the men around her and muscular as well—in fact, all the bodies they inhabited seemed to be athletic in nature. Her skin was smooth and tan, sheening with perspiration as she moved, and she had worked her hair into the same characteristic braid almost immediately.

Layden moved to one of the stations for upper-body strength and sized it up. Her Host's body seemed average height and build, though she'd never felt the muscles in her own stomach and legs as pronounced and defined as they were now. She still hadn't gotten a good look at her face—not that she was itching to. She walked to a bar bridging two poles and leapt up to grab it, pulling her body up till her chin touched. The movement was difficult, awkward, and a bit painful. It felt like the muscles didn't want to listen to her brain's command. It didn't surprise her. She barely felt in control of her walk, let alone these detailed movements. Her fingers slipped off the bar after her third repetition.

"Layden, is it?" the Commander asked, coming up behind her. "I believe you can do more than that."

"I don't know. Her muscles don't seem to be used to this." She shook her arms out.

"*Your* muscles listen to *your* brain," he said pointedly. "Stop thinking of them as someone else's, or as their own entity. They're yours right now, and you have more control than you think."

Layden considered this for a moment then grabbed the bar again. Again, the motion was awkward and painful, and she slipped off after a couple of repetitions. The Commander shook his head and pointed her back to the bar. Inwardly she chaffed, but then she looked up and saw that four pairs of eyes were watching her along with the Commander, and the fire of competition lit within her, urging her on.

Layden took a deep breath and jumped back up, this time mentally chanting to her muscles. Telling them they were hers. Willing them to listen. Again, it was slow starting, but this time, as she continued to pull up and let down, her arms became acclimatized to the motion. The movement became smoother and smoother.

"Six, seven, eight," the Commander began counting for her.

She could see the group out of her peripheral vision as they watched. She kept going, telling her mind to focus. Thirteen. Fourteen. Fifteen.

"That's it, girl," the Commander spurred her on, his tone grainy and forceful.

Soon Layden lost count, but she was no longer worried about her muscles disobeying her. She kept them going till they physically failed, and she slipped off the bar against her will.

"There you go. Tomorrow, you hit twenty," her Commander said emphatically. He gave Layden a strong pat on the back and moved to Mathis at the station beside her.

Even though Mathis's body was different, she still recognized his look of disdain mixed with envy. Ignoring it, she took a seat and caught her breath.

Exhilaration dared to rise in her chest, the words of the Guardian echoing in her head. *One could get used to living in a Host body.* She was beginning to see how that was possible and how unlocking that skill could be crucial to her progression through the Trials. A new world seemed to open before her.

The Commander kept them moving for a good two hours before showing them their new living arrangements, with the promise of a shower and a hot meal on the horizon. While Layden and the others had slept in their old quarters the night of the Transfer, they weren't permitted to return any longer. Layden was thankful she'd had the foresight to lock the Guardian's book in her study chest before the presentation. Before that, it had been beneath her pillow.

The Year Fifties barracks were located indoors and close to the sparring plaza. It was a narrow hall with shared rooms and a small mess hall at the end. Layden and her unit had the last empty room. Each room had five bunks, two stacked on the right, two on the left, and one standing alone along the back wall. Layden was quick to grab the top bunk on the left, and Manni slotted down below her. Mathis and Abisen grabbed the right side, and Yuna took the back wall.

For a moment Layden felt sorry for Yuna because they'd unanimously decided she was the odd one out. Layden thought maybe she should try and reassure Yuna—it would only be kind and a gesture of good will—but deep in Layden's chest, an uncomfortable feeling was beginning to burn. She didn't quite understand it, but it bordered on disapproval...maybe even disdain at Yuna's weakness. It wasn't Layden's fault that Yuna was the only one in Quain to advance; nor was it her responsibility to make Yuna feel welcome. Layden had enough to worry about.

She climbed onto her bunk and looked over her things for a moment. A change of clothes, a bar of soap, a towel, a small pouch of personal care items, and a portable console. She'd never had one to herself, but it looked like this one was assigned to her. She put it down and gazed around. This part of the compound smelled mustier, slightly damp with the scent of bodies packed in close together. But it seemed clean enough.

She picked up the soap. It was crudely cut, rough, and smelled strong. Why had they been given their bathing things here? She didn't see a door to a shower anywhere. Abisen appeared to be having the same thought as she handled the soap in her hand, but, unlike Layden, she didn't waste any time contemplating it. Rather, she grabbed her things, slipped out of her bunk, and exited the room. Layden threw a look at Manni who had noticed as well, and they silently grabbed their things and follow her lead.

Abisen led them down the hall. As they passed the other open doors, Layden spied the rest of the candidates standing about, talking, or using their consoles.

When Abisen made it to the end of the hall, she walked through a door opening into a large, circular room, tiled from floor to ceiling.

Layden and Manni followed. There were many showerheads descending from the ceiling, but no partitions that Layden could see. The room smelled strongly of their new soap and a cleaning agent of some kind. Around fifteen people were already showering—men and women alike, in clusters of five—their units obviously.

Yuna and Mathis trailed in behind Layden, their expressions mimicking her own. She didn't even want to disrobe in front of her own group, let alone complete strangers. They'd been given complete privacy the entirety of their time at the Conservatory, and the divide between male and female dorms had been strict. Now they were supposed to just…throw in together like this?

But Abisen—with what looked like a bit of forced bravado—took the initiative and moved to an empty corner. Manni and Mathis followed, though less confident, leaving Layden and Yuna to stand around awkwardly.

"Well, they're not exactly our bodies, are they?" Yuna said timidly, before joining the rest.

She had a point, but that didn't exactly make Layden feel better.

"Just focus on the water till you get used to it," Abisen said glancing sidelong as Layden joined them.

Layden placed her soap and towel on a ledge and stripped off her clothes, then tossed them into a large hamper that sat at the edge of the room. Mimicking the others around her, she stiffly pulled on the showerhead to activate it, trying to do what Abisen said. *Just focus on the water. Easy.* The heat was nice after their vigorous morning of exercise, and she began to relax as it washed over her.

"Hey there, save some hot water for the rest of us," a voice spoke beside her.

Layden turned to see a man from another unit leering jokingly at her as he undressed. Mortified, she turned away, taking her soap and lathering it between her hands.

"You all just transferred?" he asked.

Abisen—clearly sensing that Layden was unable to speak—mercifully intercepted the question. "Yeah, last night," she said.

"Last night?" He surveyed them all. "Oh, hey, you're the advanced recruits, aren't you?"

"That's right," Abisen replied.

"Ah. I'm Jared. This is my unit, K-Unit. Or den Kepner. Welcome," he said as he turned on his shower.

Layden thought that might be the end of it, but a woman beside him chimed in.

"Hey, isn't Layden Prier supposed to be with you—is that you?" She was looking at Abisen.

Abisen was notably irritated. "No. The name's Abisen," she said curtly.

"Ah, my mistake. You seemed like the lead," the woman replied.

Layden heard Mathis scoff, and her own cheeks went hotter, if that was possible.

Abisen glanced around at all of them, eyes settling on Layden. "That's Layden," she said. "And we don't have a *lead*. Not yet at least." She returned to her shower.

Layden finished rinsing and turned off her shower. She grabbed her towel and wrapped herself quickly.

"That's cool," the man named Jared said as he whipped his hair back, sending water flying.

The woman didn't seem to take the hint, however. "Is it true you have, like, visions?" she asked, addressing Layden directly.

Layden had already started to leave, but she felt she had to pause to answer with a nod; the last thing she wanted was to make more enemies by coming across as arrogant.

"What are they like?" The woman persisted, making the man beside her switch places so she could move closer.

Layden's tongue was tied again. She didn't want to talk about her visions, especially surrounded by a large group of naked people. But it was more than that. She found she didn't even want to think about them.

"It's hard to explain," she said, sidling away. "Besides, it's been a while since I've had one."

Since before the presentations. She had a momentary shiver of fear that she might have lost the ability when she moved between bodies.

"Excuse me, I'm gonna go get dressed." She left before anyone else could stop her.

Back at her barracks, she pulled on her clean clothes and rung out her hair. It was long and very dark, almost black. She wound it up in a bun on her head and bound it with a band she'd found in the small pouch on her bed. She noticed a small mirror on the back of the door and went over to examine her face. Her face was handsome looking, with a strong jaw and tanned skin that was tightly lined with sun and age. Her eyes were brown, and her lips were a natural pink but were interrupted by a scar that angled across the right corner of her mouth. A similar scar angled across her left eyebrow, as though it might have been part of the same injury.

As she stared at her face, that new and uncomfortable fire in her sternum smoldered. Her behavior in the baths had been unacceptable. She'd come across as weak, vulnerable. Pathetic. She needed to get it together, and fast—she couldn't afford to be the squeamish, bashful wallflower, paralyzed by conversation and ashamed of the one thing that made her stand apart.

Den Kepner had been looking for a leader. They'd expected her prowess to match her talents. She'd shown them the opposite.

"I'll do better," she said to her face in the mirror.

At that moment, the rest of her crew came in through the door and Layden had to step back. She retreated to her top bunk, watching as her group spoke casually with one another. Why couldn't she be at ease like they were? Their conversation was light and familiar as they dressed and even Yuna seemed more talkative now. Layden kept herself looking occupied as her team equipped themselves with their portable consoles and hung up their towels.

"Breakfast?" Abisen asked the room. "Coming Layden?"

"Go on, guys. Layden and I will catch up," Manni intercepted as the other three began to leave the room.

Layden climbed down from her bunk.

"What's wrong?" Manni asked her immediately.

Layden looked up at him briefly. "I'm fine," she answered, though her tone said otherwise.

"Was it those people in the shower? They didn't mean anything by it."

"No. And yes. I'm tired, Manni. I was just getting things in order, and now everything has changed again."

"It has for everyone," he said practically. "Though I'm not gonna complain about having some energy and a shorter shower routine."

"It's not only the body, or the new course, or new people, or even the fact that I have no clue if I can still have visions in this Host—"

"It's the Guardian," Manni said, his Host's dark eyes fixing on her intensely.

"What?"

"The Guardian. You spent six months struggling—and I mean, struggling—to earn his respect, and now he's not even with us."

Layden couldn't respond, but the hot tears coming to her eyes told her he was right.

"Look. You're someone who has always needed the approval of your superiors. It's who you are, how you get your bearings, how you order your world. But, maybe, just focus on the task for now. Let the rest sort itself out."

So, he didn't feel the same way she did—he might even feel the opposite—but at least he understood.

"Okay. Yeah. I can do that," she said. "Though I *had* hoped the mythological creature worship was over."

"The mythological creature bit has a lot going for it, Dennie," he said with a half-smile. Her nickname sounded even stranger out of the mouth of this gravelly-voiced, middle-aged man, than it had before. Manni seemed to think so too.

"Look, Layden," he adjusted. "I'm here, remember? I'm your constant and you are mine. Not our unit, not the Guardian. Yeah?"

She considered his face. It wasn't Manni's, but it was a handsome face; his eyes held a hunger she wasn't sure she'd ever seen in Manni's, making her wonder to whom exactly the hunger belonged.

"Yeah, okay," she said weakly. For some reason his words didn't comfort her like usual.

"Come on, let's go eat. I'm so hungry the cantina food might actually taste good today," he said, striding out of the room purposefully.

Layden waited for a moment before following. There was a time when she would have agreed with him wholeheartedly—they had always been each other's constants. But while she'd agreed to stick with him no matter what she was feeling this time around, she realized with a twinge of sadness, and a bit of wonder, that perhaps her constant had changed.

chapter seventeen

"**W**HAT IS THAT?" MANNI whispered into the dark of the barracks. A quiet kind of beeping was pulsing throughout the room.

"Sounds like it's coming from Layden." Abisen said, her speech slurred with sleep.

Layden sleepily lifted her head and checked the small shelf to the right where she kept her things. It didn't take long to realize her console was glowing and dinging, even though it was face down against the shelf. Layden flipped it over and silenced it, watching as a message floated to the surface slowly.

"Visitor. Door."

Who would want to see her at this hour? Then she looked at the clock and realized that, while they'd only just turned in, their day had been so exhausting she'd fallen fast asleep in five minutes.

"I got it," she whispered, but it sounded like everyone had already gone back to sleep. Layden descended the small grooves in the wall that served as a ladder and slid the door open as silently as she could.

To her complete surprise, the Guardian was standing on the other side. The actual Guardian, not the Commander. A strange sensation flooded her, and she found herself sighing in relief, as though she'd been holding her breath since her recent Transfer.

"Guardian? What are you doing here?"

In response to her question, he gazed at her, seeming unsure. "Layden Prier?"

It occurred to her that he didn't know what her new Host looked like, because he hadn't been there for her second Transfer.

"Yes, it's me. What is it?" she asked, becoming slightly alarmed. "Is something wrong?"

"You did not come to our evening session."

"What?" she asked, still shaking off the sleep.

"You did not think your training was complete simply because you advanced a level? If anything, you will need the training more."

"No one told me," Layden managed. She slipped back to her bunk and grabbed her warmer outer layer, tugging it on as she exited.

"I sent a message through your portable interface. Be sure to monitor it from now on."

"Yes, Guardian." Layden followed him down the hall.

"Have you had any more visions?" he asked.

Layden couldn't help but sigh. He wasn't wasting any time. "No," she said sourly as she walked by his side.

It was strange viewing him from this angle, now that she was no longer a short, older woman. He was still taller, but she wasn't craning her neck to see him either. She wondered if it was strange for him to see her in a different Host as well, or if the change was a relief for him.

"You should also use your portable console to inform me the second you do," he said curtly. "Even if it happens during lessons." He seemed moderately irritated, but she didn't think it was because of her. Perhaps he disliked the change of Guardianship as much as she did. After all, he always did seem to take his duties seriously.

His stride was quick as usual, but for once, Layden was able to keep up. She felt spry, and not just because this Host was in better shape than her last. Layden marveled at how light her feet felt now that the

Guardian was back. Why was that? It was possible Manni was right, that she oriented herself by the approval of those in authority—she'd only just started making progress with the Guardian, and it was an exhausting prospect to have to start over with the Commander—but it felt like more than that.

After all she'd gone through with the visions, and the sensitive truths she'd been learning about the Council, the Guardian had become more of a stabilizing force than she realized. And it felt good to have something stable in the midst of the chaos. She hated to admit it, but even Manni had been more of a variable as of late.

"How did practice go this afternoon?" The Guardian interrupted her thoughts.

"Awful," she said before she could stop herself.

He turned his head as he walked. "Elaborate."

"We're supposed to be 'increasing our interdependency' as a group and learning how to communicate, but we spent the entire day trying to figure out who would take point."

"I see. Who has attempted the lead so far?"

"Manni didn't seem interested; I don't know why. Mathis didn't step up either, but he also made it difficult for anyone else trying to, especially me."

She paused and chanced a look his way. She didn't want to put too fine a point on it, but it was largely the Guardian's fault that Mathis had it out for her. Ever since that day in the Library, Mathis hadn't wanted anything to do with her.

"Abisen *tried*," she continued delicately.

"Unsuccessfully?"

"Kind of."

She didn't exactly feel good about giving him the "scoop" on the others. It felt a bit like cheating. And while this new, and admittedly unnerving, fire within her goaded her to take advantage of the Guardian's ear, another, quieter part of her didn't want to betray them.

But he was asking, and anyway, was he even their official Guardian anymore?

"Why do you think that was?" he insisted.

"Well," she began carefully, "Abisen is extremely confident. She always has been. But she was abrasive and didn't seem to know how to involve the group in the plan. She just expected us to follow whatever she came up with."

"And the rest did not?"

"Not exactly." She nearly laughed.

"What?"

"I don't know." Layden sighed and rubbed her eyes. It had been a long and demanding day, and she was exhausted. "I'm not good at this stuff."

"What *stuff*."

"Understanding people. Their behaviors, their meanings, their needs."

The Guardian stopped as they reached the edge of the sparring plaza and gazed out over the track.

It was a beautiful night outside. The air was cool, and she could smell the dew settling on the fake turf, a crisp, clean scent that almost smelled plastic. As dusk disappeared, the moon began to rise and take over for the sun, revealing the night sky.

"If you are to improve at something, you must practice. You may struggle to interpret things, but you are not blind. You are perceptive. And you know your teammates, having been with most of them since childhood. Analyze the behavior, based on what you know of the individual. *Stop* avoiding the hard work, and tell me, from your perspective, why did your team fall apart under Abisen's leadership?"

Layden swallowed hard and followed his gaze onto the field. He was right of course. She wasn't great at it, but that didn't mean she could give up trying to learn. She took a breath.

"Manni is smart and has a lot to share, but he doesn't seem to *need* to lead. He just wants the best plan. If we allowed him input, he'd follow easier."

"Good. What else?"

"Yuna...is strong, but I imagine it's hard for her to be on her own among us all."

"What would she need?"

"Direction? Reassurance."

"And Mathis?"

Layden's heart sunk, and she sighed, shaking her head. "For me to be out of the picture, probably."

"Why would he want you out of the picture?"

"Because you turned him against me!" she couldn't help but quip, his persistence frustrating her.

"Nonsense."

"Nonsense? You told him to have nothing to do with me!"

"I told them all to have nothing to do with you. Why is it that he is the only one who listened? Think!"

Layden wanted to scream at him, not a new emotion she admitted, but never had she been so close to listening to it. She thankfully held her tongue, fairly certain he still had the right to dismiss her at any turn.

"You do not have time for the others to come around and ask you to lead them. If their way is not working, then you *must* take the lead. Understanding your team will put you there," he continued.

"Mathis is insecure, which makes him jealous," she said simply, though she felt like a child saying it out loud. "When you singled me out—multiple times—but didn't dismiss me, he began to believe I was a special project of yours. Now he grumbles at my every opportunity, failing to understand the real situation."

The Guardian was silent for a moment and glanced at her in the cool moonlight. His expression was peculiar when he spoke. "And what is the real situation, Layden Prier?"

Layden went quiet again. Now that she thought about it, she wasn't sure anymore. It wasn't that she wasn't grateful for the Guardian's attention, but she truly didn't understand why she was getting preferential treatment. All five of them had been advanced, hadn't they? And she was no longer a distraction, which was the reason she'd been set apart to begin with. Maybe Mathis, Abisen, all of them, were right after all.

"Can I ask, will the others be meeting with you too?" Layden changed tact. She was fairly sure she knew the answer, but it was the least aggressive way to ask what was on her mind.

"I was not illuminated on the schedules of the rest of your unit," he responded evasively.

"Same as mine. Will they be offered additional training?" she asked again.

"Being that you all advanced forward, you five are no longer under my care. However, I have been tasked with your individual training, Layden, and I will continue to do so."

"But that is the whole point! We're supposed to be learning unity and cohesion. If I receive special training, no one is going to want to work with me," Layden countered, her voice unable to conceal her aggravation.

Rather than reassuring her, the Guardian's countenance changed, and he turned to face her square on. Even in the low light she was arrested by the intensity of his gaze. When he spoke, his businesslike, though familiar, tone was replaced with a low and quiet growl.

"Listen closely, Layden Prier," he began. "I will do *everything* in my power to bring you ahead in these Trials. However, it is not my job to make others follow you. If you decide you do not want my help, if it is too...uncomfortable...for you, then say the word and we will pass these hours in silence. Believe me when I say, if I had not been ordered to watch you like a child, I would spend my time on any number of other useful endeavors."

Layden met his eyes, despite the hot tears prickling her own, but was unable to speak.

"Now," he continued, "if I am to see you succeed, *you* must learn to hold a tension between their approval and their respect. You must make it plain to them that you *will* lead them. Not because you are liked and not because you demand it of them. But because you are the most qualified. The only way that is going to be true is if you grow a spine and start believing it yourself. And if you learn to trust me implicitly. You may not like me, but I am the only one here who can get you to the end of this. Do you understand that?"

His tone had moved beyond derisive and had almost turned imploring, as though it were crucial he get through to her.

Layden's cheeks flushed with emotion. Deep in her chest the fire roared, stirring her to lash out in her own defense, but she could not bring herself to do so. In the back of her mind was a whisper that told her...that he was right. This was his job, his main mission. To see her to the end. And in that regard, they would always be on the same page.

"Yes, Guardian. I'm sorry," she whispered.

There was a moment of silence where he seemed to collect himself under the dying light. He exhaled through his nose resolutely. "No apology is needed," he replied finally, straightening up. "Just your commitment."

Layden nodded curtly and moved onto the track as he gestured.

"Now, do you remember your fastest lap time?" he asked her.

"Yes," she said warily.

"Good. Go beat it."

A thin layer of mist hung outside Miranda's window though it was well past midday. It was an eerie fog, but thankfully only the first of the season. When days like these became more regular, it meant the Monsoons were only months away. She'd learned to read the warning signs years ago.

She was safe, of course. Everyone in the facility would be, because it had been built to withstand such weather, before the weather had even begun. Those in the Outlayers had their precautions too. But safety wasn't the thing on her mind, no matter how dangerous the Monsoons were known to be. When the mist came kissing the panes of her window, all she could think of was all they had lost, and how they had no one to blame but themselves.

The Sterility, the floods, the collapse of mankind...she'd seen it coming for decades before the Council was even a twinkle in her eye. So, she'd made her moves. Played her cards. Made her alliances. And because she did, humanity existed today.

Still, she was growing weary. Immortality had its price, and it seemed the price was exhaustion. Not the physical kind, for her daughter's body had quite a bit of life left, but the mental kind. She was tired of fighting every day for what was rightfully hers.

And these new recruits, she inwardly scoffed. *They will be no different.*

They might understand at first, maybe even be willing to join the Council. Others had been. But it wouldn't last. Sooner or later, everyone let her down. She turned and pulled a picture frame off her desk. The photograph was of herself and a group of eight others. Her Council members, back before...well, everything. Perhaps they'd been through too much together. Perhaps they'd lingered too long in a good thing and now...

Miranda shook her head and straightened up. They would be here any moment, and she couldn't be looking out of sorts. *It's just the mist*, she told herself. Melancholy Mist. She might have written prose about that in her younger days. But that was long, long ago.

The knock on the door finally came.

"Enter," she called loudly.

Two men entered the room, first Miles Goaden, then Jeremiah. The men were comparable in height, but Commander Goaden was superior in mass, a brawny, militaristic type who looked odd forced into the traditional tunic. But he wore it out of respect for her. Jeremiah's was more of a practical physique, leaner; both were a fine example of the Council's principles on bodily stewardship. They stood before her desk now, arms behind their backs in civil respect.

She smiled warmly. "Good evening gentlemen. I won't keep you long, as I know you both have a great deal to do. I would like an update on our advanced recruits."

There was a small pause, but then Goaden spoke. "Yes, ma'am, but with all due respect, why is Guardian Cherut here today?"

"With all due respect," Jeremiah repeated tersely, "the advanced recruits originated from my season. Who better to lend insight into their progress?"

Goaden's eyes narrowed but he said nothing.

"Yes, it's true," Miranda said. "I called you both here because the two of you have overlapped in some areas. It is the nature of this kind of thing, and I figure it's best to be very black-and-white about all areas that are gray."

Neither man responded to this. She wasn't sure Goaden even understood her; he was brilliant at what he did, but he was a bit of a blunt instrument. Jeremiah's face, however, grew dark. He always understood.

"Guardian Cherut," she began, "I understand you have taken to training Layden after hours." Surely, he had to know she would know that. Behind his calm facade, she saw a flicker.

"Of course," he said measuredly. "You instructed me to keep a close eye on her. I assumed if you wanted that to cease, you would have said as much."

"I am not against it, but I'd like to know what Commander Goaden thinks. These five are now in his care."

As Jeremiah shifted his weight, the Commander stood there, clearly surprised. He didn't seem to know about this activity, nor expect to be asked his opinion on it.

"Who am I to argue with the Council?" he said at last. "I will do whatever you instruct me to do."

Good soldier, she thought wryly.

"Grand Councilor, if I may," Jeremiah began, "while these five are indeed, under Commander Goaden now, I must remind everyone involved that there are several compelling reasons each intake stays with one Guardian. I think my presence with these recruits is necessary for continuity, but also for monitoring. Commander Goaden has no understanding of these students and their original personalities. He cannot possibly be expected to see any abnormalities or subtle cases of Host rejection, being as he has no foundation to work from."

"Foundation or not," Goaden interrupted, his professionalism seemingly slipping, "I'm not a rookie, Jeremiah. I can spot such abnormalities a mile away."

"I do not doubt your abilities, *Miles*," Jeremiah's formality dropping in kind. "The fact remains. One cannot perceive a variable if he is unaware of the constant."

The Commander's face grew annoyed, and words—more likely than not, unproductive words—poised on his tongue.

"That's enough," Miranda interjected.

The men turned back and faced her again.

"I see your point, Jeremiah. But I, too, have every confidence in Commander Goaden's ability to handle any issues that arise. I would not have placed them under his care if I didn't."

Jeremiah's mouth pursed, but he nodded his concession.

"Here is what we will do. I'd like you both to continue as you have been. Jeremiah, you may continue to work with Layden after hours and keep a close eye on those visions of hers. As an extra precaution—because it would be a shame to waste good recruits due to carelessness—you will spend one day a month with all five of them, to ensure everything is up to standard. Outside of that, the five of these advanced students are in your care, Commander."

Both men nodded, the Commander looking relieved and Jeremiah appeased.

"I caution you, though, Commander," Miranda continued, "not to let pride get in the way of what we are trying to accomplish here. Jeremiah does know these students. Not only from the last season, but from their days at the Conservatory. You know how fast personalities are changing at these ages, not to mention all the extenuating influencing factors. If you have any odd feelings, any doubts at all, speak with him. Use him as a resource. Do you understand?"

Goaden straightened up and nodded. To his credit, she didn't think pride entered his motives at all.

"How is the Defense League faring with the new patrols to the Outlayers?" she asked him.

"Very well, Grand Councilor. The men and women have been briefed and are on a healthy rotation. Though we'll need more numbers eventually if we're going to keep it up."

"That is entirely up to the people in the Outlayers. If they cannot behave themselves, then we must enforce order ourselves. There must be no more of these incidents. All of our residents, whether in Nyine City or out in the docks of the Outlayers are under our protection. I will not leave a single one vulnerable to the baser exploits of humanity. We must, as always, strive for a more elevated nature."

"I understand, Grand Councilor," Goaden affirmed. "It will be so."

Then as an afterthought, she said, "You may sift through the disqualified candidates and bring them back into purpose should you have need. Had you any in mind?"

"Emmanuel Prier, Councilor. He'd be a valuable addition."

"He is not yet disqualified."

"If that becomes the case, I will happily have him in our intelligence division."

"Noted. Now, if you'd be so kind as to leave us, I have a few things to discuss with Jeremiah," she said.

The Commander nodded briefly, casting a subtle look between the two of them, and left the room. Jeremiah remained where he was, avoiding her eyes.

When they were alone, she spoke again. "How are things going since your recent visit to the Outlayers? Have we made the necessary repairs to their damaged bunkers?"

Jeremiah hesitated. "The problems I encountered were not ever going to be solved quickly. The wear is extensive, and, while our infrastructure teams are repairing around the clock, I have serious reservations about letting the Outlaying population stay there throughout the Monsoons. The foundations are in the worst state. They are likely to crumble the moment the waters rise."

She pursed her lips. "I have been thinking...what of Mathis Prier's thesis?"

"Converting the bunkers into ones with buoyant foundations?" Jeremiah asked.

"Yes."

"I believe that would take even more time."

"We have a full season yet," she replied.

"A single season to repair and outfit bunkers with new technology, troubleshoot, and prepare them for habitation...I am not sure that is a viable option."

"What would you propose then, Miah?"

Jeremiah was quiet for a moment, seemingly without any proposition to make.

Miranda reached across the piles on her desk and lifted the report he'd filed after he last returned. "You yourself said the foundation is the problem. Allowing them buoyancy gives them a better chance at surviving the Monsoons. Start retrofitting the bunkers with Mathis's technology. Fill in the missing specifications with our city's original flotation devices. His designs were impressively close to ours, but he missed a few crucial considerations, while, admittedly, improving others."

"Should we have a contingency if the bunkers are not outfitted in time?"

"I'm open to suggestions."

He paused, and she thought she could see his pulse quicken in his neck. "Bring the people to Nyine City to shelter-in-place," he said, his voice thick and stiff.

Miranda raised an eyebrow. That was a bold proposition, and he knew it. Her eyes roved his face carefully as she tried to discern beneath the surface. She took in his features—the stern brow, green eyes, dark, slicked-back hair. Sometimes her mind went blank around him, and she found she could not read him. It was as concerning as it was unprofessional.

Still, he did not seem to be hiding anything.

"Which Outlayer is in the worst condition?"

"Outlayer One, ma'am."

She cringed inwardly. She hated it when he called her that. It made her feel even older than she actually was. And she was old.

"Layden's Outlayer," she said.

Jeremiah hesitated almost imperceptibly. Almost. "Among others, yes."

"That won't do." She stood and walked to the large windows behind her desk. "If we must, we can bring the people into the city to shelter for one season only. Work with Johnathon and Richard, but you are responsible for calculating contingencies for rations, accommodations and travel. And if we must triage, the current candidates' families must be the priority. Our candidates cannot believe that we have failed them."

It was true she had a whole Council of individuals to help with these things, but these days, they were becoming stretched thin...and, at any rate, she preferred to work with Jeremiah.

"Yes, ma'am," Jeremiah replied.

Miranda exhaled deeply and turned slowly, fixing him with her eyes. "Miah, I have asked you to call me Miranda," she said coldly.

Jeremiah froze where he stood, not blinking. After a moment, he cleared his throat quietly and responded. "Yes...Miranda."

His eyes were steely with discomfort, and his neck had gone a splotchy red. It made her smile inwardly. It felt good to have broken him of this finally, even though she would have preferred he uttered it of his own volition. Still, he'd get used to it.

"Very well. I would like you to begin your rotation with the students tomorrow, but there is no need to take a full day—the latter half of their morning session is enough. Explain your role to them from now on. In addition, I have a specific task for you." She reached into a drawer and drew out five folders. "Here are the Council's decisions on the outcome of the students' theses. I want you to discuss these with them and monitor their reactions. Then report to me tomorrow evening."

"I train Layden in the evening. Do you wish for me to cancel?" he asked, not quite concealing his annoyance.

"Give the girl a night off, Miah. I'd say she's earned it."

"Very well."

She could tell he disagreed. He'd work them all to the bone if he had the chance. Not that she was of a different mind, most of the time. "I look forward to hearing what you observe," she said. "You may go."

Jeremiah nodded curtly and left.

CHaPTer eIGHTeen

L AYDEN WAS STRUGGLING TO stay awake. She'd been out with the
Guardian till just after midnight, which wouldn't have been too
different from the study hours she'd kept before, except her days were
now much more physically active. Her body hurt and she felt tired to
her core. In the mess hall that morning—a separate kitchen at the end of
the Year Fifties' barracks—Layden had tried coffee for the first time. The
aroma was comforting, a roasted scent, strong and somehow familiar.
However, as coffee beans were all but nonexistent, the resemblance was
limited to the properties of caffeine and color alone. Layden hadn't cared
for it, but as she watched Manni and Abisen sitting up straight and
taking notes with alacrity, she began to regret not finishing her cup.

"Excuse me, Commander," Manni asked, bringing Layden back to
attention. "Maybe you can clarify something for me. The systems you're
describing are well-thought-out. Something's just not quite right."

Layden had to pause and recall what they'd been talking about.
Defense systems, was it? She looked from the Commander to Manni, a
slight unease rising in her chest at his interruption.

"Continue," the Commander prompted, not unkindly.

Manni's Host sat forward and pointed at the board with his writing
utensil, his gruff voice filling the air with confidence. "Nyine City is
surrounded for miles by sea, and we all know the ocean is home to
predatory wildlife completely unknown before the floods, not to mention unpredictable and at times, treacherous. Swimming or rowing out

further than one mile from the city can prove to be a life-threatening endeavor, and to travel from the city to the outlaying provinces requires strong vessels able to withstand the days' long sea voyage."

"Thank you for that summary, Emmanuel," the Commander said. "Now, what exactly is your question?"

"My question is, why? Or rather, who? Who are these fortifications meant to protect us from? The people in the Outlayers? That's hard to believe, seeing as their very survival—from Monsoons, exposure, sometimes starvation—depends on their supply from the city. Not to mention they have little technology and no weaponry to speak of. So, it's unlikely. That leaves outside forces. Everyone here knows there hasn't been another living soul heard from in over a century. And for that matter, these tactical exercises we're doing, they're militaristic in nature, but why does Council need a military to begin with?"

Manni's words trailed off, his pause giving the Commander a chance to correct him. The Commander, however, did not respond.

Manni continued. "I suppose I wanted to know if we had any real threats to our safety. If not, wouldn't our time and resources be better spent in other areas of development?"

Layden had been watching Manni closely, listening to his words. Maybe it was because his new Host—this brooding-featured, middle-aged man—carried a kind of authority, but she found herself prickling with jealousy at his focus and eloquence. There weren't many times in her life where she'd felt truly jealous of Manni, not even with all his accomplishments and charisma. So, this was a strange feeling that now burned within.

But it didn't matter. Layden knew he would soon be put back in his place, because his question was out of line. At its heart, it implied the Council was wasteful. Or worse, that they were lying.

"Excellent question, Emmanuel," the Commander said.

What? Layden sat up straighter. If she had ever spoken like that in the Guardian's presence, she would've received a swift verbal lashing.

"You've studied the histories of the wars-that-were, am I right?"

Manni nodded in confirmation.

"I figured as much. You have a bright mind and sharp instinct for strategy, which often comes as a result of studying our past. Not half the men in the Defense League have that sense of understanding, and, in my opinion, that's a sound recipe to repeat the mistakes of the past."

Manni looked like he was fighting the urge to be flattered. To his credit, he maintained his composure. "You didn't answer my question," he said directly.

"As I said, sharp. We do have a military, yes. You know the Defense League to be responsible for the infrastructure within Nyine City, as well as peacekeeping in the Outlayers. However, they are also prepared in the event of a large-scale attack."

"Right, but an attack from *whom*?" Manni persisted.

"Allow me to answer your question with another—because I believe you are bright enough to know for yourself. Imagine you have a family and a home that you've been told to leave behind. Could you honestly tell me you'd do so without a thought to their protection and welfare?"

Manni turned briefly to look at Layden, his face troubled and contemplative, his eyes lingering strangely. After a moment, she shot back a noncommittal shrug. She saw what the Commander was getting at, but it was a little hard to imagine in their current life phase.

"No, of course not," Manni answered finally.

"Of course not," the Commander echoed. "Because, though we live in a peaceful, well-governed society, there is something instinctual within us that would protect what was ours."

Manni didn't answer, his attention frozen on the Commander.

"I know you understand this. After all, in your thesis...how did you put it? Everyone deserves a chance to protect what's theirs?"

Manni nodded slowly and swallowed hard before studying his hands on the table.

Layden marveled at the Commander. He was open and honest, and yet he had used Manni's own point of view to show him that he actually believed the thing he was challenging.

She supposed she was so conditioned by the Guardian's curt and chastising responses that she'd forgotten there could be others.

"Nyine City holds technology that the world-that-was had only dreamed of. It is the key to managing the Sterility and bringing new life into the world that had all but gone extinct. Our greenhouses sustain Nyine City and the four Outlaying Provinces, providing consistent staples in a flooded world. To say nothing of the children collected each year, who become the Grand Councilor's primary responsibility the moment they join the Conservatory. Can any of you honestly say the Council has nothing to protect and no reason to protect it?"

This time the whole room went silent, and Layden felt her heart swell at the burden of the Council.

"Learning to protect the things that matter is never a waste. Wouldn't you agree, Emmanuel?"

Manni nodded. Behind his eyes, there was the faintest trace of pride, as though he finally understood what he was a part of. Layden's heart dared to hope. Until that moment she hadn't realized how much his skepticism of the Council was standing between them. Maybe now, all the furtive comments and suggestions the two of them leave could end, and they could go back to sharing the same goal. The same future.

"I think that's a good spot for a break. Stretch out and be back in twenty," the Commander said, eyeing the room.

Layden felt relief wash over her body. While the Commander's open repartee was an engaging and refreshing change from the Guardian's, her eyes were fighting against her. While the others stood to stretch or take to the hall, she slouched forward, her head finding the table. The surface was cool against her cheek and had a metallic scent she'd come to associate with the compound. Her eyes closed easily.

The Commander must have read their theses then. He clearly had a grasp of Manni's true motives. She couldn't help wondering what the Commander thought of her own thesis. A thrill of competition pounded in her chest again, but she tried to suppress it. She'd made Manni a promise to choose him over whatever she was feeling.

Still, she pictured the Council's faces as she had presented—looming before her up on their platform and staring down at her. The Grand Councilor had been in the middle, her serene smile not befitting the atmosphere. The others had regarded Layden sternly and looked unconvinced, their eyes boring into her from above. The room had its familiar scent of treated wood and clean but stale carpet, and the light had been streaming in from the window in the pitched roof.

Wait. It had been nighttime, hadn't it? Not day.

Layden shook her head, hoping the memory would fade. That's when she realized that the scene before her wasn't just an image in her mind's eye. It was no longer a memory.

This was a vision.

She watched as the Councilor's mouth opened like she was about to speak. What was she saying? Layden couldn't make anything out, even as she craned her head forward to hear.

"Layden?"

The words she heard didn't match the mouth speaking—Layden watched closer.

"Layden Prier? Is everything all right?"

In an instant, Layden snapped back to reality. She was standing in the middle of the classroom, her face angled toward the ceiling, tense with anticipation.

Awareness flooded back, and she noticed all attention was on her. One would think she'd be used to that sight by now, but she couldn't shake the discomfort of all those prying eyes. She steadied herself against the nausea that washed over her, determined not to end this moment in humiliation as she had so many other times. How could she handle this differently than before? She wanted to bolt again, to hide. And yet, she was tired of that too.

"I'm sorry," she said as she took her seat again. "I don't have any control over when they happen."

The Commander stared at her for a moment, then he simply nodded, probably unsure what else to do. Layden looked at her group. They stared back at her, appearing slightly unsettled. They didn't seem to have gotten used to it either.

Though Layden could barely think straight, she pulled out her console and tried to focus. Another vision? She'd almost believed they were finished. She couldn't figure out if she was relieved or not.

Thankfully, as though sensing he was needed, the Guardian showed up at their door. He seemed to sense the hesitant energy in the room, for he paused as soon as he entered.

"Commander," he said finally, "if you don't mind, may I take these five for the second half of the session?"

The Commander nodded graciously and gestured that they could leave. The five of them stood and followed their Guardian into another empty classroom nearby then took their seats at a small conference table in the center.

"Thank you for joining me," their Guardian said, sitting at the head of the table. "For the time being, the Council has determined that, while you are in the Commander's care for this Generation, it is in your best interest to meet with me once a month for basic psychological assessment. This way, I can reassure the Council that there are no dangers from advancing you at this pace. Additionally, even you are owed a little continuity."

"Are there any concerns we should be aware of?" Abisen asked.

"Not as such. There are your basic Host-rejection issues, which if not caught early can be serious. No risks that you have not already been made aware of."

"Is there a reason we should worry about having skipped a Generation?" Mathis this time.

"None. The levels are not developmentally progressive. There are some basic concepts we wait for recruits to master before passing them on. However, the Council is apparently not worried."

The group was silent for a moment.

"I do not want to waste any more time, so let me continue on to the main reason I am here. The Council has tasked me with informing you of their decisions regarding your theses. Abisen, I would like to begin with you."

The Guardian slipped her folder to the top of the pile and flipped it open, then he reviewed a few pages before speaking. "The Council was very impressed with your findings. It seems they went forward with developing the prototype almost immediately."

"That's great," she said, her voice uncharacteristically emotional.

The Guardian flipped to the last page and spent a few moments reading before continuing. "One moment, I want to make sure I word this right. It seems they have determined that your bio-monitoring system is ideal for the Trials. They would like to use it to monitor the bodies in stasis, as well as the Host's bodies. Our scientists will be reviewing brain waves to further understand what is active in the Host brain from the time your consciousness possesses the body. Among other things, of course; vital signs, etc."

Abisen glanced around at the others. "I'm sorry, what do you mean, *what's active*?"

The Guardian paused for a moment. "Their plans are a little ambiguous...I suspect Reginald is in charge of the project. He does not often share details."

"*The* Reginald? As in Reginald Hargrave Jr.?" Mathis said, sitting up straight.

The rest of the group's interest was clearly piqued too. Reginald Sr. had been the lead scientist who bypassed the Sterility and pioneered the Host technology. His son, Reginald Jr., was known to have continued his work. Layden felt her blood run cold as she wondered if Reginald Jr. was truly his son, or if his father had also used the Host technology to extend his own lifeline.

"Will I be made aware of the findings?" Abisen asked.

The Guardian stared at her blankly and then over her file. "It does not mention anything about that."

"It's just, well, if the system isn't successful, am I in danger of..."

"Being released?"

Abisen nodded.

"It is unlikely that would be cause for dismissal, as your thesis has already warranted your advancement. Whether or not the Council can use your system does not mean as much as what they saw in you through your ideas."

Abisen seemed to relax slightly. "Okay. Well, I am pleased to hear the Council is finding a use for it."

The Guardian smiled thinly before continuing on. "Mathis, the Council was struck with your creativity. However, you undersold yourself. The concept for sustainable, floatable dwellings that rise with the tide could do more than just improve living. This could potentially save the Outlayers."

"Save them?" Abisen interjected. "Were they in danger?"

"I suppose you five have the right to know, though I caution you against sharing, in case things do not go as planned. If something is not done in the next season, our emergency bunkers will not be fit to house the Outlayers population come Monsoon season."

"What?" Yuna's voice sounded small.

"What's wrong with the bunkers?" Manni asked.

Layden remembered the Monsoon bunkers—small, compact structures built by the Council and existing just off the perimeter of the Outlayers. She and her entire Outlayer had evacuated to their bunkers every season during the Monsoons, that is, until she went to live at the Conservatory. The time spent within the bunkers was far from pleasant—cramped spaces, odorous with sour, anxious sweat, and canned rations provided by the Council. And yet, the alternative was worse. The Monsoons were unpredictable, and at times entire sections of the docks in the Outlayers would vanish beneath rising waters for weeks on end. It was bunkers, or death.

"For one," the Guardian answered, "our meteorologists are predicting this will be the most violent year we have seen in a long time and the bunkers' foundations have been in a state of extreme disrepair as of late. As a result, the Grand Councilor has decided to fit the bunkers with Mathis's technology as soon as possible. Without the flexibility of buoyancy, even if we did make repairs, the Monsoons would tear them right apart again."

"So, they're trying to update and repair all the bunkers...in six months. How many are there?" Manni asked.

"Will there be enough time for both?" Yuna again, her voice turning urgent.

"We are hoping so," the Guardian said hesitantly. "However, if not, the Grand Councilor has decided to open the city to the Outlayers for the duration of the Monsoons."

"Really?" Yuna's honey-toned voice was full of awe, her eyes wide. "They've never done that before. Wouldn't that put a terrible strain on our resources?"

"All four Outlayers? Will everyone even fit?" Abisen asked.

The Guardian wiped his brow, as though momentarily in discomfort. "We will do our best. The Grand Councilor wanted you to know that should a triage situation arise, your families will be given priority."

"Really?" Manni seemed surprised.

"Yes. So, you see, everything is under control."

There were a few moments of silence as Layden surveyed the faces of her peers. It wasn't that she wasn't concerned for the people in the Outlayers; she knew the Council would take care of them. It surprised her, however, to see the others in doubt. She looked across at Mathis, the only other one who'd remained silent. He was picking at his nails and seeming bored. Did he trust the Council too, or did he just not care?

"Always happy to help the Council," he said, rather pompously.

"Yuna," the Guardian continued, placing Mathis's folder aside for another, "the Council approved experimentation on your concept for expedited plant germination in the greenhouses. The botanists were intrigued by your idea, and I have been told they are already into beta tests. Additionally," he paused to read the file carefully, "it seems you have solved a problem they have had for a while...they are quite pleased."

The Guardian, however, did not look pleased at all. His face had gone pinched.

"Yes?" Yuna asked. Her voice quivered, but Layden didn't know her well enough to tell if she was nervous or excited.

"The resources here in Nyine City are planned to the microunit, so we have never had much to give the Outlayers in the way of food. As it stands, we provide medicines and nonessential goods, rations for the Monsoon seasons. With the work you have done, that can now change."

"Well, that's good, I guess," Yuna said with a smile.

"The Outlayers don't need food from the city..." Manni said, eyes narrowing slightly. "We have our own economy. Fishing and deep diving. We trade with the city sure, but that's different."

The Guardian continued speaking, but only to Yuna. "This has been the idea for a while—to be the Outlayers' sole provider. In this way, the Council can keep a tighter record of what comes in and out of the provinces and ensure the people have what they need always. We simply have not had the means until now."

"Oh, I see," Yuna said, her voice becoming small again.

"But...if you give a man a fish..." Manni trailed off, catching Layden's gaze.

The others looked at him as though waiting for him to finish, but Layden caught his reference to the old adage. It used to be common wisdom that if you provided all a man needed, he'd never learn to take care of himself. To take a mostly self-sufficient community and make them dependent...surely that's not what the Council wanted. Right?

"They will still be allowed to fish," the Guardian continued slowly. He didn't seem to know how to address Manni's half-spoken concern. "There is a new edict stating that any unique food cultured or caught outside the city can be sent back to the city in return for nonessential goods. But there will be a peak fishing season, and they will be limiting hours as well. Apparently, our marine and fishery departments have had concerns about overfishing. The Council must weigh all these concerns."

Layden met the Guardian's eyes and nodded her understanding. But an uneasy feeling turned her stomach.

"All right," Yuna said. She didn't seem to know if this was a good thing or not, but nor did she seem to want to voice an opinion.

"Emmanuel, I would like to move on to you next."

Manni nodded, his brow knitted, and his lips drawn in a firm line.

"Well," the Guardian began, "the Grand Councilor foreshadowed this for you on the night of the presentations. They have decided your tracker, while intended for physical possessions, is also ideal for gathering census data."

"Census, as in population?" Manni asked.

"That is correct. Effective immediately, everyone in a permanent body, both inside and outside the city, will be paired with one of these trackers. The Council saw immense value in having a tangible way to keep its people safe and accounted for."

Manni's face went white. "But it's not intended for multiple objects. Who will be accepting all the signals? How will they distinguish between them all without being overloaded?"

"They have worked around that, of course, a modified version of your concept. A console will intercept all signals as an intermediary. From there, any person with access—an extremely limited list—can request signals from anyone they need, using the brain wave technology you outlined."

"Who is allowed that information?" Manni asked.

"The Grand Councilor, of course, and anyone she approves. She says she owes you a great debt; you have done a great service to Nyine City." The Guardian's voice had become toneless and professional, devoid of personal emphasis.

Manni nodded tersely with a tight smile. "Hopefully she remembers that in six months," he said.

A couple of them laughed, but it was forced, on edge.

Layden was glad to hear her peers were helping the Council so greatly—and she thought what the Councilor had said about Manni was high praise indeed—but something was sitting heavy on her heart. They had come up with concepts to win the Council's approval, and they had. But the five of them hadn't a clue what could, or would, be done with their ideas, nor did they have any say. Layden couldn't quite describe it, but she felt out of control, even a little irresponsible. Should they have taken better care to safeguard their original ideas?

Then again, they weren't the ones tasked with protecting and sustaining humanity, as the Commander had reminded them. The Council had every right to adapt these concepts and make them work for everyone. Right?

"That leaves Layden," the Guardian said. "It says here that the Council greatly respected your point of view on the Collection and Conservatory, as well as on the tensions between the families and the children chosen for the Trials. The Council says you have demonstrated an acute sensitivity to dynamics hidden from most people."

Maybe it was the way he was reading, cautiously and on edge, but Layden found herself waiting for the "but."

"These dynamics have created some unsafe and unproductive incidents, and they believe your diagnosis is accurate."

Layden let out a breath. "Well, that's great," she said. "So, they're going ahead with my changes?"

"It seems," the Guardian continued, eyes back to the folder, almost avoiding hers, "that they plan to circumvent the problem entirely."

"What does that mean?" Layden asked.

There was a moment as the Guardian paused and appeared to collect his thoughts. He could have been reading the file, except his eyes weren't moving.

"All of you know," he began again, "that when a woman is of child-bearing age, she must travel to Nyine City to receive the vaccinations and gene modifications that allow her to carry a fetus full term. Then, toward the end of term, she must journey into the city again to have the child. What you may not know is that the child stays in the care of the doctors here in Nyine City for a full month post-delivery. We used to allow the mothers to stay during that time, but we do no longer have the space. Now they are sent home for the duration, and the child remains. Even with all we do, the percentage of parents who have a living child at the end of the month is less than sixty percent. The Sterility is aggressive and often mutates around our precautions, resulting in less-than-healthy infants."

"Yeah," Abisen said, "that happened to my baby brother."

Everyone looked at her. In all the time Layden had known Abisen, she'd never volunteered such personal information. Then again, Layden had never asked either. The Conservatory's motto to always look forward was beginning to feel like an excuse to avoid confronting the painful parts of their past. And for the first time, Layden wondered why.

"Yes," the Guardian said quietly.

"I'm sorry," Layden said, confused. "What does that have to do with my thesis?"

"The Council has decided that all newborn children will remain in the city, living at the Conservatory in a new facility for infants, until their potential has been assessed at the age of five seasons. Your programs and assessments will be adapted to look for promise in the initial stages of childhood. If a child shows no promise by Collection age, that child will be up for readoption by his or her birth parents, or by the general populace.

"The Council believes there will be less attachment developed if we intercept these bonding principles at infancy. Additionally, most women have already prepared themselves for the possibility of not receiving their child back at the end of the month. The transition would be smooth. At least, smoother than it is now," he said.

His words flew out without pause or variance, but even Layden could tell he did not agree with the Council's assessment. Judging by the silent room, she wasn't sure anyone else did either. Her own mind was racing with a dozen objections—and yet she had learned over the last twenty minutes that the Council would have thought of an answer to her every protestation.

She tried to take her own advice—reminding herself that the Council knew best what they all needed. But this time, it didn't reassure her as it had before. Maybe because this was her own idea, now twisted away from her intention, or maybe because their own Guardian's face was tight with discomfort and unease. Either way, a chill ran through her.

"There is one more thing," the Guardian spoke into the silence. The faces of her unit, slack and white, turned to look at him. "I have the details for your final assignment at the end of the term. It will be an obstacle course run, much like the ones you will encounter in your afternoon sessions. The stakes are obvious; do well and the Council will consider you for another advancement. You have done well so far, but that does not mean any of you should lessen your efforts. The Commander may seem rational, but even he is subject to the Council's decisions going forward."

Layden watched the others nod. But the Guardian didn't seem quite finished.

"Also, while the Council will be evaluating you individually, do not be misled; in this Generation, they want to see you succeed as a group."

Layden looked around the room. They weren't doing too well as a group.

The Guardian seemed to read this in their furtive glances, because he looked at them individually and said, "Whatever issues you are having, you had better work them out now."

CHaPTer NineTeen

I F LAYDEN WAS HONEST, the outcome of their presentations had
left her feeling largely unsettled. But over the course of the next
few weeks, the pace of training picked up significantly, and their
afternoon sessions took the forefront of her attention.

In addition to the physical demands of their course run practice,
Layden felt the weight of holding together a group whose individuals
were buckling under the pressure. After the Guardian's stern warning, they'd made the official decision that Layden would lead, but that
didn't mean they made it easy on her. They were all challenging, competitive individuals, and they were not holding back in that regard.

Her unit had stopped talking to her except when communication
was necessary, and she strongly suspected that they'd ignored her
distress call during one of the course runs and left her behind. At
first, she'd been furious, but ultimately, she didn't blame them. After
all, it had happened on the afternoon they'd learned Layden was still
receiving separate lessons from the Guardian.

However, while that may have been the start of the tension, the
last few weeks had held their own flavor of dissention. There was
something about their new environment that made them all self-cen-
tered, bordering on cut-throat. They were supposed to be developing
as a team, but Layden could almost tangibly feel the others' ulterior
motives, which said something, as she wasn't usually great at reading
people.

Mathis was desperate for recognition, and Abisen had a singular belief in her superiority. Yuna had become withdrawn and secretive, most nights disappearing for hours. Even Manni was enigmatic and often silent. In fact, his darkness disturbed her most because he kept it locked away, hidden behind his eyes.

Nor was Layden a saint in all of this; she had her own competitive impulses...often roaring alive within her chest at inopportune times. The only thing that kept her from acting on them was the Guardian's constant demand that she produce group cohesion.

Her end-of-day conditioning with him had continued as he said it would, and it was stretching her to her mental, emotional and physical limits. The biggest rest he'd given her was the half hour she took to explain her third vision to him, and she'd belabored the details so she could stay sitting as long as possible. But as grueling, tedious, and draining as their sessions could be, the things he said before had begun to make sense.

It was a huge challenge to make her Host body cooperate to the level of expectation, and it took everything in her to make it follow her complex commands. Though this body seemed to listen better than her last one, just listening wasn't good enough. A split second of delay could cause individual or group disqualification in their course run.

Of course, this seemed easier for some. Abisen and her Host seemed almost one person sometimes; she had the fastest reaction time of any of them. Layden was a close second, only because of the extra hours of training, and had Manni been receiving the same attention, he might have surpassed her by now. The others still struggled. Mathis lagged constantly, and Yuna was far behind them all. Layden suspected she was putting in extra training as well, but, for the life of her, it wasn't helping.

Most of their runs took place in the course she mistook for a labyrinth on her first day there. It wasn't as complex as a labyrinth, however, nor was it designed to confuse the runner. In fact, after a few times through, Layden knew the layout. It was divided into four, imprecise quadrants, each with eight open squares mixed in among the paths. While nothing was exact, Layden had been able to orient them all through the course fairly well the last few times. It wasn't necessarily the path of the maze that was proving difficult.

In each run, there were four challenges hidden within four of the thirty-two squares. These challenges changed location each game. If a square was empty, you could rule it out and move on, and, honestly, that wouldn't have taken them too much time to get through. Still, there were other factors. Many of the paths were blocked by physical obstacles, slowing them down. To get through the whole course and find all the challenges, the name of the game was speed and coordination.

Which was exactly their problem. Because no matter how fast they worked, Layden and her unit were still helping Yuna and Mathis through most obstacles, and mid-game they were always out at least one player due to miscommunication or overzealousness. They lost points for both. Not to mention, run by run, her unit was growing increasingly competitive and dealing with their losses poorly.

The number one ranking team was K-Unit, led by Jared, the first people they'd met in the showers on their first day. K-Unit moved as one, quick and agile, and they were far more familiar with each other than Layden's unit could ever hope to be. The biggest difference was that they seemed unequivocally dependent on their leader. They responded to his command without a second's hesitation. Watching their runs, Layden knew she was doing something wrong in her own leadership. She just didn't know what. Yes, her team followed her, but they did so begrudgingly, and certainly not without hesitation.

Regardless, the days to the end of the term were counting down, and they were running out of time. If she couldn't get the group to work together as one, she needed a new strategy.

Thankfully, the night before the final course run, she'd had an idea.

The five of them now sat at a table in the small, private mess hall, the air heavy with the smell of their overcooked protein porridge and the bitter, roasted coffee. They had been the last ones assigned to a course run that week and were up that afternoon.

"I'd like to try something new today," Layden said quietly.

Though they had all begun to eat, they stopped and looked up at her. Most of their expressions seemed interested, though mixed with surprise, and in Mathis's case, his standard glare.

"The way I see it, we're losing time trying to find these challenges. Yuna and Mathis are quick to solve them when we do, but we're wasting our resources trying to find them...as a team."

"What other way is there?" Abisen asked coolly.

"Manni?" Layden turned to him.

The attention shifted to Manni. That morning during their private study time, Layden had tasked Manni with a special project while she drew up her plans for the afternoon. Manni had looked at her strangely at first, but in the end, he had nodded listlessly and ducked away to get to work. She only hoped he'd been successful.

"It wasn't easy," he said. "I had to get the Commander to let me into the labs. And I had to tell him our idea to get to do it."

"What did he say about it?" Mathis asked immediately.

"Something about the other teams turning belly-up if it worked."

The others seemed more intrigued now, and even Mathis's lips curled into a reluctant smile.

"We're going to use Manni's thesis idea," Layden said. "I had him program his brain wave technology in line with several small beacons."

"We've tried signals. We still run into the same problem. Getting all the team to the same place takes too much time," Abisen said impatiently.

"I know we have," Layden answered, "but this is different. We're going to play to our strengths. Look, it's no secret, we're behind these other units in our physical abilities. Maybe not individually, but as a group, definitely. There's no way to change that except time to practice...which we don't have. So, I propose we take our three most physically capable members and set them loose on the track. They would split up into three of the four quadrants and hunt down the obstacles. I propose those three people be myself, Manni, and Abisen. We're the fastest and hardly ever need help through the obstacles."

"And what do *we* do? Just wait around?" Mathis asked, his sneer a picture of resentment.

Layden held up a staying hand. "This is what I'm thinking. I've sketched out a map of the concourse." She pulled out a sheet of paper and laid it on the table. "As you can see, there's the main path and the sections. I've drawn it from memory, but I'm certain there's a central route that runs down the middle of the course. It has some turns sure, but it's more or less a straight shot through. It's just that no one ever takes it because they get all twisted up finding the squares for the challenges."

"From memory? How can you be sure that's accurate?" Yuna asked.

"It's Layden's memory," Abisen said. "I'd wager it'd be as good as any map the Trials would put out."

Manni chuckled quietly and nodded his agreement.

"If it's wrong, then make notes, and we'll fix it for next time," Layden said dismissively. "The best part is, if I'm not mistaken, this middle path rarely has obstacles."

"So, what, you guys run, and we just walk to the end?" Mathis asked.

"No. Like I said, you and Yuna are the strongest at figuring out these challenges, so we'll need you once we find them. The three of us runners will search for the challenges and activate a beacon when we find one. That should transmit our location as knowledge and let you guys know to come find us. Once all the challenges have been found, we finish the run together."

"But what if there's an obstacle we can't get through on the way to the challenge?" Yuna asked.

Layden paused for a moment, annoyed she had missed such a big hole. Leaving Yuna to find her way through an obstacle on her own wasn't a strong option.

"And what if some of the challenges require more than two people to figure out?" Abisen asked.

Layden hadn't thought of that either, but now that she had, she remembered a couple that had needed more than three people to solve.

"Doesn't sound like you've thought this through at all," Mathis said derisively.

Layden clenched her jaw and met his eye. "If you don't want to listen to me, then don't. Quite honestly, I don't care anymore. But if you want to make progress, then maybe try contributing to the solution instead of adding to the problem."

Mathis shut his mouth and sat back sullenly. Layden released her breath and looked around. Judging by their faces, the group dynamic could go either way, but when no one spoke, she returned to thinking.

"What if we take it two quadrants at a time?" Manni finally piped up, tapping the map. "So, say I stay with Mathis and Yuna on the main path, and you and Abisen run through the first and second quadrants and find the challenges. When you find one and activate the beacon, all three of us in the middle make our way to the beacon. Then the runners are free to find the other challenges, and no one has to wait around for Yuna or Mathis—no offense."

"That's great," Layden said, poorly concealing her gratefulness.

"Still seems like a lot of waiting around," Mathis said, though less hostilely. "Are we sure this isn't going to be wasting time rather than saving it?"

"It may feel like it because you're the one waiting," Layden conceded. "But think of it this way—you and Yuna won't have to struggle through any obstacles you don't have to. And the ones you do, we can probably make easier for you by going before you. After you've finished a challenge, you simply move to the next beacon. Once the challenges are found, I think we'll make up any time we lose waiting."

"It's certainly worth a shot. Not like we can do any worse," Manni agreed.

"We need some sort of plan if one of us gets disqualified, or if we need help with a challenge from one of the...runners," Abisen said.

Everyone looked to Layden for her answer.

She met their eyes, trying not to be distracted by the sudden shift in atmosphere. The team seemed cooperative for the first time since they'd been transferred, and more than that, they were looking for her opinion because they wanted it, not because they thought they had to. She tried to think quickly.

"Mathis and Yuna will have a beacon as well," she said at last. "One they can activate that'll connect to the runners only. That way one of us will know to come back. Do you think you can do that, Manni?"

"Yeah, no problem. I've already rigged a handful of them and set the brain wave patterns for each of us. Just in case. It's simple installation and programming from here on."

"Okay." Layden recapped, "So, if everyone agrees, I propose Manni and I will be the runners. We can cover the most ground at this point.

Abisen, you stay with Yuna and Mathis because I trust you to be the most capable of escorting them through the obstacles. The three of you will wait between the first and the second quadrant on the main path. Manni and I will run in, find the challenges, leave the beacons, and move on. The three of you will find the challenges and alert us if you have any problems."

The three of them nodded their concession to this.

"There's one other thing," Manni said. "I can program multiple beacons for multiple people, but I didn't find a way for one person to receive multiple signals, even though the Council apparently did. I can make it so you're able to receive those signals, but you can only get one at a time. So, once you've made it to a challenge, you'll have to deactivate that beacon to receive any other signals. Got it?"

The others nodded.

"Good. Let's get these things installed," Manni said.

The rest looked to Layden one more time, and it took a few moments for her to realize they waited for her benediction.

"Let's go," she said.

cHaPTer TwenTy

T HERE WERE A LOT of variables, but Layden had to trust their intuition in the field. They were new to being a group, but this kind of critical thinking was what they were bred for. Manni had set them up quickly, and his confidence seemed to incite optimism.

The time to beat was 2:15:34.

Layden's skin prickled with anticipation—and the smallest hope—that they might stand a chance. She and her unit pulled on their gear, strapping on thick vests and utility belts assigned to them. There was no telling what a challenge or obstacle might hold, but they'd been outfitted for a wide range of physical scenarios. Most they'd been trained for, but there always seemed to be something for which they weren't.

"Listen up," Layden began, "Manni and I have four beacons each, just in case. You guys have one collectively. I'm already getting periodic updates of your position as...right in front me." She paused to take in the sensation, strange and abrupt in nature but also familiar, like a long-lost memory. She marveled briefly at Manni's genius. "Are the three of you getting anything from us?"

"No, nothing. That's good, right? Cause the beacons aren't on?" Yuna said.

"Right. Here's a test," Manni said. The beacons were about the diameter of a golf ball, round and flat with a button embedded that gave a satisfying click when pushed. It also had adhesives on the back so they could stick them to walls if needed.

Yuna, Abisen, and Mathis all looked up at Manni at the same instant, as though just remembering something. They'd clearly gotten the signal.

"Great. Turn that off for now, Manni. Remember to deactivate the beacons when you find them so you can receive the next signal."

"We know, Layden. We've got this," Abisen reassured her.

"Okay," Layden said, though she felt less than sure. At any rate, the time for talk was over. "Let's go then."

The five of them jogged through the entrance, aiming for the center of the course, wasting no time with the many turns that led away from the main path and staying as straight as they could. By the time they came to the main split between the first and second quadrants, only a matter of minutes had passed. Layden nodded at Manni and watched as he ducked to the right, picking up his pace significantly.

"I'll see you on the other end," Layden said before leaving the group. The image of her team, standing motionless as they watched her leave, hovered in her mind's eye. She couldn't help but doubt the wisdom of her plan.

Then the fire in her chest reared up and reminded her of her Guardian's words; the only way this worked was if she grew a spine and believed it herself.

"It'll all be worth it if we find the challenges," she muttered aloud.

The first two squares she came upon were empty. She might have been disappointed, but she hadn't run into any obstacles along the way either, so she'd made good time. When she finally did encounter an obstacle, it was on a path she knew led to a third square. A tower at least twelve feet high stood in the way between her and the square. Layden slowed to a walk, approached it, and looked it over carefully. There were small grooves for climbing, but it wouldn't be an easy one. The top ledge looked coarse and craggy, but she couldn't tell exactly what material it was made of.

She unspooled some rope from her vest and attached a three-pronged grappling hook to its end. After giving it a few swings, she lobbed it to the top of the tower and felt it catch. She gave a tug first and then put her weight on it, swinging a bit. That would have to do.

Hand over hand, she ascended the rope, using the grooves for her feet, hoping the hook would hold. Thankfully, it did. She made it to the top in relatively no time at all, but she couldn't help thinking of Yuna climbing the tower—her own arms were shaking and resisting slightly—should she leave her rope? No. Surely Abisen could manage it. She retracted the rope into her vest then peered over the other side. A hanging rope ladder led the way down.

"Perfect," she said to herself.

The ladder was bolted to the ledge of the tower but not to the ground, so she pulled it up and then slipped it down the side she had just come up. She didn't need it to descend, and it would be a lot of help to the others. It didn't quite reach the bottom, still being anchored to the far side of the tower, but it was better than nothing. Layden would have to drop. She lowered herself down as far as she could and let go.

The impact was a little rough, but she'd live. An update washed through her mind that the group of three were still waiting between the two quadrants. It came to her as old knowledge, like a thought that just popped into her head.

The third square had no indications of a challenge either and she had to admit she was beginning to worry. The longer she spent searching for challenges, the longer her team stood around looking, feeling, and being useless.

"You can't do anything about it. Just find the next square," she told herself.

Another update. Evidently Manni wasn't having any luck on his side either, because the other three were still on the main path.

Then, along the next path she came across three back-to-back obstacles: a deep pit she had to swing across, a fallen wall, and a giant bog that spanned at least ten feet of the path in front of her. Layden found her muscles growing weary and her lungs tight, and she hadn't even found a challenge yet. As she climbed out of the foul-smelling bog, the slickness running off her gear like it wasn't really liquid, she stopped for a second and begged the air for a challenge.

Walking cautiously into the fourth square, she exhaled in relief. Her hopes had been answered. Her hand fumbled for a beacon in her vest pocket as she walked further into the large space.

A series of platforms, pullies, and towers cluttered the square, and a large net hung from a beam running across the open-air square, anchored from wall to wall. The net swung slightly in the light breeze, taunting her with its mystery. She could see a door at the other end of the square that they'd probably need to open—no doubt the objective.

Layden knew, had it been only her solving this challenge, it might have taken a while. Thankfully, she didn't need to. She just needed to mark the spot and move on. After glancing around, she picked a tower in the center and stuck the small beacon to it. Then she pressed the beacon's button with her thumb. She paused and waited for an update. Nothing at first, no movement. Then suddenly, she knew they were moving toward her again. Her heart leapt. She could almost see their movement in her mind's eye.

It had worked! They were on their way.

Okay, on to the next square.

Layden made it through several empty squares and a handful of moderately challenging obstacles before she received the knowledge that her team had left the area of her first beacon. She hoped they had re-membered to deactivate it, or they wouldn't get her next one.

Her "memory" of their location was working perfectly, and she hadn't gotten any alarm beacons from the team indicating they were stuck. All was going well. She checked the small disc on her vest that was keeping time. They were only forty minutes in! This was very good.

The obstacles began to thin, which in Layden's experience meant there probably wasn't a challenge around, but she made herself check the eighth square just in case. When she entered the space, she felt a chill run down her spin. Despite her expectations, it appeared there was indeed a challenge.

Never cut corners! That competitive fire roared within. It would have ruined everything if she had.

The ground in front of Layden was flooded, and frozen over, the surface before her reflective like glass. Layden stepped out tentatively, her heart skipping a beat as the ice beneath her toes cracked delicately. A small mound stood a few yards away in the center of the square with a chest on top. Their objective would probably be to cross the ice and get the chest open. The ice wasn't completely transparent, but as she stared closer, Layden thought she saw something dark swim beneath the surface. Could it be that those who constructed this run had dug out the ground straight down to the water below Nyine City? She shuddered again thankful she didn't have to find out.

Layden took another beacon and switched it on, then stuck it to the wall beside her.

The trio was nearby. Perhaps they'd been trying to make their way back to the main path and had gotten lost, but they seemed to be winding their way toward her. That was fine; she'd intercept them and regroup for a moment. She took to a sprint again, turned a few corners, and found them within two minutes.

"Hi," Layden said breathlessly. It was just Yuna and Mathis.

"I was trying to find the main path, but I got turned around," Yuna said, looking harried.

"Where's Abisen?"

"Just as we reached the first challenge and deactivated your beacon, Manni set off one on the other side. We were pretty confident about what to do in the last square, so we told her to go."

"Were you okay though?" Layden asked. It bothered her that Abisen had left the other two behind when she'd been explicitly instructed to look after them.

"Yeah," Mathis said, holding up a small brass key. "It was a simple timed circuit. Pull this lever, hoist up here, door is open, run in and grab the key. Would have been rough with one person, but wasn't too bad with both of us."

"Well, you have your work is cut out for you ahead. Follow me." Layden broke into a run and led them back to the frozen ground. She didn't want to leave them just yet. If Abisen and Manni were working on the other side, they had time.

Yuna and Mathis scanned the square. Then, all at once, their expressions shifted—as if a long-buried memory had surfaced.

"They turned off the other beacon. Abisen must be at Manni's challenge. We can see this one now," Mathis said.

Layden nodded her understanding and took the beacon down from the wall. She switched it off and pocketed it again. "So, what do you think? Do you need my help here?"

Yuna surveyed the ground carefully. "It looks like a false floor," she said.

"What do you mean?"

"I mean, there is a path that's solid, we just have to find it. It's not easy to see, but there will be some way to reveal it," she answered.

"Light?" Mathis asked.

Yuna nodded and unhooked a small flashlight from her belt. She shined it across the glassy surface and the ice began to show differences in opacity. A foggy, clouded path began to emerge.

Mathis turned and grinned at Yuna.

"Mathis, I suggest you go. One false step and something tells me you'll fall straight through that 'false floor.' Also, there's something in the water." Layden said.

The two looked at her without blinking, but she could see the fear register on their faces.

"Bring the key. I have a feeling it's for that chest," Layden said.

They both nodded, and Mathis took a small step out onto a patch of cloudy ice. It held.

"Yuna, come here for a second?" Layden said. She took Yuna by the arm and led her back out to the path. "Remember this route, okay? You're close to the main path. All you need to do is head out straight from here, take your first right, and then an immediate left. One right and one left then keep going straight to reach the main path. Got it? I'll be waiting for you."

Yuna nodded her understanding, and Layden gave her a pat on the back before making a run for the center of the course.

She arrived in a matter of minutes and found Manni and Abisen waiting. Judging by the fact that they were out of breath, she gathered they had just arrived.

"How'd it go?" Layden asked.

"One challenge in my quadrant, in the eighth square. I didn't have any more squares to investigate, so I decided to wait around for the team. Abisen showed up minutes after I turned my beacon on."

Abisen held up a short, black dagger. "This was buried in the wall behind some cleverly concealing greenery."

"Is that what you were supposed to find?" Layden asked, confused.

"I'm assuming so," Manni said. "The square was almost completely empty except for the foliage on the walls. Abisen noticed there were various kinds and colors. Once we realized that, the section hiding the dagger stood out fairly obviously."

"Yuna and Mathis are working on the second challenge in my section," Layden filled them in. "It should be easy if they can stay steady on their feet. Yuna knows the quickest way to get back. I ran into them, lost, on their way out to the main path."

"That was lucky," Abisen said flippantly.

"Probably wasn't a good idea to leave them on their own," Layden said. Hearing her own voice, she realized it sounded snarkier than she meant.

"They're a little clumsy. They're not children. And didn't you just do the same?" Abisen responded defensively.

Anger flashed like a firestorm in Layden's chest, and harsh words rose to her mouth; they were Abisen's responsibility, and she'd abandoned them. What kind of a teammate did she call herself anyway? This was exactly why they kept failing.

But then a small whisper interrupted, laying a blanket of snow over the flames and extinguishing them. *Stay together.* It had been a while since she'd felt its prompting, and, this time, she decided to listen.

"You're right, I did," Layden said, exhaling the remaining frustration. "You helping them through obstacles and keeping them from getting lost is key to us winning this, though. It's important."

She could tell Abisen had been rearing for a fight, but at Layden's words, the hostility seemed to leak out of the air.

"Sorry," Abisen conceded. "I'll stay at my post next time."

"I think I hear them," Manni said touching them both on the shoulder.

Just then Yuna and Mathis came out of the second quadrant onto the main path. Mathis was drenched from head to toe.

"He fell in," Yuna said. "Once he opened the chest, the whole mound collapsed beneath him. He barely made it up to the path again."

Mathis was shivering. "It's a shield." He hoisted it up for them to see.

It was matte black and looked heavy. Why would they need that?

"Are you good to carry that, Mathis?" Layden asked.

He nodded and slung it on his back with a bit of cord.

"All right. We've made it through three challenges in an hour. We might actually have a chance at winning this," Layden said.

The team seemed to gain a second wind at her words.

"What's the plan?" Abisen asked.

"The same as before. Follow me." Layden began to run, keeping in mind the others weren't as fast, and led them through the course to the third and fourth quadrants.

"Manni and I will go through the remaining squares to find the last challenge. Since there's only one left, activate the distress beacon when you're all together, so the other runner will know to stop searching."

Manni gave her a nod and took off again without waiting for further prompting. Layden followed suit.

This was it. They were so close. An hour in and they only had one more challenge to go! That was unheard of. She began to feel light on her feet.

She rounded a corner and saw the first square a few yards ahead of her. Unfortunately, it was blocked by an obstacle. A thick, black liquid, steaming and reeking of burnt rubber and mildew, coated the path before her. Above it, a slack rope ladder stretched horizontally like monkey bars on a playground, its corners anchored to the sandstone walls. The rancid sludge didn't look deep, but when Layden dipped her rope in it, the tip of the cord shriveled up with a hiss. That was new. Layden had heard of members being disqualified for becoming stuck in an obstacle, but there had never been anything harmful before. Maybe the muck wasn't as bad as it seemed.

Layden wedged a foot onto the wall and pushed herself into a jump to grab the ladder above her. The movement was awkward in her Host's body, even with all the training she'd put in, and she almost didn't make it. After hanging for a moment, she hooked her legs through a rung and pulled herself on top of the ladder. Judging by how the ladder sagged low, she thought it would be safer to crawl along the top rather than dangling below. When she reached the last rung, she lowered herself back through a gap between rungs, almost clear of the caustic pit.

But at the last moment, her hands slipped, and she fell flat on her back with a crash. Her shoulder rolled in the hot sludge, which burned straight through her vest and seared her skin.

Layden cried out in pain and reflexively rolled clear of the sludge. Without thinking, she brushed at the greasy substance with her hands, but the sludge only got on her gloves and burnt through to her fingers as well. Inhaling sharply, she wiped them on the ground frantically, trying to alleviate the searing pain. When that didn't work, she pulled a small bottle from her side and poured what little water she had onto both hands. She breathed in relief as the black sludge cleared, and the pain subsided.

Layden fell back and took a deep breath, the smells of dirt and sweat and the black tar lingering in her nostrils. What would have happened if she'd fallen in completely? For the first time in these course runs, she felt real, visceral fear. Fear itself wasn't a stranger to her, but it had always been an ambiguous, unknown fear. Fear without a face. This hot sludge and, more significantly, the implication that the Council wasn't beyond concocting obstacles that could physically harm the recruits...well, that certainly added a face. Furthermore, it confused her.

Layden realized in an instant that her team was at the last challenge. Relief washed over her. That had been mercifully quick, and it was good that it was, because she was reaching her limit. All she had to do was make it to the end, and they'd be out. She checked the last square for good measure then headed out a different path, one that avoided the sludge, toward the others.

Just as she made it back to the main path, the others emerged from the fourth quadrant. In Manni's hands was a sleek, matte black helmet.

What was all this about? Three matching pieces to a suit of armor? The Commander had briefed them that the safety precautions would be removed for their last course run as an extra challenge, but she hadn't given any thought to it. The runs hadn't been that dangerous before. In the light of the last obstacle, however, she was beginning to see things differently.

"Good job. Let's go," Layden said, having no energy for anything else.

"What happened to you?" Abisen gestured to Layden's shoulder.

It was still emitting steam, and her face was covered in cold sweat. "I'm fine," Layden answered dismissively, walking along the path toward the exit.

"How'd you get that?" Manni persisted.

"I'll explain later." Her chest felt tight, and she didn't have words for her thoughts at that moment.

Layden led them to the end of the course then she stopped to check the time. One hour and thirty minutes... They'd done it! She felt the adrenaline of success course through her veins. She pushed the door open and stepped out onto the fake, plastic-smelling grass turf on the other side.

She didn't know what she expected to see—cheering, happy faces, or something that reflected the victory she felt on the inside, but she didn't see any of those, obviously. The other units sat under a covered patio where they'd been watching Layden's team's progress on screens. They were not happy to see them at all. There were some accusatory looks on their faces, but mostly they just seemed angry. Especially the members of the highest-ranking unit.

"One hour and thirty-five minutes! That's a record time. Phenomenal teamwork." The Commander was waiting with a large grin on his face his thick arms folded across his chest.

Layden couldn't help but give a small, relieved smile.

"Sir! That wasn't teamwork," Jared shouted, standing angrily. "That wasn't group work at all. They should all be dismissed for such a hack of a run!"

"That proves what I've been thinking for months—you do not understand, nor have ever understood, leadership, Jared," the Commander said, rounding on Jared with a change of attitude. "You charge through every course the only way you know how—your way—and your team keeps up. Because they're exceptional. But what would happen if your teammates couldn't keep up? You'd leave them behind in the dirt. There's nothing wrong with understanding the dynamics of a group and using them to your advantage." He turned back to Layden and nodded in approval. "I saw more team cooperation, communication, and cohesion today than I've seen all week."

Layden felt her cheeks go hot. She glanced at her team, expecting to see envious faces, angry faces, like she always did. Instead, they seemed proud. Abisen was smiling with a tired kind of satisfaction, and Manni was looking at Layden differently, the darkness behind his eyes fading into kindness and respect once more.

"Layden's unit, go. Hit the showers before I change my mind," the Commander said.

Layden walked with her team up the hill toward the complex. They were moving at a crawling pace but seemed in high spirits. Manni walked ahead of Layden, talking with Yuna about something, but when he turned and looked at Layden, his smile fell. He subtly ended his conversation and fell back in step with her.

"Hey," he said.

"Hey, Manni," she responded evenly.

"You okay?" He gestured to her shoulder.

"Oh, yeah. Of course."

"An obstacle?"

She nodded. "I think we'll find the next course...different."

Manni didn't say anything, but she knew he read her meaning. "I know this has to be getting old," he said tentatively, "but I owe you an apology."

She slowed to a stop and angled herself toward him.

"I left you behind," he continued, "two runs ago. Or I told the team to," he said bluntly.

Layden had to process his words at first, but once she did, that fire reignited in her chest. She'd suspected they had, but hearing it was his call hurt way worse.

"I lost my way again...became preoccupied with winning. And leading. I don't know what came over me, but I thought it would be easier if you were out of the picture. Even for a second."

"I thought you didn't care about leading," Layden asked, hotly.

"Of course I care! I didn't want to fight you for it. At first. Then I did."

Layden thought about this for a moment and generally understood his frustration. Surely, she'd be feeling the same thing if their roles were reversed. "Fair enough," she said, tightly. "Even though you were the one who made me promise to trust you. Despite what I was feeling."

Manni looked at the ground. "I know. I tried."

"You *tried*? It wasn't even three months ago that you told me you were my constant, Manni. Then the first chance you have, you turn on me. How do you expect me to feel about that?"

"It wasn't my first chance."

"Oh, that makes me feel better."

"You don't understand what it's like, Layden! I tried to stay objective about you. When I learned you were still getting training with the Guardian, and attention for these...visions, when you were so clearly better at leading than Abisen, I told myself every time that you were still you. That you needed me. But you don't need me, Layden. You don't need any of us. You are flying through these Trials, on your way upward and outward, and there's nothing I can do about it. That is hard to watch, and harder to stomach."

There was a moment of silence as Layden took in this view of her, perplexed at how someone who *knew* her could have it so wrong. True, there was a chord within her that roared with fiery pride at how she was coming across—strong, independent, successful. But another part of her was sad—no, not just sad. Torn. Manni's words tugged at a deep place inside her that longed for connection, the kind that had made them both feel a part of something bigger, together. A connection that had made her feel safe, as long as she had him. They had had that for longer than she could remember, and the thought that they might've been losing it, without her even realizing, scared her.

She wrapped her arms around herself as if to ward off the creeping darkness that came with his words. "I never wanted you to feel left behind," she finally said, her voice softer now. "But I can't stop. I can't just—hold myself back because of how it makes you feel. I have to keep moving forward. We both do."

Manni nodded, the features of his middle-aged host going morose in a complicated way.

"Maybe we should have left when we had the chance," she said after a while.

Manni turned to face her fully. It seemed to surprise him that those words had come out of her mouth, and she was surprised too. But she didn't take them back. Manni's expression was odd, almost hopeful, but when his mouth opened again, his words were not what she expected.

"You did some great work out there. We won because of you."

"We won because of all of us," Layden said. "And we'll all do it again at the end of next week. Something tells me, for this final run, we'll need to be more in sync than ever."

CHaPTeR TWeNTY-ONe

"GET DOWN! GET DOWN now!"

Layden reacted instantly, hitting the ground at the sound of Manni's voice. Her face pressed so roughly to the ground, she inhaled a nose full of the sand that covered the path, and she coughed reflexively against the stinging in her nostrils.

During their past course runs, she had learned that even a split-second hesitation could be the end of her run. In this case, there was a slightly more literal sense to that truth. She craned her neck up and saw the source of Manni's warning—a projectile lodged firmly in the wall above her.

"The Commander said there'd be new dangers, but I didn't expect that."

Manni reached down and helped her up quickly, his Host's strong arms lifting her with ease. His steely eyes were alert as he scanned the path. "I haven't seen any of the other team yet," he whispered.

"And you're complaining?" she whispered back.

Shortly after they'd received the order of their next and final course run, they'd also learned that they'd be sharing the course with another team. In addition to the increase in physical danger, the two teams were now competing for the same prizes, with full permission to discourage the other at any cost. This was the final course run of the Generation...and the stakes were high.

"I'm just worried the others have run into them." Manni said.

Layden paused to receive a thought. "They seem fine. Abisen, Yuna, and Mathis are still together and working their quadrant," she said, knowing this as innately as she knew how to breathe.

Manni nodded and motioned her forward.

With the other team now in the mix, leaving teammates on their own was no longer a safe option, even though it had worked best for their group before. None of them were strong enough to handle hand-to-hand combat with the other team, and K-Unit, the team they'd been paired with, were out for blood. Layden's last run had moved her group up in the rankings which meant they were second place to Jared's team, and in the arena with them. Jared had seemed disturbingly excited about that, so it couldn't mean good things.

But nor had Layden's unit had any success traveling together as a group, and an offensive attack while they were clumped together could just as easily take them all out at once.

So, after much debate, they decided to split into two parties. But there would be no going rogue, and no waiting around. They would all be "runners" in a sense, searching out the four quadrants and then meeting on the main path when all the challenges had been found. Layden and Manni were together, and Abisen was with Mathis and Yuna again.

It was true, Abisen had her work cut out for her, escorting the other two through the obstacles, but Yuna and Mathis were quick with the challenges, and Layden banked on that making up for the lost time. The beacons would be used to signal the completion of their quadrant, and they had agreed to avoid the other team unless they had no other choice.

There was one more tactic that Layden hoped might give them an edge. In the final hours before they were due to report for this course run, Mathis had a brilliant idea. They would begin their search at the *end* of the course and work their way backward to the beginning, ideally reducing their chances of encountering the opposite team and competing for the same squares.

Abisen had voiced the concern that they'd lose time getting to the other side of the course, but Layden had felt confident she could bring them to the third and fourth quadrants quickly enough.

And she had.

Now she and Manni were well on their way through quadrant three, investigating as many squares as quickly as possible. There was no guarantee the challenges were loaded evenly, and it was unclear if there were four challenges as usual, or eight, to accommodate both teams. So, for now, they weren't taking any chances.

"Hope they're having luck on the other side," Manni said, exhaustion in his voice.

He tucked his most recent prize into his vest. It was a small, circular, mechanical device that didn't seem to be on, nor did it respond to anything they did. But they didn't usually waste time speculating about the challenge prizes. Whatever the object was, it would make sense eventually.

They headed back out and wound through the corridors until they found another obstacle in their path. The black ooze again. Except this time there was no rope ladder across the top, only a set of swinging ropes hanging from an erected beam. One false move and the person crossing would be disqualified immediately. Layden knew there'd be no continuing with such injuries.

"Here, I'll go first. When I reach the next rope, I'll give it a push back to you," Manni said, twining his forearm around the thick cord in front of him.

"Maybe I should go," Layden replied tentatively. She wasn't "not good" at the challenges, but, realistically, Manni was more qualified to continue alone. More of a complete package.

"Nah, my arms are longer and stronger. I have a better chance of making this." He didn't even look back at her.

Just as he was about to swing, a member of the rival unit, a woman, appeared on the far side of their obstacle.

Layden and Manni had cleared five of the eight squares and solved a challenge already, and they hadn't encountered anyone yet. So, seeing the woman sent electricity down her spine.

The woman stood still for a moment, and then, most peculiarly, darted away down a different path.

Was she alone? Was it possible her team had split up as well, trying something more like their opponents' strategy? Or would her whole team be right around the corner?

"Do we keep going?" Manni asked, seeming as paralyzed as Layden.

"What other choice do we have? Her being there is a good indication there's a challenge. Right?"

"Maybe. Either way, we have to know for sure."

"Let's go in case she's bringing others back," Layden said urgently.

She and Manni crossed the obstacle with a newfound energy, swinging and passing the ropes back and forth to each other, and finally jumped to the solid ground at the other side. Layden felt a wave of relief when they fully cleared the sludge—just being near it made her shoulder twinge—and entered next square.

It was mercifully empty of the other team, though it clearly housed a challenge.

Layden assessed the square quickly, trying to process all she was seeing. There was a beautiful fountain at the center of the square with water cascading from the top, and in front of it sat a small table with two porcelain jars: one small, one large. Other than that, the square seemed to be clear. Layden walked forward to get a closer look. Lifting one of the jars from the table, she could tell it was empty, though it looked like it had had water in it previously, possibly from when the woman had been there.

"Look," Manni said, moving beside her and lifting the larger vessel.

There was a small, almost indistinguishable outline in the shape of an oval etched into the surface of the table. In the center of the oval, were four vertical lines. Layden ran her fingers over them. Tally marks?

"A compartment?" she asked.

"Yeah, maybe." Manni pressed down on it, but it didn't budge.

"Well, what are these jars for? Search the area," she said, taking the jar with her. After a quick jog around the square, it was obvious there weren't any other clues.

"Okay. Well, there are two different sizes here, so maybe it's a weight thing?" He inspected the jars. "This one has five lines on the bottom. And yours has three."

"Hold on," Layden said, something coming back to her. "Yes, I know what this is. I've read about it."

"What do you mean, read about it?" Manni asked.

"Well, you remember when I told you this course resembled a labyrinth from Earth-that-was? A maze?"

"Uh, yeah, kind of."

Layden's mouth twisted. Manni may have looked fifty, but sometimes he sounded just like the freshly post-adolescent boy he should have been.

"The Aquarius Conundrum," Layden said, her eyes shifting beyond him as she fought to remember the details.

"I don't follow."

Of course, he didn't, she thought. She hadn't explained it yet. Is that what she sounded like all the time? With all her questions and confusion. No wonder the Guardian was always annoyed.

"It's a famous logic riddle. We're given a three-liter and a five-liter jar, and the oval on the table requires a four-liter weight to push it down or open it or something. It won't budge for anything above or below that. So, we need to use these two jars to make exactly four liters."

"Okay. Do we fill up the five-liter jar three-fourths full?"

"We can try that...but I bet it has to be a little more precise," Layden said. "Go fill the small jar to that line at the top."

Manni went over and did as she said. He brought the small jar back to her from the fountain, and Layden poured it into the large jar.

"All right, so we know for sure this is three liters."

"Great. Now just need one more liter? But we can't eyeball it?" Manni asked.

"Right. Give me a second. I remember my book saying something...that the solver needs to think of the space that's empty, just as much as the space that is filled. That's the trick."

"Okay...there's two liters left empty in the large jar and three empty in the small jar," Manni said. "So, if we fill the three again and empty it into the five..."

"Yes! Because the large jar will only take two more liters, that would leave a single liter in the small jar. Which is what we need to make four," Layden finished. She filled up the small jar again and emptied as much of it as she could into the large one, leaving exactly—well, she hoped exactly—one liter in the small jar.

"Right. But the large jar is full now," Manni said.

"So, empty it," Layden said, unable to hold back a laugh.

Manni paused briefly and shook his head. "'Soons, that's clever."

"They don't call it a puzzle for no reason."

Manni poured the water out to the side, and then Layden transferred her single liter into the large jar.

"Now we just fill the three-liter again and move it to the large jar...and there! Four liters."

"Great. Put it on the weight," he said.

She could hear the excitement in his voice, though he kept it off his face. Once again, her fascination with the world-that-was had proved useful, despite the Guardian's countless admonitions that it was ultimately a waste of time. Perhaps she'd point that out to him later.

Layden placed the vessel on the center oval and waited. At first nothing happened, but then the oval began to sink down until the rim of the jar was level with the surface of the table, and a small compartment appeared below the table. Inside the compartment was a pair of matte-black, leather greaves. Part of her was exhilarated at the win, the other part unnerved because they looked like her size.

"What are those for?" Manni asked.

Layden didn't want to know, but she had a feeling the greaves belonged to the helmet, shield, and dagger they'd won in their other run. She had thought about bringing those items along today, but she hadn't heard anything about that in the rules, so she hadn't. The other team hadn't brought anything with them either. Still, she hoped she hadn't made the wrong choice.

"Come on, let's go," she said.

Layden and Manni had just finished reviewing their last square when they got a signal from the other party. Layden saw it on Manni's face the moment she received the brain wave herself. The others were on the main path.

She took a moment to orient the two of them before entering a full-on sprint headed the fastest way she could remember. Within minutes she and Manni had rendezvoused with the other members.

"We had two challenges on our side," Abisen said as soon as she saw them.

"Well, so did we," she informed them. She chewed her lip as she considered whether or not that was a good thing.

"So, do we think there are more than four challenges?" Abisen asked, apparently sensing her worry.

"I've never heard of them loading the course so unevenly. It would have been a total waste of time to start at the beginning," Mathis pointed out.

Layden considered this but didn't say anything.

"We didn't see anyone from the other team...if there were no challenges, maybe they were still looking in the first and second quadrants?" Yuna speculated.

"We saw one woman, on her own. She was at the challenge just before us. She didn't attack us though. Nor did it seem like she'd solved it herself," Manni added.

"So, they sent runners of their own, did they?" Mathis said with a hint of mockery.

It didn't matter to Layden what the other team did, but she needed to stall so she could think. "What did you find?" she asked.

"A four-digit number...a code of some sort maybe?" Yuna produced a small strip of paper.

"And these," Mathis held out six black pellets.

"What are those?" Layden asked, peering into his hands.

He shrugged.

"Can I see?" She took one and rolled it between her fingers. It had a solid, grainy texture. She passed it to Manni who gave it a sniff.

"Smells like...flint. Like charcoal or something," he said. "Stand back."

The team gave him a wide berth, and he threw the pellet to the ground with some force. It erupted with a loud pop and smoke rose from its destruction. The entire path was covered in a black cloud for almost a minute as the team backed away and watched.

"Why would they give us those?" Abisen asked.

She looked annoyed, but Layden could sense the same emotion she was feeling beneath the surface. Fear.

"It doesn't matter right now," she said, gaining control of herself and, hopefully, the situation. "We have a decision to make. Do we go back and look through the rest of the course, or do we push through and finish the race?"

"What's the time?" Yuna asked.

"We are fifty minutes in," Layden said.

Despite the anxiety of the moment, she was proud of her team, and she could see they were proud of themselves. They had successfully split up and conquered four challenges in under an hour. That was by far their best course run yet.

"It would make sense to double the challenges with two teams in the course. Maybe one of you can go back and check a few quadrants to make sure? Would it take that much time?" Yuna suggested.

"Just looking through empty quadrants, no. But there are still obstacles. And what if there *are* challenges?" Manni said.

"And what if we run into the opposing team. Being a lone runner would guarantee our disqualification. None of us are strong enough to handle a fight at this point," Abisen added.

"We can afford one loss without being penalized. The Commander said so." Mathis this time.

"I don't want to lose anyone," Layden said firmly. "And frankly, it makes me nervous that he accounted for that this time around."

"Yeah, it feels like the sort of thing the Commander would plan. We're used to four challenges, but he was purposefully vague this time around. I bet the course was loaded with plenty so both teams had a chance at getting a prize. Besides, I suspect these prizes are meant for something coming up. I think we need to go back," Manni said.

"I agree," Abisen agreed.

The two heavy hitters. Now Layden wouldn't be able to disagree without "pulling rank." That annoying surge of fiery energy burned behind her sternum, urging her to do just that. To take control. To use her authority. It took everything in her to breathe and suppress the emotion. But she did. By now she knew what came of listening to it, and it was nothing helpful.

"Okay. But I'm the one going." she said.

"That's ridiculous," Abisen said sharply.

"Yeah, I should go. I'm more expendable," Mathis said quickly.

His face didn't register bitterness, and he seemed earnest to contribute, but Layden shook her head curtly. "No one is expendable."

Mathis hesitated but then agreed with a nod.

Finally, the right words came to her. "Personally, I'm against sending someone back at all, but we're running out of time. The rest of you exit the course. The run won't officially be over unless I am either disqualified or I make it through the exit myself. But at least you'll all be safe from the other team. You'll know I'm down if the run ends."

"I'm coming with you," Manni said determinedly.

"The whole point was that just one of us would go; we can't be out two members," Layden resisted.

"Who said we're gonna be out? Maybe the other team has already moved on. And maybe there are challenges that need more than one person. We'll stick together. We have a better chance of making it that way," he said.

"Fine. We've wasted enough time. Abisen, take these with you," Layden said, handing over the greaves. She gestured to Manni, who passed over the curious electronic device. "Don't wait for us...I don't want you all taken out while loitering by the exit," she said.

The others nodded.

"Whatever happens, we did great today," Layden said. There was a time when they might have resisted such a compliment from her, but it didn't feel that way now.

"Be quick," Mathis said.

CHAPTER TWENTY-TWO

L AYDEN AND MANNI SWIFTLY worked through quadrant one, easily discovering two more challenges. However, it didn't take long to realize both had already been solved, their prizes claimed. One room held a large, crumpled bag on the ground; the other, the shattered remains of a pillar. After seeing the wreckage, she and Manni decided there was no point in investigating further. They'd only be wasting more time.

Still, it was reassuring to know they hadn't missed anything. The purpose of these prizes remained a mystery—and the fact that the course run hadn't ended, despite the other team being nowhere in sight, was yet another.

As they sprinted back to their team, a bloodcurdling shriek tore through the air, freezing them in their tracks. This wasn't a cry of surprise—it was one of raw pain. And it belonged to a man.

"What was that?" Layden asked, alarm surging through her, adrenaline spiking.

"Did that sound like Mathis to you?" Manni asked, his face turning ghostly pale.

Layden's mind raced to the worst-case scenario: that the other team had been lying in wait, striking when they were at their most vulnerable.

"Come on," she said, grabbing Manni's hand and sprinting harder.

After a few minutes, they reached the exit. Neither team were there, but something was different. Two large floor lockers on either side of the door stood open. Layden rushed over and peered inside, only to find them empty. There was a small keypad on the front of the locker, much like the ones she had in the study rooms to store her books—that must have been what the four-digit code was for. It was unclear what had been in the locker.

"What is that?" Manni said. His face was like stone as he listened to new noises coming from the other side of the door.

Layden didn't know, but she wasn't going to wait to find out. She lunged forward and opened the door, rushing through with Manni close behind.

What she expected to see on the other side was the covered patio area with tables and chairs, and screens displaying the course run for the other teams. Instead, she saw another large arena. Walls as high as the course, floor covered in sand-colored dirt. The air smelled like sweat and dust...and something metallic. Like blood.

Her eyes couldn't take in the sight fast enough. She watched as bodies raced around the arena, maneuvering, retreating, and advancing as a deafening barrage of rifle fire hurled their way. There were barricades and walls, ramps and ropes. Layden could only assume these were there for cover. She and Manni rushed forward and ducked behind a crate as something whizzed past their heads.

At first Layden thought it was K-Unit shooting at them but then she saw a member of Jared's team rush by her crate and roll to cover nearby. Layden peeked over the crate to try and discern the situation. Blocking the exit was a row of giant soldiers standing along a platform and defending the door.

Layden jumped as a shot fired in her direction, and Manni pulled her back to the ground.

"Who are they and why are they shooting at us?" Manni yelled over the deafening noise.

"We have to find our team!" Layden exclaimed.

She did another quick scan before finally locating them huddled behind a barricade to the left. They weren't moving around like the other team. Layden pointed them out to Manni and then broke into a run. More heavy fire assaulted them as they slid behind the barricade, shots trailing behind them and kicking up dirt. Layden exhaled in relief.

But that relief was short-lived. As soon as Layden turned to her teammates, she realized something was terribly wrong. "What happened?" she asked immediately.

Abisen was stripping Mathis of his shield. He was not moving. His face was covered in sweat, and he looked pale—terribly pale.

"Is he okay?" Layden asked Abisen.

Abisen's face was all business, as she pulled the black pellets out of his pockets. "He volunteered to go ahead. Tried to make it to the door."

Layden was wrong. Abisen wasn't in business mode; she was in shock.

"The guns..." Yuna interrupted, her eyes wide and hyperaware.

"What about the guns?" Manni prompted urgently.

"It's live ammunition," Abisen said tonelessly. "He didn't make it further than five feet before he was taken down. We had to drag him back."

Layden looked at Mathis and realized what was happening. She could see the ground beneath him growing dark red with blood. "Why wouldn't the Commander..."

"Warn us?" Abisen snarled. "I guess he did, didn't he?"

"Come on, let's try to stop the bleeding," Manni said, moving everyone aside.

"What's the point?" Mathis said weakly. "It's not my body anyway, right?" He gave a kind of crooked half-smile.

It made Layden nauseated. She gave Manni a dark look. She wouldn't say it out loud, but they both knew a brain did not live long if the heart stopped pumping blood to it. She helped Manni tip him forward, ignoring his loud yelp of pain, and finished stripping off his vest. She could see the shot had gone straight through and out his back.

Manni took his own vest off and slipped the shirt off his back, then he replaced his vest quickly. He rolled up the shirt in his hands, slipped it underneath Mathis's back, and moved Yuna's hands to hold it there.

"We need to end this and get him help. Now," he said urgently, reaching for the helmet and the greaves. "Where did you get the gear? We didn't bring it with us."

"From the locker before we entered," Abisen said absently.

Manni didn't respond as he tried to put it on.

"It won't fit you," Abisen said. "It really only would've fit Yuna, but Mathis wouldn't let her go. The only things he could use were the shield and dagger."

"What do you mean it won't fit?" Manni asked, suddenly angry.

"It's meant to go to the team lead," Abisen said quietly, nodding at Layden.

Layden felt a sense of resolve steal over her at this revelation. Good. Now she wouldn't have to convince anyone that it should be her. Soundlessly, she took the greaves and slipped them on over her shins. She positioned the shield next to her, and then, as an added thought, she slipped Mathis's vest over her own; double thickness might protect her a little more. She shoved the pellets in her pockets and finally placed the helmet on her head.

Something was wrong. The helmet visor was black, and she couldn't see through it. She slid it off.

"What's wrong?" Manni asked.

"Salt it, it's useless! I can't see anything," Layden growled angrily.

"That doesn't make any sense," he said, just as frustrated. He grabbed it and looked it over.

She glanced over at the other team. She recognized Jared in similar armor, though it looked like he had different pieces. And he did not have a helmet.

"It's fine. I'll have to do without it," she said more bravely than she felt.

She rose to her haunches and moved to the side of their barricade, then peeked out at the row of attackers. There were four tall soldiers in head-to-to-body armor. They were equipped with arm-length firearms that sounded like thunder when they fired. Layden was horrified that Mathis had been hit by something coming out of that.

"This is insane!" she exclaimed over the sound of gunfire.

K-Unit seemed to be standing strong, yelling and giving directions, running around the course like they were searching for weaknesses. But they had not advanced the whole time Layden had been behind the barricade. It didn't look like they had guns and Layden only saw a few pieces of armor. Then, suddenly, a massive boom rang out through the arena and K-Unit let out a different kind of shout—one of victory—as one of the soldiers fell to his knees and tumbled off the platform. K-Unit did have a weapon apparently, and it was enormous. Layden couldn't see it clearly, but it looked like a rifle the size of a toddler.

"I'm gonna make a run for it while the soldiers are distracted." Layden yelled.

"Wait!" Manni grabbed her vest and tugged her backward.

"What?"

"On the helmet—look, there's a circle."

"A *circle*?" she repeated, transparently irritated at missing her moment to advance.

"Where's the small device we found?" he asked.

Yuna gestured that Abisen take over for her and then dug in her pocket to produce the small black device. Manni grabbed it and slipped it into the same-sized groove on the side of the helmet. Instantly, the helmet came to life, lights shining from inside. Layden began to hope as she slipped it on and discovered that she could not only see through the visor, but that it was now giving her information.

"It's feeding me all kinds of data about the arena," she relayed.

She focused hard, trying to figure out what kind. It was...everything! Down to minute details about the composition of material in their clothes and the heart rates of those around her. She wasn't wearing the helmet more than thirty seconds before she felt like she was going mad. She couldn't process everything it threw at her; it was too much.

Just as she was about to take it off, her fiery companion of drive and steel rose up. It commanded her weakness to leave and for Layden to stand firm. At the same time, the gentle whisper on her heart urged her to remain calm. Only in that moment did Layden realize both voices had been influencing her, but never had they agreed. She was momentarily unnerved as she marveled at these internal presences. Up until now, she'd taken them for intuition, a sixth sense maybe...but now, she wasn't sure. But she didn't have time to dissect this.

Instead, she did what the voices said.

Focus. Slow down, and focus.

Layden returned to her corner of the barricade and stared at the line of defense. She fought against the surge of information coming into her brain and focused on one of the soldiers. Only one. Suddenly the helmet was working for her, analyzing the rate of fire—50%—the weak points of the armor—shoulders, behind the knees, the neck—even his angle of firing, which was relatively horizontal and didn't seem to vary.

The helmet also relayed the composition of the people...they weren't even people! They were animatronics, firing at an entirely predictable rate and trajectory. She had been so overwhelmed, she hadn't even noticed they weren't real people. Layden did a quick analysis of the other soldiers, and she discovered if she took out the middle one, she could avoid the others' fire and make it up to the platform to disable the rest of them.

"Okay," Layden said. She was speaking through her helmet, but she figured they could hear her because they gave her their attention.

"I'm going to get the other team to take out the one on the far left. Once he's down, this is what I want you to do. Keep low to the ground, don't rise higher than four feet, and move from the left of this barricade along the wall of the arena and to the farthest ramp on the left. I want you to *wait* at the side of the ramp. When I've taken out the last soldier on the left, use the ramp to mount the platform and leave. Do you hear me? We need to get Mathis out before the other team decides they want to take us down to win the course run. Got it?"

Manni clenched his jaw and nodded at Layden, and Yuna helped Abisen prepare Mathis for moving.

Layden remembered the pellets in her jacket and took one out. "I'm going to black out the area so the other team can't see where I'm moving. I'll cover you all when it's time to move."

"We're ready, Layden. Go end this," Abisen said.

Layden took a pellet and threw it into the middle of the arena, then she ran into the smoke. It didn't deter the bullets of the animatronic soldiers, but she stayed low and managed to avoid them. She crossed to the other team in a few seconds, crashing into their midst in a cloud of dust.

They startled but then quickly snarled hostilely. One man grabbed her shoulders and held her in place, but Layden didn't bother fighting him.

"That giant weapon of yours? It's the only one that can take them down!" Layden said, not wasting any time. "I need you to take out the far-left soldier, so I can get close enough to get rid of the rest of them."

"Why should we trust you?" Jared yelled. He was wearing a breastplate and some gauntlets and wielding the exceptionally large gun.

"I'm sure this is probably all good and fun for you, but I have a friend dying over there. We need to get him out."

The man behind her loosened his grip on her arms and Layden shook herself loose, taking off her helmet so she could look at Jared directly.

"No one said today would be safe," Jared hurled back, but she could tell he wasn't as unmoved as he wanted to appear. After a moment he spoke again. "The gun...it takes a long time to cool down."

"You got the far-right soldier already, take out far-left, as soon as it does," she repeated now that he was listening properly. "Then I'll take out the middle two, and you can advance. Fair? Then no one else gets hurt."

"But your team wins, don't they?" he spat.

"Hey, it's anyone's game now. You're all able-bodied, and we're down a man that we'll have to carry out. I'd say that evens your odds," Layden said. It made her sick to barter with this man for Mathis's life, but she kept it from her voice.

Jared looked at her for a moment and then hauled the gun onto the shoulder of another team member. "You heard her, Michal. Concentrate your fire on the left soldier!"

Layden felt relief flood her. She looked over at her team and nodded that the plan was still on. She put her helmet back on.

After a couple minutes, the big gun operated by K-Unit had cooled down. "Aim and fire!" Jared shouted.

The far-left soldier didn't stand a chance once the large firearm unloaded on it. Within moments it fell in a crumpled heap of dust and rubble—but Layden didn't wait to see it fall. She signaled her team to move then threw three pellets in their direction as she ran toward the platform, providing a cloud of cover for them all. She ran low and used her helmet to avoid the gunfire from the remaining two soldiers.

The helmet also made her aware, that the other team was aiming the giant gun at her for its next round. She threw down another pellet at the front of the platform and leapt up under cover of the smoke. Taking out her small dagger, she darted out of the smoke to the next soldier on the left. She sliced through the thin slits between the chest pad and arm guards. The soldier's arms dropped to its side, ceasing fire, then fell forward with a crash. She left the other to keep firing at K-Unit.

Layden turned and ran to her team as they hovered by the ramp. She had told the other team that she would disable all the soldiers and let them out—and she still intended to. But she needed K-Unit to stay where they were until she got Mathis to safety.

"Let's go!" she shouted.

Yuna, Manni and Abisen wasted no time carrying Mathis up the ramp and through the exit door.

Layden stayed in the smoke for a moment to make sure her team had all made it through. She couldn't see the other unit, but she heard the large weapon charging. She stood up tall, clearing the cloud, and lifted her hands in surrender.

"Let me honor my agreement!" she shouted.

When the gun fired, it was not at last remaining soldier but at her. Her helmet went ballistic, shocking her with the incoming threat. Layden dove out of the way in time and laid panting for a moment on the ground. She knew she should go through the door, but just because the other team had tried to kill her didn't mean she was about to do the same. She slipped over to the last soldier and disarmed it quickly. With the gunfire from the mechanical soldiers silenced, the arena fell quiet.

The members from the other team stood, and the large gun began to charge again.

"Hear me out!" Layden knew she had a few moments to speak. She took off her helmet and placed it on the ground as a sign of surrender. "My team member is out, and I promised I'd give you a shot. It's only fair you leave before I do."

Jared lowered the gun, and she could see his expression was visibly annoyed, and that he'd rather pass on her gallant offer. In the end, he seemed to want the win more.

"You bet your salt it's fair." He turned to his unit, gesturing for them to move up on the platform and out the door. They followed his direction, but he lingered behind. "Fair or not, that wasn't a very bright move. This place doesn't care about your team member, or that you wanted to save him. They care that you win."

Layden's throat closed up at his words. She hoped he wasn't right, even if his words had the ring of truth to them. "Then it's not worth the win," she choked out.

Jared walked forward and hopped up on the platform then stared at her for a moment. "Hope you know what you're talking about," he said, advancing even closer.

Layden recoiled slightly, unsure why he lingered. He almost looked like he was considering letting her through first. Ultimately, he turned and ducked out the door, giving her a strange look as he left.

A loud siren went off and announced the end of the run.

Layden and the others gathered before the Commander in a small room inside the compound. K-Unit was loud with the noises of victory, while Layden's teammates were pale and quiet. She knew they were mostly worried about Mathis, who had been rushed out on a stretcher, but she also knew they were sore about the loss. She didn't blame them. Had it been lesser stakes no one would have begrudged her call to be fair and honor her word. She wouldn't have begrudged her own call. As it stood though, she couldn't help but feel she'd made a terrible mistake.

It had been the final course run, the one that ultimately determined their place in the Trials. As she looked up and saw the Guardian enter the room, she could barely hold back her tears. She tried to decipher his face for an indication if she'd done right or not, but both he and the Commander were inscrutable.

Finally, the Commander spoke. "Quiet down, you barrel of monkeys. It's time to discuss the results."

"What results?" The woman who was often seen with Jared spoke. "We won. That's the result."

This solicited a round of cheers from K-Unit—well, most of K-Unit. Jared was oddly quiet.

"Sera, silence yourself," the Commander said.

Sera. So that was her name. Layden laughed sadly within. After all this time, she was embarrassed to say she hadn't learned any of their names besides Jared's. She was astounded at how fast she'd let them be known only as her competition.

"Sir, if I may say something," Jared said, stepping forward before the Commander could speak.

"I'd rather you not," he said gruffly.

However, Jared didn't seem like he would be stopped. "Layden's team should win this one. She was there by the door; the rest were out. She let my team leave."

"Jared, what are you doing?" Sera shoved him in the shoulder.

"Layden only let us out first because she promised she would give us a chance. We didn't earn that chance. The win is theirs, fair and square."

There was silence for a moment.

"As admirable as your concession is, we do not look for acts of mercy and honor in this round. I'm here to judge you solely on your team effort and your success in the runs."

Then he turned to their Guardian, and they exchanged a glance. "That being said, we think Layden's solution was extremely team-oriented, even if it didn't involve only her team. Additionally, the rules state that a team can still win with the disqualification of one team member."

There was silence as everyone looked to Layden and processed what this could mean.

"But I wasn't disqualified," Layden said.

"It could be interpreted," the Guardian interjected, "that your choice to get Mathis to safety before yourself was an intentional self-disqualification. A substitution, as it were. If you had left Mathis behind, your team, no doubt, would have won the course run. As it was, he was a disqualified person who crossed the threshold, while you stayed behind in his place."

Layden couldn't quite believe her ears. Were they actually arguing for her team to be the victors?

"I'd agree with that assessment," the Commander said.

"I would too," Jared said, though it looked like it took everything within him to say it; and Layden understood why. By forfeiting their victory, K-Unit was forfeiting their security within the Trials.

"Layden's Unit, I'm pleased to announce the Council has deemed you worthy of advancing. K-Unit, your fates will be decided at the end of the week." The Commander finished.

Layden looked back at Jared and his team, whose faces were now white as a sheet. She watched as Jared tried to swallow, nodding that he understood. Then he cast a look around and gestured for his team to leave. He followed behind, lingering as he passed Layden. He offered his hand. Confused, she took it hesitantly and met his eyes, seeing a deep fear beneath the surface of his Host's aged face.

"Sometimes it's not worth the win," he said quietly.

Layden paused for a moment and then nodded slowly.

Then, almost as an afterthought, Jared leaned forward and laid a kiss on her cheek. "Goodbye, Layden Prier, and good luck." Then he turned and left.

Layden's cheeks went hot, and her eyes followed him out the door then instantly darted back to the rest of the room. If anyone noticed, they did not respond.

The Guardian had the same dispassionate look he always wore as he took a few steps forward. "I'll take it from here, Commander. Thank you for seeing these five through this Generation."

Chapter Twenty-Three

As Layden stood beside Manni at the edge of the track, much as she had six months ago, she couldn't help but feel as though nothing had changed. But it had. Everything had. The length of her hair alone indicated as much. As she watched the approaching clouds, Layden gathered the wild locks and pulled them to the side, casting a look to Manni as she did. Because of the growth enhancements, when they returned to their bodies this time, they were the equivalent of seventeen years in development. But she didn't exactly feel that way. In some ways, she still felt like the girl who began the Trials, timid and scared and obsessed with the approval of all those around her. In other ways—ones she couldn't begin to comprehend or process—she felt older, with a mind full of skill and knowledge and wisdom beyond her season. At moments, it was almost too much to reconcile.

Her team had been given a full week to reacclimate, mainly because of Mathis. The medics had stabilized him, but he needed time to recover before they transferred him to his own body. He wasn't in a coma, but he was heavily sedated, and the Council was adamant all five of them advance together.

After Layden had gotten her team out of the arena, Mathis had been rushed to the infirmary. Their victory had come as a surprise, and, honestly, a relief. But she didn't want to hear congratulations. She hadn't wanted to celebrate. Her friend had been hurt, and for the first time, she began to wonder if the ends justified the means.

Her friend. Did she just think of Mathis as her friend? She lived a crazy life, but that was one of the craziest things to happen yet.

"Do you think he'll be okay?" Layden asked as she observed Yuna and Abisen work a plyometric exercise under the burgeoning clouds. It had been her idea for them to get some fresh air, but now that she was here, she didn't feel up to working. Not to mention, the threatening storm clouds reminded them all that the Monsoons were upon them, and that made her instinctually want to go back inside.

"Yeah, of course," Manni said. "He's in the best place he could be."

He stooped down and pulled some synthetic grass from the ground then broke it apart in his fingers. Thunder rumbled in the distance.

Layden began walking, and Manni stood and followed.

"Mathis hates me, you know," Layden said.

"Nah," Manni replied. "He knows how the Trials are, too. It's not like any of us have been ourselves from the start. It's an environment too full of pressure for friendship."

"Maybe," Layden said. "But we try."

He looked sidelong at her and nodded slightly. "Yeah, we try."

"But?"

"Well..." He looked like he didn't want to say anymore, but he did. "When I'm me, I have no problem being friends with you. Or Abisen. Or Mathis, for that matter, even if he is a jerk."

Layden laughed despite herself. "Don't," she chided. "The man is in the sick ward for taking bullets for us."

Manni shook his head and exhaled, then stared off into the distance. "There's something here, isn't there?"

"What do you mean?"

"Something's going on. As soon as I'm in that Host's body, everything about me becomes a little more removed. A little farther away. It's like I'm a sponge to whatever the atmosphere is. I change. I hate how much I change."

Layden glanced at him but didn't respond. She *did* know what he was talking about. She was not a competitive person. Nor was she as paranoid and morose as she'd been when she was in her first Host. And yet, it seemed that maybe there were other influencing factors at play. She didn't even want to go into the competing voices she'd been hearing since day one of the Trials. In the last Generation, those voices had seemed more separate from her than ever. Maybe she really was going crazy...

"I don't know. I'm trying to figure it out," Manni continued. "Maybe we're accepting different hormone signals from the bodies we're in, or maybe we're more sensitive to the mood of the Generation because we're so out of control."

"Maybe. They're our minds, though, right? Shouldn't we be able to control those emotions? Whether there are different hormones or not?"

"Control our actions maybe. I don't know if we have much control over our emotions. Especially if they're unique to our Host's chemical makeup."

"True," Layden said.

It would be interesting if she could find a way to block out that part of the process. How much easier it would be if everyone could be in control of all those chemical reactions.

They stopped walking as they came upon Yuna and Abisen.

"Are you two going to work out or what? Your bodies are gonna be soft and flabby next time you're in them," Abisen said sternly.

"They will be no matter what," Layden said. Regardless, she started to stretch after tying her hair with a band she had kept from her last Host. Her chest ached momentarily at the thought of her. Layden didn't miss her per se; the feeling was closer to nostalgia. Possibly a bit of trauma. She wasn't sure how to respond to it.

"Come on then, teacher," Layden goaded. "Give us a good one."

But Abisen wasn't listening; her eyes were trained beyond Layden, focusing on the doors leading into the compound.

"Mathis!" Yuna shrieked.

Layden hadn't heard Yuna speak that loud the entire time she'd known her. She watched as Yuna broke into a jog and went to meet him, and the rest of them followed, meeting Mathis as he entered the sparring plaza. It felt strangely good to see him again.

As they got closer, Layden could tell something wasn't right. He wouldn't have carried any injuries with him through the Transfer to his own body, but something was off all the same. His face was pale, and he moved slowly. He gave only a small embrace to Yuna as she clumsily hugged him. Layden observed the two of them, looking familiar and close. It caught her slightly off guard. It hadn't occurred to her that during all their forced pairing, they'd probably developed a relationship of some kind.

"I'm glad you're all right," Abisen said, taking her turn to hug him.

He'd grown in the last six months, finally shooting up as tall as Manni.

"Mathis," Layden said cautiously, but warmly.

He looked at her briefly and gave a tight smile.

"Did they fill you in?" Abisen asked.

He had the look of someone waking from a deep, deep sleep. When he didn't respond, Abisen turned to Layden, her brows dipping in worry, then nervously decided to plod on in explanation. "We're skipping another Generation," she said with forced enthusiasm. "All of us. We're heading to the Thirties."

"You all right, man?" Manni gripped Mathis's shoulder comfortingly.

Mathis seemed to shake himself out of it a bit and forced another smile. "Yeah, of course," he said quietly. "Just exhausted."

"Well, let's go eat." Yuna took him by the arm and led him away.

Layden thought that was a promising idea and followed them. After a few feet, she realized Abisen and Manni were hanging back. Layden turned and lingered.

"Oh, don't wait up. I have to speak to Manni," Abisen said, waving Layden on.

Completely put off, Layden awkwardly walked back up the plaza by herself. Before she entered the double doors, she turned around briefly. What were the two of them talking about? Abisen was saying something to Manni, and there was laughter. Then she took his hand in both of hers and said something else. Layden couldn't see their expressions because of the lighting of the plaza, but she didn't miss it when Abisen moved to her tiptoes and planted a kiss on his lips.

When Layden awoke the next day, it was groggily and reluctantly, stirred only by rays of sunlight streaming across her eyelids. Yes, sunlight.

Her new room was on the outer edge of the complex, affording her a window and the first sunlight greeting in nearly a year! She rose quickly on her elbows and peered out the window next to her bed that overlooked the glassy water below. Even as the mist and clouds continued to roll in, threatening to choke what little morning light there was, it was a beautiful sight. She took it in and felt a tug in her heart to give thanks, though she didn't know to whom exactly. The Council, she supposed. It was their room after all.

Layden laid back down and breathed in the scent of her clean, silken sheets, almost feeling peaceful. That is, until she remembered all the things of yesterday: Mathis's strange return, Abisen and Manni's kiss, the awkward dinner that followed, then finally the summons for their Year Thirties Transfer. Layden didn't know which had bothered her the most.

She shook her head and pressed her palms to her eyes. She wasn't exactly sure why she was upset about the kiss between Manni and Abisen, but she certainly was.

It wasn't because she had feelings for Manni, not those kinds of feelings anyway. He meant a lot to her, of course; he was the closest thing she had to family. Even he'd gone out of his way to insist to her that the kiss hadn't meant anything. *Just a thank you between friends*, he'd said. And, of course, it didn't. Where would he and Abisen have found time to develop that kind of intimacy?

Still, Layden felt jaded. Jaded by the thought that those around her were developing meaningful relationships, and, once again, she was on the outside. And Manni...he should've known better. He should've known that it was hard for her, and that she wanted to *belong* more than life itself.

Then, again what exactly did she expect from him?

She'd admitted to herself, a little angrily and late at night, that she thought he'd be there for her forever. Exclusively. After all, he'd vowed something along those lines. But did that mean he'd be there at the expense of a romantic relationship? What about a family? Honestly, she hadn't thought that far. After all, at the start of the Trials they were just over fifteen seasons—and while the end of the Year Thirties would bring their eighteenth birthdays, their whole world had become preoccupied with survival. At least Layden's was.

After climbing out from the sheets and downy comforter, she moved around her room, angling for a better inspection. To the right of her spacious bed, she had a wardrobe housing different kinds of clothing.

She wasn't sure if the many choices were meant for special occasions or daily use, because, as long as she could remember, she'd only ever worn one style—excepting the white ceremonial gown for her Transfer.

There was a small desk on the opposite side of the room, littered with stacks of papers, a few journals, and several books. She didn't need to get close to tell they were the contents of her locker in the study room two seasons ago. She walked over and riffled through them momentarily, finding the small, green book among the clutter; the one she'd taken back from the Guardian. She surveyed the book for the hundredth time, still ignorant of its contents.

Layden wrapped herself in a robe that was hanging on the wall and opened the door to the corridor. No one else was out that she could tell, though she did see steam coming out from under the door directly across from Manni's room, which happened to be right next to hers. There was also a door opposite Layden's chamber, and it had her name on it. That was a thrill to see, she had to admit.

Crossing the hall, she opened the door and found a spacious bathing chamber. Relief flooded her. While she'd gotten used to the coed showers—to some degree—she was happy to move on from that experience. A large pool-like tub sat within the middle of the floor, its edges flush with the cool, cream tiles, and a long counter stretched along the wall to her right. There seemed to be infinitely more products on this counter than on the one in the communal baths in Year Seventies. And certainly, more than the bar of soap they'd been given in Year Fifties. A small corner of the chamber was sectioned off by glass doors, and peering through them, Layden could see wooden walls and a single wooden bench. A personal sauna? The whole room had the aroma of heated logs on a fire and clean, polished tile.

She wasn't sure what her schedule would be for the day, but nothing sounded better to Layden than the peaceful rush of water as she drew her bath. She turned the little knobs along the side of the tub—all of them, for she suspected they all added something—then she stood and slipped off her robe. As she did, she caught a glimpse of her reflection in the mirror that stood above the counter.

Her breath caught in her chest. She'd never seen anyone as beautiful as the woman that now stared back as her reflection. Her Host was singular in beauty, with smooth bronze skin completely devoid of sun damage or fine lines. Her dark hair was long and silky, looking elegant despite the mess she had made of it that morning. Layden immediately pulled the hair loose from its tie, worried she might cause it to break or tangle. Cherry lips and heavy lids, thick with a fan of lashes, symmetrically populated her face. Layden reviewed the curves of her legs, waist, bust, and shoulders, all in flattering proportion. She wasn't rail thin or heavily muscled like the last two Hosts she'd occupied, but she could tell she was in good shape.

An excitement overcame her momentarily, tingling throughout her skin and bringing a strong confidence she hadn't felt before and a sense of pride. She'd never felt this beautiful in her life. In fact, she had never given much thought to beauty. Now that she had it, it was intoxicating.

It wasn't as laborious as she thought it would be to take the first—how long was it? One hour? Two?—out of her day to take care of her new Host's body. Creams for the skin, the lips, and under the eyes; tonics for the hair, nails, and backs of her thighs. Once she got started, she found herself increasingly interested in what each product was said to do. She could see the magic they worked almost immediately, and the result was deeply satisfying. Not to mention, spending the first twenty minutes of her day soaking in a fragrant salted bath was much preferable to running on a track, though she did miss the endorphins that came from the latter.

Back in her room, the sunlight was now completely gone, replaced by dark and brooding storm clouds. She finished the breakfast that had been waiting for her and slipped on a form-fitting thigh-length dress over a pair of leggings, trying to ignore the rain whipping against her window, when she heard a knock on her door. Immediately her mind jumped to the Guardian. Had he come to collect her for special training again? She rushed to the mirror she'd found inside the wardrobe and smoothed her hair, then went to the door. She opened it with what she hoped was a calm breath and was greeted by a man she didn't recognize.

"Manni?" she guessed after a moment.

He gave her a wide and inviting smile. His Host, like her own, was extremely handsome. His eyes had a bright amber hue, and his dark hair and eyebrows complimented his skin tone well. He was tall and muscular, but not in the same way as his last Host had been who had been all brawn and callouses. He was now smooth, toned. Sculpted.

As handsome as her friend looked, she felt oddly disappointed it was him.

"Hey," Manni greeted her, breathlessly.

Layden couldn't tell the meaning of the look in his eyes—it was unfamiliar in more than just his Host's features—but the butterflies in her stomach told her this look was something new. She lifted her chin in a greeting and flashed a smile then took a step back and did a half turn. Her skin prickled with elation.

What are you doing? she asked herself. *Showing off,* she answered.

Manni shifted his weight awkwardly and gave an uneasy laugh.

"These new Hosts are something else, aren't they?" she said to try and recalibrate the moment back to normal.

"Yes. They are," he replied haltingly. "And how about that bathing chamber? Did you realize where you were?"

Layden shook her head.

"Remember the ones at the back of the communal baths? The door on the opposite side leads into the Year Seventies bathhouse."

Understanding dawned on her, and excitement rose within. She remembered how badly she'd wanted her name on one of those doors. Now she had it. "I've always wondered why we never saw anyone go in or out, and why they stayed in there so long," Layden said. "I suppose they leave through the hall most of the time."

"Well, they're ours now. We could cut through the bathhouse any-time we wanted," Manni said with another flash of a smile.

Could it be he, too, wanted to show off? That wasn't like him, but then again, she wasn't behaving like herself either. Maybe she should make more of an effort to. This new dynamic was...strange.

"Do you know where we should be heading to now?" Layden took a steady breath.

"I think so. Follow me."

"Where to?" Layden asked. "Food was already delivered to my room. Though I wouldn't call that an actual meal." While surprisingly filling, Layden had finished her breakfast in a matter of bites, so it lacked a mea-sure of satisfaction. She assumed it was among the genetically engineered foodstuffs made with the perfect proportions of protein, oils, fats, and minerals. It was supposed to be great for weight maintenance and loss because it was exactly what the body needed; no more, no less. Personally, she wasn't a fan but knew she should be honored; not just anyone was given those rations.

"How about we go explore bit?" Manni asked.

"Explore? Where? What if someone tries to find us, or if we're needed somewhere?"

"Layden, relax. We made it this far. I think we have more favor than you realize."

Layden saw something flash in Manni's eyes. Pride? Well, why shouldn't he be proud? They *had* made it far. Maybe they did deserve to claim a little freedom. "All right," she said finally.

He offered his arm to her, and they exited the hall. Layden was on edge for the first few minutes, but after passing several people without being reprimanded, she began to relax. She stuck close to Manni's side, enjoying the feeling of his arm against her ribs and the scent of their baths lingering in a cloud around them both. They had never held on to one another like this, but it felt natural, like their Hosts were filling in the blanks on behavior they knew nothing about.

Layden glanced up at him from the side. She was grateful they were still on good terms after all they'd been through. Still, she couldn't help but wonder in what way this fresh Generation would strain everything she knew and cared about. Deep down sat an ominous foreboding that things could change at any minute.

Her thoughts ran back to the Guardian. What would he think if he caught them wandering around, wasting time? A quick, self-conscious thought warned her to separate herself from Manni's side before that could happen.

Manni opened a door to a closed-off hallway that ran perpendicularly with windows at either end, and doors with glass windows lining the corridor across from them.

After a quick search for people, Layden broke free from Manni's arm to cross the hall and peer through a window. Once sure no one was inside, she pushed the door open.

"These rooms are immaculate," she said airily. She found herself slightly annoyed at the sound of her new voice. It lacked...substance. She tried to lower it, to push it out from the chest. "Laboratories?" That was better.

"That's right," Manni said casually.

Layden watched him as he moved through the room, running his hands and eyes over a myriad of items on the tables.

"What do you two think you're doing?"

Layden started and turned around. "Guardian," she said with relief. Why did he insist on surprising them like that? Why couldn't he just enter a room like everyone else?

He seemed to need a moment to register who stood before him, but after casting a look to Manni, he appeared to figure it out.

"Layden Prier? Emmanuel?"

"Sorry, Guardian. We just wanted to look around." She hated how much like a little girl she sounded around him, no matter what age her body was.

"I did not recognize you. The photos I was given of your new Hosts did not do you justice," he said.

His words hung in the air, and Layden was left to infer what exactly that meant.

"Wait here. I was sent to find you and bring you to this very place," he finished officiously.

"Does that mean you're back with us for this next Generation?" Layden asked, her tone syrupy with hope she didn't mean to show. She cleared her throat and leaned back against a desk, her attempt at casual. She had to get control over this new voice...

The Guardian lingered at the door and regarded her for a moment. "Yes. There is no need for group work in the Year Thirties. It seemed the prudent option to follow through, that is, with the rest of my workload...lessening."

While that statement was more than a little unsettling, Layden was relieved they wouldn't have to meet another Guardian. She gave him a small, almost imperceptible, smile in response.

The Guardian's brow furrowed slightly, but then he turned to Manni, gave a curt nod, and left.

Layden started to chew her lip but stopped when she felt the gloss react to her gnawing, reminding her to lay off. She straightened and looked around. The room seemed to be for one individual—one console, one work desk, one lab bench—but there was so much equipment at their disposal. Half of her was intrigued, the other half nervous.

"The Commander let me in here when I was developing the beacons for the course runs."

Layden turned her attention back to Manni. "Do you think we'll be asked to further our theses?"

Manni shrugged. "Not sure. Sounds like the Council already moved ahead the way they wanted."

Layden nodded. Good. She didn't want to help them with how they were applying her idea anyway.

The thought startled Layden. It came to her in an instant, as though she had thought it a million times, as though her opinion had already been decided. But this was a surprise, as she hadn't allowed herself to think about the results since they were revealed almost six months prior. Apparently, however, her subconscious had.

Layden and Manni passed the time in an awkward, charged silence. She could tell he was uncomfortable about something, but that was the extent of her perception. Nor did she feel in the mood to pry. When the Guardian returned with the other three, she was relieved.

Layden immediately tried to determine who was Abisen and who was Yuna, and it wasn't hard. Though both were stunning with their well-tailored clothes and shiny hair, Abisen always stood a little taller than Yuna probably ever would. They had lighter features and a slighter build than Layden, though neither of them seemed to know how to hold themselves yet. Did she? Something in the way everyone's eyes were lingering on her told her maybe she did.

Mathis was equally handsome and also in his mid-thirties, but he did not stand tall. In fact, he seemed to be having a tough time greeting any of them at all. As Layden looked closer, she wasn't sure he'd even bathed that morning. The others looked well-groomed with a sheen over everything, like they had been dipped in a fine coat of sealant. Mathis, however, looked disheveled, his hair briefly combed and his clothes likely pulled on in a hurry. Not to mention his complexion was quite drained.

"Now that we are all here, please take a seat so I can explain the next few months," the Guardian said briskly, avoiding their eyes. No, avoiding hers.

The group moved into the room and took their seats on small stools that bordered the large workbench. Layden sat in front of a bio-microscope, the kind that didn't just see through dissected sections of flora and fauna but also provided significant readings on genetic composition and alterable genes. She remembered it from her tour of the greenhouses, but she hadn't ever thought she'd get to use one.

"As you may have noticed, in this Generation you have been given an incredible insight into the production of our line of Long-Life products."

"Long-Life products?" Yuna asked. She spoke softly, her tone low. It suited the body but not Yuna.

"Yes. Much of what you are now using on your skin, eyes, hair, teeth, etcetera, was developed in the early days of the Council before Host inhabiting was discovered. All the products were designed to prolong the human body longer than it was...well...designed for. The Hosts you are in are undergoing an experimental trial that began three decades ago.

Doctors and researchers are meticulously recording the effect of these products from infancy till death. We will not know the full effect until these bodies are of old age. Only then can scientists gauge just how long these products buy humanity."

"Surely there are easier, more scientific, ways to know those things," Manni said, appearing slightly put off.

"It may be a redundant test, but it will be useful in time. The subjects are not complaining. As it stands, they have already been recorded as a full eight years younger across the board than they actually are."

Layden felt her skin prickle at the thought. If she failed to take care of this Host, she would be neglecting years of someone else's work and study. She cast a glance at Mathis, hoping he realized what was at stake when he chose not to bathe, but he seemed to be barely listening. He cast a shifty look around the room, bringing his hand up to rub his forehead. Why was his manner so distressed? She wondered if the Guardian noticed.

"In that vein of work, you will be subjected to a series of examinations throughout your stay. Those researching these products have been gracious enough to lend the bodies to the Trials, but in return they must have full access to your Hosts for their studies."

Yet another shiver ran down her spine. She didn't like the idea of being under the microscope any more than they already were.

"What kind of tests are we talking about?" Abisen asked gruffly. Abisen had a confident personality, but she seemed to be slightly at odds with her Host body.

"I would not lose sleep over it." The Guardian glanced at Mathis. "Most of you have already faced far worse. Take the day to familiarize yourselves with the labs. Feel free to request books from the archives via the desk console, and your midday meal will be brought to you here. I will come tonight to collect you for your first round of tests."

He paused for a moment, surveying them all. "I am sure it is obvious what is at stake. The Council has entrusted you with a dear prize of theirs. In no way could you have been given a more...valuable Host. You would do well to treat them as your very own body. Better than. Hopefully by now, you realize what that takes."

The others nodded, but Layden couldn't help but fixate on Mathis from the corner of her eye. Her awareness of him and his unkempt state burned in her mind.

"That is all. If you have further questions, feel free to summon me via your consoles. I will be in my office. Layden knows where that is," he said as an afterthought, though still avoiding looking at her.

As the others rose to find their own laboratories, Layden ran to catch the Guardian.

"What is it, Layden?" He paused to receive her question, moving aside as Yuna, Mathis, and Abisen passed through the door.

Layden took a step closer, but she felt the Guardian shift and distance himself again. "I just wanted to talk to you," she began in a half-whisper. "Have you noticed Mathis isn't quite himself?"

The Guardian stared at her for a moment, his eyes searching her face. Her Host's face. "Yes. In fact, I did." It wasn't a reprimand. He, too, was concerned.

"He's been like this since he came back," Layden said, conspiratorially. "He said hardly anything at dinner yesterday before the Transfer. I thought maybe he was just shaken from the experience in the course runs, but to carry it into his next Host like this..." Layden let her words trail off delicately.

"No. You are right," the Guardian said after a moment. "These are the things we look for among our recruits." He suddenly seemed truly worried.

"Well, I am sure you'll get to the bottom of it," she said, reaching for his arm. "No one else knows us better." She hoped her face conveyed the gratitude that warmed her chest at having him back among them. The Guardian's breathing change slightly as he stared back at her.

"Thank you for your insight," he said finally, pulling his arm from her carefully. He straightened and glanced over to Manni. "Emmanuel, may I have a word with you?" he asked before turning to leave.

Layden turned to see Manni in the corner of the room, busy with one of the instruments. She hadn't realized he was still there. Her cheeks flushed with embarrassment, and she cast her eyes to the ground as they both exited the room.

Why did she do that? She'd *never* initiated contact with the Guardian. He was their *Guardian*. What was worse was that Manni had seen it all. Mortified, she moved to a bench and sat down, stunned into silence. Her mind spun in circles, trying to think of how to explain the moment to both her friend and her Guardian, but when neither of them returned, Layden resolved to move on and get to work. Or at least she would try.

chapter twenty-four

L AYDEN WAS CURLED UP on the floor of her room when she
heard a knock at her door.

The Monsoons assailed the panes of her window with their brute force, and she listened to them with eyes closed. Her cheek pressed against the thick, soft carpet as she breathed in the chemical scent of its fibers mixed with the smell of her own bile. Part of her secretly hoped the windows would give in and the rain would flood her room.

She couldn't do this anymore.

The vision had hit her full force and taken her by such surprise that she had thrown up her perfectly proportioned evening meal and then laid sobbing on the floor for what seemed like hours. She cried because she was tired of losing control, but also because she was relieved. She'd only had one vision during her last Generation, and her fear of losing the...gift? had been weighing on her more than she realized.

At the same time, she also wanted the visions gone. Even though they were the main reason for her advancement, she was afraid of them. Afraid of what they meant or didn't mean. Afraid of their power over her life.

Layden hugged herself tightly as a residual shudder ran through her body. She'd heard something this time. There'd been sound in the other visions—wind rustling, distant dripping and crackling, the deep unintelligible voice—but her last vision of the Council before her, with their muted, wordless mouthing, had been silent up till now. She wished it had stayed that way.

The knock came again. Layden startled and dread filled her. Somehow, she knew it was the Guardian, but he was the last person she wanted to see. Not only did she feel vulnerable and weak, but she was still humiliated by her earlier behavior. Nor did she want to share the recent development of her vision. However, there'd be no hiding it if he saw her like this.

At the same time, she knew if she didn't answer, he was liable to override her door and come in anyway. Layden stood up shakily and wiped her face dry, not bothering to make herself any more presentable than that. Unlike this morning, when she'd encountered Manni outside her door, this time she was correct in assuming it was the Guardian. Though she'd dreaded seeing him, a space between her ribs expanded momentarily in relief.

He seemed guarded at first, but when he noticed the state she was in, he stepped forward, clearly concerned. "What has happened?"

She knew what he was hoping to hear, and she resented the eagerness in his expression.

He took her by the elbow and led her to the chair by her desk, settling her gently upon it. "Another vision?"

She nodded weakly as he poured her some water from the pitcher beside her desk.

"Was it a new one?" He seemed confused, possibly by how overcome she was. Perhaps he thought new visions were more intense than repeated ones. There was no difference.

She shook her head.

"Did you receive...more of it then?" he asked.

"Not exactly," she said enigmatically.

He watched her for a moment, but she couldn't say more. He glanced around her room. "We will bring someone to take care of this," he said, gesturing to the carpet. "Was this after your supper?"

She nodded.

"Come. The clinicians are waiting for us now. We will find you something to eat while we are there."

"I don't want to eat," she said listlessly. She didn't know what to do.

Neither did the Guardian apparently, because he came back over and stood beside her silently. At length, he knelt beside her. "What did you see, Layden?" he asked quietly.

"Heard," Layden said. "I heard what the Council said."

The Guardian seemed surprised. "You are sure this was the same vision? Not a dream?"

She nodded again.

"Well," he said haltingly, "what did they say?"

"They were telling me..."

"What?" he prompted.

The small voice within her told her she must tell him. Even if she didn't want to. At this point, she'd learned to trust this prompting, for only bad things happened when she ignored it. For that reason alone, she explained.

"I had been officially accepted to the Council. Or rather, I would be if I desired it. There were still some things I had to know, and then I would be free to make my decision," Layden said.

She saw the Guardian's face grow white. "What did they tell you?" he asked urgently.

Layden shook off his question. "I didn't get that far. The vision ended before then."

"So, that was all?" The Guardian's brow knit in confusion.

"No," Layden said.

"What is it then? Why are you so distraught?" he asked insistently.

"They told me congratulations. That I was the only one to have made it this far. That they were sorry for the loss of my companions, but that I was braving it well. And I didn't feel anything about that. I wasn't sad about it. I didn't even seem to care."

Layden stared off into space as she spoke. She hated the way she had felt in the vision. She'd been resolved and single-minded; she hadn't felt a single pang of loss or regret for the people she had left behind. Not even Manni.

She was a monster.

"And?" the Guardian asked gently.

"Does there have to be anything else?" she shouted, her voice becoming shrill. "You heard me. I didn't care. I will lose everyone I care about, and somehow I will not care!"

"Layden, calm down." His hands steadied her shoulders.

"I don't even know who I am anymore! I didn't know that person standing before the Council."

"What makes you think it was you?" the Guardian asked.

"What?"

The Guardian let his question hang in the air but did not repeat it.

When *had* she made the switch to thinking these visions were about her? The one in the cave had felt personal; she'd always felt that. And this one...well, she supposed, at first, she had wanted it to be her. After all, the Council was telling her everything she'd ever dreamed of as a child. However, upon closer thought, there wasn't any considerable evidence to prove that it was her in the vision. In any of them.

"I guess...I don't know."

"Last time we talked, we decided we did not know what these visions are. Do not trouble yourself to try and understand them. That is the Council's responsibility."

"What do they think?" Layden asked, beginning to feel hopeful.

"There has been some small precedence for this kind of thing. It is more likely to be a connection to another living person, rather than a prediction of the future. There are those who believe visions are echoes of the past."

Yes. Surely there would have been others who had similar visions—otherwise why would the Council have been so ready to believe her? More importantly, there were people better equipped than she to determine that. She sighed a deep, shuddering sigh and buried her forehead against his chest, crying in relief. She remained this way for a long time, with the Guardian's arm around her.

Finally, he spoke. "Come," he said softly. "We can talk about this later. The others are waiting."

The Guardian had taken good care of her that night, in his own way. He had set out a change of clothes and sent the others ahead, so she'd have time to recuperate. When she arrived, there was food for her to eat, and the others were already underway with their testing. She didn't know what he told them, but they didn't even react to her tardiness, nor did they ask any questions.

The upside was that she was so emotionally drained, she didn't spend much time worrying about the procedures at hand. Thankfully—like the Guardian said—she'd been through worse. Either way, Layden found her mind elsewhere: on her visions, on the Council, but mostly on the kindness of her Guardian. She felt a powerful desire to thank him, and yet, what would she say? That she appreciated a moment of humanity in one of her lowest? On the surface, one might say it had been uncharacteristic of him, and yet, if that was the case, why had she expected nothing less? Somewhere along the line, under her very nose, this had become their dynamic. He was, despite everything, there for her.

Regardless, she didn't get to say thank you, for he didn't show up again that night. Or the following day. Or the remainder of the week for that matter. Layden wondered a couple of times if she should page him from her console. But it felt like the first time he had disappeared, and she knew it wouldn't help.

Without the Guardian there to tell them otherwise, the five plunged into work. At this stage that mostly looked like reading and exploring the instruments in the lab rooms, waiting for an idea that would be worth pursuing. In this season, they were asked to create something of value for the line of Long-Life products, but, once again, any great scientific achievement would do. Layden paid detailed attention to the caretaking routine outlined for them in their baths. She hoped something missing would present itself as an idea, but so far, the process seemed perfected. There wasn't an inch of skin unaccounted for.

In relatively little time, Layden found herself appreciating, even enjoying, that process. In fact, it wouldn't be a stretch to say she was quickly becoming dependent on it. Developing beneath the skin was a strong sensation she had no words for. It drove her toward the pursuit of perfection. When she did poorly, it nearly overwhelmed her with discomfort, a nagging sensation she could do nothing to appease. When she made progress and her percentages climbed in the daily tests, it prickled in elation, washing over her body like a fresh wind and deep breath. She wasn't sure what was coming over her, but she had her theories. Maybe it was the watchful and calculating eyes of the doctors that made her hyperaware.

Or maybe it was because this was the first time in a while she had any measure of control.

Control.

Layden sat up straight at her desk, an idea coming to her. She patted the papers in front of her, looking for a utensil to write with, then scribbled furiously once she found one. Then she read back over what she had written. Yes. That could be something. After all, the Long-Life products were concerned with the external human body. Did any consider the human mind? Or the human heart? How much age was stacked internally because of emotional stress?

Maybe she could find a way to suppress some of those subconscious, uncontrollable urges, fears, and insecurities. Like the ones that made her push people away because she felt inferior and sure to fail...the ones that made them all so competitive that they betrayed one another...the ones that would make a candidate violate a natural boundary with her Guardian simply because she *needed* that attention...yes, there had to be a way to suppress those.

"This is human nature you're talking about," Manni countered after she had called him into her lab to share her idea. "Surely one can't suppress the entirety of human nature."

"I'm not talking about the whole of our emotions," Layden responded impatiently. "Just some of the subconscious impulses we're not aware of. Ones that if we *were* aware of them, we might act differently. Make different choices."

She could see in his face that he was not on board. Which wasn't good, because she needed his help. But someone else on her team might be, and maybe they could help change his mind. Layden called the others to her lab through the intercom, and tried not to notice Manni's dark expression as they walked in.

"What is it?" Abisen asked, taking off a pair of gloves.

For some reason, this threw Layden. Was Abisen already into the hands-on stages of development? She *was* the most scientifically minded of the lot of them. Except maybe Yuna, which Layden always seemed to forget.

"Layden wants to take out the emotion centers in the brain," Manni said flatly.

Layden turned to him harshly with a slight flip of her hair. "Not all emotions," she reiterated sharply.

The expressions of the other three seemed alarmed, but no one interrupted, so Layden took that as permission to continue. Or at least opportunity.

"Each of us here has been the victim of subconscious, uncontrollable impulses while under the influence of the Trials. I know this because I've seen us all act in ways we normally wouldn't have acted. Within these harsh, survival-oriented situations, there are factors beyond our control. Baser impulses. Instinct. My proposal would put a damper on those emotions, dulling them enough so one could maintain control over how one responded to any situation. As I'm not strong at neuroscience or biology, I plan to use Abisen's pill to help me locate the correct signals and hormones...if you'll show me how it works?"

Abisen pursed her lips in response, as though she smelled something foul. Yuna had put her hand to her mouth, and Mathis's color was drained—though to be fair, that was how he always looked lately.

"What? You don't think there'd be a market for this? Think about the toll that anxiety and fear take on a person. If one could choose to act independent of those factors, I think we could add years onto people's lives."

"But...they're emotions Layden," Abisen said. "They're not bad. They're human. You're talking about suppressing defense mechanisms hardwired in us through millions of years of evolution. Instinct, survival."

"So, what?" Layden countered immediately. She stood up taller and glanced around at the group. Beyond the respect they'd begun to show for her leadership, she knew at this point that her Host's physical presence carried an authority of its own.

"Would that really be such a bad thing? Why is instinct so valued? Blindly making decisions based on hormone signals and physiological responses is the opposite of what the Council stands for. Logic, reason, and control, that's what they care about. I gather the Council would love to be free of the baser side of humanity—one might even say it's our next evolutionary step. After all, it was the very unpredictability of human nature that led to the world being destroyed."

"Maybe she's right."

All heads swiveled toward Mathis. It was surprising to hear him speak at all, let alone to hear him agree with Layden. So much so that no seemed able to say anything else.

"I think she's right," he said again. He cleared his throat. "And I'd like to be the first."

"The first?" Layden asked hesitantly.

"Yes. The first, for you to use this on. Or if, you know, you need someone to test it."

The silence in the room grew thicker, and a small voice within nudged her to be cautious. There was something going on with Mathis. And the others had valid concerns; she would be wise to listen to them. But there was something else within her, something louder, telling her to take the win and forget the rest. She felt blind in that moment to anything but this ambition. "Okay," she said. "I agree to that, Mathis."

With Mathis on board, Layden wouldn't really need anyone else to help if they didn't want to. Manni dropped his head and left the room without saying another word. Yuna followed behind him, her body language defeated. Only Abisen and Mathis remained.

"Okay, Layden," Abisen said quietly. "I'll help you understand my pill, but only because I don't want to see you botch this and hurt Mathis. Also, objectively, I can see your point."

"Thank you," Layden said gratefully.

"Even if I think you're a moron for putting this in the hands of the Council."

Layden was startled by her words. Such open distrust of the Council was brazen, even for Abisen. And yet, Layden didn't have the words she normally would, to counter her. "It won't be like that. This doesn't have to be something given to everyone. It can be by choice. A modification."

"Because your intent was so carefully considered last time?" Abisen asked, her eyes steely.

Layden couldn't answer. In the back of her mind was the whisper that Abisen was right. Even Layden herself had recently admitted she wasn't happy with the way the Council had used her last idea, however, that didn't mean she was ready to throw all her hard work, all her efforts, and her desire to join the Council out the window. She shook her head and looked away.

There were a few moments of silence before Mathis spoke. "Layden, I'll be in my laboratory. Let me know when you need me."

Abisen followed behind him, not giving Layden another look.

Layden paused before following them out the door and proceeding straight to Manni's lab. He sat at his desk looking over some papers, but she could tell by his ragged breathing and unmoving eyes that he wasn't concentrating.

"Abisen and Mathis are on board," Layden said, leaning against the frame of his door.

He didn't look up at her but picked up a pencil and started writing something.

"Is it really such a terrible idea?" She moved into the room. "You and I were just talking about how horrible it's been to feel out of control these last three seasons. Imagine if we could help one another. If we could help everyone with that."

Manni stopped writing and put his hand to his forehead, sighing heavily.

"Come on," she pleaded quietly while walking to his side. "You know I'm shoddy at neuroscience. I could use your help."

She paused, her pulse pounding in her neck, that itching desire to win him to her side, to win the Trials, highlighting her only way forward. "I...need you, Manni."

Manni finally met her eyes. It felt like cheating, saying those words, because she was beginning to realize the dynamic of their relationship that she'd been blind to for all the seasons they'd been together. She may have once needed him like oxygen. But it was clear now he needed her too, maybe even more than she did now. And what was more, he needed her to *need him*.

"All right. If only to keep you from hurting Mathis."

Layden sighed in relief. "Thank you."

Manni turned away, his cheeks blotchy and red. "Call me when you're ready." Then he returned to his work, as much of a goodbye as could be suggested without saying it.

"The things I'm hoping to find are more specific than you'd think. I'll try to focus my thoughts on them, and you watch which areas of my brain are active during those moments. Once we find what we're looking for, Abisen is fairly sure she can program her pill to search it out more systematically."

Layden sat forward in her chair and allowed Manni to attach the electrodes to her temples and forehead. Mathis, while he hadn't said much to her in the last month, had kept his part of the bargain and showed up. He sat beside them now, watching.

"How will I know that I've found the right thing? How will you know? After all, didn't you say these feelings were subconscious?" Manni asked.

"Well, that is the tricky part. We'll record in five-minute segments. By the time I realize a feeling is the one I'm looking for, it has become conscious. So, we'll have to back up the findings and see where the emotion starts."

"All right. Tell me when to begin," he said.

"Okay." Layden started thinking. "Go ahead."

Manni selected a button on the console beside him and sat back, watching the monitor passively. Layden waited, but all she could think about was how she hoped they would find something significant. If she didn't make progress, she might lose Manni's help. Not to mention, it had already been a month, and she was just breaking out of research. If the Guardian had been here, she could've asked his advice, but she'd given up expecting him to show. Regardless, if she didn't come up with anything good soon, no amount of visions would save her from dismissal.

Manni reached over and paused the recording.

"Why have you stopped?" she asked, concerned.

"That's time," he said simply.

"Oh. That went fast." She felt oddly vulnerable.

"There was a lot of activity," Manni told her. "Primarily in your lateral septum. This here is a small neural circuit that connects the lateral septum to other brain structures in a manner that directly influences anxiety and anxious behavior."

Spot on, Layden thought. Anxiety. So, that's what her brain must look like half the time. Maybe she should get a printout. Still, she was impressed that Manni was able to read it so clearly—she was lucky he had decided to help her.

"Was that what you were hoping to find?" he asked, turning her way.

"No," she said. "I mean, yes, partly. But not quite."

The thoughts she had weren't positive ones, but they were normal and understandable. Too conscious. How exactly was she planning to dredge up the feelings she'd been talking about? Maybe she should talk about them and see what surfaced.

"Go ahead and start again," she said.

Manni reached over and tapped the console.

"The thoughts and emotions I'm talking about, the ones that concern me, are much less on the surface," she began, hoping if she explained them something underneath might be triggered.

"Subconscious," Manni reiterated.

"Right," she said. "But they seem to be more than a subconscious run of thoughts. They're impulses, reactions that make me behave in ways I wouldn't have before."

"Impulses. So that would be subconscious thought and feeling in connection with autonomic nervous system—specifically the sympathetic nervous system—of the body," he instructed. "Fight or flight—our response to stress—*is* largely a physical reaction, hence the nervous system connections. However, the command center is located mainly here, in the hypothalamus, and in portions of the cerebellum and temporal lobe of the cerebral cortex. If you're experiencing those kinds of emotions, they should appear active here," Manni said, directing her to areas of the brain.

She remembered some of this from her studies with the Guardian, but she probably wouldn't have been able to recall it like he had. "All right, so, I'm gonna try and remember, and maybe feel, some of those emotions again. Watch the screen, and if those areas light up, we'll have a bit more direction."

Manni nodded again. Beside him, Mathis had turned a shade of ash, and his eyes seemed bleary.

"When I first arrived here, I was terrified," Layden began. "We all were, but that was understandable. Soon I realized there was more to it than that; there was a gnawing feeling...of isolation. Intense loneliness. Both feelings were new to me, and stronger at times than anything I'd experienced before. They made me act in ways I never would have."

Layden thought she should be able to feel the things she spoke of, but she couldn't; they were merely a memory. She looked at Manni who shook his head. Nothing there.

"It was the same kind of thing during the last Generation. Except that time, I felt like I had to be the best, at any cost. It was more than just normal competitiveness; it was intense, like thick disdain for any measure of weakness within me, and a push to be the best. I had no control over when it would rear its head. I know you understand that Manni."

Manni didn't answer, but she could see on his perfectly sculpted features that he was ashamed of that memory.

Tell me now, Manni, what would you give to have had control over that moment?

"Still nothing, Layden. Really think about how you felt. Try to feel it again," he said quietly.

Layden tried, but again it was only a memory. None of those intense emotions remained. It was like they'd been washed away with the Generation. Maybe she'd need to go more recent. The horrifying moment with the Guardian surfaced, the moment when she'd tried to be...familiar. Charming. She cringed inwardly.

Any other time she would've pushed the memory from her mind with a shudder. How she'd touched his arm, smiled with her eyes, and leaned in close. His breathing had quickened, but he'd pulled away stonily. Clearly, she'd crossed a line, but why had she dared in the first place? As she let herself stew in the humiliation of it all and pondered this question, a different emotion surfaced.

Desire.

Desire for what though, the Guardian's attention? No, it was more subtle than that. It was the desire to be wanted by another. To be thought beautiful. The feeling overcame her momentarily, and she felt herself wishing the Guardian were here now, or that any of them would look at her that way. Immediately the thought shamed her, but this time Layden didn't fight it.

"There," Manni said, sitting up straight. "What was that?"

"What?" Layden asked hopefully.

"There was a basic emotional reaction here in the temporal lobe—the anterior cingulate cortex—but then a flash over here. Something entirely different. It pulsed steadily and then faded."

"Was it in the section we talked about?"

There was a pause as Manni replayed the recording. From the corner of her eye, she saw Mathis sit back.

"No," Manni said. He stayed silent for a moment.

"Well, what was it?" she asked.

"I...I don't know," he said. "No one really does. That part of the brain is...uncharted."

Layden was about to ask how that was possible, but in the next moment, Mathis spoke.

"I know what it is," he said softly.

Manni and Layden turned to look at him.

"Layden, I think you'd better let me sit in that chair now."

CHaPTer TWenTY-FiVe

M ATHIS HAD ONLY BEEN in the chair for several seconds
before that same section of the brain began to pulse like a
strobe light. Except with Mathis, it continued to do so for the full
five minutes. When the time was up, they had to shake his shoulder
to bring him to, and even then, it was with a faraway look in his eyes
that he returned.

"Thank you, Mathis," Layden said, unable to keep the excitement out of her voice.

"How did you know?" Manni asked, trailing off.

"When Layden was describing those emotions," he said quietly,
"I knew I'd had them too."

His manner was slightly enigmatic, but Layden wasn't exactly
concerned about it. She had what she needed, and now she could
begin the next stage of research. Mathis apparently felt the same way,
because in the next moment he stood and walked out the door.

Layden moved to a table close by where she began to record their
findings.

"Layden," Manni said, bringing her attention back. "Those
things you described..."

"What things?" Layden asked, already distracted with planning
her next step. She could hear his cautious tone and could tell he was
about to steal her joy at having a breakthrough.

"We've all felt those things."

"And?" she prompted, only thinly veiling her annoyance. After all, that's exactly what she'd been saying.

"Do you think maybe these emotions have been induced by the Council somehow? Or even the Guardian?"

"Induced?"

"Yes. Like, somehow, we were made to feel that way. For the sake of the Trials?

"How?"

"I don't know. Like, maybe they put something in the food or water."

Layden thought about this for a second, and offense rose within her. If that were true, then it would undermine her whole premise. "What a thing to say," she said coldly.

"It's not an outlandish idea."

"I don't think the Council is drugging its recruits for sport, Manni. They may have different motivations than we're used to, but they're not..." Layden paused, unable to find the right words. The truth was, she didn't truly know what the Council was capable of. Still, she would say anything she could at this point to move on with her research. With such a big breakthrough, it was all she could do to keep her excitement at a respectable level.

"I never said for sport," he said quietly. "But I see I shouldn't have brought it up. I'm sure you'll be fine from here on, and if you aren't...well, you can figure it out."

Layden watched him leave, wondering why they were trying so hard to hang on to something that had clearly changed. All his words said he'd be there for her no matter what, but his actions said something completely different. Not only had he apparently harbored thoughts of betraying her more than once, but he was constantly doubting everything she said and did. What's worse, he made her doubt herself. It was exhausting.

She walked to her console and requested a page for the Guardian again, though he'd yet to respond to one. The console informed her he was unable to receive her message.

"Well, then don't bother offering to be around!" she shouted at the console.

She took a few deep breaths before becoming aware she still had some congealed gel on her temples from before. With a shudder just short of repulsion, she decided to hurry to the baths and wash them off.

Layden had intended to take a quick shower, and to maybe reapply some of the more essential products before heading down with the others for their tests, but as she sat in the warm water, she felt the sudden, itching, compulsion to complete the entire process again. By the time she finally reached the labs, she was a full hour late. The staff didn't seem too troubled when she explained the reason; they nodded with a kind of resigned look and then guided her to a bed between Manni and Abisen.

"Where have you been?" Manni asked. Was that worry in his voice?

"I was in the bath," she said.

"For two hours? Didn't you do all that this morning?" he asked.

"Yes, well, perfection is the tip of the iceberg, isn't it? Beneath the surface is all the hard work and time and care and sacrifice," Layden recited as the clinician inserted a small needle into her arm to take blood.

"Do you think it'll help?" Abisen said, obviously overhearing their conversation.

"What do you mean?" Layden replied.

"Do you think the extra time will improve your stats? I can't seem to get above the ninety-two percent mark on anything. I feel like the clinical team is getting angry with me. They keep mumbling that I'm ruining all their work," she whispered, eyeing the nurse who was setting up the body scan above her.

The scan was the best part of the night in Layden's opinion. All that was required of her was to lay still as imperceptible lasers made tiny scan after tiny scan.

"Well, we'll see, won't we?" Layden heard her tone turn slightly haughty, but she didn't bother correcting it. Truthfully, she'd thoroughly enjoyed the second routine, however, even more truthfully, she disliked how much she enjoyed it. It was like there were two competing selves within her: one urging her to stay longer, care more, and be more tediously aware, and the other one that knew there was more to do in the day than take meticulous care of her body. Her *Host's* body.

That's why it's so important that I make progress with this advancement, Layden thought as the nurse began to take skin samples. If Layden could pinpoint these impulses and learn how to suppress them, they'd be under her control, not the other way around.

She glanced over to see Manni nearly asleep under his scan. He looked very tired. Despite the constant wellness lectures they'd been receiving, he'd been working too hard. There was a battle within him much like the one she had within her, she could tell—give in to the nettling needs of her caretaking process or fight through and work.

Manni's theory about how they'd been slipped something to make them feel the way they did swirled around her brain until she found herself angry again. Not that she didn't see where he was coming from. All the emotions she'd described seemed to be shared among them, granted, with nuances. And those emotions seemed to disappear with each new Generation.

But that didn't mean she wasn't on to something, either.

"Time to relax," the nurse said, setting up the scan above Layden. They'd hurried through her tests so she wouldn't be here too much later, which she appreciated.

As she closed her eyes, she overheard the lab technician speaking with Yuna. He was giving her an additional cream for the callouses developing on her hands from her work at the lab. Layden couldn't help imagining what Yuna was doing. Then he spoke to Mathis about increasing his protein intake; he was testing deficient. The clinicians were puzzled about this—his food intake was precisely calculated—but thought that perhaps Mathis was exerting more energy than the original Host had. Layden had other theories; mainly that he wasn't eating the precisely calculated protein.

To Manni, the technician demanded he turn in earlier. Layden saw that coming. She also knew Manni well and suspected he wasn't going to listen. For Abisen, there were no comments for the day. She was doing well and had risen a full three percentage points. Layden watched her reaction through half-closed eyes, seeing elation light Abisen's beautiful features as she climbed out of the bed.

"Well, that's a relief," she said, tossing her hair.

Was that what Layden looked like when she did that? She closed her eyes quickly as the others looked her way, hoping they'd think she was asleep and leave her. They did.

With the lab now mostly empty, Layden felt she could truly relax. She willed the scans to come out positive. She needed them to be.

Layden ignored the beeping from the console beside her, not willing to lose her steadiness yet; the wrong amount by a microunit and she'd have to start all over again. Anyway, it was most likely Abisen or Mathis and they could wait. However, when the pulsing buzz of her intercom didn't stop, she realized it wasn't coming from her room only. As she listened carefully, she eventually heard each console silenced as her coworkers answered the call.

The Guardian. It had to be.

She slipped her hands out from the vacuum sealed chamber she'd set up and swiveled to the console, then she tapped the screen.

"Your presence is requested in the common room to discuss the further requirements of your projects."

It was a prerecorded message, voice only, but it was clearly the Guardian.

Requirements? There'd better not be anything restricting her from what she'd already done. She'd ignore it if so—it was his fault for not getting those *requirements* to her sooner.

Did she have time to finish what she'd started? She really shouldn't leave it half done. Then Abisen appeared in her doorway and waved her along; Layden sighed and pulled off her gloves and left her lab.

Layden turned the corner, trailing a few feet behind the others and entered a midsize seating area. The common room was meant to be a place to rest and reenergize, but the only thing they'd used in it was the coffeepot. They didn't eat outside their planned meals and were far too busy to just sit. As a result, the place looked clinical and unused. It was a nice thought though.

The five of them settled around the table, though Manni walked to the kitchenette in the back and poured them all cups of the coffee substitute before sitting. A few minutes passed in a silence that was charged with tired and preoccupied energy, until, eventually, he arrived.

The Guardian strode in with his usual air of cold efficiency. Upon seeing him, Layden realized her current annoyance had to do with more than being interrupted from her work. It had been two months since any of them had seen him, and now he simply showed up like he'd never been gone. A large part of her was angry. She'd felt, in no small terms, abandoned.

"Good afternoon," he said to them all, taking a seat at the head of the table.

Layden glanced over to see if her feelings were reflected on Manni's face, but all she noticed were bags under his eyes. She'd overheard how the lab techs had come into his lab and escorted him back to his room the last few nights, administering a sleeping aide as well. But he still looked tired. Perhaps he'd been getting up earlier.

"I wanted to thank you all for your patience in the last months. I am sure it was not easy to carry on in my absence. I assure you, I would not have left you had I not absolutely had to."

Layden tried to check her anger and took a closer look at him. Had the Council sent him away again? She could see in his eyes and face the same tired look she'd seen after he had gone missing the first time, two seasons ago.

"I am sure you are all well on your way with your projects now. Has the Council assigned someone else in my stead?" he asked.

Why wouldn't he know that? They shook their heads.

"Then they must have thought you capable enough on your own. As I mentioned before, the Year Thirties do not have any group requirements; it is largely an independent venture. I trust they knew you would be fine." He paused for a moment.

Layden felt like he was waiting for them to accept his half-apology, and she worked hard not to react. Before, she would have nodded eagerly, made him feel listened to and respected, but this time she kept her face stony.

"Regardless, I have returned. If any of you need to run your ideas by me, please do not hesitate to do so."

The others nodded readily, and Layden felt her stand dissolve. She couldn't be the only one angry, or she'd look like a petulant child. Especially in this Host, with her naturally pouty lips and airy voice.

"I have come to inform you that you will be presenting in two and a half months, just before the end of the season. Following your presentations, the Council will deliberate on your placements. You have made it this far and it is the Grand Councilor's hope that, no matter whether you are invited to join the Council, you will decide to stay within Nyine City and help toward the betterment of society. Perhaps even train the next recruits."

Layden knew she should be relieved to hear this finally confirmed, that there were options after the Council, but she wasn't. Despite her doubts and all she'd learned, could she truly be happy with a secondary life? Back in her body, but rejected by the Council?

"While they are deciding, you will be permitted to return to your own bodies, though you will be sequestered. Deliberation can take a few days, so prepare yourself. I hope I am clear that while your chances are good for receiving a placement outside the Council, they are not one hundred percent. Do not take the next couple months lightly. You still need to excel at this final presentation."

The others nodded again. They seemed confident that their discovery, invention, or whatever they were working on was worth putting their name on. The only one who didn't seem engaged—as per usual lately—was Mathis.

"You will be given a full day to display your work, along with any trials you may have been working on. You will know your order shortly. Does anyone have any questions?" he finished, standing before them.

"If someone on the Council counters our idea, do we have time to change our project?" Abisen asked practically.

"In a way. It would depend on the nature of the critique. If the problem is fixable before the end of the day, and corrections would not change the inherent nature of the project, then, yes, you are free to adjust. However, should something fundamental be lacking, you will not have time to resolve that. Save yourselves the nightmares. Triple-check your work. If you feel comfortable, share the premise with someone else now."

"We're allowed to share?" Yuna asked.

Layden hoped so because she'd practically broadcast hers to the entire group. She felt momentarily exposed at that realization, but the upside was she already knew where everyone stood.

"As a general rule, no," the Guardian said.

Layden shifted uncomfortably and tried to keep her face neutral, though she felt her cheeks going hot.

"However, you five have been together for more than three seasons. If you do not trust each other now, perhaps you never will."

It almost sounded like a challenge, the way the words fell off his lips, crisp and curt. The others seemed to share her thoughts, because they looked around at each other, their expressions unsure. They hadn't exactly been encouraged to trust.

"I will let you all return to your work."

Layden stood with the rest and walked past the Guardian without giving him a glance. She felt his eyes follow her, but she didn't linger. After entering her lab, she shook the meeting from her mind and pulled on a fresh pair of gloves. The sample before her looked like it had decompensated, so she opened the vacuum and disposed of it. Unfortunately, that little meeting had cost her half a day's work. She was setting up her materials again and giving her workspace a cleaning when she heard him enter the room.

Not looking up from her activity she said, "Yes, what is it?" Her voice was more callous than she felt.

He didn't answer but moved further into the room until he was standing beside her, observing her activity over her shoulder. Her skin prickled with awareness; he was standing close. He smelled as he always did, like fresh air...and earth. Dirt. That's what it was. She hadn't been familiar enough with the scent when she'd first noticed it, but after all her time outside on the concourse, rolling around in the artificial dirt, she realized she'd smelled it before. Not artificial dirt though—he smelled like the real thing. He smelled like earth.

It had been during a tour of the botanical labs when she was in the Conservatory that she'd first experienced the musty scent of real soil. The whole place reeked of it. Not that it was an unpleasant smell, just so unfamiliar to her senses that she couldn't smell anything else. Every time since, when she smelled it on the Guardian, it had seemed out of place, but familiar. Now she knew why.

Well, not exactly. Why would he smell like fresh earth? Did he do work at those labs? Surely, he must supervise them or have business there. Layden shifted slightly, an involuntary urge to gain some distance.

"Did you need something from me?" she asked again, casting him a sideways glance.

"Where did you procure an endocrine gland?" he asked.

"I requested it," she said warily.

He didn't speak again, so she pressed her eyes to the viewer and tried to resume her work.

"Which hormone are you extracting?"

She was surprised he knew what she was doing. Then again, why wouldn't he? He probably would've been the one to teach her. Had he been around.

"Any hormone," she said shortly.

"To what purpose?" he asked again.

Layden sighed and pushed back from the viewer. "If you're interested in my work, you should've been here two months ago."

She felt the urge to flip her hair off her shoulder, but she stopped herself. Half of her had wanted to deny him the satisfaction of defending himself. She'd wanted to stonewall him with silence. But she hadn't been able to stay silent. It infuriated her that his tone of instruction hadn't changed one iota from the last time she'd seen him.

"Look," she said, staring into his narrowed eyes, "I don't have time to fill you in. I'm incredibly behind. I was just informed my timetable was moved up a month."

His jaw clenched as he listened to her. "Two months should be plenty of time if you apply yourself."

"Maybe it would be, but I have less time during the day than the others, and while I don't know what they're attempting, I can guarantee it's not as groundbreaking as what I've decided to do. And as you know," she continued, stopping him from replying, "I am absolutely abysmal in the sciences, so I can't even imagine why I thought I could do this!"

"Why do you have less time in your day?" he managed to interject.

She found his interest in this tangential part of her rant maddening. "Because I have this wonderful new...compulsion...to complete the cleansing process in the evening as well as the morning. If I want to make it to the tests on time, I have to leave the lab an hour early. And is any of that helping my marks? No. In fact, last week they dropped three percentage points!"

"Your marks?"

"Yes. The tests. On my Host. That we do every night. The ones you'd know about if you were around. You'd think the marks would be higher now, but they're not. They're actually dropping." Layden's mouth was running without her permission. She didn't want to share any of this, but it seemed once she started, she couldn't stop. "And you, you're supposed to be our Guardian, *my* Guardian. Every step of the way you've fought to be with us, and then you leave, for two months, during the most crucial time of our Trials!" Her voice was becoming louder, but she couldn't seem to check it. "Do you even know how Mathis is doing? Or Manni? It's your job to know! I'm not the only one unravelling."

She stopped herself finally and stood there shaking, hoping the others hadn't heard her. Hoping that they wouldn't come to gawk as the Guardian reprimanded her for speaking so disrespectfully. Again.

Much to her surprise, no one came, nor did the Guardian react as she expected. He exhaled through his nose and trained his eyes on the floor, his jaw clenching and unclenching in that familiar way she'd once taken for a sign of anger. Now she knew it was simply a physical component to him processing his thoughts.

"There is no excuse that would relieve you of your anger," he said quietly. "To explain where I have been would not help, nor would the assurance that I was needed more where I was."

"Wonderful, thanks," she said contemptuously, turning back to her work. Her hands were shaking too much to do anything serious, so she tidied her station instead.

"Layden," he said sternly.

There weren't many times he'd called her by her first name only, and it had a way of softening her anger quickly. She turned toward him.

"I'm here now," he continued simply.

Layden regarded him for a moment, then sighed. She sat on her stool and pushed back from the bench, allowing the silence to linger.

"I am working on a suppressant," she finally responded.

"What are you trying to suppress?"

"It's complicated," she answered evasively.

Now that he was asking, she was positive he wasn't going to approve of the work she was doing. He didn't prompt her to say more, but he didn't leave either.

"There've been certain impulses. Emotions. Reactions to situations here in the Trials that I haven't been in control of at all. Times when I haven't felt like myself. None of us have."

"What do you mean, haven't felt like yourself?" he asked.

"It's no secret that stressful situations bring out the worst in our nature. We go into instinctual, survival modes, and we behave oddly, contrary to what we'd normally do—it's like we aren't *ourselves*."

A ray of comprehension dawned across the Guardian's face, and he walked around to the areas she'd set her research in.

She took that as permission to continue. "So, I'm creating something that would suppress those...instinctual impulses. Not eliminate them—" she said quickly before he could object. "I understand this is human nature I'm tampering with. At the same time, how much more could humanity accomplish if we weren't constantly betraying our values for our more primitive, selfish needs? After all, the Council takes care of us, right? We don't need to fear for our individual lives like we might have before. At least, not outside the Trials," she said the last words lightly, almost as a joke, but the Guardian didn't seem to share her humor.

"What I'm saying is, these impulses are relics from a different time, when we needed to survive. Now all they do is hold us back."

"And you don't think," he began, picking up a few of her papers, "that these impulses have helped you at all?"

"Maybe. Sometimes," she said carefully. "But there are also times where they've been massively restrictive. And...compromising. I simply want to get us to a state where we're a little more in control of them. Where we have more of a choice."

Her motives had started out broad, but what she didn't say was how personal her quest had become. She couldn't tell him that her need for physical perfection was consuming her every thought, or that she had a tough time even concentrating on her work.

"I see," he said finally. "Well, I have no doubt that this endeavor will be extremely valuable to the Council. I only urge you to carefully consider the societal implications of your creation."

"I think it's a bit late for that now, don't you?" she said with a small laugh. It was light, flirty. She hated it.

"It is never too late, Layden Prier, to do the right thing." He set down her papers and stared at her.

Her pulse quickened as she met his eyes. The itch under her skin told her to ignore him and push on, that she was so close and had only to finish her premise to get everything she'd ever wanted. But the quiet whisper she'd come to view as sound judgment surfaced again and told her to ask...

"Do you think I should...stop?" She obeyed, her voice quiet. It was hard enough for her to consider, let alone voice, but she hadn't been wrong trusting that whisper yet.

The Guardian held her gaze for a long time, before looking back at her work. "Well, that is the nature of invention, is it not?" His tone was slightly lighter. "Sometimes it is hard to tell what is right and what is not. This could indeed be the breakthrough humanity needs. Something that would keep us from ever facing the end of the Earth again."

"Yes, it could," Layden said, relieved he could see that at least.

"Just make certain you are certain," he said.

"Yes, sir," she answered absentmindedly.

"Guardian," he corrected quietly.

"Yes, Guardian." She wondered why, after all this time, he insisted on being called their Guardian. Maybe his role meant more to him than she realized.

"Any additions to those visions of yours?" he asked.

It had become kind of a ritual to hear him ask.

She shook her head. "Nothing new, since, well—" She stopped short. It was hard to remember that night on the floor of her room. The pain she'd felt, the mercy he'd shown.

The Guardian seemed to be remembering the same moment for he did not insist she finish her thought. Instead, he exhaled quietly and nodded.

"Very well," he said. "Page me if you need me. I will answer this time."

Layden couldn't help but smile in forgiveness.

CHAPTER TWENTY-SIX

T HE NEXT TWO MONTHS went by faster than any other time in Layden's life. Every day was precious, and every hour counted. So, it was distressing when the Guardian insisted on taking a half day every week for psychological evaluations. Then there was that whole day they lost in stasis so the doctors could conduct a series of internal scans, which the Guardian insisted was a necessary precaution for them all since he'd been away for so long. Layden suspected it all had something to do with Mathis, but she noted that even she felt better after going under for a while, her compulsion to bathe calming to once a day.

Despite all this, the tension among the group continued to rise as their presentations neared. Yuna was scheduled to go first, followed by Mathis, Abisen, and Manni, with Layden last. Layden was relieved she wasn't first, but Yuna didn't seem bothered. Or maybe she was. Layden realized she had no idea how to read Yuna. This was slightly bothersome, mainly because Layden had been with her nearly three seasons, and after the Trials, she might never see Yuna again. That thought was enough to prompt a visit that afternoon when Layden found herself in need of a break.

Layden walked down the hall to the lab at the end where Yuna had set up shop, suddenly feeling awkward. How did one get to know someone intentionally? She'd left it so long she didn't know where to start. She was about to turn around and abandon the venture when Yuna noticed her at the door.

"Layden?" she didn't try to hide her surprise.

"Hey, Yuna. Just thought I'd come say hi," she said haltingly.

"Really." Yuna stated more than asked.

Layden ignored the tense air and began to look around. All awkwardness left her in an instant as she took in Yuna's work. How had this big of a project been going on just down the hall without her knowing? Giant tanks of water stood all around, some taller than Layden, others standing on tables. Within each was a host of beautiful plant life floating in an eerie light. Other tanks were blacked out except for a dim light at the top. The scent of seawater filled the air, along with a musky dampness that reminded Layden of the sea-soil she used to collect for her mother a lifetime ago.

"What is all this?" Layden asked in awe. She walked to one of the blacked-out tanks and opened a small viewing panel. There was a tall, bright blue plant within, leaves stretching upward like seaweed.

"Aqua flora," Yuna said.

"Water plants?" Layden asked, taking a stab.

"In their very basic sense, yes." Yuna's words sounded a little stilted.

"What are they for?"

"The same thing all other plants are for," she said simply. "Food, medicines, oxygen."

"Oxygen? Under water?"

Yuna gave a small smile. "You don't do a lot of botany, do you?"

Layden's cheeks flushed, and she shook her head slowly. "My mother used to grow plants in sea-soil we'd collect for her," she offered lamely. "For food, trade, and stuff. In other words, not really, no."

Yuna seemed to consider this for a second before continuing. "All plants produce oxygen. Phytoplankton alone were estimated to produce fifty to eighty-five percent of the Earth's oxygen even before the floods. It is likely the main source of what we breathe today. However, with most above-water plant life gone, we could always use more."

"So, that's what you're doing?" Layden asked.

"Why are you here, Layden?" Yuna asked reservedly.

"I wanted to see how you were doing," Layden replied quietly.

It felt like Yuna was biting her tongue by the way she was looking at her, but after a moment, Yuna took a breath and walked to one of her tanks.

"The light wasn't the problem," she began, as though Layden might've suspected it was. "Most plant life, minus seaweed, is dependent on the red spectrum to progress physiologically, and the red spectrum can penetrate through water as low down as fifteen meters. So, there's a bit of precedence for underwater cultivation. Unfortunately, in all cases, the plant life had to be protected from the actual water in dome-like structures and was still dependent on above-ground soil. So, that research isn't helpful to us."

Layden nodded, allowing her to continue.

"I've been genetically engineering a sort of bio-case for plants that can shelter above-ground crops like berries, wheat, and beans, underwater. Within the case, I create each plants' ideal environment, producing pockets of oxygen and regulating the light. The cases aren't plastic or glass though. They're plants themselves, and they function as any underwater plant would, taking the same light spectrum as, say, seaweed, and thriving on the nutrients from the ocean floor. Then the bio-cases convert those nutrients into whatever the plant inside requires. The properties of the case itself allow it to filter the appropriate light spectrum. When harvested, the cases look like this—bulbous and multi-colored—I'm calling it bulb-weed. Though, the product inside isn't that different from the ones we grow above ground."

"Yuna," Layden said, her mouth agape, "that's incredible."

A smile grew on Yuna's perfectly symmetrical face. "Thank you." She turned back to her plants and touched a tank fondly. "I have some things to work out still, like how to make them self-producing. The bulb-weed exists solely for the plant inside, so it doesn't need to reproduce. But I can't find a way to make the plant inside pollinate in any meaningful way while within the case. It may be they'll need to reproduce as one unit. I just don't know how to do that yet."

"So, what does that mean?" Layden asked.

"Huh?" Yuna said, apparently having gotten lost in her own analysis. "Oh, well, nothing more than what I'm doing now. We'll have to be the ones to plant each bulb-weed, which might prove difficult at the depths we're talking about."

Layden glanced around, sure there were many nuances to the project; the assorted colors played into what kind of light spectrum was absorbed, she remembered that. Layden's color, at the moment, was impressed.

"I think this could really turn things around for Nyine City," Layden said.

Yuna nodded excitedly, but then her smile fell. "I am hoping it won't be only for the city." She made some notes at her bench. "I think the Outlayers could use this as a way to be self-sustaining."

Her real meaning wasn't lost on Layden. Yuna had been responsible for the exponential growth in the greenhouses, which had resulted in the Outlayers increasing their dependency on Nyine City. No doubt she was trying to undo that situation.

"Well, keep an open mind," Layden suggested gently. "You don't want to be disappointed."

Yuna's face went hard as she looked at Layden. "Did you need anything else?" she asked coldly.

"No," Layden said, taken aback.

"I better get back to my work then."

"I didn't mean to offend you," Layden said. "I am sure the Council will value your discovery in many ways. I wouldn't be surprised if they offer you a place right away."

"Yes. Well, if not, I'm sure it will be fine."

"Yeah...maybe the Council will let us work near each other." She gave a nervous laugh.

"Please, Layden. I may be quiet, but I'm not an idiot."

"I'm sorry?"

"There may have been a couple of times when I believed we were in this together, but that was a long time ago."

Layden didn't say anything, so Yuna added, "Do you remember that speech you made on our first day in class? About rallying together. I honestly thought that might've been real. Then the first chance you got, you pulled ahead for yourself. You all did. I did too."

Layden didn't know what to say.

"I don't blame you," Yuna said evenly. "Maybe I was the fool to believe we could have fought the Council's games, and trust me when I say, no one is to blame for playing the game. But where does that leave us? A group of players doomed to be outplayed."

There was silence as Yuna sat on a stool and returned to her work. At any other time, Layden might have refuted her, defended the Council, but it didn't even occur to her this time. She'd learned too much to say she understood the Council like she'd originally thought.

She chewed her lip as she remembered the class Yuna was talking about and her speech of unity. Her gut twisted as she wondered what the last three seasons had been like had she *really* known Yuna—her thoughts and heart. If Layden had chosen this friendship instead of...everything else she was "supposed" to choose.

Suddenly, it came rushing back to her. Layden hadn't realized at the time, nor was she sure how she knew now. That day in the classroom, when she'd first felt the bone-shattering loneliness of what they were about to embark on, there'd been one tangible moment of kindness. A woman had held her hand.

Now Layden knew without a doubt, that woman had been Yuna.

"I don't understand," Layden said to Manni.

She had just made it to his office and sat down, interrupting his work. He had seemed surprised she was there, but he didn't tell her to leave.

"I'm not the way Yuna sees me. I'm not a liar. Or two-faced. I'm just doing the best I can. We all are."

Manni didn't say anything as she rose again to pace the room.

"Everyone thinks I'm the Council's pet project, but they don't see all the difficulties that comes with it. These dumb *visions*...they make no sense to me, by the way, and they probably mean even less. Everyone thinks they're something special, and they're probably nothing but fish fodder!"

"Layden..." Manni paused and glanced around before closing the door. "I know you better than anyone does."

Layden didn't answer. There was a time when she would've conceded that point right away. Not these days. There was one other who'd seen more sides of her than anyone, and who—for better or worse—seemed to understand them.

Manni didn't sense her hesitation, however, and continued. "I don't believe that these visions were your doing, and I don't believe you spur them on for attention, no matter what others say."

"Is that what others say?" Layden asked, heat rising to her cheeks.

"Let's face it, when it comes to the Council, you have a blind spot. You always have."

"What does that mean?"

"It means you believe the Council is...everything. You believe it so blindly that no other option is going to be acceptable to you. I saw it in your eyes when the Guardian told us that even if we made it through the Trials, we might be placed elsewhere. That thought had never truly occurred to you."

"That's not true. I think about it constantly," Layden said.

"You fear it constantly," he countered.

"It's not fear...it's..."

"What?"

"Being with the Council is all I've wanted since I was five seasons old!"

She paused for a second, but when he didn't say anything, she continued. "So, yes, I suppose that makes it hard for me to entertain anything outside joining the Council. I mean, can you? Could you stomach being stuck here as a Guardian as drove after drove of students came through, getting a chance to do what you'd failed to do? Those are the choices in front of us. And I won't be made to feel bad about trying my hardest to get what I want."

"We could've left! Made our own choices!" Manni slammed his hand on his desk. "We had a way out, and you said no."

"You're not listening!" Layden exclaimed hoarsely. "Left and gone *where*? Done *what*? You're constantly running for the door, but have you thought anything through? If you ask me, you're the one making your decisions out of fear." Layden paused and caught her breath. "I get that not knowing is scary. I feel it too. I get that every day the moves of the

Council become a little murkier, and we become a little more out of our depth. But I just won't be governed by fear."

Manni practically spat in mocking laughter. "All you *do* is fear, Layden! You're afraid of not being noticed, but then you're afraid to stand out. You're afraid of disappointing *anyone*, but most of all you're afraid to fail. And do you know why Yuna feels the way she does? Because those fears have made you sabotage every relationship you could've had. You used to be brave, Layden, and strong! I used to believe in you. Before the Council ever thought you were *promising*, I thought you were..." He didn't seem able to finish. His face was flushed, and he looked like he was having trouble swallowing.

Layden looked down and away, unable to escape his words, but unable to acknowledge them, thick, hot emotion constricting her throat. For a while they sat in silence.

Then Layden spoke again, her voice thin and quiet. "I was one of five, Manni. The youngest. No one wanted me around. I was just a pair of working hands to my mother, and I barely knew my father. It wasn't the same for me as it was for you, okay? *Nobody asked for me back*. For a while, I got to have you, and that has meant everything to me. But even that is changing. Soon, I'll have no one. I don't want to have no one—forever." The words escaped without her full permission. "Don't you get it? The Council is my chance at being...someone, to somebody. Forever."

Manni didn't speak for a while as he let her wrestle with her rebel tears and regain composure.

After some time, he stood to his feet. "You know, Layden, for someone with visions, your sight is pretty shoddy."

"What does that mean?" She sniffed, all fight gone from her veins.

His manner had changed as he watched her cry. His voice was soft and sincere, but also distant as the moon. "I truly hope they're everything you need them to be."

Originally, Layden had had it in her mind to talk with each of her team members before their presentations happened at the end of the week. After all, it might be the last chance she got. However, after the way the first two conversations went, she decided to keep to herself. And she wasn't the only one. Tensions were running high.

Their final week of preparation went by quickly and quietly. The morning of the first day of presentations, Layden didn't see Yuna leave, nor did she return at the end of the day.

Mathis was gone the next day, and Abisen left on day three. Layden wanted to speak with Abisen before she left, but Layden was too scared. In her head, the conversation would have gone something like, *Thanks, Layden, you were a good leader, but let's not pretend to be friends.* Even the hypothetical speech hurt.

That night in bed as she cried confused tears, Layden realized she had to let them all go; it surprised her that she'd been holding on.

On the eve of his presentation, Manni and Layden sat in the lounge sharing the rations of their last meal together. It seemed odd not to be working, but there was nothing worth doing at that point. Things were still raw from their earlier confrontation, but when it came down to it, it would take something a lot worse for them to ignore each other that last night.

"I think you were right about one thing," Layden said into the tense silence.

"What?" Manni speared some protein with a fork.

"I don't think I ever truly allowed for the possibility that I might not make it on to the Council. Even now, I'm so close I can taste it, and I've never wanted anything so badly in my life. It's only just becoming real that this time tomorrow I'll know, and they *could* say no. That history even favors that result."

Manni put down his fork gently and looked at her from across the table. His face was unreadable, but his eyes held the tiniest bit of empathy.

"You know, I'm not blind," she continued. "I know you think I am. I get that the Council has made some choices we don't understand, and I'm not ignoring that. The Grand Councilor herself...at one point I wanted nothing but to be like her, but over the last three seasons..."

Layden stopped short of saying what was on her mind. She couldn't go into all she'd learned *and* defend her desire to be with the Council. Maybe that should have been a red flag, but she was too tired to see those things clearly anymore. And too tired to care.

"I guess, in the end, I have faith that they know what they're doing. It's like looking through a keyhole. I can only see what's visible through the keyhole, but they're seeing things with the door wide-open. With the walls knocked down, even. I have to believe the decisions they are making will be justified when the door opens."

"Why do you have to believe that Layden?" he asked in a whisper.

She was quiet for a moment as she looked at his face, his strong jaw and bright eyes. She could almost see Manni's soul peering out from behind those eyes.

"You know, when I was young, my brothers," she began softly, "they were the world to me. Even if they barely gave me the time of day." She shifted in her seat, and a smile came to her lips unbidden. "I remember one day when we were on a deep dive, I almost drowned. I was being stubborn and wanted to finish the dive. I never had before."

"I thought you didn't know how to swim."

Layden couldn't help but laugh. It was a deep, belly laugh that matched the smile spreading across Manni's reluctant face.

"Yeah, well, my oldest brother, Rye, got really mad at me. I thought he was mad that I screwed up the dive. Then, when the others left, he told me I was stupid to risk my life for a bag of dirt." She felt her eyes prickle with tears.

"You were only five," Manni said, no doubt mistaking her tears for hurt.

"It was the first time Rye had ever said anything that indicated I was...worth anything. To anyone."

"Ah," Manni said slowly.

"Before I left for Nyine City, he pulled me aside. Told me that I was the kind of person who would give everything for just about anything I cared about. He told me that was a good thing. I still can see the look in his eye. Like he admired that in me. But he also said...that I had to make sure that the *anything* was worth my everything."

When Manni said nothing, she wiped her eyes and took a shaky breath. "I've given my everything to the Council, Manni, for years. They have to be worth it. They just do. *None* of us have any other choice."

Manni sat back in his chair and let out an almost imperceptible sigh. There were words on his lips and behind his eyes, but she knew he wouldn't say them. After a moment he rubbed his face with his large hands. "Did the Guardian tell you where he went this last time?" he asked quietly.

Layden paused, her heart stopping in her chest. "No. I didn't ask. Wouldn't let him talk, more like."

"I asked him last night. He told me the Council gave the order to bring our families to the city. They're here," he said, shaking his head.

"Safe from the Monsoons. Only a few hundred feet away from this very room."

Layden couldn't say anything to this. Of course, the Guardian went and took care of those in danger from the Monsoons. Why hadn't she put that together? She knew she should be more shocked that her family was in the city this very moment, and she could imagine a part of her that might have once cared. But that part felt distant, even after retelling the story she had. They weren't her family anymore, hadn't been for a long time. All she could feel now was how horribly she'd treated the people who had been there for her in every way that counted.

"Maybe you're right about it all. I mean...just when I think I have the Council figured out..." Manni said, pausing before shaking his head again. "Anyway, good luck during your presentation." He stood to leave. "And if I don't see you again, be safe."

"We'll see each other again," she said, though the words sounded hallow. Those days were over.

"Goodbye, Layden." He turned and walked out without another glance.

CHAPTER TWENTY-SEVEN

M ANNI LEFT EARLY THE next morning to present his ideas to the Council. Layden knew very well that he would be gone that morning, but the reality felt different. Would she see him again? Why hadn't she said more before he left? She didn't know what kind of friends they were at this point, but the space between her ribs that grieved his loss told her that he was important, and that he always would be.

She tried to reassure herself that he would do well, but she didn't even know what he'd been working on. She'd never even thought to ask. She completed her morning ritual in a haze and headed to the labs with the aim of distracting her wandering mind.

Finally, sometime in the afternoon, Layden received a private message on her console telling her to go to the common area. Already weary of tweaking her presentation, she wasted no time in doing so. When she arrived, she found the room empty, so she walked over and poured herself a mug of coffee. As abhorrent as she'd first found the stuff, it had been one of the few luxuries items they'd been allowed, and it had grown on her. As she sat there, sipping from her mug, it occurred to her that it was close to her eighteenth birthday. She and Manni had postured that they would be twenty when they saw their bodies again. If she made it past this last Trial, however, she would get it back a full two seasons earlier than planned. It was a nice thought, but not even this realization could stop her spinning mind.

Finally, the Guardian arrived; she almost knew he was there before she saw him. He had that kind of a presence. Layden's Host was tall, almost as tall as the Guardian, which had been a new perspective, because she was accustomed to being short. No matter her height, though, the Guardian was still the most prominent figure in the room.

"Hello, Layden," he greeted.

Layden gave him a nod and gestured for him to take the adjoining lounge chair near a small coffee table. He did so obligingly but did not recline as she did, rather he sat forward as though ready to stand at any moment. She wondered briefly if she'd ever seen him relaxed.

Yes. She had. Out in the courtyard that one peculiar night, when he had spoken to her like a friend.

"I have come to give you some basic instructions for tomorrow. You are to prepare as you would any other morning. That may seem unnecessary as you will be leaving this Host soon, but it is a day-long showcase. You do not want anything nagging in the back of your mind, something you have left unfinished."

"All right," Layden agreed.

"As soon as you are done in the morning, report to the Council immediately. Do you have much to set up?"

"No, hardly anything at all."

"I see." He seemed a little concerned about that, but he didn't say as much. "Following your presentation, you will adjourn to the side chamber and await the summons from the Councilors. They will take the day to review your project."

"What if it doesn't take them a full day to evaluate?" she asked.

"They will do you the favor of considering every aspect they possibly can. It rarely takes less than a day."

Layden nodded, though her stomach was a pit of nerves. She'd prepared hologram stations displaying recordings of her work at every step so they could see the various procedures she'd done. There wasn't much else to her presentation. Nor was her concept inherently complex. They would either like it, or they wouldn't.

"Is there anything else?" she asked.

"I believe by the end of tomorrow the Council will have their placement recommendations for the five of you. The others have not received their results yet, as the Council prefers to compare candidates to find the best placements."

"Recommendations? That sounds like we have some choice involved," she said.

"Well, yes," he said his words trailing out cautiously. "However, Layden, the Council does not make the recommendations lightly. You would be wise to follow whatever they have planned for you. Do you understand me?"

Layden thought she did, but he was looking at her so pointedly, she wondered if perhaps she didn't.

"I can't imagine a situation where I wouldn't," she said carefully.

"Even if you could, my advice stands."

She thought she could read concern deep within his eyes, but he was veiling it well. Only because she had grown to know him could she sense it. An ominous feeling grew over her.

But in the next moment he stood to his feet and made to leave.

"Guardian," she said, her voice coming out urgently. "Will you be there tomorrow?"

He considered her for a moment and then gave the faintest of grimaces. "No, Layden. I have done my job. Tomorrow is up to you."

"So, this is goodbye," she said, standing as well.

He turned toward her, clasping his hands behind his back, a posture she'd come to know well. He didn't respond but rather looked at her steadily.

"I just mean, I wanted to thank you. I know I haven't been your favorite, and I'm sure you're ready to move on. But you saw us through well. You saw me through well." Layden wanted to hug him, to thank him for everything, the way she hadn't hugged Manni or the others before they'd left. She didn't want to leave things the same way, but she couldn't bring herself to cross that boundary again.

"On the contrary," he said slowly, "you have been one of the most exceptional candidates I have guarded. It has been my honor."

Layden felt that mourning space between her ribs fill briefly with warmth. Such direct and uncurbed praise alone could have lasted her through many winter months. So, she wasn't prepared when the Guardian crossed to her measuredly, his green eyes holding hers unguarded. He offered his hand, and she took it carefully, feeling his fingers fold over hers firmly, then his other hand enclosed over the top. The grasp was not businesslike or obligatory, but warm, intimate. Like a friend.

"Take care, Layden Prier," he said, his voice low.

And, as was his way, he left swiftly.

Layden opened the door to the waiting room and stepped through. She hadn't been able to stop the shaking of her hands the whole time she spoke. It was natural she'd be nervous, but it wasn't just anxiety; she had also felt the adrenaline because she knew, as she spoke, she was doing well. She saw the Grand Councilor's face light up when Layden presented the final product, explaining its test rate at one hundred percent. Herself, Manni, and Mathis had all reported decreased subconscious impulses, an effect that felt much like being on the outside looking in. Her product didn't dull the senses, simply let the person choose more directly how they wanted to act.

She had almost heard the catch in their collective breath.

The door she had exited led to a hallway that wound behind the Meeting Hall, dead ending at a large room. The space within contained a table in the middle, a few lounges, a kitchenette, and some doors that led out the back. As she looked around, one of the doors opened, and a familiar face came through—Abisen.

"Layden!" she exclaimed in surprise before walking across the room to embrace her.

"Is this where you've been this whole time?" Layden asked, looking around. "Where are the others?"

Abisen's smile fell a little, but she called out for the others to join them. "Layden's here!" she said, a measure of relief in her voice. Perhaps the time apart had made them miss her.

Abisen moved to the kitchenette and put a kettle of water on the stove as Mathis and Yuna came out and greeted Layden warmly. Mathis even managed a small smile. That's when it dawned on her.

"Mathis..." she said, surprised. "It's actually you!"

His smile was all relief as he nodded. She felt daft for not realizing immediately, but the others had been transferred back to their own bodies. She couldn't help but notice how light and at peace Mathis was, and she wondered again what exactly had been going on with him that last season. She was about to ask him but thought better of it. She didn't want to muddy the joy in the air with a murky topic. Another time maybe.

"How soon after did they give your bodies back?" Layden asked.

"Not too long. I think most of us went the next day," Abisen said, pouring some mugs of tea for everyone.

"I think the lab techs knew we wouldn't be able to sustain our previous lifestyle here in this *bunker*," Mathis said. He grabbed his mug and took a seat with the others around a coffee table, then he opened a small box at its center.

Layden peered down at a stack of assorted cookies, their fragrance wafting out and almost making her swoon. She couldn't remember the last time she'd had sugar. It was a rare treat as it was, but once the Trials began, whatever small amount they'd been given had ceased. Should she indulge? In the back of her mind, she was still too concerned about the body of her Host. Would she get another chance, though? Probably not...still, she'd better wait.

"Where's Manni?" she asked. "Is he at his Transfer now?"

The three exchanged looks, and Yuna and Mathis busied themselves with selecting their cookie.

Abisen, however, set her mug on the table and gazed at Layden steadily. "Manni never showed," she broke the news quietly.

Layden glanced at the others. "What do you mean?" she asked, though she knew exactly what Abisen meant. "The Guardian told me the Council wouldn't make their decisions till we'd all made our presentations."

"We thought at first...well, if you didn't show up either, there was a chance that maybe the Council had offered the two of you a placement, but not us three." Abisen finished, dropping her eyes to the floor.

Layden suddenly understood their excitement upon seeing her. Her stomach flipped, and panic rose in her chest.

"Layden, before you let your mind go there, the truth is we really don't know what the Council does during this time. Anything could have happened. Including something good," Abisen said. But her voice wavered, and she quickly stood and made herself busy elsewhere.

Layden knew she wasn't the only one who cared about Manni, but at that moment, she also realized that he was the only one who truly cared about her. She couldn't lose him now. Not after how they'd left things. She just couldn't.

The problem was, she was completely powerless to do anything about it.

A short while later, Layden was summoned to return to her body. Like Mathis had predicted, the Council didn't want Layden to ruin her Host in a place with the most basic provisions. So, regardless of the outcomes, Layden would at least have her own body for the day. Exhilarating as that was, Layden felt weak as she made her way back to their lounge room after the Transfer. She'd been hoping to see Manni somewhere along the way, or even to be escorted by the Guardian who might know something about where he was. Alas, she'd seen no one.

There'd been an immediate lightening upon returning to her body, though she'd have to readjust to more changes yet again. Thankfully, she seemed to have left behind the neurosis concerning the care of her Host body. That change was a relief.

"Welcome back," Mathis said with a small smile.

"You missed a message while you were gone. They've begun to summon us for their conclusions, and if we're lucky, our assignment. Yuna's already gone through," Abisen said.

"Did they say anything about Manni?" she asked.

She couldn't not ask, but Abisen shook her head.

"So, we wait?" Layden sat down at the small table again.

Mathis nodded gravely.

Layden supposed she was becoming used to the waiting. At least she'd be able to enjoy a cookie.

Eventually, Layden was, again, the last one in the room. It quickly grew stale without company within it. Thankfully, she didn't have to wait long in the silence—the Council, once their minds were made up, seemed relatively quick in delivering their verdict. A couple of stone-faced men wearing the dark blue garb of the Defense League escorted Layden down the hallway and into the Meeting Hall. She'd never met a member of the Defense League and didn't know what it meant for them to be there now.

Layden took a breath and prepared herself for the Council. They were already seated when she entered and watching her with attentive expressions. Even in her anxious state, she noticed that one seat, toward the end, was empty.

"Layden Prier." The Grand Councilor welcomed her with a large, perfect-toothed grin.

Layden did a small bow.

"I trust you are feeling well. How did your body fare this last season away from you?"

It was an odd question if one thought about it, but not for the life she led.

"It was well taken care of and seems to be in good shape," she said graciously.

"Good. Good. It appears healthy. A little exercise and we'll have it in tip-top shape."

Layden didn't have anything to say to that, so she simply glanced down the row of Council members, unable to conceal her unease.

"Layden, is everything all right?" the Grand Councilor asked.

What a question.

"Yes, of course," she began. "I just...where is Emmanuel? None of us have seen him."

The Councilor's smile faded slightly. "Emmanuel Prier," the Councilor answered softly, "gave us reason to doubt he'd be a safe addition our ranks."

"What do you mean, safe? He's not dangerous—I've never trusted anyone more," Layden blurted out, alarmed.

"There were questions about his loyalties over the course of his Trials," the Councilor answered carefully but firmly.

Layden wanted to protest, but she couldn't. She knew Manni's propensity for doubting the Council better than anyone, the times he'd asked her to leave, his attempts at tampering with their security system. And yet, why would the Council have brought him along this far if they'd had doubts about him? Layden wanted to ask, but her jaw was stiff with fear.

"But not you, Layden," the Grand Councilor moved on without a pause. "You have always displayed the utmost perseverance of loyalty in the face of challenging concepts. Perhaps even information that disturbed you?"

"What do you mean?" Layden managed, fighting a welling up of tears.

"Your Guardian was in the habit of sharing things with you he probably shouldn't have. Rather than stopping him, we decided to use it to gauge your loyalty. And you never gave us a moment's doubt. To have doubted a little would have been human, but we never sensed resistance or hesitation on your part. This kind of loyalty is a trait we do not see often, but which we have come to highly value. Your trust. Your faith. Tell me, Layden, are you still receiving visions?"

Layden's brain barely followed the topic change, but after a moment she nodded. Her mind was racing furiously. She didn't want to talk about her visions; she wanted to know more about Manni. And was the Guardian in trouble too? She heard the other Council members murmur, and a few gave approving smiles.

"Well then, I believe congratulations are in order," the Councilor said with her low and officially smooth voice, "to the first person to succeed the Trials in fifty years."

Layden's blood ran cold in an instant.

In another situation, she might have been excited, elated, or relieved to hear these words. But she wasn't. In addition to the news about Manni, these were the very words that had started her vision.

"We are sorry you are the only of your group to make it to where you stand. However, we've seen you keep your distance and think you've been wise. You will be able to brave the separation better because of it. Now before we continue, there is one last choice you must make. Your last 'Trial' as it were. You see, in order to offer you a place among us, we must lift the veil completely. Are you ready?"

Layden knew these words well. She had heard them repeatedly as her vision replayed itself, but she'd never made it past them. A rush of revelation overtook her as she realized the visions *were* about her, and they *were* of the future.

She also knew now that she was not the ambitious monster she'd seen all those nights ago, for the coldness in her heart at that moment—the moment she'd loathed and feared— was not callousness for her friends' fate, but a steely resolve that got in the way of her feeling anything else.

"Yes, Grand Councilor. I am ready," she said.

Chapter twenty-eight

T HE GRAND COUNCILOR SMILED. "Your concept on suppressing subconscious impulses—the instinctual tendencies
that cause us to act outside of our own character—did that concept
arise within the Trials?"

"Yes, ma'am."

"From experiences you had?" she asked.

Layden nodded.

"I thought so. Well, Layden, it is customary to ask you to do
one last thing for us, before we move any further. You see, we, too,
experience those impulses."

Layden was nonplused. "Yes, ma'am. We all do. It's our nature,"
she said reassuringly. She hadn't expected the Council to have risen
above such impulses, which is why she knew they would like her
thesis.

"However, this is not human nature, Layden. At least, not in the
basic sense of the term. The feelings you targeted in your studies are
something completely different. And I must admit, this particular
issue has been a problem among the Council for a long while. It
seems you have inadvertently solved that problem, for which we are
resoundingly grateful."

Several Council members nodded emphatically and murmured
among themselves.

Layden was confused and no longer completely following. In the back of her mind, she had a powerful desire to find the Guardian and Manni with an urgency that was hard to ignore.

"Up until this moment, I thought perhaps it had been your intent all along to solve this problem for us. After all, we know that your Guardian shared with you how the nine of us still live indefinitely within a Host of our own."

Layden jolted back to attention. She was surprised the Councilor would bring that up. In what way was Layden's suppressant related to that horrible fact?

"Perhaps he shared more with you?" The Councilor tested tentatively. Layden's puzzled face seemed to be her answer. "Never the matter. I will not beat around the metaphorical bush anymore," she said with a slow, stretching grin. "Layden. The impulses you've experienced are not subconscious impulses of the primitive mind. Rather, they are the subconscious impulses of the mind of your Host."

Layden stared blankly. What had she just said? The subconscious impulses... "My...my Host?" Layden stammered.

"Surely, you must have wondered where the mind of the Host goes when you are occupying its body. The answer is that it doesn't."

"It doesn't what?" Layden said, feeling foggy-brained and thick tongued.

"It doesn't go anywhere. It reverts to a specific part of the brain that had, up until our creation of the Generational experiments, been largely unused. The mind of a Host can exist there in a dream-like state for a time, safe from degeneration. The impulses you felt—the hopelessness, the competitive drive you mentioned, the neuroses—they have existed within the perimeters of each Generational level—the Seventies, Fifties, Thirties—because they belonged to your Host. Not to you."

Layden stumbled backward a few steps. It felt like someone had shoved her head underwater and she couldn't breathe. "I don't understand. We all felt that way. It wasn't just me," she protested.

"We select specific personality types for each Generation. Each is meant to give you a different mindset, a unique perspective. Ones we learned from dearly and at great cost through our years of discovery. Self-reliance and independence, an uncompromising desire to excel, the pursuit of perfection. True, you all might have felt a nuance of these mindsets; people are not cookie cutters. However, the themes were similar."

"Why...?" was all Layden could get out. She didn't want to know more, but she had to.

The Councilor seemed patient. "At each Transfer, did you not feel a piece of your last experience come with you?"

The question seemed rhetorical, so Layden concentrated on remaining standing instead of answering.

"This is why we made sure you returned to your own body in between each Generation, so you could retain those perspectives for your future self. So they could shape your identity. In this way, you become more than just you. You become you, and Mairi. And Deena. And Jocelyn."

The sound of those names on her ears was almost too much to bear. It had been hard enough to see her first Host walking and talking before the Transfer, but to learn that she'd been alive within Layden's mind the entire time was mortifying. And the other women, with names and personalities, shoved to the back of their own minds while a stranger took command for months and months...

"Did they know...were they aware of what I was doing and thinking and saying?" Layden asked frantically. She could imagine how violated they felt, but she felt just as much so.

"The mind lives in that section of the brain in a kind of stasis, as I mentioned earlier."

"So, it's like they're asleep the whole time?"

"Yes and no. The longer a body is a Host, the more likely the mind of the Host will...wake up...so to speak. First, the personality changes and intrusive thoughts are small, and the automatic reflexes of the subconscious, minimal. With a fully awake mind, however, well, there's no need to explain to you how two minds competing for the same space can be extremely uncomfortable. Your friend Mathis knows a little bit about this."

Layden was only half-processing the Councilor's words, but as she did, something horrible occurred to her. "Wait, you've all been within your Hosts for...decades! How can you possibly—?"

"How can we live this way?" the Councilor preempted.

Not exactly. Layden's sympathy wasn't exactly for the Council.

"We discovered the hard way that most subconscious minds will rebel eventually. This makes it hard to function, to hear your own thoughts; to distinguish what is yours and what is theirs. We have been calling these moments *occurrences*, rather than conflict, in respect of the original Host mind. However, at this point in time, living with these rebellious impulses has been our most difficult struggle. The more practiced the Host mind gets at sending signals, the more dangerous those thoughts can become. You may have noticed we are short a member today. Our dear Henry recently took his own life at the promptings of his Host."

Why was the Councilor telling Layden all of this? She could not take a seat on the Council if it meant she'd have to live within a Host's body forever. And why would she need to? She had her own now. What was the point of all this revelation?

"Thus, we found that a *willing* Host was necessary."

"Willing," Layden found herself repeating.

"Yes, Layden. You once asked your Guardian what the Council looked for above all in its candidates. Sadly, so many have fallen to the wayside because they lacked this one crucial quality."

Layden looked between all the faces that stared at her.

"Loyalty."

"Loyalty?" Layden asked. She felt like a parrot repeating back the words of the Councilor, but she had none of her own.

"Yes, Layden. And without knowing it, you—above everyone else we've ever watched—have proved yourself loyal to us repeatedly. There were times when we thought your loyalty to others might overshadow your pursuit of this call, but you've always chosen us. You understand us. Now, Layden, we choose you. I choose you."

"I don't understand," Layden said, feeling lightheaded.

"It's a wonderful thing really, because when you join me, I will receive your visions. I wasn't sure they'd transfer from Mairi, but we hoped. What a valuable tool you are adding to our governing powers, and you will not go unrewarded. The name Layden of den Prier will go down in history. Your sacrifice, your gift, your honor. It will be you who rules with a mighty and selfless hand. For no one but any of us will know any differently."

"But I won't....it won't be me," Layden said emphatically.

"No, Layden, it will be better than you. It will be us. You and me and pieces of the lives you have touched during the Trials. Mairi, Deena, Jocelyn."

Layden swayed on the spot, but someone from behind came to steady her.

"Please, take a seat. We have given you a lot to think on."

Layden sat in the chair that had been provided for her and drank from the glass of water given. She did so in a fog. She needed time to think, but her head swam. What could she do? She couldn't imagine a lifetime of being enslaved in her own mind. How could anyone be called to be a *willing* Host? Then again, the Councilor had said Layden had a choice, hadn't she? Layden *did* have to be willing. If she wasn't willing, would they let her go?

"Where are the others?" she croaked out.

"You don't need to be concerned with them. You will see them soon enough," she answered.

Layden didn't know what that meant, but it didn't matter. She knew one thing, and she knew it with absolute certainty. In the face of being offered what she'd always desired, she had come to find that the dream was a nightmare. This was *not* what she had meant when she talked of living as one of the Council forever. It was no longer a mystery why there had been no others added to the Council since its initial change in leadership. No one in their right mind would agree to this! She was sure her friends wouldn't have either. If they couldn't make it past the Trials, then neither would she. She stood to her feet.

"Yes, Layden? Have you something to say?"

"I've made my decision," she said as strongly as she could.

The Grand Councilor did not respond, her eyebrows rising mildly.

"I am sorry, but I cannot be the Host you want. Loyalty or not, I am unable to choose a path that leads to enslavement. You may have judged my character correctly; I am loyal, I do feel I understand you, and I do want to belong more than anything else. But you have also misjudged me. I am not spineless, nor am I without a place to belong. I may have been blind to it before, but in the face of what it is *not*, I see it clear as day now."

There was complete silence in the hall. The faces of the Council members looked unimpressed, stoic, and the Grand Councilor's smile faded, though only slightly, its shadow remaining in its place.

Layden felt uneasiness steel over her again.

"Oh, Layden," she said quietly, "you always had a way with your small speeches. However, that is not the choice you have to make."

Layden's blood ran cold. "You said the Host had to be willing. I'm not willing."

"Not yet. I believe you'll feel different, however, when you learn that your friend, Emmanuel, is on schedule to be Sectioned. I know you are familiar with this term, but I will explain clearly," the Councilor continued, her voice no longer gentle. "His mind will be taken from his body, boxed up, in a fashion, and sent where all other troublesome persons go. People who know too much. People who cannot be trusted. You see, the body has a kind of loyalty to its mind. Without the mind, the body isn't even fit to be a Host. In this day in age, it's such a waste to destroy a body, though, so, we keep them stored, in case we find a way around that."

Layden sank to the ground and gagged violently. She probably would have thrown up if she'd had anything real in her stomach. "He did nothing wrong! How could you do something so monstrous?" she yelled at them.

"That is your choice, Layden," the Councilor continued unaffected. "Agree to be my willing Host, and instead of a formless, restless, dreamless eternity, he will live out a life of menial labor, having only to serve his term as a Host like the rest of the failed candidates."

"I don't understand! You said you couldn't trust him," Layden countered, reeling from all this information, things she'd been desperate to know for a full three seasons. Now she wished she didn't know any of it.

"Your suppressant will take care of any rebelliousness, especially if it's only for a season."

"But *why*?" she cried out again. "Why do you need me to be willing if you will use the suppressant on me anyway?"

"Because you are far too valuable to risk losing, Layden Prier. You have solved a problem for most of the Council—and your friends will be the first wave of test subjects for long-term use of your suppressant; we can no longer wait around for the willing. However, your visions could be the key we've always needed to solidify our rule and ensure the future of humanity—for we will be able to *see* the future. It's very possible that to retain your visions, I may not be able to use the suppressant. It's a risk I can't take."

Layden sat before them, her body shaking with anger, sobs rolling out when she could not stifle them anymore. Had this been what the Guardian meant? He had told her to make sure she knew what she was doing. But there was no way she could have known. She'd handed the Council a tool that would keep this practice thriving for years to come.

No, surely, he couldn't have known the scope of this horror. After all, he had told her it would be wise to do whatever the Council suggested for her. There was no way he would ask her to do this if he'd known.

And yet, none of that mattered. She had to make a choice. A lifetime of her enslavement, or a lifetime of Manni's.

Finally, she stood, shaking all the way up. She managed to look the Grand Councilor in the eye. "Very well," she uttered with as much disgust as she could manage. "You have your *willing* Host."

The Councilor's smile returned.

Even though Layden had agreed to be willing—as willing as she could be—she was immediately seized gruffly by the two men from the Defense League who had been standing by. So that was what they were there for. Their fingers gripped her shoulders so tightly she had to fight crying out in pain. They lifted her off her feet and began carrying her out of the room. Was it happening now? No! She wasn't ready!

"Will you let him go?" she yelled back at the Councilor. "Please, just let him go!"

The Councilor's expression did not change as the men carried Layden through the doors and around the corner.

"Stop, please!" she shouted at the men carrying her, but they didn't pay her any mind. While her body had grown, she was still small and weak, her withered muscles nothing against the brawn of the Defense League.

Soon enough, too soon, she was in the Transfer chamber. She'd just been there not hours ago, back when she had no idea what was ahead of her. Back when she didn't know the true horrors of the Council. The men set her down and headed for the door without so much as a word.

"Please!" she said rushing behind them. They turned and closed the door in her face before she could reach them and locked it behind them. Layden sank to the ground with a sob, then sat there unmoving.

"I'm so sorry," she cried helplessly.

She didn't know who she spoke to, only she knew she held the names of the people she had violated in her mind. Had she known their minds were present the whole time, she never would have... But was that true? It's very possible she still would have. She'd already done many things to win the Council's approval. If she had learned this at the beginning of the Trials, she might not have even cared.

Well, she *did* care now. A resolve overcame her, and she stood up, looking around for something, anything. They'd regret leaving her alone. She found a sharp needle on one of the tables next to a small vial. She didn't know what was in it, nor did she know if it was enough, but she filled the syringe as full as it would go. She'd have to risk it. If she couldn't take the Councilor down, she'd take herself out of the picture.

Layden stopped in her tracks. What about Manni? If she took her own life, they would *section* him. She let out a roar of frustration. She couldn't do that to him! She would have to make this weapon count in another way. She moved to the door and stood beside it, waiting for the Councilor to enter. Where would be the most effective place to take her down? The neck...? Layden shuddered at the thought. Could she do this?

She heard footsteps approaching.

I'm not ready!

Yes, you are, a small whisper answered.

The door opened, and Layden swung around immediately, aiming the needle upward toward what she estimated was the height of the Councilor's neck. But her arm was blocked immediately by a strong hand. She was aiming at the wrong part of the body, as the man before her stood taller than the Councilor.

"Guardian!" Layden rasped out in frantic relief, collapsing against his chest. "Help me! Please, help me! Get me out of here."

He caught her as she crumpled again and took the needle gently out of her hand. Then he moved her over to a chair and sat her down. She clung to him like a child, crying and shaking. His scent of earth and course soap acted like a balm to her nerves. She was so relieved to see him, but she knew she wasn't out of danger yet.

"Please, you have to save Manni! They're going to section him—you have to help! You have to find him!"

"Emmanuel is safe," the Guardian said without looking at her.

Relief flooded her. The Grand Councilor had kept her part of the deal. "Please, Guardian, we have to leave," she said weakly.

The Guardian leaned back and lifted the syringe up to the light, staring at it closely. His expression became alarmed. "This is far too much, Layden. You could have killed someone."

"That was the *idea*," she said urgently. "Please, let's get out of here."
A cold fear was beginning to wash over her again. Why wasn't he mov-

ing? Why wasn't he rushing her out? He couldn't possibly be helping them, could he? Surely, he didn't know about the Hosts, that had to be it. That's why he'd always felt on a different side from the Council. He had been. He didn't know what was happening. Right?

Or did he? Why did she believe so strongly that he would save her? She'd been wrong about so much else today. Did she even know him at all?

Yes, you do, the voice within her whispered. *You do know him.*

So then why was he releasing some of the serum back into the vial and approaching her with the syringe? Why wouldn't he look at her?

"What are you doing," she asked, recoiling as he came closer.

"Trust me. This will help." He grabbed her arm and inserted the needle before she had a chance to pull away. His hands were very practiced. The pinch came and a rush of cold flowed through her veins. The room began to fog and sway. She felt the Guardian lift her up and move her to the chamber on the left.

No! She screamed in her mind, but she couldn't talk. Or move or think.

"That's it, just relax," he said gently, setting her in the chamber. He strapped her in and closed the door.

She could still see, but a black fog was growing from the corners of her mind, closing in on her view. The Grand Councilor walked in. The Guardian greeted her with a small bow. A kiss on her hand. The Councilor smiled and took off her outer robe. She walked gracefully to the chambers. Layden could hear her stepping in. This was unbearable. She screamed at the Guardian in her mind. *Traitor! Monster! Liar!*

Then she heard the rustling as the Guardian attached the wires to the Councilor, and a hum as the machine switched on.

It was in that moment that Layden realized she had no wires attached to her own head. Nothing set up at all—just the straps to hold her in place. The black was closing in, but Layden fought it. It was her last view with her own eyes, her own toes against the cold metal beneath her. Her last breath with her own lungs. The black finished its work, and she saw nothing. It was over.

CHAPTER TWENTY-NINE

L AYDEN PRIER WAS CRAWLING out of her skin, knowing she
was no longer alone in her body.

It was strange to be awake but have no control. Paralyzed within
your own form. Where was she? Rather, where were *they*? The Grand
Councilor was lying down, in Layden's body, on something soft,
but the room was dark and dingy. It smelled damp. The Councilor
was awake surely—for Layden could see out her eyes—but she didn't
hear any thoughts. She didn't hear the Councilor's voice, or even feel
her move. How did this work exactly? Layden hadn't expected to be
so present... How much time had passed?

Someone was coming into the room. The Councilor moved her
eyes reflexively to the door to see who it was.

"Manni?" Layden heard her voice speak. Her voice, surely commanded by the Councilor.

Then again, no, it had been her thought too. Her voice and her
thought.

"Layden!" Manni said, rushing over and kneeling at her side. He
lifted her up by her shoulders and hugged her closely.

Layden was overcome with confusion at first and then wild,
mad, uncontrolled elation. The Councilor was not with her at all!
She alone possessed her body, and she commanded it herself.

"Manni?" she said again, gathering him further into a hysterical embrace. Her body shook from head to toe, and deep sobs escaped her throat as she tried to stand. "What happened? Where am I?"

"Hold on, the drug you were given was a paralytic. You'll be a bit groggy for a while."

Layden leaned back.

"You're safe. We're in the Telling Tower," Manni explained.

"The Telling Tower?"

"Hello, Layden." A tall, gangly man with dirty blonde hair entered the room. He looked familiar, but she didn't know why. He walked over and helped her stand. "I'm Tobias," he said offering a hand. "You're safe."

"So everyone keeps saying," Layden said, unconvinced. Who was this man? His clothes were strange. There was a lot of equipment attached to them, almost like the vests they wore during their year Fifties training.

"What's going on?" she asked forcefully.

"Would you like something hot to drink?" Tobias led her to the next room, Manni helping to half-carry her over to a small, makeshift firepit. There was a woman stirring something in a pot above the fire. She gave a smile, then turned to the side, poured a cup of something, and offered it to Layden. Layden took it as Manni helped her sit.

"Welcome, Layden," the woman said. "It's so good to see you again. You've grown into an exceptionally beautiful young woman."

Layden squinted in confusion. "I'm sorry? We've met?"

The woman laughed and looked at Manni. "I thought you said she had a good memory, Manni."

Manni smiled and shrugged.

"You were young, I'll give you that," the woman said.

Layden wracked her brain. She hadn't seen them in years, but she had always assumed she'd recognize them when she did. "You're not my...?"

"Your parents?" the woman finished. "No, Layden. I'm sorry."

"Then, who?" she asked.

"Drink up. We'll explain everything when he gets here."

"When who gets here?"

No one answered her. The woman busied herself with the pot, and Tobias began to organize some things at the crude, wooden desk in the corner. Layden glanced down at her drink and took a sip. It was hot and herbal-tasting, like roots, and felt good on her throat, which was hoarse from all her screaming. She shuddered at the memory.

She'd made it out, but how? Was this all a dream? Was she doomed to wake and find herself in the Councilor's control?

You're safe, a voice repeated in her heart. *You too*? she muttered to the whisper, failing to believe even its steady reassurance.

"He's here!" Tobias said.

Layden heard footsteps beneath them ascending the steps of stairs unseen, until finally a man appeared in the door frame.

Layden recoiled instantly, spilling her drink. "No! Get away from me, you *monster*!" she yelled, standing up and backing away.

"Layden, calm down," Manni said, rising quickly. He reached out and held her still, as she frantically tried to get away. "Jeremiah got you out! He got us both out."

It took Layden a second to process what Manni said as their Guardian stood at the door, clearly on edge and waiting for her permission to enter. Jeremiah. That was his name; she remembered the Councilor calling him that. How he had helped her, though, she couldn't recall. All she remembered was that he had drugged her, loaded her into the chamber, and...

And what?

Nothing. She'd woken up here, with friendly faces, known and unknown, telling her repeatedly that she was safe.

Of course, the Guardian had helped. There was no other way.

"I'm sorry..." she trailed off. She sat back down, shaking slightly.

"It's all right, dear. Have some more, it'll calm the nerves," the woman said, pouring Layden another mug of tea. "Jeremiah, please come in. The food is just about done."

"Thank you, Connie. I am not hungry. Tobias, may I have a word with you?" the Guardian said.

Tobias nodded, and the two of them moved to the back room and began talking in urgent voices.

"Well," the woman named Connie said, ladling out some stew from the pot. Her eyes followed the men, but she kept any worry out of her voice. "We might as well eat."

Layden crossed her arms and clenched her jaw. Why would no one tell her what was going on? She wasn't a child. She was nearly eighteen seasons and had been through enough to be treated like an adult. The woman seemed to sense Layden's impatience.

"You truly don't remember me?" she asked.

Layden surveyed the face again. She shook her head.

"Well, I was younger," Connie said, a bit self-consciously. "My hair was lighter. Not as light as Constance's, of course. No one knows where she got that hair."

"Constance?" Layden sat up straight.

"These are her parents, Layden," Manni said. "They came to get her back that night. I know you remember that night."

"I don't remember you being there," Layden said to Connie.

"You don't remember me there either, do you?" Manni asked.

Layden turned to him, confused by the question.

"I was there too," he clarified.

"No, I don't remember that," she said quietly.

"These people said they'd be back for us," Manni said.

"There will be plenty of time to explain all that later," Connie said, giving him a staying look.

Layden accepted a bowl of the stew and took a few tentative bites. Even in their makeshift surroundings, it was better than any food she was used to.

Tobias reentered the room, the Guardian on his heels.

"We move out within the hour. If we leave now, we'll raise suspicions, but it's unwise to wait longer than that," Tobias said.

Layden watched as her Guardian ducked his tall frame back through the door. She knew he had saved her, but for several horrible moments, she'd believed he'd betrayed her in the worst way. Unfortunately, that feeling lingered.

"Why don't you go get some rest, Layden. You have been through a lot, and I'm afraid the journey won't be a short one," Tobias said.

"Where are we going?" Layden asked, hoping to be answered this time.

"Somewhere remote, where the Council won't be able to find you," Connie answered.

"For now," Tobias said.

Connie threw him a sharp look. "Go on, Layden." she said, taking Layden's bowl from her. "Go lie down. The blankets are clean and warm."

Layden stood and did as she was told. She had many more questions, but she knew they weren't going to be answered, not now anyway. She settled down onto the small pile of blankets in the next room and closed her eyes. She *was* tired. Every limb ached. Her new party's voices echoed in the next room, bringing her a strange, nostalgic comfort as she pulled a quilt up to her chin.

"Layden," a voice spoke into the darkness.

Layden opened her eyes again and saw the Guardian.

"I need to speak with you a moment before you sleep. If I may?" He moved forward, pulled a chair from the corner of the room, and sat in it.

Layden propped herself up on her elbow.

"I owe you an apology," he said, his voice low and quiet.

"You saved my life...apparently. I can only be grateful," she said, though, in truth, she felt owed one as well.

"I am sorry I couldn't explain what was happening at the time," he said, meeting her eyes directly. It was the most direct look he'd ever given her, actually, and he seemed different now, outside the confines of the compound. Even his rhythm of speech seemed more relaxed, as though he wasn't holding back a myriad of words. "I wanted to, many times. But for obvious reasons..."

"You've been with these people the whole time, haven't you?" Layden asked.

There was a small pause. "Yes."

Layden broke his gaze and looked at the wall, her jaw clenching in frustration. She understood why he'd had to lie, and honestly who was she to deserve the truth? She probably would have ratted him out had she known. Still, it felt like a betrayal.

The Guardian exhaled quietly. "I am sure you have questions, and I promise to answer them all on the journey. It will take several weeks. For now, you should rest."

Layden didn't respond. Now matter how she felt about him, the threat of the Councilor was still fresh on her mind; she didn't care where they went, or how long it took. "Well. Thank you for getting us out."

He took in her words and nodded briefly, then he stood to leave.

"Guardian," she said to keep him there. As conflicted as her feelings were, she didn't want him to leave.

"Please, it's Jeremiah. I am no longer your Guardian."

"Were we able to get the others?"

"Others?"

"Yuna, Mathis, and Abisen?" she asked.

The Guardian shifted and glanced around the room. "Unfortunately, they'd been taken to an area I didn't have access to. For the plan with the Councilor to work, I needed to play my part to the very end."

Layden felt the heat drain from her face. "But the Grand Councilor is going to use my suppressant on them and make them Hosts to the Council. I can't let that happen!"

"I know you feel responsible. I wanted to stop your research. However, our plans were based on you making it through to the end. I knew what you had stumbled upon would more than ensure that. So, I allowed it. I am more responsible than you."

"What are we going to do?" she asked. "We have to go back in."

"We need to regroup. Recuperate. You need to get stronger; your muscles have atrophied again and are unused to you. If our plan works, we may be able to save them. At the very least, their sacrifice will not have been in vain, and we can stop this from happening to many, many others. Now, please, rest up. We leave soon." The Guardian stood and left the room before she could stop him with another question.

Layden laid back down on the blankets and tried to go to sleep but the faces of her friends hovered in her mind's eye and tormented her.

Her friends. She would make it her mission to save them, if it was the last thing she did. At that moment, Manni walked in and crossed to a mat in the opposite corner of the room, then settled in. He probably thought she was sleeping, which she desperately wanted to be, but couldn't.

"How long did you know?" she asked into the silence.

"Since Constance," the answer came back.

"Why didn't you ever say anything?" She tried to stop the emotion from choking out her voice.

"I was told not to. We both were. Not even to each other. I thought that would be difficult, but you didn't seem to remember anything afterward. It was like you blocked it all out. There were a couple of times, during the Trials, when I thought that maybe you knew. That I only had to make a move bold enough, and you'd admit you'd known all along. But I was always disappointed."

"I was a coward. I was protecting myself even back then," she said, disgusted.

"No. You were a young girl, Layden. You're not responsible for that."

She was, however, responsible for Yuna, Mathis, and Abisen. She'd been saved from that horrible fate, but they hadn't. It was almost unbearable.

There was a silence for a while and Layden thought Manni had fallen asleep. Until he spoke again. "The Council told me what they were going to do to me. Told me I had one hope of salvation."

"Manni, don't," she said quietly.

She didn't want to talk about it. She didn't want gratitude. She didn't deserve any.

"I knew you would choose me. I hoped you wouldn't, but I knew you would."

"You did?"

"Yeah," he said.

There was more silence. Then he whispered, "Because you give everything for the things you care about."

EPILOGUE

T HE NIGHT AIR WAS crisp on his skin, and the wind burrowed into his bones. He looked across the deck at the young woman standing at the bow. She clung to a blanket wrapped thick around her shoulders and gazed out into the black water as though she could see in the dark. Her hair had grown long, and her body frail in stasis, but she stood with a command unique to the young woman. Not a girl anymore. Maybe not as old as he, no, but full of as much heartache. Full of as much inner conflict. And as many secrets.

She had better be worth it.

The Commission believed she was. Worth leaving the others behind in the hope that eventually, they could stop treating the symptoms of the Council and eradicate the disease. Emmanuel—while biasedly close—had been convinced that, when presented with the truth, Layden would make the right choice. And to his credit, she had. But Jeremiah had never been so sure.

She was a peculiar one. At times, maddeningly bold and brash, at others, unbelievably weak and soft. Both moods often manifesting at precisely the wrong times. He had feared for them in those moments, knowing more than any of them, just how tormented she could be. But then that boldness would surface; the flash of outrage and alarm he'd watch her quell many times in an attempt to please the Council. To please him. And a still, quiet whisper would remind him that there was One in higher control than even the Commission. That there were things

Jeremiah didn't understand, and that he was wrong to doubt them. His hand palmed the small green book tucked in his cloak. He'd managed to rescue it and wondered if now was the time to return it. But he had a feeling it would be too much at the moment.

Then again, even now she seemed to bear all the change, the news, the revelations with an eerie calm he hadn't expected, or understood. What he'd give to know what she was thinking at that moment. Did she fear? Did she still wrestle with her old loyalty to the Council? Would she compromise them all, everything they'd done? They'd waited years for this opportunity, needing to time it exactly right so it corresponded with the night Layden was summoned before the Council—and yet, she could undo it all in the next hour if she wanted.

The ship they were commandeering was already approved for departure to the Outlayers with its first shipment of the new bio-engineered produce, but it wasn't supposed to leave for another hour. So, they'd have to wait it out to avoid suspicion. Still, it was a much better cover than the one they'd had before Yuna dazzled the Council with her genetic botany and humanitarian spirit.

His heart froze at the thought of her. And the others. His orders had always been to retrieve Layden and Emmanuel only, but that decision had a high cost. Three more lost, and to an even more harrowing fate than many others. Yuna, Mathis, Abisen…they weren't banished to slave labor in labs, greenhouses, or the underwater piping, awaiting their time to Host. Nor were they Sectioned—their minds separated and cut off from their physical form—a still doom leading to sure madness. No. They were permanent Hosts now, to the Council, with no guarantee of freedom until their bodies perished. Some thought Sectioning was worse, but Jeremiah was not so sure.

Pushing violent memories to the back of his mind, he drew in a deep breath of fresh sea air—his last for at least two days, as he'd be stowed away with the rest of them. It wouldn't take long for them to find the Councilor in her unconscious state and once they did, there'd be no hiding that he'd been the one to betray her. His life would be just as wanted as Layden's.

Go. Speak with her.

"No," Jeremiah answered the persistent nudge in his breast, "I've nothing to say."

She is not to blame, it persisted.

Jeremiah paused and with a steely look in his eyes, obeyed. He walked forward a few steps, coming up behind Layden, but she didn't hear him among the buckle of the ship against the docks.

"You shouldn't be out in such plain sight," he said.

He couldn't help his officious tones. He still felt responsible for her in many ways. She didn't startle, but he could tell by the rigidity of her shoulders that he had surprised her.

"And you shouldn't sneak up on people," she said quietly. There was a coolness in her voice, and while it didn't waver, when she turned and glanced his way, he saw a thorough account of her feelings within. Anger, trauma, fear. Anger. He supposed he didn't need to read her mind after all, being he'd always been able to read her face.

Jeremiah shifted under the weight of her gaze and moved beside her as she returned her stare to the water. He could see by moonlight, her harsh profile, a drawn brow, the muscles of her jaw tensing in restraint.

They stood in silence for a moment, contemplating...too much? Nothing? The vast briny deep? She'd never seen real land, he thought to himself. This glassy surface of water was all she'd ever known. All she'd ever seen. She couldn't possibly understand what she was missing, but he pitied her all the same.

Layden was grown and raised by the Council. In their houses. In their school. It was only natural that she'd regard them as her only chance at belonging. Her only home. For her to have chosen, even indirectly, what she did, meant she'd been shaken to her very core. Her entire world view had been thrown to the winds in one, traumatizing, moment.

A hatred deepened in his heart.

It does not help to hate them. It clouds your view.

"My view is fine." Jeremiah said crisply.

Layden looked over at him and he received her unsure eyes, realizing he had spoken aloud.

"Yes. Mine too," she said, carefully, "though winter is knocking."

She gathered her blanket closer around her. He resisted his reflex to comfort her and instead watched her shiver.

"We had better get you underdeck. There's no telling when they will be alerted to what we've done. We leave within the half hour," he said, turning away abruptly.

"Guardian?" she asked.

He turned back to see the fear he'd wondered about, plain as day on her face. He found himself hoping again that she was what they all needed, but this time for entirely different reasons.

"Come," he said, taking her by the elbow and leading her away, "our journey begins."

Samantha Rae Ortiz is the author of *Behind the Veil*, and the Whispers of Eden Series.

She lives in Albuquerque, New Mexico and when she's not writing (editing, marketing or publishing!), you can find her reading, playing with her children and watching movies with her husband.

Samantha also pastors and serves at her local church, loves a good Excel spreadsheet and has a to-be-read list that's far too long.

Keep an eye out for the next in the Whispers of Eden series, *Uncovered Earth*.

www.samantharaeortiz.com
info@samantharaeortiz.com
@samantha.rae.ortiz.books

ACKNOWLEDGMENTS

I WANT TO START off by acknowledging my reader. Without you, these would be but words in a document—and for a long time they were! You are the dream, and the reason I write, and I'm grateful you'd take a chance on my debut novel. I hope to talk with you one day and get to know you, as you've gotten to know a piece of me over the last 300 pages.

MY TEAM: First off, I want to thank my developmental editor, Laura Burge, whose expertise and encouragement gave me the confidence to release *Behind the Veil* independently! To Joanna K. Harris, my copyeditor, I am so grateful for your incredible, mind-boggling thoroughness. This book would not have been as strong without you. To Hannah Linder, my cover designer, who effortlessly captured the heart of *Behind the Veil* with her art, I'm so grateful. And a thank you to the artists I found through Fiverr who did all the concept art.

MY SUPPORT: To all the author friends I've found this year, and my wonderful Kickstarter Campaign backers—this literally would not have happened without you:

E. A. Hendryx, Karyne Norton, J.A Webb, Kevin King, Stephanie Winter, Jennifer Woodward, Philip Wilder, Ellen McGinty, Jennifer Frankovic, Candace Kade, D.E. Carlson, Kitty and Greg Belle, Kelly Outzen, Jody and Frederick Doyle, Hector and Ashley Mancha, Matthew and Stacey Ortiz, Matthew and Sally Taylor, Christina Romero, Thomas Doyle, Robert Ortiz, Giselle Trejo, Sandra Ortiz,

Kathy Brasby, Bec Fletcher, MadiJoy, Sandra Toga, Brenna R. Campbell, Kandi J. Wyatt, Liesbeth Blackstone, Anonymous, Natalie Pelletier, Lina Lopez, Megan Hines, EL, M. Armstrong-Willinsky, Angela Morse, Amanda Dowdican, Alicia Aragon, Megan Gilbert, Kathleen Tennant, Darlene N. Böcek, Pastor Anthony Ortiz, Ashley Morelock, Alana Fisk, Annarose Willhite, Christy Patterson, Rachelle Y. Sperling, Celeste Richardson, Hannah Rissler, Katie and Mason Schrack, Adam and Laura Burge, Pamela Hart, Bobbi Halverson, Z.R. McCormick, Katie W., Terry Steinke, Vicki Goode, Mindy Hite, Steven A. Guglich, Marissa Childs, Angela Miles, Whitney Phillips, Eddie and Amy Leighton, Natalie Ulibarri, Angela Miles, J.L. Hendricks, MarcAnthony Salas, Amanda Cipiti, Rick Tester, Patricia Sung, Kim, Jeroen, D.T. Powell—to all of you, your support made this possible!

Next, to my incredible Beta Readers, Kitty Belle, Kelly Outzen and Jody Doyle—the three women who have read every word I've ever written, long before they were "validated" by the act of publishing. You've been the wind in my sails on hard days by letting me know I was capable of creating stories and characters that you could fall in love with.

And lastly to my husband Robby, and beautiful children Eliana and Malachi, who have endured many hours of "mama lost in her writing, editing, revising, and dreaming." While I pride myself on being interruptible for each one of you (and interrupted you have!) you need to know what it means to me that you support me this way. I wouldn't be who I was without you.

To Jesus, without whom I wouldn't have had this dream, let alone known how to walk toward it, let alone kept going when it seemed over. I owe you more than the words on any page.